The Darkest Place

JO SPAIN

Quercus

First published in Great Britain in 2018 by Quercus
This edition published in 2019 by

Quercus Editions Ltd
Carmelite House
50 Victoria Embankment
London EC4Y 0DZ

An Hachette UK company

A CIP catalogue record for this book is available
from the British Library

PB ISBN 978 1 78648 396 6
EBOOK ISBN 978 1 78648 398 0

10 9 8 7 6 5 4 3 2 1

Printed and bound in Great Britain by Clays Ltd, Elcograf S.p.A.

Praise for Jo Spain

'Reliably assured plotting, sympathetic characters – and
something horrifyingly dark lurking at the edges – make Spain's
latest DCI Tom Reynolds title a deeply satisfying read'
Sunday Times

'Irish crime fiction's current hot-ticket . . . busy, imaginative,
cleverly structured and zippily-paced'
Irish Independent

'Deft plotting and expert handling of tension make
for an intelligent mystery'
Guardian

'Fiendishly clever . . . and a big fat twist is lobbed into
the ending like a hand grenade'
Sunday Independent

'A very intelligent whodunnit'
Best

'Dark, funny, well-plotted, sinister. Superb'
Will Dean, author of *Dark Pines*

'An engrossing and compelling story that will have you
reading well into the night as you keep telling yourself,
"just one more chapter"'
My Weekly

'Wonderfully drawn characters and more secrets and
motives than you can shake a stick at'
Caz Frear, author of *Sweet Little Lies*

'A fabulously entertaining whodunit, with a sly wit
and a wonderful detective duo'
Sunday Mirror

Jo Spain is a full-time writer and screenwriter. Her first novel, *With Our Blessing*, was one of seven books shortlisted in the Richard and Judy Search for a Bestseller competition and her first psychological thriller, *The Confession*, was a number one bestseller in Ireland. Jo co-wrote the ground-breaking television series *Taken Down*, which first broadcast in Ireland in 2018. She's now working on multiple European television projects. Joanne lives in Dublin, with her husband and their four young children.

Also by Jo Spain

The Confession
Dirty Little Secrets
With Our Blessing: An Inspector Tom Reynolds Mystery
Beneath the Surface: An Inspector Tom Reynolds Mystery
Sleeping Beauties: An Inspector Tom Reynolds Mystery

Those we love. Those we miss. Those we lost.

Christmas 2012

CHAPTER 1

Forty years was too long to wait for somebody to come back from the dead.

But still, she liked to get everything ready. Just in case.

Every year, she carefully arranged the candles and red bows and holly trimmings on the dark mahogany mantle. She placed the little crystal snowflakes on the ends of the tree branches. She removed the tissue paper from the delicate Murano glass baubles they'd bought on their honeymoon in Sirmione. It was amazing, really, that they'd survived so long.

Every year, every Christmas Eve.

Were he ever to return, the house would look just like it had the day he should have come home. The day he'd vanished.

Miriam Howe had made it her life's work to make time stand still. When it came to Christmas, anyhow.

This year should have been no different. But it was.

Sighing, she reached into the box of precious things and took out the old stockings. One at either end of the mantelpiece for the children. Children who were no longer small; no longer here. They would come on the 31st, apparently. If they'd all recovered from the harsh exchange.

I'm sick of this charade, her eldest had snapped. *I want a normal Christmas for my kids, not the shite we had to put up with. I want giant plastic reindeer and dancing snowmen and I want to get hammered watching the soaps on telly. He's not coming back. He never was. Move on, for fuck's sake.*

Of course, she understood Jonathan's anger, even if it hurt to have what she'd always considered a special occasion parsed so viciously and flung at her. The children had been very young at the time. It was difficult to feel the absence of a man they'd barely known. Their mother's four decades' worth of prayers had far outlived the actual memories of their father.

Miriam lowered herself gingerly to her knees and began to organise the nativity scene beneath the tree. Her grand-daughter had pulled baby Jesus' head off last year and he'd been glued back together haphazardly by her son-in-law. The little Lord Jesus' tiny head sat at an odd angle now, slightly crooked.

A bit like mine, Miriam thought.

The clock chimed.

5 p.m.

Any minute now there'd be a knock on the door and it would be him.

Even after all this time.

The last bong sounded and Miriam closed her eyes.

The sound of the brass knocker clanging on the front door filled the house.

Miriam's eyes snapped open.

Quicker than she'd got down there, she stood up, wincing as she hobbled a few steps until her legs righted themselves. By the time she'd reached the hall, the small heels of her house shoes clicking on the varnished oak floor, she was walking erect. Miriam liked to carry herself the way a woman of class and good breeding should. Spine straight, shoulders back, chin up. Whether twenty-six or sixty-six.

If it were him, he would see the woman he'd left behind.

Older, greyer, slimmer, but still tall, confident, proud. Miriam Howe, unflappable.

Ha. She'd been distinctly flappable ever since that Christmas Eve in 1972.

She opened the door.

The sensor-activated porch light was still on, throwing its glow over the long pebble drive and onto the elderly man who stood at the door.

He was facing away from her, staring back at his silver Audi, so all she could see for a moment was the familiar hunch of his shoulders in the old-fashioned black winter coat, the striped grey scarf and wool bowler hat. He was still strong, even in his early seventies.

Her stomach lurched.

'Miriam!' Andrew turned, suddenly realising she was there. 'I didn't even hear the door open. Happy Christmas!'

She forced a smile.

'Happy Christmas, Andrew.'

She allowed him to kiss her chastely on the cheek, his beard tickling her soft skin, his scarf scratchy against her neck.

'I was just wondering if I should bring the presents in from the car, but if the children are not here yet, they can wait.'

'They can wait,' she parroted.

Jonathan and Vanessa were forty-six and forty-three, respectively. But for Andrew, too, they were forever frozen in time as the cherubic little six-year-old and three-year-old that everybody had cried for when Conrad had gone missing.

'Come in,' she said, ushering Andrew inside, as she did every year.

And he ooh-ed and aah-ed at the winter wonderland in the sitting room, as he did every year.

She took his coat and winter garments, poured the brandy and handed him a sugar-dusted mince pie on a porcelain plate. They sat by the fireside. And waited.

'Where are the children?' he asked, as it approached 6 p.m., the exact time when she'd rung and he'd answered and she'd asked if he knew where Conrad was.

There'd been a pause, back then, which she'd filled nervously.

'It's just, I expected him by now. He always puts Jonathan and Vanessa to bed on Christmas Eve. I thought, maybe the ferry was cancelled?'

'Miriam . . . I . . . he's not there? He's not here, either.'

Everything changed utterly.

'They're not coming,' she answered his question now. 'They wanted Christmas in their own homes this year. We . . . we had words.'

'It's understandable, Miriam,' Andrew said, gently. 'It's been so long.'

'I know that. But . . . forty years. It's . . . I don't know. It feels significant. Like something might happen.'

'Maybe it is happening. Maybe the children have made it happen. They're drawing a line. Perhaps . . .'

He left the rest of the sentence unsaid.

She didn't reply.

Every year, Andrew kept her company through the most painful hours. He was selfless. In all respects. She wouldn't be able to bear it if he became one of those people who lectured her, who told her to live her life and stop waiting. He knew her better than that. He'd been waiting with her. They'd all been friends, after all.

'You're wearing the pearls,' he said.

Miriam lifted her hand unconsciously to her neck and smiled. The last gift. A beautiful double string from Conrad for her birthday. Chosen because they brought out the grey in her eyes.

'Hmm,' she said, and ran her fingers along the polished jewels.

The phone trilled in the hall, the old-fashioned ringtone melodic and sharp at once. At the same time, the clock began to chime.

Miriam and Andrew looked at one another, eyes wide.

Surely not.

The children would never ring at 6 p.m. on Christmas Eve. Nobody who knew her would ring at 6 p.m., the very time she'd learned of her husband's disappearance.

Andrew followed her into the hall. She walked fast but didn't run, because, despite the instinct, she knew she would likely trip and kill herself in her haste. Wouldn't that be ironic?

But she was terrified the phone would stop ringing before she got to it. And she was so relieved when she picked it up and said, breathlessly, 'Miriam Howe,' and heard a voice on the other end.

She listened, her heart thrumming in her chest so hard she thought it might beat right out of her body. When the caller finished speaking, she let go of the receiver and it fell from her hand, the cord catching in her fingers so it dangled over the floor like a suspended bungee jumper.

'What? What is it, Miriam?'

Andrew was as pale as a man who'd seen a ghost.

And that made sense. Because a ghost had just entered the hall.

'It's Conrad. They've found Conrad. Andrew, they've found him.'

Then she fainted.

CHAPTER 2

Final Diary Entry
St Christina's asylum, 1972

It's almost over.

Thank God, because I cannot stay here much longer. I've seen too much, changed too little. The small kindnesses were never enough and my attempt to stop what is happening has come too late.

Much too late for Minnie.

I've tried to be good. I've tried to be strong. I've tried to be human.

There's no room for any of that here.

There was never much hope, even when I decided to take action. You cannot reason with the unreasonable. You would think I'd have learned that lesson already, here of all places.

The poor souls in our care cannot help their madness. But the people who run this place are just a different sort of insane. They hide their true nature from polite society and only show themselves in private, away from those who'd hold them to account.

They are the sickest in this asylum, the most depraved.

They are crazed with their power over others.

I can't take it any more.

Just a few more weeks.

I've done what I can for the patients.

Now I must save myself.

CHAPTER 3

There had been no need for him to ring on Christmas Day. None whatsoever. It was part of the campaign to drive Detective Chief Inspector Tom Reynolds nuts. And it was a campaign his boss, Joe Kennedy, was winning.

They'd been having pre-lunch drinks – Tom, his wife Louise, their daughter Maria and little Cáit, their granddaughter, the life and soul of the gathering and her only on the milk.

Tom's old boss and even older friend, Sean McGuinness, was there too. He'd decided he couldn't do the first Christmas without his beloved June in his own home. He'd balked at being fussed over and mollycoddled by his sons and daughters. And he'd seemed to be enjoying the day with Tom's family, as much as he could, right up until the goose was mentioned.

I just said the goose fat was doing lovely things to the roast potatoes and he started to cry, Louise told her husband, after Sean disappeared upstairs claiming he'd something in his eye. It transpired that June had been a traditionalist – turkey and ham every year, no exception, even when the electricity had gone one year and it had been deli slices of turkey and ham. The change in the Christmas roast had brought it home to Sean. His traditions had been abruptly and cruelly cut short.

Tom's driver, Willie Callaghan, had then called by with a doll house three times the size of Cáit and trying to fit that in the door had distracted everybody. Willie abandoned them soon after, claiming his wife had threatened to kill him if he came home smelling of booze, accusing them of being drunk with a laugh (not even half true).

Then Tom's fellow officers, Ray and Laura, had popped in. Tom tried and failed to make them stay for lunch. They had two more houses to call at and by the sounds of it, would be eating in both. Neither had been able to break it to their respective families that they'd be having dinner elsewhere that year – let alone daring to have it on their own – now they were a couple. They'd just called in to show solidarity with the inspector and remind him how much he meant to them.

It had been a tough six months.

It started with a leak to the papers the previous August, spun to imply that DCI Reynolds had somehow botched an investigation, albeit one that had resulted in the arrest of a serial killer. First, the press landed on the nugget that Tom had actively suspected a fellow member of the force of being guilty of the multiple murders. He'd gone against Garda protocol to haul the relevant sergeant into police headquarters and interrogate him without a union rep or solicitor (partially true, Tom conceded. Though there was no 'hauling', and the Guard had come in willingly, innocently . . . unaware of the inspector's motives). Then there was the small matter of a young member of his squad attempting to interview – alone – the man who eventually turned out to be the real culprit, and being kidnapped and nearly murdered in the process. Laura had been working on her own initiative and Tom's quick thinking had saved her, but none of that was mentioned in the reports.

Words like *maverick, arrogant* and, worst of all, *egomaniac*, were being thrown about in tabloid columns. All of that Tom could have swallowed, albeit unhappily, hoping it would pass. But the door-stepping of his family by a particularly nasty piece of gutter-press scum had torn it.

The investigators were never the story. That was Tom's career motto. It was the role of his team to do their jobs and stay in the background. People above the inspector's pay grade, and better-looking than he, could deal with the media. Tom's family and *where they lived* was sacrosanct. To print that photo on the front page – the shock on Louise and Maria's face as they were confronted at their garden gate – it was all Tom could do not to hunt down the journalist and beat him to within an inch of his life.

Kennedy had been giving him rubbish cases ever since.

You said yourself you don't want the spotlight, so let's keep you out of it, he'd said. *The regional divisions can handle murder cases for the time being. Just until this blows over.*

Christ, how the chief loved it. Tom doubted he was even properly investigating the man the inspector believed to be the source of the leaks, the Guard he'd 'hauled' in during the serial killer investigation. Kennedy wanted Tom on the back foot and, even though he'd done nothing wrong, that's where the inspector was.

So Christmas week, Tom had switched off completely. He needed a break. On Christmas Day he was content to be in the company of his loved ones and good friends, to have a few beers, to play *Guess Who?* with Cáit, and just enjoy the holiday.

Then his phone had sprung into action.

'I'm terribly sorry to ring you today,' Kennedy said, straight away.

Then why the hell have you, Tom almost said. He didn't, though, because it had already crossed his mind that it must be something big to make a call on Christmas Day. And if it was big, then the isolation period might be over. It wasn't just about the inspector: his specialist murder investigation team was made up of detectives he considered to be the finest on the force. They hadn't been entirely relegated, but with their boss offside, they were rudderless. They had been separately assigned to cases that their collective brains would have solved quicker, which was how Tom preferred to work.

Nobody was happy.

'What's happened?' Tom said, willing to indulge Kennedy out of sheer necessity.

'Have you been watching the news this week? You've heard they're digging around the old asylum on that island off the Kerry coast?'

'Yeah,' Tom replied. He didn't even need a minute to recall. Since Kennedy had started isolating him, the inspector had been hyper-aware of the news, watching and listening to nearly every bulletin to see what cases he wouldn't be assigned. 'St Christina's, isn't it?'

'That's the one,' Kennedy said. 'They found that mass grave last week.'

'I heard. Shocking. But there's nothing irregular, is there? Didn't a lot of these places bury dead patients in hospital plots?'

'Indeed. The problem is there's a body in the pit that shouldn't be there.'

Tom's ears pricked up. And yet he had the good sense to not sound too enthusiastic.

'Oh. I see. A missing local, is it?'

'Not exactly. Are you familiar with The Honorable Mr Justice Peter Mythen?'

'The Supreme Court judge?' Unconsciously, Tom raised his

glass of pale ale to his lips and sipped, suddenly tense. 'He's not . . . ?'

'God, no. His sister is a woman by the name of Miriam Howe. Forty years ago, her husband, Dr Conrad Howe, went missing. He was thirty-two years old at the time and a senior clinician at St Christina's. We think – well, we're fairly certain – that it's his body that's been found.'

Tom's shoulders slumped, just in time for his heckles to rise.

'Forty years ago,' he repeated.

'Yes. I know – it's a cold case. But . . .'

'There's a cold case squad.'

'There is. But at the time, this was sensational news, Tom. And Miriam Howe is still a very respected woman. Then there's her brother.'

'So now I'm a rent-a-cop for people in high places?' Tom took another gulp of ale. Kennedy was going to turn him into an alcoholic.

Across the room, Louise was running her finger around the rim of her glass and watching him closely, lips pursed. Kennedy didn't know it, but he lived every minute on borrowed time.

Louise had it in for him.

The inspector smiled at her reassuringly. It was Christmas Day. Peace and goodwill and all that. She tightened her lips even thinner and turned back to her conversation with Sean.

'I know,' Kennedy said. 'You're angry and you've every right to be. You've put up with a lot these last few months, Tom. And I've been giving you lesser cases. You're entitled to feel pissed off. But look, forty years old or not, this was – is – one of the most high-profile disappearances of the last century. Will you go and talk to Howe's widow, Miriam? I think that when you meet her, you'll want to take this on.'

'Do you know her?' Tom said, antennae buzzing.

'Not her, personally. I know Peter.'

Peter. First-name terms.

'You said we *think* it's Howe who's been found. Shouldn't we wait until we're sure?'

'It's been explained to Miriam that we have to perform DNA testing but there are compelling reasons to believe it's her husband. Talk to Moya Chambers. She's in charge of the autopsy. I've told her to put a rush on it.'

Tom sighed. What could he do? Kennedy was his boss and, yes, while this was a . . . could you describe a forty-year old case as cold? Frozen, more like it. This was an historical, frigid, probably unsolvable noose of a case, but Peter Mythen was a Supreme Court judge. The inspector had to look into it. Even if it turned out that this Howe bloke had just fallen into the bloody pit. And even if it wasn't Howe at all – the fact a body had turned up on the same island he'd gone missing from – well, that didn't bode well.

None of that made Tom feel any better about Joe Kennedy. Forty years old, and it couldn't have waited until St Stephen's Day? Or the New Year? It wasn't like the case was getting any staler.

'I'm not expecting you to do anything today,' Kennedy said and it was all the inspector could do not to bang the handset off the wall. 'But if you could call out to Miriam in the next day or two and then visit the island. I've asked Emmet McDonagh to travel there too, to take care of the forensics.'

'Did you ask him today?' Tom asked, incredulous.

'Last night.'

That cheered the inspector up no end. Now he understood why Kennedy had rung him on Christmas Day. It must have taken at least twelve hours to recover from the verbal blast he would have received from the head of the Garda Technical Bureau.

'He was . . . delighted to assist,' Kennedy lied.

'As am I,' Tom lied back. 'Is there much point in me going out to the island, though? I mean, I might want to take a look at the grave at some stage, but it will be more important for me to start identifying witnesses from the time. The island just housed the asylum, didn't it? And that's been closed down for years. There can't be anybody left there to talk to, surely?'

'That's the thing. You're right, the hospital trustees owned the island itself and there was never a general population living on it. But the staff did when it was in operation and some of them remained there.'

'Really? Beside a run-down, deserted psychiatric hospital?'

'Yes. That alone would make you wonder, wouldn't it?'

Tom found himself in the very rare position of agreeing with Kennedy.

'And,' his boss continued, 'they resisted the island being sold back to the State by the hospital trustees. Signed a petition and everything.'

'They didn't want the place dug up,' Tom said.

'Looks like it.'

The inspector nodded slowly to himself.

'This will be good for you, I think,' Kennedy added. 'Get you back investigating properly again while keeping you out of the media's gaze. You and your family. You will give my best to Louise, won't you? And do apologise for my intruding on Christmas Day.'

His boss rung off and Tom felt his blood pressure rise by more than few blips. That had been a dig, dragging up the coverage of his family. Kennedy would never learn and it looked like Tom would never cease to be bothered by it.

Over on the couch, Louise and Sean felt the air shift but said nothing. Tom gave Ray and Laura a nod and the three of them left the sitting room. When the door closed, Louise turned to Sean.

'This has to stop,' she said quietly. 'Ringing Tom on Christmas Day? On top of treating him like crap for the last few months? He's like a schoolyard bully. Why is he getting away with it, Sean? Surely Tom has friends in there who can put a halt to it?'

Sean took a large gulp of wine and returned her earnest stare. She was only younger by twelve years or so, but Louise Reynolds carried her age well, a woman of nearly fifty who could pass for early forties. Her hair was long and dark, her skin smooth and tanned, eyes brown and kind. She looked nothing like his June, and yet she reminded him of her. It was that fierce loyalty and the desire to protect all those close to her.

A defensiveness he felt for Tom Reynolds, too.

'Tom has plenty of friends,' he said. 'But Kennedy outranks him and people don't like to interfere in other departments. Tom was offered the promotion, you know that. He turned it down.'

'They can't keep punishing him for it,' Louise protested. 'Not like this. He wasn't ready, Sean. He likes where he is. And he'd no idea the sort of man they were going to appoint when they didn't get him in the role.'

'I know that. Look, I'm not happy, either, Louise. About any of it. But I can assure you, change is coming. Trust me. Kennedy has gone and pushed this too far. He's been stupid, trying to marginalise Tom the way he has.'

'So, why . . . ?'

Sean shook his head.

'Kennedy is nothing if not strategic. He was clever, when all this started. The media stuff about Tom had to be handled and Kennedy is a master PR man. That's why he got the job. But he failed to contain it – either willingly or because he isn't as good as he lets on. And people are starting to notice Tom's absence. Change is afoot. I mean it, trust me. I can't say any more. Not at the moment, it's all being finalised. But, Louise, there'll be good and bad in it for your husband. And he'll have to swallow the bad if he wants the good.'

Louise said nothing. She'd known Sean for over a quarter of a century. Of course she trusted him, even if he was speaking in riddles. She'd trust him with her life. But he'd been through so much recently. His face was still lined with grief; those shrewd eyes that could sparkle with such humour were a tiny bit duller, a little less lively. His shock of grey hair was thinning – a loss that had started in the years leading up to June's death, after she'd got her diagnosis of early-onset Alzheimer's – and he'd shrunk. The Sean that Louise knew was a tree trunk of a man. Even in his early sixties, he'd looked like he could stop a train with his hands. But the Sean of late was more hunched over, like the weight of the world was on his shoulders.

He held her gaze and in that moment she saw something. A kindling.

There it was – the spark in his eyes that had been absent. And she smiled.

Sean had something to fight for and it was her cause too. She believed him. He'd fix this.

CHAPTER 4

'How's the head?'

Ray groaned, all the answer Tom needed. December 26th and they were en route to Miriam Howe's home. Ray had turned up at the inspector's that morning looking distinctly green, his suit freshly pressed but his normally good-looking face pale and tired. The combination of cold air and the coffee Louise had pressed on him was doing its job.

'Improving. I tried to cut down on the drinking yesterday when you said we were going out to meet this woman today, but Jesus! I didn't stand a chance with Laura's family. I thought mine were bad, but they've got nothing on hers. Her da brought out the *poitín*. He had it under the kitchen sink. I mean, illegal hooch, and he's an ex-Guard.'

Tom laughed.

'He's a Kerry man, Ray, and it was Christmas Day. And tell me something: as a current serving detective sergeant, did you have a drop?'

'I'm trying to impress the man. It would have been rude not to.'

'Very rude. How's Laura?'

'In the lucky position of sleeping it off. She said she'd call into the office later for an hour or so.' Ray grinned. Tom always knew when Ray was thinking about Laura. His face lit up with it.

And the two of them deserved it. Their relationship had been a while coming. The inspector reckoned it wouldn't be long cementing itself into something permanent. That's what his all-knowing, all-seeing wife had predicted and she rarely got it wrong.

'How does she feel about me whisking you off for a romantic island getaway during Christmas week?' Tom said.

'Well, I've had to break it to her that the whole curly-haired, curvy, gorgeous thing hasn't been doing much for me. I'm looking for a George Clooney lookalike. A tall, grey, bearded, mature . . .'

'Mature? How dare you!'

'You're, what, fifty? Fifty-one? I hate to break it to you, but if it weren't for modern medicine, you'd probably be on your way out. Hang on, isn't it your birthday this week?'

Tom raised his eyebrows. He wasn't about to mention it was today.

'Yeah. And let's not talk about it. I'm still recovering from the trauma of the surprise party last year, a whole two months early. We've family coming over on the 28th and New Year's Eve, that's more than enough for me. I'm starting to feel old. Look at me, driving a Toyota Avensis like an ageing taxi driver. I don't know why I let Louise talk me into this.'

'Perhaps because every car you bought on your own broke down as you were leaving the garage forecourt? Anyway, to answer your original question, Laura is feeling pretty pleased with herself. Putting her in charge of the squad when we head off to that island – that was a nice touch.'

'Ha! As in charge as Kennedy will let her be. Still, of everyone in the team remaining in Dublin, she's the one most capable of telling him to go and f— Is this the turn? I can't see anything in this rain.'

'We left your house ten minutes ago, how can you be lost?'

'Different postcode, different universe.'

They turned down into Dublin's Strawberry Beds, the famous, fertile valley that stretched between the north bank of the River Liffey and the west side of the Phoenix Park. The inspector's home was on the other side of the Park, on the slightly less famous, certainly a few degrees less wealthy, Blackhorse Avenue.

The Howe homestead nestled on an elevated slope close to the river. Down here the Liffey was a more like a beautiful rural stream than a capital city river. They drove along the gravel drive and pulled up outside the tall Georgian-type house. Miriam Howe opened the front door and stood awaiting their arrival, a man beside her.

Tom took in the house's expensive redbrick front and mullioned windows as he and Ray bounded the few steps up to the porch. There was proper money here. Miriam Howe had done well, despite her husband's disappearance. Maybe because of it? And who was the man with her? It wasn't her brother, the judge. Had she had the husband declared dead and married again?

'Mrs Howe?' the inspector said, extending his hand.

She gave his hand an efficient shake. Everything about the woman was dignified and proper. You could tell. Old school. She probably rode horses side-saddle.

'That's me. It's Detective Chief Inspector Reynolds, yes? And you must be DS Lennon? This is a friend of mine and my husband's, Dr Andrew Collins.'

'Andrew will do,' the man said, shaking their hands in a finger-breaking grip. He was tall, his beard the same salt and pepper as Tom's, his eyes clear and shrewd.

'Come in out of the rain,' Miriam said, and led them into the house.

Miriam brought them to the sitting room. There, Christmas decorations had been arranged tastefully. The baubles and candles had the air of much-loved family heirlooms about them. Back home, the inspector's tree was adorned in multicoloured red, blue, gold and green, with a plastic train track running around the floor and a giant inflatable Santa Claus in the corner, all for his granddaughter's benefit.

Tom felt his heart go out to the woman. He may have had to take a call from Joe Kennedy on Christmas Day, but poor Miriam Howe had received far worse news on Christmas Eve and it was evidently a holiday she went all out for. It wouldn't have mattered that she probably had her husband dead and buried in her mind after forty long years. The fact of it would have been devastating.

'I'll fetch the refreshments,' Andrew said, as they took their seats around the fire. Embers smouldered in the grate. The fire needed to be stoked, but the homeowner was distracted.

'I can't believe they found him on Christmas Eve,' Miriam began, as soon as he'd left. 'You know it was Christmas Eve when he disappeared?'

The inspector noticed that she fiddled nervously with the double string of pearls around her neck. He watched as her slender, wrinkled fingers traced each jewel, back and forth along the rows.

'Mrs Howe, I believe you were told that while there are indications that the body we found is your husband's, nothing is positive until we have conclusive DNA evidence,' Tom said, and hated himself for it. This woman had lived with so much uncertainty for so long. It seemed wrong to bring her this close to the conclusion and tell her she must wait a little longer.

'It's him,' she said. 'I know it's him. Even while I've spent every minute of every day waiting for him to return, in my heart of hearts, I knew he was dead. He wasn't the sort who would just leave. Conrad was so dedicated, so loyal. And yet, that man, that bloody man, he claimed Conrad had just run away. That he'd abandoned me and the children . . .'

'Which man is this?'

'Oh. The head doctor at St Christina's, Lawrence Boylan. My husband's boss. He was absolutely insistent. And he knew nothing about our life! About how happy we were. He destroyed my husband's reputation and even tried to destroy me with his nasty assumptions. I mean, it was obvious that Conrad had never left the island. Oh, thank you, Andrew.'

The doctor had arrived back with a tray of tea things and fine china cups.

'I was just telling them, Andrew, how Conrad never left that island. And Lawrence insisted, didn't he? In spite of all the evidence to the contrary.' She turned back to Tom. 'I haven't been able to think of anything else since I heard. If they'd listened to Andrew and myself, they might have searched the island properly to begin with. They might have found Conrad immediately. What if he didn't die straight away? What if . . . what if he slipped and was in pain, waiting for somebody to find him?'

Tom worried the woman was going to pull the pearls apart, her fingers were now moving so frantically. He could almost hear the string snapping and the grey beads spilling onto the floor.

'Miriam, we did look,' Andrew said. 'Where Conrad was found . . . where that body was found . . . it was put there. Chief

Superintendent Kennedy told you. If it's Conrad, it wasn't an accident.'

'Of course,' she said, nodding slowly. 'You're right.'

Andrew nodded back.

They were very familiar with each other, the inspector noted. Had the loss and grief pushed them closer together? Or was there more?

'It does appear that the man we found died in suspicious circumstances,' Tom said, gently interrupting. He'd had a brief, abrupt call with Moya Chambers, the State Pathologist, that morning. She'd told him to ring again in a day or two, but said for now he could assume that the body in the pit hadn't ended up there for innocent reasons and that she was ninety-nine percent positive it was Conrad Howe.

'I'm curious as to why you're so sure he didn't leave the island when he disappeared,' the inspector continued. 'Can you tell me a little about that?'

'Andrew, why don't you . . . ?' Miriam said. 'Andrew was there, you see, at the time. I was here, waiting. When Conrad started working on the island, we'd agreed to maintain our home in Dublin so he could eventually move back to one of the larger hospitals. I don't think we realised how long his residency would last for, or perhaps we'd have changed our plans. I guess we both knew that even if he worked in Dublin, we wouldn't see him from one end of the week to the next. But that Christmas, we were missing him terribly. He hadn't been home for a few weekends by that stage. He'd broken his arm and didn't want to travel for a while. He'd promised to be home on Christmas Eve. For the children. He was looking forward to it.'

'That was his plan,' Andrew took up the tale. 'But he never left Oileán na Coillte. Miriam rang that evening and said

Conrad hadn't arrived home. The ferry had left early that afternoon; we had assumed he was on it. Immediately, we thought he must have got held up on the other side, that his car had broken down or there'd been an accident. But then . . . then we found his car, still parked in its spot outside the hospital.'

'That must have alarmed you,' Tom said.

'It did and it didn't. We were still at the point of making rational excuses – maybe he'd had a few drinks and decided to get the train on the other side of the ferry, that sort of thing. We started ringing the hospitals, hotels on his route home, that sort of thing.'

'That must have been hard, having to make all those calls at Christmas time,' Tom said, looking directly at Miriam.

She gave a brief nod. It had been horrific, but she wasn't the sort to wear her emotions publicly, the inspector realised. She would have tried to be stoical, practical, for her children's sake if nothing else.

Some people would perceive a woman like her as cold. He knew better. He hoped her children did too.

'And they came to nothing,' he said. 'So how long before you started to think he hadn't left the island?'

'Not long at all,' Andrew said. 'While we were searching and making more calls, one of my colleagues spoke to the ferry operator, Mannix Senior. We couldn't get hold of him until the 26th, but when Mannix arrived that morning, Dr O'Hare was waiting for him at the dock. He asked how Conrad had been on Christmas Eve, had he shown any signs of being ill or distressed, anything like that.'

'And what did the ferry operator say?'

'He said Conrad had never boarded the boat. Only two people

left the island on Christmas Eve and neither of them were Conrad Howe.'

'Who was on the boat?'

'The senior nurse, Dolores O'Sullivan, and the head orderly, Owen Reid.'

'I see,' Tom said. 'And was that the only ferry of the day?'

'Yes. The weather was worsening and even that trip was only undertaken because we needed provisions on the island for Christmas Day.'

'So why, with that knowledge, was this Boylan fellow insistent that Conrad had left?'

'Oh, his theory was that Conrad had left the island the previous day.'

'And you don't think he did?'

Andrew shook his head.

'I'm positive he didn't. I saw him early on the morning of the 24th out at the cottage on the headland. I'd gone on a walk to the far side of the island to clear the cobwebs. I didn't speak to him – I was enjoying the peace and quiet, being alone. I saw him from a distance but I'm certain it was him. I'd know Conrad anywhere.'

'Did anybody else see him that day?'

'No. That was the problem. Dr Boylan insisted I was mistaken. Conrad had finished work the previous day and hadn't returned to the hospital, so as far as everybody was concerned he could easily have left on the 23rd. He lived on the hospital grounds but not in the building itself. It wasn't as easy to keep tabs on everybody back in those days, without mobile phones and so on. Half the cottages didn't even have landlines. Anyway, Dr Boylan doubted my account and started to spout the nonsense that Conrad had simply walked out on his life. That he'd had some sort of breakdown.'

'Well,' Tom cocked his head, 'it's clearly redundant at this point, anyway, but Boylan's theory could have been easily discounted, surely? Wouldn't the ferryman have confirmed whether or not Conrad had taken the trip the previous day?'

Andrew's cheeks flushed red. He was still angry at being doubted, that was obvious.

'Unfortunately, a good many of the staff left on the 23rd. Nobody remembered seeing Conrad, but Boylan's assertion at the time was that he could have easily made himself invisible on the crowded ferry if he'd wanted, especially with most of the people on it in good spirits and distracted by their own Christmas plans. "Good spirits" being another term for tipsy. Dr Boylan was in the habit of giving everybody, from senior physicians to the caretaker, a bottle of whiskey for the festivities and we'd had the annual staff party earlier that day.'

'I see. I'm sure you wish you had the opportunity to point out to Dr Boylan how wrong he was.'

'He *will* have the opportunity, Inspector,' Miriam interjected. 'Dr Boylan is still alive.'

'Is he? He must be a great age, if he was in charge of the hospital in 1972?'

'Yes. He's eight-two. He still lives there, on the island.'

Her voice was bitter when she spoke about this Boylan character. Tom immediately wondered if there was more at play than simply ancient anger at the man for not taking her husband's disappearance seriously.

As though reading his thoughts, Miriam nodded and withdrew a small leather-bound book tucked between her leg and the side of the chair.

'I think there will be a lot that we'll be confronting Dr Boylan about, now Conrad has been found.'

She placed the book on the table.

'A few years ago, I found this diary, Inspector,' she said. 'At first, I had no idea what it was. As the years went on, Conrad's script was illegible most of the time, a typical doctor's hand. He'd leave me a note and I'd have to remind him I wasn't a chemist, I couldn't translate scrawl. But the words on these pages were written deliberately, with care.'

From her pocket, Miriam withdrew a small card with flowers on its front. She opened it and showed it to Tom.

'I hope you don't mind if I don't let you read it, but it's personal. Conrad used to send me little love letters when we first started seeing each other. I found a box of them around the same time I found the diary. He'd write the notes neatly, slowly – he took care over his words. It's the same with the diary. It's like he wanted to carve into history what he was witnessing. And it is a history, you see, of his time in the hospital.

'He'd hidden this diary in our attic. I don't think he presumed I'd ever see it. He wouldn't have wanted me to know what was going on at St Christina's. It was only when I was having the roof insulated that it turned up.'

'May I?' Tom asked. Miriam nodded and he picked up the diary.

The inspector flicked through the next few pages and saw what Miriam meant. Much of the writing had been inscribed with an angry pen. It was cramped, tiny penmanship, not the flourish of a confident doctor signing off on a prescription or a patient's file. These were Conrad's most intimate thoughts and, from what Tom could see at a glance, they, like the handwriting, had become steadily uneasier as time passed and the entries had mounted.

'What's in this diary?' he asked.

A patch of reddening skin peeked out from under the woman's high-collared blouse, a betrayal of emotion in a woman not disposed to showing it.

'The answer to who murdered my husband, Inspector. I told Lawrence Boylan years ago what my husband suspected and he just ignored me. I told the police, too, after I'd found the diary, but they said at the time that it proved nothing. It was just a man's recollections of unpleasant practices at a hospital where he himself worked.

'But it is more than that, Inspector. Somebody at the hospital was doing very evil things. My husband confronted whoever it was. I suppose that's why he was killed.'

CHAPTER 5

'You do realise, don't you Tom, that psychiatry and psychology are different disciplines? Not that I'm unenthusiastic about this little trip a mere two days after Christmas, but I feel the need to check that you are aware of the difference between what I do and what would have been practiced in this hospital.'

'Yes, Linda, I'm not completely ignorant. I still think you'll be of use, even with your more limited qualifications.'

'You're very funny for a big, thick, plodding policeman.'

'Children!' Ray said, trying to concentrate on the road. They were on the road to Carnbeg, Kerry. The village was the last mainland outpost before Oileán na Coillte, the island home of St Christina's. 'We're nearly there. You've kept it civilised all this way. Don't make me pull over.'

'He started it,' Linda said.

'I apologise,' Tom said. 'There was no need to get upset. One day you might turn into a real doctor. Jesus Christ, ouch!'

Linda McCarn, the state's leading criminal psychologist, had smacked the back of his head. As the inspector rubbed the sore spot, Linda fixed her brown corkscrew curls with the aid of the rear-view mirror and winked at Ray.

'Pavlovian response. Now he'll associate insulting me with pain.'

Ray shook his head. It had taken him some time to think of

Linda as anything other than batshit crazy. She didn't help her cause. The woman was in her late fifties and came to work most days looking like she'd picked her clothes off the backstage rail of a vaudeville theatre.

'For your information,' she drawled, in her well-to-do south-side Dublin accent, 'there are some who consider psychology the more challenging profession. We can't just prescribe drugs to fix a problem. We have to use . . .'

'Your wands?'

'Tom, why did you ask me to accompany you on this trip? Was it just to abuse me?'

The inspector smiled. The continued presence of people like Linda and Emmet McDonagh (even while those two couldn't stand each other) after Sean had retired had made Joe Kennedy's reign that bit more bearable. Linda was eccentric and a little overwhelming, but also a huge asset to the team and an absolute tonic for a bad mood.

'I asked you because I do very much appreciate that this is an area you are far more familiar with than I. I know St Christina's was a hospital of its age, populated more with psychiatrists and traditional medical doctors than your sort, but still . . .'

Linda sighed.

'God. You've a lot to learn about these sorts of places. Isn't that the sign for Carnbeg?'

Ray hung a sharp right, taking the narrow road that led towards the village.

Tom looked at the clock display on the dashboard. They'd left Dublin at 10 a.m. and had stopped for less than an hour. It was 4 p.m. already. They'd driven to the edge of Ireland.

'We should have flown,' Linda said.

'Ray's afraid of flying,' Tom replied.

'Well, yeah, that and it would have been impossible to get a last minute flight from Dublin to Shannon on the 27th December for anything less than remortgaging HQ,' Ray pointed out. 'Aren't we suppose to worry about a little thing called resources? By the way, I've sorted us out accommodation for tonight, presuming we don't stay on the island. There's a B&B in Carnbeg. We can call in there first and leave off our overnight bags.'

'I love it,' Linda said. 'Ménage à trois. And, I have to say, Tom, your deputy has become even hotter since he made himself unavailable. On the other hand, that beard puts ten years on you.'

'Ray was never available to you and Louise thinks my beard is sexy,' Tom retorted.

Linda patted his shoulder.

'Is that what she's told you? Look, it's hard being partnered with a Tom Hardy lookalike. We all know you grew that beard so you'd feel more masculine.'

'Why did you grow yours?' Tom snapped childishly, a little stung.

Ray laughed.

The B&B was easy to find, being the only one in the village.

The building was 1950s in style, a three-storey, street-front affair with a light blue-painted front wall, lace curtains in each window and a statue of the Virgin Mary on the front windowsill. The owners, a youthful dark-haired brother and sister in their twenties, explained how they'd inherited the place from their grandparents, who still lived there and dictated the decor.

'I don't mind,' Sabrina said, smiling as she showed them their rooms. 'It has a certain flair. Now people try to recreate an authentic fifties style – we have the actual furnishings, including our grandparents. Granddaddy still dresses like a Teddy Boy. They're the "Mr & Mrs Higgins" on the sign over the door.'

Then her brother broke the news that there was no way they'd be getting across to Oileán na Coillte that evening.

'I thought there was a late afternoon ferry,' Tom said. 'We did ring ahead.'

'There is,' Colm said. 'But he won't sail now. Too windy. He'll bring you in the morning.'

'Who is *he*, exactly? He's not the man who's always ran the crossing, by any chance?'

'God, no. You're thinking of his father. Mannix Sr ran the ferry when it was profitable, or so Granddad says, anyway. He's dead ages. His son, Mannix Jr, took over the business but uses the boat these days mainly for trips over to the Aran islands. He only does the island once a week or when he gets a summons. He's in his late thirties and . . . eh, the strong, silent type. You'll see. You'll be lucky if you get ten words out of him tomorrow.'

Colm offered them some dinner, as Sabrina brought them into the B&B's living room.

In the corner sat a wizened little man, bald as a coot, shoulders hunched, gnarled hands clasped across his stomach. His feet rested by an electric two-bar heater. He wore black drainpipe trousers, a black tee-shirt, a red drape jacket with a velvet collar and white socks. He was eighty, at least.

'Granddad, we have some guests this evening,' Sabrina said. 'Is Grandma in bed?'

'What are you on about?' the old man replied. 'She's in the pub. We're not dead yet.'

'You keep hanging on in there. Our guests are heading out to the island, Granddad.'

'Is it a good distance by sea?' the inspector asked.

'You wouldn't be swimming it, put it that way,' Sabrina answered. 'But it's not too far. A couple of miles.'

'Not far enough,' Mr Higgins grunted.

'It's just a piece of land, Granddad.'

Mr Higgins shook his head.

'Funny, I can't remember you ever suggesting a little trip over for a picnic, Sabrina. Even when you were a youngster and could brave anything. Nor your folks, for that matter. You do know what it's called, don't you, lads and lassie?'

'Oileán na Coillte,' Ray said, wondering what was so strange about that.

'No, lad. That's the modern-day version and sure, we all call it that these days, even those of us who know better. The island's proper name is Oileán na *Caillte*. There are plenty of woods, *coillte*, on the island but it was never named for them.'

Ray looked to Tom who, in turn, looked embarrassed. He'd spoken near fluent Irish at school level but couldn't for the life of him remember the difference between *coillte* and *caillte*.

'Island of the lost,' Linda informed them, then turned back to their host. 'Has it always been called that, or did it get its name because of the asylum?'

'Interesting question,' Mr Higgins said.

'Why's that?' Ray asked, looking from the old man to the psychologist, completely *caillte*.

'Considering what went on at that place.'

'You know a lot about St Christina's?' Tom asked.

'Don't get him started,' Sabrina said, 'with his fairytales.'

'Ah, child,' her granddad replied. 'The stories about that place aren't a word of a lie, as well you know. Other kids grew up with threats of the bogeyman. Those of us who grew up in

Carnbeg had St Christina's. I suspect this lassie here knows what I'm referring to, am I right?'

Linda nodded, her face resigned.

'In a manner of speaking,' she said. 'Our reputation when it comes to care of the mentally ill is not exactly laudable.'

'No,' Mr Higgins shook his head. 'Some people never saw the need for those places at all, mind. My mother, God rest her, had madness in her own family. An older brother, not right in the head. It would never have occurred to her or the wider family to have him shipped off to an asylum. But then, we Kerry folk believed in more traditional cures for that sort of trouble.'

'I can see you're going to be well-entertained,' his granddaughter cut in. 'I'll go give Colm a hand with dinner.'

Mr Higgins waited until the door to the small sitting room closed before speaking again.

'She's sceptical about this kind of thing. Did you ever watch *The X-Files*?'

Tom nodded, bemused.

'Sabrina and Colm are the Scullys to my Mulder. No matter what happens, even if it's in front of their own two eyes, they'll doubt it. Young people. They'll believe everything they read on Facebook but not a tale passed generation to generation. Have you heard of the taking of the waters? Gleann na nGealt?'

'Can't say I have.'

'They used to say it was an old wives' tale. Gleann na nGealt translates to Valley of the Mad. It's so called because there's a well there, believed to have restorative powers for troubled souls. Legend has it that Gall, the King of Ulster, drank from the well and ate watercress from its beds and was cured of his insanity. Many older Kerry people believed in its powers. My mother would have brought her brother there regularly.

The thing is, years ago, a group of scientists got interested in the tale and they came to test the waters. Guess what they found?'

Tom shook his head.

'Lithium,' Mr Higgins said with satisfaction. 'A high concentration of it.'

The inspector laughed.

'I see.'

'I've thought of bottling up some of the water to use in my wife Betty's tea, but I'm a'feard the boiling would kill the drug.'

'I think you might be right,' Linda agreed. 'Far wiser to put it in the glass she uses for her teeth at night. Let it absorb.'

'Aye. Anyway, the point of the story is that folk round here wouldn't have looked too kindly on St Christina's and what it was used for. Even if it was good for business.'

'Was it always an asylum?' Tom asked.

'That building was, yes. Oileán na Coillte was never properly populated, though. Too small, too exposed and that bit too far from land. But more importantly, the treacherous water around it made it inaccessible until the jetty was built and the ferry could get in and out. In the late 19th century, the Earl of Dunree was gifted the island by the British monarch. He didn't want to waste it, so he put in the harbour and landscaped a portion of it so he could build a holiday home. It's quite a pleasant place in the summer, by all accounts.

'Anyhow, this fellow wasn't the worst and wanted to use some of his money for good. He constructed the hospital and put in the road infrastructure and accommodation and so on. He was well-intentioned. The few asylums already in existence were bursting at the seams. You know who built the first one in Ireland?'

Tom shook his head.

'Jonathan Swift. The writer.'

'I'd no idea.'

'Most people don't. Anyway, they caught on quick – asylums. And the earl believed the location of St Christina's would be therapeutic in itself. Of course, he'd never spent a winter on the island.'

'What do you mean by that?'

'Oileán na *Caillte* – it was the island's name long before the hospital was built.' Mr Higgins nodded to Linda. 'In winter, they say the fog falls so heavy there that you can't see your hand in front of your face. Storms rage so forcefully you can be blown from the cliffs into the sea. And the Atlantic winds bring weather so cold the marrow in your bones will freeze while you're thinking about taking your next step. I've never been on it, so I only have the fables, as Sabrina says. But the island was given such a damning name because for centuries, fishermen and ignorant travellers had been lost to the sea around it. Of course, once St Christina's got up and running, the name took on a new meaning. Very few who went into that place ever came out for good.'

'Was that normal?' Tom asked, directing his question to Linda. 'To build a hospital offshore?'

'Yes and no. You know how it is. We Irish spent centuries thinking up new and ingenious forms of incarceration for much of the population, Tom. We had institutions for everyone and we especially liked to hide away unwanted family members. Where better than on an island?'

'Unwanted?' Ray said. 'That's a bit harsh, isn't it?'

'Oh, but they were, Ray. You must know this. Patients with dementia, deformities, nervous disorders, domestic violence sufferers, homosexuals, epilepsy, depression. Their families couldn't deal with them and they had to go somewhere. There was also a very good reason for the asylums, economically speaking. Local towns and villages would have relied on the business they provided. This country was almost solely dependent on agriculture for so long. Asylums were big business. They were huge providers of employment.'

'You know your stuff,' Mr Higgins said.

'I'm in medicine. I'm a psychologist.'

'Which, apparently, is very different to a psychiatrist,' Ray added. 'What was Conrad Howe, by the way?'

'He was a psychiatrist,' Tom said. He'd checked that very thing that morning.

'They wouldn't have really respected the field of psychology back then,' Linda said. 'Howe and his colleagues would have treated insanity mainly as though it were physical, like a broken limb or a stomach complaint. There was a constant effort to *fix* people. Those who couldn't be fixed – well, they were just kept locked up. Forgotten. By their families, and by the world.'

'Lost,' Mr Higgins said.

'Yes. Lost. And Ireland had the highest number of people lost to asylums per capita, in the entire world.'

'Really?' Tom raised his eyebrows.

'Really,' Linda nodded. 'In the sixties, when Howe started working in St Christina's, the numbers were at their peak. We'd over twenty thousand people incarcerated in psychiatric institutions in any given year. Do you know how many people would have been in prison each year around that time? Numbers in the hundreds. Even today, you've about fifteen thousand people in the prison system and that's with a much higher population. Back then, you'd walk a long way before you found a family who hadn't at one point sent somebody in for a *rest*.'

'Jesus,' Ray said. 'Thank Christ I wasn't around back then. I know more than a handful of people who'd have ended up in straitjackets, by the sound of things.'

'That's only the half of it,' Mr Higgins said, ominously. 'Going by the stories I heard, the place was absolute hell. Nobody in this village is surprised that doctor was killed over there. We're only surprised more bodies haven't turned up.'

CHAPTER 6

Diary Entry

I've been so nervous since agreeing to take the job in St Christina's.

I don't want to appear ignorant. I've a lot of experience but mainly in general hospitals. This is very different. The senior doctors, even the nurses in some cases, will look down on me unless I can distinguish myself, regardless of previous experience.

Even though this is my first residence at a psychiatric institution, I'm clearly suited to dealing with the more troublesome patients. I'm gentle, yet strong. And changes are afoot in specialist mental health treatment. I can see that in what I've read about St Christina's. It's exciting, alluring. This is a progressive movement that I sincerely wish to be part of.

I felt the anxiety and anticipation bubbling in my chest as we crossed the bay to Oileán na Coillte. The sea was uncharacteristically smooth, according to a fellow traveller, a delivery man bringing crates of non-perishables. He told me the hospital is fairly self-sufficient for most foodstuffs, having an extensive fruit and vegetable garden within its grounds, but that contracts for the other necessities are much coveted. His trips run to once a month but are almost profitable enough to be his sole business. The only downside, he added, was the ferry trip – an unreliable journey, with nobody able to predict when the sea would be calm enough to travel. Often the weather turned quiet waters choppy and dangerous in the blink of an eye.

This trip was peaceful, though. It was almost balmy, the sun shining upon us, the island bearing down, its trees swaying gently, sandy stretches lit golden, cliffs rising magnificently towards the clouds. We arrived in the small harbour safely and the pedestrian passengers alighted first.

The quiet, that's what I noticed. I've heard the locals on the mainland refer ghoulishly to the island as haunted, but my first impression was just how silent and peaceful the whole place seemed. Back on the ferry, I could hear the sound of engines ticking over as the few small vehicles waited to disembark. But on dry land, with the vehicles gone on to their destinations, the only sound was of the waves lapping behind me and the circling gulls.

It is exquisite in its isolation. Beautiful. Within minutes, I understood how the solitude here would be good for a disturbed soul and what drove the Earl of Dunree to build this place of rest and recovery.

Dolores O'Sullivan, the senior nurse at St Christina's, was sent to meet me. I was the only new employee on the ferry that day. The two silent, sullen passengers who had stood at the rail with me and watched our approach were a mother and daughter, I discovered. The daughter was being admitted to the asylum. She had seemed serene on the crossing, tranquil, no sign of the inner turmoil that must surely exist. They walked ahead of us, the two relatives, apparently familiar with the path. Something else I learned – that some patients leave St Christina's, but more often than not, they return.

I remarked on the girl's tender age, perhaps nineteen at

the oldest, and her solemn, placid disposition, as Dolores and I strode a hundred yards or so behind, tracking their footsteps on the solitary path from the short pier.

The nurse had been listing instructions about the asylum's routine, the duties I would be assigned, my lodgings. I wasn't put off by her bored, sharp tone; I was accustomed to the clipped manner many nurses have when speaking, the deliberate enunciation and delivery that brooks no dissent. She paused in her monologue at my sudden observation and stopped short on the path.

'I am aware,' she said, 'that this is your first time working in an institution that deals exclusively with the mentally ill. And I understand you know best how to do your job. But as the senior nurse, please, let me give you some advice. Do not be lured into feeling sympathy for our patients. Do not assume to know their characters on the basis of a few short meetings. With each and every one, be aware that you could be dealing with a dangerous individual. It is our job, our sole job, to attempt to right the minds of those admitted to our care. Where this cannot be achieved, we must ensure they pose no danger to wider society, to themselves or to us. Sometimes it can take a while for it to sink in – how different a psychiatric asylum can be to a regular hospital. The cases of insanity we get here are generally more complex than in the general hospital system. It's best you know some things from the start.'

I nodded.

'Like that girl ahead,' she continued. 'She has been admitted to us several times because she persists in prostituting herself to men in her town. She's been at it since she was fifteen. She was even promiscuous as a child, her mother tells us. You might not think there's any harm in that but the girl has had recurrent bouts of syphilis. If we don't treat her sexual urges, she will keep getting it and will eventually go mad from the disease – more so than the madness that already exists in her. You wouldn't think it to look at her, would you?'

I stared at the back of the figure walking into the distance and shook my head. The insane patients I had dealt with previously were all quite obviously mad. But that was why I was here, wasn't it? To challenge myself, to learn, familiarise myself with the new and unexpected.

The nurse smiled.

'See?' she said. 'It's shocking. I know, having worked in Dublin, you probably think you've seen it all but we really do get the most extreme cases here. Nothing is what it seems.'

I thanked her for her observations and we continued on.

Dolores is attractive. Blonde, not peroxide as I see a lot of women trying for these days, but natural, her hair parted in the middle and rolled into two plaits that sit like Danish pastries on the sides of her head. She is big-boned, as you would expect for a nurse in such a place, but not manly – just a strong specimen of her sex. Despite her stern, efficient tone, her eyes are kind. I can see she is professional but also caring.

'Have you ever had problems with a patient?' I asked.

'No,' she said. 'But that's because I am always alert.'

Soon the building itself loomed large before us and I was struck quiet by its enormity and magnificence. Four storeys high and a basement level, its windows barred with iron grilles from what I could see. The front door, heavy and tall enough to serve a cathedral. I was silenced, as was my companion, even though she is used to the place. She let me take it in.

St Christina's is daunting to the uninitiated. It's both austere and oppressive. I wouldn't quite describe it as ugly but it's not welcoming. The building's façade has somehow managed to absorb and reflect the pain and misery contained inside its walls.

Yes, the island has a strange sense of wonder and wild charm but entering the asylum I had only one thought.

How terrifying this place must seem to the vulnerable people who arrive here involuntarily.

CHAPTER 7

The inspector shivered as he read the last sentence and closed the diary. He rubbed his eyes, tired from concentrating on the tiny handwriting. He could read no more tonight, even though he wanted to go on. Howe had used some type of fountain pen for his account and the ink had leaked in places, blotting out sentences and forcing words to run into each other. It was at once fascinating and frustrating.

He was an excellent journalist, that was without doubt. Though his flair for the dramatic might make him an unreliable witness. Tom sensed he'd learn much from the diary if he struggled through, perhaps even garner potential suspects. But it would be an effort.

He rested the book on the chest of drawers and sat back in the comfortable rocking chair. His room was to the front of the B&B. Outside, he could see the Christmas lights twinkling invitingly in the pub across the road. Linda and Ray had gone across for a nightcap. And here was the inspector, sitting in a rocking chair in his room and it not even 9 p.m.

He was ageing faster than Rip Van Winkle.

A few minutes later, Mr Higgins knocked on Tom's door with a double measure of Tullamore Dew and a glass of water.

'I thought you might fancy a sup before bed. I nicked this from my grandson's cabinet. Him and Sabrina are conspiring with the wife to keep me off the spirits but they don't know how good I am at picking locks.'

'Sounds like you're running rings around them, Mr Higgins. Will I feel happy after I drink this water?' Tom eyed the liquid suspiciously, wondering about the well from whence it came.

'No happier than after drinking the whiskey,' Mr Higgins grinned and retreated down the hallway.

The inspector did feel aglow after a few gulps, even while his throat burnt a little. If he had a cigar now, he'd be right at home. He picked up his phone and opened the search engine.

Conrad Howe's name gave him no hits older than the last few days' headlines. Forty years was too long, even for Google. The case might have been sensational at the time but, ultimately, it had only been a high profile disappearance, not a murder. Not significant enough to be recorded in the annals.

Well, it was making up for it now. And it was nice for the inspector to see something else splashed all over the tabloids.

Tom resisted the urge to search for his own name. He'd gone down that rabbit hole a couple of times already and still felt a bit dirty from it.

He accessed his emails instead and got a pleasant surprise.

Laura had managed to source a few original articles from archives in *The Irish Times* and had mailed them through. The girl was brilliant, Tom thought, opening the first one.

The January 1973 news report ran through the salient facts of Howe's vanishing a couple of weeks previous. A small, grainy photograph was included and the inspector zoomed in as much as his phone would allow, but the image lost all definition. All he could make out was that Conrad Howe wore glasses. The next article came almost a year later and marked the anniversary of the doctor's disappearance. This time the photograph was of Miriam Howe and two small children. A boy and a girl, Tom saw.

Laura had included a message:

Lots of medical papers and articles written by Howe but didn't think you'd find any of it relevant. Have attached one piece here from a colleague about how well-respected he was in his field, thought you might find the last paragraph interesting. The author is dead, I checked.

Tom opened up the file, retrieved from a medical council journal dated 1967.

Leading Young Psychiatrist Joins Staff at
Avant-Garde Asylum
By Dr Kristoph Melvin

Dr Conrad Howe, former trainee psychiatrist in residence at St Bartholomew's general hospital, Dublin, has become the latest high-profile recruitment to the staff of the progressive and radically run St Christina's hospital for the mentally ill.

Howe, one of the youngest qualified psychiatrists in the country, has previously written papers on the need to revolutionise treatment of the insane, including the undertaking of intensive therapy sessions with patients. His experience to date has involved treating patients among the general population at St Bart's, but Howe has expressed his desire to move onto more challenging case studies.

Tom's eyes scanned the next few paragraphs of the article, all referring to medical drugs and treatments of which he'd never heard. He didn't slow down until he reached the end, the section to which Laura had directed him.

It will be interesting to see how Howe adjusts to life on the island where St Christina's is housed. This author does not wholly subscribe to the theory that remote care is the best care, but I recognise that I am in the minority as far as current medical trends go.

More fascinating will be Howe's relationship with Dr Lawrence Boylan, the esteemed director of St Christina's. Howe is one of the youngest, brightest, most ambitious lights in the field of psychiatry, an accolade that, up until now, Dr Boylan has held. Will the two collaborate to do great things? Or will they, as with many great minds before them, clash on how patient care must advance?

The medical world will watch with interest.

Hmm,' Tom murmured, when he'd finished re-reading the piece. He sent Laura an email back thanking her for the research.

A door opened in the pub across the road and a local stumbled out onto the street, still singing the pop song the band were playing inside.

Tom smiled. He felt like company now but couldn't be arsed going over.

He rang Moya Chambers, the state pathologist.

'What news from Coventry?' were the words she used to answer the phone.

'No, no,' Tom replied. 'You have that all wrong. I'm not being punished. Not any more. Apparently, this case is the most sensational to hit our shores in the last, oh, forty years or so.

Laura found a whole two articles on it from the time. I feel privileged to be awarded the honour of solving it. In fact, I've a notion if I use the right words and fall to my knees, Kennedy will build me a time machine and send me back to 1972 to interview key witnesses.'

'Why not 1971 to prevent the crime from occurring?'

'Good point, but a little too existential for my tiny brain. Are you drinking?'

Moya sounded more relaxed than the last time they'd spoken. He'd got her at a good time. When he'd rung that morning, an assistant had answered and politely told him the state pathologist couldn't come to the phone. In the background, he'd heard her shouting, *Tell him I'm up to my fucking elbows in corpse and I'll get to him when I get to him.*

'It's the 27th of December and I've been working non-stop right through Christmas. I consider it my God-given right to be three sheets to the wind and, after all, I'm performing autopsies on the long dead. Who's going to complain? Are you drinking?'

'Not a drop. I'm on the job.'

Moya snorted her disbelief. Tom smiled. Moya was tiny, all Dolly Parton curls and bosom, but she had a tongue like a whip and ran her department like an army general. Given she practically lived at the hospital, he considered it was probably her due to do what the hell she liked there.

'I suppose you're ringing me for the conclusive findings on Conrad Howe?'

'I was merely placing a call to wish you an early New Year's blessing but if you happen to have Dr Howe's cause of death, I'm happy to discuss work, even at this late hour. What have you got? You told me we could be confident he was murdered. Why, exactly?'

'I'll tell you what I've got, Tom. I have a forty-year-old corpse. I spent most of the day extracting DNA from the clothes remnants and the skeleton.'

'What are you matching it to?'

'His children. They arrived in Dublin today. I can't match dental records because his dentist died in 1980 and nobody, for love nor money, can tell me where the records ended up. I blame that on Christmas week as opposed to an actual disappearing act. And while his widow hung on to some of his clothes, she didn't keep his toothbrush or hairbrush. Which, to be fair, would have been weird if she had.'

'Jesus, Moya, I'm in the arse end of Kerry about to head over to this island to see where Howe worked and conduct interviews with people who hopefully knew him. Are we sure it even is Howe? His wife will be devastated if we've led her on a merry dance.'

'Tom, if this were the age before DNA, I'd tell you the skeleton was found in the remains of Conrad Howe's clothes, including what I'm convinced is a doctor's coat with his name pin attached. He had his house keys, confirmed by his widow, by the way, keys to the asylum, his wallet and a much-damaged but still identifiable picture of his wife and children. He matches the age, size and, obviously, sex of Howe and he's been in that pit about forty years.'

Moya hesitated and Tom waited. He knew there was more. He knew Moya Chambers would not risk her professional reputation on a misidentification, no matter how eager anybody else was for information.

'You are certain,' he said into her silence. 'But reluctantly so.'
She sighed.

'Mm. I'm told this woman has waited four decades for news of her husband. She's probably nursed the hope that he'd just turn up. Be found alive and diagnosed with amnesia, sheep farming in Wales or something. A tearful reunion, that sort of thing. But I'm certain this is the last remains of Conrad Howe.'

'What clinched it for you?'

'The arm. Thanks to the efficiency of Kerry General, I have an x-ray that was taken of Conrad Howe's arm when he broke it, a few weeks before he went missing in '72. I spent Christmas Eve looking at the arm of the skeleton we found. It's the exact same break.'

'Kerry General?' Tom said. 'Couldn't he have got it treated in St Christina's? He was surrounded by doctors.'

'The staff at St Christina's would have used Kerry hospital for their medical treatments. Serious stuff, anyway. So, that's what I have but, look, the DNA will prove it absolutely.'

'And the cause of death?'

'That's harder. The neck is broken.'

'But that could have happened when he was thrown into the pit?'

'Correct. Or he could have been flung from a high window beforehand, there's no way of knowing. If the method was strangulation, it's near impossible to prove with a skeleton. Stabbing, equally difficult to establish. The scraps of clothing aren't drenched in blood but I have picked up traces. I'm testing the bone samples for foreign chemicals, to see if any poisons were ingested or if I can detect unusual quantities of a drug. If he was shot I'd have expected to see shattered bone fragments or some form of bullet trajectory damage, so I think we can rule that out.'

'So, why are we so sure the man was murdered and didn't just die naturally? Maybe whoever found him panicked and put his body in the pit. Stupid, but not criminal, unless I can charge him or her with unlawful burial and withholding knowledge from the widow?'

'Did Kennedy not explain to you? Christ, that man! He's been on my back the last forty-eight hours. Look, the bodies that were sent over to Kerry were all buried in hospital bags – naked, zipped up and tagged with their names. It was an unmarked, mass grave, but its inhabitants are distinguishable and record-ed. Except this one. Howe's body was wrapped in plastic. Fully dressed. Personal belongings in situ. Nobody gave Howe a bur-ial. He was being hidden. Okay, maybe it's like you said and somebody just dumped him in there after an accident – but wrapped in plastic? Seems a little excessive to me.'

'Right,' Tom said. 'That is revealing.' Kennedy hadn't told him that. Kennedy had told him very little. As usual.

After he'd hung up, the inspector felt unsettled. If the person who'd disposed of Howe's body had used one of the hospital bags, it probably never would have been noticed. His wife would never have known the truth of why her husband had vanished. And a possible murderer would have gone to his or her grave, with people being none the wiser.

The inspector didn't like those sort of what-ifs.

He fell asleep thinking about the various things that could have happened to Howe. And his final thought before he drifted was this: he hadn't been strictly accurate with Moya. He didn't need a time machine to interview the key witnesses at the time of Howe's disappearance. From the sounds of things, quite a few of them still lived on Oileán na Coillte.

CHAPTER 8

It was the cold that stirred Tom the following morning. He'd managed to kick off his blankets during the night and woke with that aching feeling in his joints of having slept with limbs clenched. He was pulling the covers up from the floor to try to get some warmth back in his bones, not knowing what time it was, when there was a rap on the door.

Half-blind, stubbing his toe on an unfamiliar bed leg, the inspector made his way across the room and opened it. It was Colm.

'It's 6 a.m.,' he said. 'We've the breakfast on and Mannix Jr said he'll take you over at 7. The fire is lit downstairs. A freezing fog came in overnight and the pipes are solid. No heating, I'm afraid.'

'Can we sail if there's a fog?' Tom asked, properly awake now.

'With Mannix you can. He knows the route like the back of his hand. Only high winds keep him docked.'

The inspector got dressed quickly. He abandoned his suit jacket in favour of a thick fleece and put on two pairs of socks. Still, he knew it would take him all day to warm up.

Colm and Sabrina had laid on a full Irish breakfast for their guests and made sure they were eating before they left them alone, content they'd done their job as hosts, even if the radiators weren't working.

Tom waited until Ray had gone upstairs to grab the bags before broaching the subject he'd been wanting to raise with Linda since she'd agreed to come on the trip.

'You do know that Emmet McDonagh is over here, don't you?' he said.

She raised an eyebrow, mock disdain on her face.

'A mass grave, a murder, a Supreme Court judge's brother-in-law – why would the Chief Superintendent of the Technical Bureau be here?'

Tom grimaced. So, she knew and had agreed to come anyway. Was that a good or a bad thing?

He had every right to feel nervous. Linda and Emmet's relationship had been less *An Affair to Remember* and more *Fatal Attraction*. These days, it was based on hurling vitriolic abuse at each other. They'd acrimoniously split when, after agreeing to inform their respective spouses of their relationship and sail away into the sunset together, Emmet hadn't kept his side of the bargain. Linda had fallen out with her entire family, so prepared had she been to sacrifice her marriage.

But what she hadn't known was that, at the last moment, Emmet had discovered his wife had breast cancer. He couldn't leave.

Linda's husband had taken her back but her heart was broken. And so began a lifelong campaign of trying to make Emmet suffer, including telling his wife about his betrayal. The two had treated each other despicably ever since.

'I know he's over there,' Linda said. 'Don't worry. We can be adults for a day. In any case, I'm not interested in forensics. I'm here to help you with the history of this place and the interviews with the former doctors, correct?'

'Yes, but . . . you're sure?'

'Mm-hm. Anyway, me and him, maybe it has gone on too long. It's twenty-one years now. Twenty . . .'

She stopped, and looked so sad that Tom thought she might cry.

'Are you okay?' he asked.

She shook her head, not saying no, more to shake off whatever she was thinking.

'I'm fine. Don't mind me.' Linda smiled. 'It's Christmas. I shall be the embodiment of goodwill.'

They'd been expecting a ferry, but the boat Mannix Jr planned to transport them to Oileán na Coillte in was a tiny fishing vessel and its owner, a giant of a man, looked far too big for it.

The boat and Mannix's size were about as much as they could make out, the fog was that thick. Tom stretched his arm out just out of interest.

'Mr Higgins was right. We're not even on this island and I can barely see my fingers.' He turned to their pilot. 'You're absolutely sure it's safe to go out? Would you run the ferry in this?'

'Yup. Only storms cause a problem.'

'Why aren't we on the ferry?' Ray asked.

Mannix looked up from the knot he was untying and beheld Tom's DS like he was some sort of halfwit.

'Three passengers?' was all he said and Ray turned bright red. 'Anyway, are ye getting on?'

Tom and Ray exchanged a look, wondering if there was even room. It took Linda to get things going.

'Oh, come on, you big girls. You can't see your hand, Tom, because you're fifty-one and need glasses. And Ray, any one of these days you're going to confound us all and behave like your physique would lead us to believe.'

'What does that mean?' Ray said, squeezing onto the small bench beside her. 'So I'm not mad on sailing in pea-soup fog in a bloody boat that looks more like a teacup. Surely that's not unusual.'

'I think,' Tom said, climbing aboard, 'that Linda is referring to the fact you're afraid of flying; you're afraid of dogs; you're afraid of blood and now it turns out, you're afraid of water. You're a big six-foot wimp.'

'I'm not afraid of water,' his deputy hissed. 'I'm afraid of drowning.'

They all grabbed the sides of the boat as Mannix climbed back in.

'Drowning's the least of your worries in this water,' he said. 'When the Fear Liath comes down, the selkies aren't far behind.'

'The what and the what?' Ray said, eyes wide as Mannix smiled and turned on the engine.

'The Fear Liath,' Tom said. 'The Grey Man. He brings the fog to lure travellers to their death. And selkies, they're like mermaids. They'll be looking to torture you for a bit, make you obsessed, before dragging you to your watery grave.'

'These are myths, right?' Ray said, casting looks left and right at the water slopping on either side of the boat.

Tom and Linda exchanged a glance, shaking their heads.

The trip across was eerily quiet; the darkness and the fog acted like a thick blanket on sound, the splashing waves barely breaking the silence. The world felt very still. Mannix was contentedly silent and the banter amongst Tom, Ray and Linda dried to a halt as they left land and headed out to sea. Even though there was something about their guide that told them they were in good hands, the boat didn't feel the safest. That, and they were all freezing.

'Nearly there,' Mannix said, after about fifteen minutes.

'A tough journey for patients, this,' Tom said, breaking the tension. The thought of land cheered him. He rubbed his hands briskly and blew on them. 'They must have been terrified.' The words of the diary had stayed with the inspector. And Howe's first trip, he remembered, had been in bright sunshine.

Linda nodded, looking straight ahead at nothing.

'Most of them probably gave up on the boat.'

Mannix had turned the engine off and was guiding the boat manually.

'Gotta bring her in slowly so I don't hit the jetty.'

'What are those lights up there?' Tom asked.

'Arnie Nolan's headlights. He's got his car at the dock. No lighthouse in these parts.'

They stopped talking and let Mannix steer the boat until they gently bumped against what turned out to be a pier. At its foot, a man got out of the car with the lit headlights and walked towards them. Slowly, his silhouette became clearer.

'Morning,' he called out from under a thick scarf and multiple layers. 'Staying for a coffee, Mannix, or are you off out?'

'Heading back home. Too late for a decent haul. Phone across when ye need me.'

'Right so. Ladies first.'

The man offered his hand to Linda and helped her up the ladder, followed by Tom, then Ray. Mannix tossed their bags up, raised his hand in a good-bye and was off, disappearing back into the dense fog.

'Fáilte go dtí Oileán na Coillte,' their host said. 'Not that you can see much of it at the moment. But at least the fog is starting to lift behind us.'

The inspector looked over the man's shoulder and realised he was right. The thick mist had receded a little on land and in the half gloomy light of the early morn, they could see the tall oaks that stood as sentries to the island and the single lonely road that led inland.

He thought of Conrad Howe arriving here all those years ago, to this very spot. The opening pages of his diary spoke of a man filled with excitement for his new appointment.

Of course, Howe had no idea what lay ahead.

He'd had no idea the island would end up being his resting place for forty long years.

CHAPTER 9

'So, your father was the caretaker for the island back in the day and Mannix Jr's father was the ferry operator at the same time, and both sons followed in their dads' footsteps. It's a bit of a family affair, isn't it?'

Tom wrapped his hands around the steaming mug of coffee Arnie Nolan had given him, allowing it to burn his ice-cold fingers just to get the feeling back.

Arnie grinned and took a sip from his own mug. Once the various layers of winter clothing were removed, a young man had been revealed. Late twenties, ginger-haired with fair eyebrows and lashes and a trillion freckles on ruddy, weather-beaten cheeks.

'It's a local affair. Half of Carnbeg would have had links with St Christina's when it was operating, between direct employment and servicing. My mother was one of the cooks.'

'Did she live in, then?'

'In a manner. She lived in this cottage. It was our family home. She has her own small place across on the other side of the island now. Had her eye on it for a while and was waiting for one of the doctors to pop his clogs so she could get it.'

'Your mother lives here still?'

'She does. I suppose she'll be on your list of suspects. Luckily, I'm a bit too young to have killed your doctor. I wasn't born until '84. But Mammy – I guess she could have poisoned him. She *was* the cook.'

He said this deadpan and they all indulged it with a smile, even while Tom was thinking *why not?*

'So, do the houses on the island belong to the hospital? What's the story with them?' he asked. 'Why did some people choose to stay? I mean, I can see it's quite a refuge from the world but it must be tough going. In the winter, especially. And there aren't too many of you living here.'

'Well, you know, this place is all I've ever known so it's hard for me to say why people would choose to stay if they'd lived elsewhere before. I go over to the mainland often enough, but this is home. Though, that's all up in the air now. The houses, including this one, belonged to the hospital. The earl who built the place left the island and all its dwellings to the trustees of the hospital. The trustees aren't individuals, in case you're wondering. The hospital was part-owned and run by various charitable and mental health organisations. When it closed, I think they just sort of forgot about the place, or maybe the island wasn't considered of value back then. Some of the former staff stayed on and there were a few patients who refused to leave.'

'Refused to leave?'

Arnie nodded.

'Seriously. Some old folks who'd been here all their lives and wanted to die here. All long gone, now. Then the State made an offer for the island. It was accepted and they've awarded a contract to a tourism agency to redevelop the place. Knocking the hospital is the first step. They plan to build a retreat on the site, an exclusive hotel. Nobody's sure what they want to do with the houses – whether we've a case to stay living in them or whether they want to sell them off too. We all pay token rent but nobody was ever allowed to buy.'

'I'm surprised they don't want to do something like they did with Spike Island,' Ray said, referring to the former prison island off the neighbouring County Cork coast. 'Turn the hospital into a visitor attraction.'

'I think it was considered,' Arnie nodded, 'but ruled out on the grounds of sensitivity.'

Linda snorted.

'Yes. Very sensitive. The government is terrified it will be sued by former psychiatric hospital patients, like it has been by the inmates of all the other institutions. When they're reeling off their fake platitudes of regret, they won't want anybody pointing out they've been ferrying troupes of tourists over here for a spot of voyeurism.'

'That's about the sum of it,' Arnie agreed.

'It would have been easier for the people who live here, though, wouldn't it?' Tom asked. 'What will happen to everybody if they tell you to move?'

A shadow fell on their host's face.

'None of us know. For me, it's my job, too. The trustees pay me to take care of the hospital's security, some of the upkeep on the island, that sort of thing. Minimal but enough to live on. The uncertainty is why we opposed the development. But there are too few of us to be enough of an obstacle.'

'How many, exactly?'

'Well, there's the former big boss, Dr Lawrence Boylan. He's in the grand house, as we call it, the earl's home. Carla Crowley – she was a nurse. We've another former doctor – Robert O'Hare. The hospital chemist is still here, Edward Lane. There's mum and then there's me. Oh, and Andrew Collins.'

'Andrew Collins?' Tom said, and he and Ray exchanged a puzzled look. 'The doctor?'

'That's him. You know him, then?'

'Only just met him, but yes. He was a friend and colleague of Howe's. We met him in Dublin. He didn't say anything about living here.'

'That's why I thought of him last, to be honest. He's not here an awful lot; he spends most of his time in the capital. But he does have a house here. I think he's one of the longest residents besides Dr Boylan. Anyhow, do you want to stay here tonight? I presume you're not going back over to the mainland? Your lot have taken one of the larger houses nearer to the hospital but I don't think there'd be enough space for the three of you. They've a cast of thousands working down at that grave.'

'Well, yes, I suppose. If we're not putting you out. We'd like to get a look around the hospital and interview the people who live on the island today. It probably wouldn't be fair to expect Mannix to remain on stand-by.'

'It's no bother. I've room if you two lads don't mind bunking together. I can fit yourself, Dr McCarn, in the room in the eaves. Sure, I'll bring you down to your colleagues now and you can get a spot of work done before lunch. How's that for efficiency?'

'In the eaves,' Linda whispered in Tom's ear as they waited for Arnie to don multiple layers of clothing again. 'Very shabby chic. Do you think I could buy this little dwelling when the government puts it on the market?'

'Don't be unkind. And remember, you're to be nice to Emmet when we see him.'

Linda fixed her hands in prayer and nodded.

'Scout's honour,' she said.

'You're mixing up your oaths,' the inspector pointed out.

'And I'm not sure you believe in either of them.' He followed her through the door to the car. He hoped she really did intend to be on her best behaviour. It could mean the difference between one murder on the island and two.

'There are no birds.'

'What?'

Tom lowered his gaze and looked at Ray. The inspector had been staring up at the large grey hospital building – square, symmetrical, Georgian in style, but with four tall storeys instead of the usual two or three associated with the period. A lower floor was visible just below the railings that surrounded the front of the building. All of the windows were encased in iron bars.

It wasn't an attractive building. Even if he didn't know its former purpose, Tom would have thought that. He realised now why the developers hadn't considered keeping the façade at least. There would be nothing aesthetically appealing about all this dull grey stone to somebody seeking a restful hideaway.

'There isn't a bird in the sky,' Ray said. 'I went to Auschwitz a few years ago and it was the same thing.'

'It's too cold for birds,' Tom said. 'And I don't think you can quite compare this place with a concentration camp. It's got a gothic creepiness to it alright, but it's still just a hospital.'

'Where's this grave then?' Linda asked.

'You can walk around to the rear of the hospital along the side there,' Arnie informed them. 'The pit is out back. The demolition lads knocked the rear perimeter wall and old staff bungalows first and were heading towards the hospital when the surveyors realised that they were bulldozing right over a grave. That's why the main building is still intact. I'm going

inside to make a few calls to let the others know you'll be visiting later. I'll come and find you out back.'

'Thanks for that,' Tom said. 'When you do, is there any
chance you could give us a quick tour inside the hospital building before we move on? Is it okay to walk around inside? It's not
falling down, is it?'

'God, no. Most of it is fine, anyway. There are one or two bits
of it locked up, they wouldn't be the safest. But that's at the
basement level. There's not much to see down there, anyway,
bar the rats. I can give you the tour, no bother. I know the place
inside out.'

'I'm not sure I'm wearing the correct footwear for this,' Linda
said, as the three of them followed the directions they'd been
given. The ground got muckier as they went. Tom looked down
at Linda's feet, surprised. The tall woman very rarely wore heels,
from what he recalled. And she wasn't on this occasion, either.
The psychologist was wearing snow white Nike runners.

He raised his eyebrows, and then winced every time their
feet landed on a particularly soft patch of mud, as though it
were his own shoes being destroyed.

It was about to get a whole lot messier.

The scene behind the hospital was a massive excavation site,
with mud hills and debris dotted everywhere. Emmet's large
team were all clad in head-to-toe forensic white suits, stained
from days of working in wet and dirty conditions.

A wide perimeter had been established around the pit with
marking tape and a huge tent stood beside the freshly dug area.
The Tech chief's makeshift lab, Tom imagined.

He spotted Emmet immediately – the man's bulk distinguish-
ing him from his coworkers. He was also the only one talking,
barking orders at minions who worked silently and efficiently.

A body was being taken from the grave, still ensconced in its hospital issue bag. One of the final few.

They waited until it had been safely moved into the tent and Emmet was back up on terra firma before the inspector called out to him.

'Ah, Tom, howya'. Greetings of the season, or what we're having of it.'

Emmet grabbed Tom's hand in his and pulled him in for a bear hug.

'That little runt Kennedy ruined your holiday, too, eh?' he whispered. 'Well, solidarity in the trenches. Literally, in my case.'

The Tech chief stood back and pushed his glasses up on his nose. It was then he noticed Tom's company, hanging back a little.

'DS Lennon,' he said, curtly, in acknowledgement. That was his only greeting.

Linda rolled her eyes.

'Hello to you, too, you old codger,' she said, then gave a worried-looking Tom a wink. 'I see you've lost some weight. Must be all that jumping in and out of that pit. It looks well on you.'

Emmet kept his gaze directed at the inspector, flicking his floppy, unnaturally dark fringe out of his eyes.

'We've almost emptied the site,' he said. 'We're just . . .'

'Emmet,' Tom interrupted. 'Linda was speaking to you.'

The Tech chief hesitated, then turned and looked at her.

'I know she was speaking to me. I have absolutely nothing to say to her. Right, Linda? I'm here. You're here. Of course you are, it's a mad house, your natural habitat. We're on this island together. But I do not want to speak to you and you do not need to speak to me.'

His words were delivered with such ferocity that Linda recoiled. Even Tom and Ray were taken aback and they'd both witnessed heated exchanges between the pair in the past.

'There's no need—' Tom began but Emmet held his hand up.

'It has nothing to do with you, gentlemen. Now. Will I fill you in on the salient facts?'

The inspector was about to protest but felt a grip on his arm.

'You don't need me here,' Linda said. 'Look, I'll just go wait inside until you're ready. I won't go wandering where I shouldn't. You heard our host – any unsafe parts are cordoned off.'

The inspector nodded. It was the best course of action. He didn't know what else to do.

He walked Linda the few hundred metres to the rear of the asylum and held the unlocked door open for her. Arnie had told them the building had been opened up for their benefit. The inspector had asked why it needed the security, considering how isolated the place was.

'The records are inside,' Arnie said. 'Not that anybody is likely to rob them but it seems appropriate, you know?'

'You will come back for me?' Linda joked, crossing the threshold into the atrium that served as the rear entrance. The jest was made from force of habit, but there was a distressed tone to Linda's voice that Tom wasn't familiar with.

'You're just going in for a rest,' he delivered his line equally lamely.

Back over by the tent, Ray was remonstrating with Emmet. The older man raised both his hands as Tom approached, the inspector's face as thunderous as his deputy's.

'No,' he said loudly. 'Don't you start as well. You've no idea what that woman has done. No idea. And now's not the time to discuss it. We've work to do. Can we drop this?'

The inspector sucked in his cheeks and swallowed the rebuke. He was here to do a job, not be a counsellor. The personal problems of two people old enough to know better weren't the priority.

'Right,' he said, and flashed Ray a warning look to let it go. 'Talk to me. What did you find in the grave?'

Emmet nodded, the matter closed.

'Good. Follow me.'

He brought them over to the side of the pit as far as they could go and not risk falling in. There were four or five body bags visible at its bottom, partially encased in mud from the burials above.

'That's the bottom layer,' Emmet said. 'The hospital used this pit over a number of years. It was dug and the bodies were laid out in a row, then that layer was covered completely and the earth was allowed to settle. The entire pit was probably covered over with sheets of wood, or something akin, while it was open. A new layer of bodies was then added, and so it continued. As Moya probably told you, each cadaver was found in those hospital bags you see, naked, zipped, buried without ceremony, but with a certain ritual nonetheless. The victim's body had none of that.

'Every layer had fifteen body bags and this was done four times. It was patterned and predictable. But the first forensic team realised there was something amiss right from the top row. There were sixteen bodies – the victim being the addition. His body was found lying at a right angle to the others, wrapped in plastic sheeting, hidden beneath the body bags. What I suspect is that he was dropped in and then somebody climbed into the pit and positioned him. The wall would have been fitted with a rudimentary ladder – we found the remains of two wooden rails staked at the side that were probably used by whoever was managing the grave.

'So, let's say the killer lifted up the bottoms of four of the body bags, the legs – the lightest bit – and placed his victim's body underneath. And, as we've discovered, the pit was due to be filled in very soon after. Whoever hid him there was clever and knew what they were doing.'

'Right,' Tom said. 'Nicely stomach-turning. So, what's been happening with the other bodies?'

'Come on into the tent for this bit.'

Emmet led the way into the makeshift morgue, where three tables held the recently removed corpses. The skeletons were visible in the zipped down black bags but the smell of death and rot had long since passed, along with flesh and organs. One of the skulls still had tufts of reddish-brown hair attached. Tom gave it a glance then turned away. It reminded him too much of the bodies they'd found in Glendalough the previous summer, young women, the victims of a serial killer.

'As soon as it was discovered there was a mass grave here, the Bureau sent over one of our regional forensics teams,' Emmet told them. 'There are records in the hospital for the site and each body bag was labelled with its occupant's name. The hospital seemed to have followed good practice in that regard, even if the method of burial is distasteful to any good Christian.'

'You mean, not buried individually with headstones, that sort of thing?' Ray asked.

'No. I mean, the hospital might have been named for a saint, but its back garden is not hallowed ground.'

'I see.'

'Anyhow, the team has been removing the bodies and

checking them against the records before sending them back to the lab in Kerry General. The causes of death were recorded as natural – well, if you can call it natural – but now post-mortems have to be carried out as much as they can be, considering we're mainly talking about skeletons here. The body bags are well-lined, but not impenetrable or indestructible. A few more decades and we'd be talking proper ashes to ashes, dust to dust.'

'That's a lot of bodies to process,' Tom said.

'Indeed. And I didn't realise the enormity of it when I got the call on Christmas Eve. We won't dwell on that. My heart can't take it. In any case, we re-examined all work initiated by the first team in light of what was found and took over the remaining excavation. We went from having a sensational mass grave to a murder site, but so far we've discovered no other bodies we weren't expecting to be there. We're opening each bag as it comes up to establish it only contains the routine corpse, nothing out of the ordinary, and we'll transfer this final lot over to Kerry tomorrow.'

'Is this the only pit? Are we certain of that?'

'We've run prods into the soil around here – there's nothing else down there. Cadaver dogs wouldn't be much use given the length of time involved. Are you thinking if there are more pits there could be more murdered bodies?'

Tom shrugged.

'We've only one disappearance that we know of, but yeah.'

'Well, I've done some homework for you. The records detail the layout and history of this grave and the dates of the burials run from 1961 to 1972. It transpires that post-1972, all deaths recorded at the hospital resulted in bodies shipped to the mainland. On the other side of the island there's a small graveyard, which we haven't touched. It's full of headstones running from the mid-1800s to the 1960s, with a few of the island's locals buried there later on. So we can speculate that the cemetery was full or reserved and the hospital looked to other forms of disposal in that 1961–1972 period, for bodies whose families had no interest in being returned. Hence the pit. There's no record for any others, that we've found.'

'Right. By the way, what did you mean by that earlier comment about deaths not being natural?'

'I think that's what you brought *her* for,' Emmet nodded in the direction of the hospital, his mouth set with bitterness. 'Have a look at the records and get her to explain the medical procedures performed on some of these poor sods before they died. All perfectly legal and all utterly reprehensible.'

'What are you saying?' Tom said. 'That some of the patients here died as a result of their treatment in the asylum?'

'That's exactly what I'm saying,' Emmet said. 'According to the records, by modern standards more than half of them were actually murdered. But it was professional murder, sanctioned by the State, so you don't need to worry your head too much about it. We just need to find out who killed the nice, respectable doctor. Not his charges.

'Who said class was dead, eh?'

CHAPTER 10

'You know what's really unsettling about that mass grave?'

Tom waved up ahead to Arnie who was waiting for them at the back entrance to the hospital.

'What's that, then?' Ray asked his boss. 'And I take it you're referring to something other than sixty bodies being thrown into unsanctified ground and a murdered corpse hidden amongst them – something more worrying than that?'

'Yes, actually. I'm referring to the fact that it's within sight of the hospital.' Tom nodded up at the building ahead.

Ray looked back at the scene.

'I see what you mean.'

Arnie led them through the glass-roofed atrium and into a long corridor that was bathed in green. Green terrazzo hardwearing floor; green painted walls, scuffed and marked by decades of traffic; and even a light shade of green on the ceiling, though it may have been a dull white absorbing all the colour around it.

They found Linda in an office towards the bottom of the corridor, sitting behind a desk and reading from a bound journal with an obscure medical reference for its title.

'Fascinating,' she said, and stood to join them. 'Most of the books in this room are probably collector's items. I hope all this material will be archived properly before the hospital is demolished?'

Arnie nodded.

'Absolutely. Some of it is worth a fortune. Dr Boylan has insisted on its preservation and the trustees wrote it into their condition of sale. He's in charge of overseeing the packing up of everything, although he's been delaying it as much as possible. Part of the obstruction strategy.'

'Perhaps don't share too much of that,' Tom said. 'Us being the Guards and everything.'

'Oh. Right. Anyhow, it's interesting you landed in this office, Dr McCarn. This entire corridor served as the staff's offices – and the records are kept in Dr Boylan's and his secretary's rooms at the other end – but this one here, so I'm told, belonged to Dr Howe. Most of the texts on these shelves probably belonged to the man himself, originally. Nobody would have liked to throw them out and his poor wife wouldn't have had much use for them.'

'Really?' The inspector looked around with new interest, though aware the room would have been much used by others in the years following Howe's disappearance. It seemed basic enough – a couple of filing cabinets, a full wall of academic tomes. Tom scanned their titles. One caught his attention and he withdrew it.

'Incredible,' he muttered, flicking to the inside page where the first edition year was printed.

'What is it?' Ray asked.

'A study on treating and curing homosexuality. 1957.'

'Do you need to do things in here, fingerprinting or any-thing?' Arnie asked.

Tom smiled and shook his head.

'No. The crime is too old. Let's have a quick look around.'

'No bother. I'll show you a corridor or two on each floor.

Otherwise it will take forever. The place is massive. We'll start at the top and make our way down. Sort of the reverse of what the patients would have wanted.'

'Eh?'

'You'll see,' Arnie said, as they left the office. 'The top floor is like five star at the Ritz compared to those below it.'

Not quite the Ritz, Tom thought when they climbed the stairs to the highest floor in the asylum. In fact, it reminded him of pretty much every hospital he'd ever encountered, just more dated and shabby. They quickly made their way through the warren of corridors, slowing on the final one so Arnie could talk them through a few rooms.

Dusty yellow curtains hung in the windows of the wards and private rooms, and white steel-framed beds stood in rows against the walls. Rubber mattresses were piled up in most of the rooms. At the end of the corridor was what looked like a patients' lounge. Here, brown, hard-backed armchairs were placed around small coffee tables, their material scratchy and uncomfortable-looking but mitigated by faded, striped cushions. Vases, cracked and chipped, were displayed on the windowsills. And in the corner, on a shelf fixed to the wall, a lone pair of rabbit ears marked the spot where a television once sat.

'It seems nice enough up here,' Ray said. 'Not what I was expecting.'

'This would have been as good as it got for the patients,' Arnie explained. 'In a way, the floors of the hospital reflected the level of insanity. The cases on the top floor were deemed the least dangerous. They'd have had access to the most modern treatment facilities, technology – well, things like TV – and so on. The hospital was modernised in the seventies, bar the basement level. That's why the structure is partially unsound.

They never strengthened the foundations to cope with the development overhead. I suppose the place would eventually have had to be knocked, even if it weren't for the sale.'

'Were they saving money?' Tom asked.

Arnie shrugged. 'What else, with bureaucrats?'

'It's got such history, though,' Ray said. 'Couldn't the developers just convert it? Invest in the existing building?'

'I think the people who'll be marketing the place will want a different tagline than "Forget your worries – stay in a former asylum".'

Ray shrugged. 'It just seems like a shame.'

'You mightn't feel as fond of the place as we make our way downstairs,' Arnie said. 'Even I get spooked in the basement. It's nonsense, of course.'

The next level was similar to the floor above, though they noted it was all wards on this corridor, no private rooms, and the patients' leisure room wasn't nearly as comfortable. The bathing facilities were two wide open communal rooms, one for men and one for women, and the toilet cubicles had no doors. Upstairs there had been individual bathrooms.

'Where did the live-in staff sleep and socialise?' Tom asked.

'One of the wings off the ground floor contains the kitchen and some staff quarters,' Arnie answered. 'But as I said earlier, there were some bungalows on the grounds. At the outer boundaries, by the walls. They were the first to be knocked.'

'Right. And how many people would have been treated here at any given time?'

'I'm not entirely sure,' Arnie said. 'I was only a kid the last time it was operational. I wouldn't even be able to tell you how many staff were here. All I'm expert on is its layout. The place was built in a corridor-style, a type of design that was fashionable for asylums in the 19th century. The earl did his homework. The administration offices were based in the middle of the ground floor, with corridors for the patients running off to either side. You can see even on these floors that there's a segregation between the corridors. That was to separate sexes but also to allow for the isolation of any particularly volatile cases. It's a clever design.'

'You do know your stuff,' Tom said.

'I read a lot,' Arnie shrugged. 'It's good to know the value of things.'

'It is a real shame they're not keeping you on as a tour guide. Anyhow, I'm sure we can get the other information on staff numbers and so on from Dr Boylan. And if his memory escapes him, the records downstairs will help.'

'They will. There's enough of them, from what I'm told. But they're well ordered. Your lot found the records for the grave quick enough.'

They were on the second floor now and as soon as they entered the first room, Tom felt a change in the atmosphere. He realised immediately what it was. These lower windows were just below the tree-line and the combination of the branches outside and the heavier grilles on the windows made everything darker. Without the winter sun shining on the glass, the rooms were a few degrees colder. And everything inside had lost its colour. The walls, once magnolia, perhaps, were now dirty and grey.

The wards contained empty bed frames and the remains of the curtains that surrounded them. They passed a large room with benches nailed to either side, bereft of any other furniture.

'It was a common belief that patients should socialise,' Linda said as they halted by the room. 'But there was no stimulation. No radio, TV, or books or games. People could go mad from the boredom. Then, if they reacted angrily or violently to their incarceration and treatment, that behaviour was deemed insanity. It was a Catch 22. They would respond to being locked up as you or I would but the very act of that would satisfy the accusation of madness made against them.'

It was on the first floor that they encountered the first of the padded cells. There was a small row of them, each with a wire-mesh glass window set in the door so those locked in the rooms could be safely observed. The doors swung open freely now and yet, stepping inside one of them, Tom felt an urgent need to keep his foot in the doorway in case it closed on him and he was trapped there.

'I can't hack going in there,' Ray said. 'It's giving me the willies from out here.'

'There's nothing frightening about a padded room,' Linda said. 'They're still in use. They're for the patient's safety, trust me.'

On the ground floor, Arnie skipped the administration offices and first showed them the wing where the staff quarters and catering facilities had been housed.

'So,' Tom said, 'would Dr Howe have stayed here? Or in one of the cottages? Who'll be able to tell us?'

'I can, as it happens,' Arnie said. 'We've been talking about him since it all kicked off. My mother says very few of the doctors lived in or right beside the hospital. That was mainly the nurses and attendants. But apparently he did live in one of the bungalows on the grounds. He had a family in Dublin and returned regularly, whereas some of the people who worked here made the island their main home. They got first priority for the proper houses around the island.'

'That makes sense,' the inspector nodded, disappointed that they'd lost the chance to examine the doctor's old residence, even if little could have been gleaned from it.

They moved on to the next corridor, stopping outside one of the larger rooms. It looked like an old operating theatre, with a single steel table in the centre and large, low-hanging lampshades overhead.

Tom looked to Linda for explanation.

'For surgical interventions,' she said.

'Like what?'

'You don't want to know.'

CHAPTER 11

Diary Entry

I think it may have been a test. Throw me in at the deep end and see how I react.

If it was, I passed, but at great expense to myself.

I managed to look calm, as though it wasn't the most disturbing thing I'd ever witnessed. Then, afterwards, I ran to the toilets and vomited. So hard, I thought my stomach itself would come up.

I knew it was going to be horrendous the moment we fetched the patient from the ward. Already in St Christina's, and even in my last post, I have helped to drag many a troubled or violent patient back to a ward or into an isolation unit for their own benefit. But this man, my God – he was terror-stricken. He fought us tooth and claw and then, on the stairs, he collapsed and cried and pleaded not to go to the theatre. Within sight of it, he began to scream again and then went into a spasm so vicious he near bit his tongue clean off.

We strapped him, with great difficulty, onto the operating table. The attending nurse tried to sedate him, but couldn't keep the needle in the vein in his hand and blood was spraying everywhere. It took another nurse practically sitting on the man's arm before the sedative could be administered. Another few minutes and the patient had calmed and slipped into unconsciousness.

By then, we were all more than a little shaken.

Though I had no experience of them, the surgeon invited me to observe the lobotomy. I had to agree, despite my shock. I wanted to learn, after all.

'What you've just witnessed,' he said, 'will never happen again with this patient. The lobotomy is the miracle cure. You need to see it in practice to fully appreciate the genius behind it.'

So I watched from the door as he drilled holes in either side of the man's head. The sound reverberated through my teeth and it smelled like the flesh was being burned. He took the scalpel then and severed the frontal lobe.

It barely took any time but felt like the longest hour of my life. Afterwards, the surgeon was at pains to ensure the man's open head wound was stitched carefully and immaculately cleaned.

'We must make sure, now he's been cured, that he doesn't die from an infection,' the surgeon said and laughed.

I laughed too, tasting acid bile on the back of my tongue.

Later, I sifted through my journals until I found articles on the lobotomy procedure. I knew, before I came to St Christina's, that it had been common. The man who popularised it, Walter Freeman, apparently undertook three thousand himself. He travelled the United States conducting the operation in front of audiences. He even performed it on children.

Were my stomach not entirely empty, that would have brought more retching.

It was pronounced at the time as the greatest advancement in treating highly disturbed patients. But it was no longer used as much as it once had been – only now on the extreme cases.

I didn't know the history of the patient but Dolores told me the next day that he was a violent rapist. I suspect she could see I was traumatised by what I'd seen and wanted me to understand the need for the operation.

And she was right. When I heard that, I felt better. I visited the patient afterwards and found him lying on the floor by his bed. The ward nurse had moved him there, because the mattress on his bed was stained through with faeces and urine. He is a complete vegetable now. But, given his crimes, yes, I can see that perhaps what was done was a mercy to him and to the women who could have been his future victims.

And, yet, I cannot help but feel that it is not very progressive. Slicing part of somebody's brain off is an admission that the patient cannot be cured – when I hold out so much more hope for them.

CHAPTER 12

As soon as Arnie opened the door to the basement stairs, the smell came up to meet them. A damp, malodorous stench of a space neglected, with just the tinge of bleach masking the worst.

'I rarely come down here,' he said. 'Most of it is shut off, but on top of that, the electrics are faulty, so I have to leave the lights off. It's not worth the risk of a fuse sparking and the whole building igniting from the ground up. And it's terrifying in the dark, no matter how much you tell yourself there's nothing here to worry about.'

Tom could understand it. He was desperate to go back upstairs and outside, to feel the fresh air on his face, to breathe. He couldn't imagine what it must have been like for the men and women who were kept in this part of the asylum – the lack of natural daylight, the freezing cold, the isolation. He was still on edge after the operating theatre.

Still, they needed this brief tour. He'd insisted Arnie at least show them part of the basement. The inspector figured it would have been pointless to come all the way over to the island and not even look at the place where Conrad Howe had worked in the years before he vanished. And he wanted to familiarise himself with the asylum so he could better understand the references in Howe's diary. The basement featured – he knew that much from just flicking through.

Arnie gave them all torches and they directed their beams into the stone cells on either side of the corridor. Most had tiny windows set high in the walls, looking up to the iron railings that surrounded the building's front. Some, however, had no windows. It was those rooms that were the most distressing.

One of the rooms held a single suspended contraption that looked like a chair, attached to the ceiling by some kind of pulley.

Tom ran his flashlight over it. The wire holding it up still gleamed in places and reflected the torch beam, giving it a movement-like quality that was uncanny.

'Any clue, Linda?' he asked.

'Yes. Let's just say, it's a story for when we're back out in the sun.'

Arnie stopped and pointed out a set of double doors ahead.

'I won't bring you any further,' he said. 'Beyond this is where the foundations are the shakiest. They stopped using it after they modernised anyway, so there's nothing there.'

'I think we've seen enough, anyway,' Tom agreed, eager to get back upstairs. He thought he'd heard a squeak. He had no desire to witness Ray's reaction to the sudden appearance of a rat and, in any case, he wanted to read a few more pages of Howe's diary.

CHAPTER 13

Diary Entry

St Christina's is not what I expected.

Parts of the asylum are actually quite modern, especially on the upper levels. I feel like I'm on familiar ground when I'm up there. The patients' lounge on the fourth floor has a radio and books and somebody usually ensures there are fresh flowers brought in regularly from the gardens.

The patients there are generally of the more genteel variety, too. Their families have paid generously into the asylum's coffers to allow them a period of rest and treatment for minor diagnoses. Some of the ladies have afflictions of the nerves and the gentlemen often have acute anxiety issues and nervous disorders. One of the men ended up here after he returned from the Battle of Aachen in 1944. He wakes with nightmares, occasionally frightening the others with his screams. Yet during the day he is calm and dignified, an intelligent chap who keeps to himself mostly.

There are a couple of patients on the top floor who moved up from the floors below. These are the patients who have shown the most promise of recovery, such as one or two of the women admitted while suffering with insanity caused by childbirth. They have become more balanced over time. Their stays are quite tolerable and eventually their families will take them out.

I am always relieved when I'm assigned work on the top floor.

I have been allocated accommodation on the hospital grounds because I have a family home to return to, but most nights I find myself sleeping in the hospital, when work runs late or I feel I might be needed.

It's then that I'm reminded what kind of place this really is.

There's so rarely any quiet.

Of course, it's noisy during the day, too. There's a constant, chattering murmur. Some of the patients are quite empty in their heads but their little tongues can't stop wagging, spouting all sorts of harmless nonsense. Many of my colleagues say they're driven half-demented themselves by the continuous babble. I don't mind it. Of all the noise in the asylum, it's the least offensive.

Sometimes the patients can get manic.

A boy grabbed me just yesterday in the patients' communal area on the third floor. He was gulping back great big sobs as he tried to tell me his circumstances and plead his case. He said his father, a respectable businessman, believed him to have designs on an older man in their village and he'd sent him to St Christina's to be treated for homosexuality. The lad is just eighteen and in amongst the sobs and the breathless story-telling I discerned that the older man in the boy's village was powerful – in fact, somebody I have read about in the papers. It sounds as though he has been behaving inappropriately towards our patient from a very young age. And him with a wife!

Had I not already seen so much in my life, I would hardly believe the young man. Instead, I felt sorry for him. It seems so unfair, the course his life has taken. But if his family brought him here and are unwilling to take him home, I don't see what can be done. I promised to speak to somebody higher up about his predicament but I don't know what good it will do. I'm still new and my opinion doesn't hold weight.

He's just one of the many sad cases. You would never believe, in the outside world, how little it takes to cross the threshold from there to here. A mere blink of an eye. We had a nasty incident last week when one of the patients became quite violent and attacked his doctor. The patient bit the doctor's leg and had to be forcibly restrained and moved to the basement. Only the very worst cases are sent there.

Anyhow, a patient, a young woman who I've grown quite fond of, told me she'd heard a very interesting tale about the man. I took what she said with a pinch of salt, of course. Minnie is twenty-going-on-ten at times. Her parents had her admitted after she suffered severe, inexplicable bouts of depression in her late teens. The scars on her wrists are evidence of how much care she needs, though she still claims she's being forcibly held against her will and would do fine on the outside.

'You wait and see,' she announced recently, winking comically and tossing her long dark hair. 'I'll fly out that window like a little bird one day and find myself a nice little flat somewhere up in Dublin. I'll get a job in a hairdressers and any time a nurse comes in, I'll spit in her tea and have a wee in her shampoo. Bloody bitches. They all need a bloody good ride, the stuck-up, dried-up old cows.'

She's always coming out with the most hilarious things and truly fantastical tales but there's no real harm in her, bar to herself. And in this instance, her story was utterly compelling, embellished with outstanding detail.

Minnie said an older patient, who was around when the man who bit the doctor was admitted, told her the man had been a farmer who'd fallen out with his landlord over money matters. The landlord was friendly with the local judge and between them, as a cautionary tale to other tenants, they had the farmer committed to St Christina's.

Minnie claimed the farmer went slowly mad when repeated efforts to gain his release were thwarted because he refused to apologise and make financial reparations to his landlord.

'I'm sure that's not true,' I told Minnie. 'And in any case, the man is quite clearly insane now.'

'Listen here,' she said. 'I might be mad as a brush but I'm not a bloody liar. That's what I was told.'

'Yes, but whoever told you it might not be trustworthy.'

'She's more trustworthy than the bastards who work in here. You excluded.' She winked at me again. 'You're the only nice one. But it's true, what you say. He's insane now. That's what happens when you keep us here. We're all going crazy wanting to get out.'

On the one hand, I cannot equate Minnie's story with the man I saw raving and screeching, pulling at the few tufts of hair left on his head, being dragged down stairs with the blood from the doctor's leg still smeared around his mouth.

And yet, sometimes I wonder. There is something so very fragile about the mind. When I look at those in here, even poor Minnie, it makes me think: is it just luck that I am here to work rather than to be 'cured'?

CHAPTER 14

'Where are they now?'

'In the asylum.'

'Why? What do they want in there?'

'To see where Conrad worked, I imagine. They haven't been in there long, they're just looking about the place. We knew they'd go there. There's no need to worry. We've taken the necessary precautions.'

'Presumably they'll want to see the records.'

'Yes.'

'I knew we should have moved them.'

'The records?'

'Everything.'

'The police won't stay in there long. We're safe. They're planning to interview everybody on the island, I'm told.'

'And what will you say to them?'

'Nothing of import. I'm involved in this as much as you.'

'Just remember that.'

'There's no need for you to remind me.'

'I know. I know, I'm sorry. I'm jittery.'

'There's no need to be. Like I said, we've taken care of everything. And remember, what they're investigating happened forty years ago. They won't figure out anything.'

'I still feel uneasy about them being inside the asylum.'

'Don't. They'll be finished in there soon and they won't find anything.'

'Maybe they won't discover anything to do with Con's death, but that's not what I'm worried about, as well you know. It's what we're doing now that concerns me.'

'I've told you, I took all the necessary precautions.'

'But . . . I don't know. I think we might need to move them.'

'What does he say? Where is he?'

(Sigh)

'He's upstairs. He didn't sleep last night. I told him to rest.'

'Let's speak to him when he wakes. Reassure him. We can rest easy. They cannot solve what happened forty years ago and once they realise that, they'll leave. We can decide then what needs to be done.'

'I hope you're right. Either way, I think it's coming to an end.'

'It doesn't have to . . .'

'No. That's where you're wrong. It does. We've done as much as we can. It's time to end things. We knew when the island was sold it would all come to a head. Nothing we've done has slowed things down. It's time to act.'

'I don't want murder on my conscience.'

'Ha! You already have. This started in 1972. You mightn't have been involved then but when you agreed to keep the secret, you took it on your conscience. I'm sorry, but it's true. What's another death? In any case, it's not murder when it's done out of charity. That's what you must tell yourself. We're not murderers.'

'No. You're wrong. I'm not a murderer. You are. And I won't cross that line.'

'Oh, but you will. Wait and see just how far you're willing to go to protect yourself. Take it from somebody who knows.'

CHAPTER 15

'My mother said she'd pop along to the house later and have dinner with us,' Arnie told them, as they sped away from the asylum. Tom looked up from the diary. It was getting too dark to read anyway.

'I couldn't get hold of Edward Lane, the chemist, but we can just call out if you like. And our nurse, Carla, has asked if she could see you in the morning, if it's not too inconvenient. She had a bad dose over Christmas and she's still in bed. Mannix says he's not running the ferry until midday tomorrow so you'll have time.'

'That all sounds fine,' Tom said. 'We'll do Lane in the morning as well, then. When we've finished with Boylan and O'Hare, I wouldn't mind coming back here to look at the records. Would that be all right?'

'Sure. This is the most exciting thing that's happened to me in quite a while. I planned to head back myself later to lock up, so I can leave you in Dr Boylan's office while I do my rounds.'

'How big is this island, by the way?' Ray asked.

'About ten kilometres squared. It's not that much bigger than Inis Meáin, the second largest of the Aran Islands. Obviously with far less population. Nowadays, anyhow.'

'How many would be on Inis Meáin?'

'Ah, about two hundred I'd guess. A metropolis compared to here. Even when there were hundreds here, they were mainly concentrated in and around the hospital. Everybody who lives in the cottages has always had a great deal of privacy.'

'And loneliness, surely?' Linda said.

Arnie shrugged.

'It has its merits.'

A low mist had started to creep in with the arrival of the evening sky and Arnie fell quiet as he concentrated on the narrow road.

'Sorry,' he said, after a few minutes of silent driving. 'We get a lot of fog being so exposed to the sea. I have to focus.'

'No worries,' Tom said, understanding. Their driver obviously knew the roads well and wasn't expecting to meet other vehicles, but still, you could never tell. Tom imagined all the inhabitants of the island lived in a constant state of caution.

He turned to Linda.

'This Boylan character, what do you know of him? In a medical sense, I mean. I thought you and I could talk to him and Ray could have a chat with O'Hare.'

'I only know what I've read,' Linda answered. 'But that's plenty in the last couple of days. In his prime, Lawrence Boylan was considered a very progressive medic. He wrote numerous groundbreaking papers on the treatment of the insane. In retrospect, a lot of what he advocated, the medical profession has since turned its back on. For example, he was a keen supporter of shock therapy in all its forms, including milder procedures like ice baths. Under his stewardship, St Christina's was considered one of the more modern asylums. The theory that caring for patients somewhere peaceful, away from the noise and bustle of a city, gained a lot of traction. There were several smaller hospitals built on the mainland in isolated rural locations trying to replicate the perceived success on Oileán na Coillte. Though, Boylan maintained, it was the water on all sides, the *cutting off* of patients, that ensured residents of St Christina's had real serenity.'

'Who could check?' Tom said. 'They were so far removed, nobody could know what was going on here.'

'Precisely. And that's how it all started to fall apart, really. There was a movement – across the world, not just in Ireland – to have families more involved in the treatment of their loved ones. Anyway, psychiatry was starting to work alongside the wider medical profession,' Linda continued. 'People were beginning to accept that the mentally ill could be treated by the whole system and not just by an elitist coterie of psychiatrists. Fewer and fewer were being admitted to asylums and when they were, it was generally less traumatic. New drugs came to the fore and the concept of counselling was universally accepted. GPs were able to prescribe stronger anti-depressants, and people didn't automatically end up in a hospital if they had a breakdown. There's still a huge stigma, but things have come on.'

'So Boylan, once avant-garde, became old-fashioned,' Tom said.

'Yes. They started to wind down St Christina's in the late eighties. All the patients were eventually removed – well, as we've heard, those who wanted to go.'

'I can imagine that could make a man very bitter,' the inspector said. 'Having your life's work questioned in hindsight. Having modern eyes cast aspersions on your advances.'

'It could and it did. Boylan wrote a lot of very angry pieces for medical journals but then he just disappeared off the scene. Either he accepted the new age or editors refused to print him.'

'You'll be able to ask him yourself, now,' Arnie said, breaking his silence. 'We're here.'

The Land Rover's headlights revealed the entrance to a driveway, tall stone pillars on either side. Sculpted horses adorned the tops of the pillars, rearing on their hind legs.

'Impressive,' Tom said, leaning forward to get a better look.

'From the earl's family crest,' Arnie told them. 'The Dunree men were all military, apparently.'

The car travelled along the short driveway and pulled up in front of a large country house, three storeys high, four tall sash windows on each floor.

'Nothing like a little pad off the Irish coast for a bit of relaxation, huh?' Tom said. 'He probably had farmers from Kerry carry the stone here on their backs.'

'You socialists and your insistence we all live in box units wearing grey smocks,' Linda mocked. 'This doesn't look anything special to me.'

'That's because your family residence is palatial,' the inspector said. 'How was it your granddad made his money again?'

Linda clicked her tongue dismissively. It was speculated her family's wealth had originated from a spot of bootlegging in America. By the time her father entered parliament and had his own children, they were a very respectable, well-to-do household and the origin of their fortune a distant, never referred to, memory.

'And Boylan lives here on his own?' Ray asked, in awe. He'd grown up on a working-class estate on the north side of Dublin. He lived in a one-bed apartment now and thought that was spacious, after having to share a childhood room with several siblings. 'I'd like a nice house, but would you not go mad in there?'

Arnie shook his head.

'He seems content. And he's not always on his own. Carla takes care of him and he gets visitors. People come across to talk to him about the hospital and the island's history. He just wants to live out his days here. Doesn't seem like a lot to ask.'

'Right so, we'll keep him company for an hour or so,' Tom said. 'Would you look at that – I have a signal. The big house has everything.' His phone had started to beep, missed calls and text messages flooding in.

'I'll swing by in an hour,' Arnie said. 'There's no need to rush, though. If you're busy when I call back, I can have a cuppa while I'm waiting for you. I'll drop your deputy up to O'Hare now.'

The inspector thanked him and helped Linda from the car.

'Just give me a sec',' he said and quickly scrolled through his messages. Most he ignored, sending one quick reply to Louise to tell her he'd been out of range. She'd sent a lovely picture of their granddaughter Cáit, her face covered in chocolate, spoon in hand and a bowl of Rice Krispies cake mixture in front of her. They seemed to be having fun.

The two missed calls from Joe Kennedy he deleted. He'd have left a message if it was something important.

'Still,' the inspector said, shoving his phone in his pocket and continuing the conversation from the car like it had never stopped. 'It takes a bit of nerve, doesn't it? To move into the largest place on the island, live there more or less rent free on your own and then think it's your God-given right to stay there until your time is up.'

'It's presumptuous,' Linda said, shifting from foot to foot to keep warm. 'Very doctor-like, you might say. The whole God complex and all that. And Boylan was the head of the hospital for so long. He's probably a right pompous arse. And it takes a lot for me to say that, darling.'

Tom smiled, grimly. Linda was at home somewhere like this, far more than he was.

'It looks empty,' she continued. 'I don't see smoke from any of the chimneys, or any lights on, bar in the hall and on that first floor landing.'

Tom followed her gaze up. As he did, a curtain twitched in one of the rooms.

'You see that?' Linda asked, and Tom nodded.

'Maybe it's haunted,' he said, dryly.

'Only one way to find out,' she said, and strode towards the door. The door opened as she was raising her hand to drop the brass knocker for a third time, and the inhabitant of the house appeared.

Tom and Linda were speechless.

Lawrence Boylan was not what they had been expecting.

CHAPTER 16

'It's a bit of a comedown, isn't it?'

Arnie nodded at the tiny cottage they'd just parked in front of.

'Your boss and the doctor will be having a silver tea service up in the mansion while you . . .'

He chuckled.

Ray smiled and shook his head.

'To be honest, I think this place is more appealing.'

Light shone from every room of the cottage into the dusky gloom and smoke billowed out of its chimney. The garden beyond the gate was filled with winter berries and perennials, a wild disorder that was attractive in its own way. Far removed from the neatly landscaped lawns of Boylan's house but more to Ray's taste.

'You're okay going in there on your own?'

As Arnie asked the question, the front door opened, casting a warm glow down the footpath. A man stood in its arc, his weight on the heavy side. His cheeks were jowly, his face well lined and he wore a flat tweed cap, evidently indoors and out. He waved cheerfully in their direction.

'I think I'll be safe,' Ray answered. He jumped out and gave the car's roof a tap as Arnie drove off.

'Hey there!' the cottage owner called out. 'Come in out of the cold.'

'DS Lennon,' Ray said, offering the man his hand when he arrived at the door. 'Thank you for agreeing to see me, Dr O'Hare.'

'Not at all. It's nice to have the company. Call me Robert, please.'

'Your accent,' Ray said, following the man into the cottage. 'That's Northern, am I right?' The lilt was distinctive, the hard vowels and softer consonants, the ring of Donegal and Scots behind it.

'Derry. I haven't been up there in a good twenty years and it's been a lot longer since I lived in the place, but I never forgot where I was from.'

O'Hare brought Ray into a small kitchen that was straining against its walled confines with untidiness.

'Excuse the mess,' he said, lifting a bundle of newspapers off the chair he was offering Ray and looking around to see where he could deposit them. He settled on a wooden table by the window, already creaking under the weight of other detritus.

'Carla is sick,' he said, by way of explanation. 'She usually comes up and does a bit for me. She'll murder me when she sees how I've let the place go this last week.'

A week? Ray thought, looking around in amazement. He was naturally neat, he couldn't imagine accumulating this much stuff in a year. And how the hell was Robert O'Hare getting all these papers to his cottage on a more or less deserted island?

'Mannix picks up back issues for me in the newsagents in Carnbeg,' Robert said, reading Ray's mind. 'It doesn't matter to me if the news is a few months or a few days old. It's the investigative articles I enjoy, anyway. That's what you miss on social media – people only share what they're interested in, not the in-depth pieces.'

'Social media?' Ray asked.

'I love Twitter, what can I say. Live on an island, but stay connected to the world. This is all very exciting, though, isn't it?'

'What is?'

'This. Them finding Conrad in that grave. Will you take a wee dram with me?'

'A wee what?'

'A dram of whiskey?'

'Sorry, I can't.'

'Oh. Right, of course. I'll make tea, then.'

Ray cast one look at the overflowing sink and the dirty crockery stacked precariously on the draining board and shook his head.

'Please. Not on my account. I'm fine.'

All he'd had since breakfast was a sandwich when they'd arrived at Arnie's. He'd quite happily drink a vat of tea. But not here. Ray sighed. He'd have to hold out for dinner and hope Arnie's cooking skills went beyond ham and cheese. He'd mentioned something about liking wine. Ray was more of a beer man but right now, he reckoned he would happily down a few glasses of red. It was just a shame he couldn't share them with Laura. God, he missed her. Her curls, her beautiful freckles, her perfume. He'd seen her yesterday morning, and still he was pining for her. A lost cause, that's what he was.

'. . . course only knew him a while, but still, it was such an event.'

'Sorry?' Robert had been talking away while he poured himself a whiskey that looked anything but wee. Ray waited to see if he intended to add water but no, the doctor seemed to like his medicine straight.

'Conrad. I only started in the hospital in 1971, the year before he went missing. I was young, twenty-three, a student doctor. And, of course, Conrad was senior by that stage, even though he'd just turned thirty-one. A bit of a prodigy, he was. He'd already risen quite highly in his previous hospital before he was recruited here.'

'So you didn't know him very well?'

'Oh no, I wouldn't say that. Conrad was very personable, very engaged with us younger doctors. And there weren't that many of us. He was always willing to give us a hand getting to grips with procedures, help us with our practical learning. He was strict too, made sure we followed our orders. But not in a mean way.'

'He was a good colleague?'

'Of course. I would have looked up to him and been grateful for his guidance.'

Would you really, Ray wondered. The last line had sounded a little rote. Was it easier to look back now and think of Howe's advice and direction with fondness? At the time, with all the arrogance of youth, would Robert O'Hare have been so keen on being told what to do all the time?

'Was there anybody who didn't get on with Dr Howe? That you knew of?'

Robert took a long sip from his glass. Too long a sip. He was thinking. But of what? An honest answer to the question? Or a diversion?

'Well, he might have had one or two clashes on professional issues. But never personal. Conrad was committed to his job. He wouldn't have had the time nor inclination to fall out with people over something minor.'

'What do you mean – professional? Like how the patients were treated, things like that?'

Robert tugged the front of his cap and nodded.

'Exactly like that. I suppose you would say that Conrad considered himself pioneering at the time. He believed patients could be fixed.'

'And what about you?' Ray asked. 'Did you not want to see them cured?'

'Of course I did, Detective. But I was – I am – a realist. Some problems can be treated to the point where the sufferers can live amongst us and you would never guess at their illness – personality disorders, bipolar sufferers, obsessive compulsions – but there are certain afflictions of the mind, particular types of psychosis, for which there is no cure. All you can do, all we could ever do, was strive to keep those people in a safe and secure environment. I suppose where Conrad would have looked at those people as the more challenging cases, I would have seen lifers on the island. Like me.'

Robert smiled wistfully and took another sip from the whiskey.

'Why are you still here?'

'On the island?'

'Yes.'

'It's my home. I love it. I worked here for almost twenty years before they closed us down. It's not like working in Derry or Dublin where, if you lose one job, you can find another and still live in your home, still have the same friends. We were like family in St Christina's. And you start to lose touch with your real family. I'd never married, either – wedded to the job, I suppose.'

'But the hospital was closed by 1990. You would have been, what, forty-two? That was very young to retire, surely?'

'I didn't retire. A few of the patients wanted to stay on and the Trustees were looking for volunteers to continue their care.

I didn't mind whether we'd five hundred patients or five. It was the same work, the same thing I loved doing, in the place I loved to do it.'

'Even now, though, you in your early sixties – I'm sure there are lots of country towns who'd love to have a doctor of your standing. Wouldn't you consider working on the mainland?'

'Ah, Detective, you misunderstand the discipline. I'm not a general practitioner. I couldn't move over to Carnbeg and start doling out antibiotics. I'm a specialist in afflictions of the mind. If I wanted proper work, I'd have to move up to one of the larger hospitals near the capital. It's too much, at this stage.'

'Right. I see. So, five hundred – is that how many patients there would have been in the hospital at any given time?'

'On average, yes. We were relatively small compared to the large asylums. You could find a thousand patients in one of the big Dublin hospitals. But we tended to service the West coast, which was less populated. We only got extreme cases from Dublin or the big cities and that was mainly because of Lawrence.'

Ray nodded. He was sweating in the small kitchen and the heat was making his eyes water. The sudden burst of intense warmth from the open stove, after being in a state of semi-freezing all day, was a shock to the system. He needed something cool to drink but he didn't have to look at the chaos in the sink to remind himself that wasn't an option. He'd just have to speed up the interview and hope Arnie returned sooner rather than later.

'I just want to take you back to the day Conrad went missing,' he said. 'I know it was a long time ago but do you remember anything?'

O'Hare stroked his fleshy jowls, drawing them down.

'We had a skeleton staff on that week – it being the lead up to Christmas. The morning before Conrad was due to go home he did his rounds, bidding everybody good wishes for the season. Most of the staff were heading to our annual Christmas party, before the ferry that evening would take a pile of them home, but he wasn't one for mixing in big groups. I think Conrad was a bit shy. Sometimes I got the feeling he preferred the company of the patients to other doctors. I was staying on because I was one of the newest. You weren't given much choice with the rota. Anyhow, Howe called up to my office especially to leave off his bottle of whiskey.'

'Why did he do that?'

The old man eyed his glass pointedly.

'I'm a lifelong connoisseur. Conrad wasn't much of a drinker and he knew the bottle wouldn't be wasted with me.'

'So, he was a generous man.'

'Aye. You could say that. You could also say that he was practical.'

'How's that?'

'Well, he didn't go buy the whiskey himself. He just re-gifted it to me.'

Ray shrugged, his body language saying, yes, you could say that. Inwardly, he made a note that the other man was quick to take the gesture negatively.

'So, nobody but Dr Andrew Collins saw Conrad on the morning of his planned departure, Christmas Eve?'

'That's right. There was a barney about that at the time. Lawrence reckoned Conrad had taken the ferry the evening before. But Andrew insisted he'd seen him out at one of the cottages on the morning of the 24th. There was an empty one on the far side of the island, and that's where Andrew said he spotted him. It didn't make a lot of sense at the time. Why would Conrad have been over there? But I guess Andrew was right. Conrad Howe never left the island. At all.'

'When his wife phoned and said he hadn't arrived home – what happened then?'

'We started to look for him.'

'Where?'

'In the hospital, of course. We began there, then radiated out.'

'Why do you say *of course*? Why would that seem obvious and not that he'd had an accident out by that cottage where Collins claimed to have seen him?'

O'Hare shrugged.

'The patients in our care – like I said, it was our job to keep them safe and also to keep others safe from them. The thing is, to do that we had to put ourselves in danger. It's not an easy job, dealing with the most insane, the most violent of society. There were always plenty of incidents, no matter how many orderlies you had or how much security you thought you'd installed. We had doctors and nurses slapped and punched, bitten, even. We'd attempted escapes; near riots sometimes. After what had happened the year prior to the Howe incident, I suppose we were all conscious that things could escalate very quickly. And we figured something like that might have happened to Conrad.'

'Hold up,' Ray said, his senses alert. 'You said, after what had happened the year prior. What are you referring to? What happened the previous year?'

CHAPTER 17

Diary Entry

An uneasiness has settled on me these last few weeks.

At first I thought it was being on the island. The forced isolation from family, so far removed from what I'm used to.

Then I wondered if it was actually the opposite – the claustrophobia of having to live amongst my co-workers, never truly escaping from their company, even somewhere as remote as this.

On reflection, it is neither of these things that lies at the heart of my disquiet. I am used to working on my own and I am used to living in at a hospital.

It's the asylum itself and the patients that have unsettled my mind.

I am aware that the people who have been admitted to St Christina's are generally extremely ill and must be treated as such.

But, while many of the staff try to show compassion towards our charges, there's a collective acceptance that they have few rights. Very little dignity is afforded to these grown men and women. My colleagues do not seem to be aware of the damage this can do in the long term.

The degradations are minor, but they are daily and they accumulate.

The women are often left without sanitary towels. The wards on the lower floors are not washed frequently enough to clear the smell of urine and faeces. Patients walk to baths naked and are made to use the same water over and over. Letters from home are read by the nurses first, and visits from relatives – rare enough in any case – are refused for the most petty infringements. It goes on. Dinner is served cold. Treats are withheld. Bedtime is at 6.30 p.m.

These frequent humiliations have become a fabric of the asylum, so much so that, until I stood back and actually looked at what was happening, I almost didn't see it myself. I too was complicit with the system.

Now, every day, I try to make a little change. I talk to the patients like they are human. I pass on little messages and packages on my rounds. Minnie says my visits are the bright spot of her day. She has been feeling very down lately and this worries me. Her life on the fourth floor is so comfortable. She has no idea how bad it can get downstairs. She needs to be sure to get out of her bed and mix with the other patients, to smile at the doctors and nurses and have a good appetite. Whatever brought on this latest malaise, it's obvious she's not herself and it's only a matter of time before it's noticed. Whatever happens, she mustn't draw enough attention to warrant being transferred to one of the other floors.

I asked her yesterday if she was feeling down and if there was anything I could do to help.

'Yeah,' she said to me. 'Get me a packet of fags, a bottle of Babycham and a roast beef dinner. That should do it. I've a pain in me fanny with that watery mush they keep serving us from the kitchen. Would it kill them to give us something more solid than what a toddler eats? It's no wonder I'm fucking depressed.'

I smiled, feeling a little reassured. When she gives me lip, it means she's okay.

This care and attention I give to individual patients all has to be under the radar because I know my co-workers, so used to the status quo, would think my actions naïve. Ignorant, even. I remember Dolores' warning on my first day – though, to be fair, she is not like her colleagues. She is kinder to the patients, efficient but thoughtful.

For the others, debasing the patients has become part of the treatment plan.

While my colleagues may be mainly unaware of the effects of this routine, I fear that some of them enjoy it. It's the same in every sphere of life. There are always those who take pleasure in the discomfort of others.

I was surprised, recently, when I overheard a small group of patients discussing a staff member. He is admired and respected for his academic work and advances in the field. He treats the patients quite kindly, as far as I can tell. But this group described him differently. They spoke his name with fear. Does he even realise what they think of him? Would it matter to him if he did?

I've always thought him a little arrogant. And certainly intense. But in other respects, he is charming and friendly. He seems like the perfect doctor.

But then, I am not his patient.

CHAPTER 18

The cancer that was eating away at Lawrence Boylan had ravaged every part of his body it seemed, bar his brain. That was as sharp as a tack.

It had taken Tom and Linda a few seconds to collect themselves when the shrunken former head doctor opened his front door to them. Given the tales of his renown as head of St Christina's, the inspector had mentally painted a picture of a tall, imposing man – imperious, arrogant. A man who had steadfastly refused to accept that Conrad Howe had not left Oileán na Coillte that Christmas Eve, who had failed to see the urgency of the man's disappearance and pressed his belief on the staff, even on Howe's widow. A legend in his time, perhaps an infamous one in some circles. That was who Tom was expecting to meet.

Instead, he found a man thin almost to the point of emaciated, his creaking, fragile body hunched over on itself, swollen stomach protruding, skin taut and grey across his face and hands. And yet, the doctor wore a shirt and slacks, pulled up high around his waist. His voice was deep and clear. He kept smoothing the strands of hair on his balding head, an effort to look respectable in their presence. Or rather, in Linda's presence.

It had taken Tom all of five minutes to realise that Boylan specialised in zooming in on the most important person in the room, which, for him, was the other doctor. Struggling to breathe and walk, he'd nonetheless offered to take Linda's coat. Directing them to the sitting room at the rear of the house, he followed at a slow limp, trying to make small talk with the psychologist the whole way.

The house still retained a nod to its former grandeur, but as they passed room after dusty room, their doors wide open with no heed to the draught, the inspector realised that most of it was un-lived in. Inside the rooms, partly visible from the hall light, he could see the outlines of hand-carved Victorian-era chairs, marble-topped parlour tables, studded leather sofas and antique rugs. It was like a very much neglected museum. Soon to be a mausoleum, if its inhabitant was anything to go by.

Boylan had set up home in two rooms in the rear section of the large house – a small sitting room and an adjacent kitchen, which had been modernised, or at least brought up to date, in the 1970s. The inspector ended up in the kitchen watching the kettle boil and listening to Linda and the doctor chat.

Boylan's vocal chords gave no hint of the disease eating at his bones. And it was his bones it was after, he'd told them, when their mouths fell open at the front door.

'Sarcoma,' he said. 'Primary bone cancer. I look worse than I feel. The morphine helps, of course.'

Then he'd ushered them inside.

At eighty-two, the man couldn't have long left, anyway, the inspector reckoned. So why wasn't he in a hospital? Getting the best treatment and being cared for by experts? Was he so attached to the old place and the island that he wanted to die here?

'How are you managing day to day, Doctor?' Linda asked, as Tom carried the tea things through.

'Oh, I manage fine,' Boylan replied. 'Carla comes in and cooks and cleans, stays on top of my prescriptions and so forth. I have good days and bad. But really, I am a doctor after all. I know how to care for myself.'

'Yes, and we are usually the worst patients,' Linda said.

'Are you in the field?'

'I'm a psychologist. Not quite as talented as you.'

'Now, now. I knew it. I have seen you in the journals – you've written a few papers, haven't you? I never forget a face. You have a bright future ahead of you, young lady.'

Tom cringed and Linda blushed. Neither of them liked to point out that as the State's leading criminal psychologist, Linda was at her professional zenith. Or that she was fifty-nine and could take retirement in six years, if she chose.

'Have you read any of my papers?' Boylan continued.

'Several,' she said, not adding she'd scanned all of them in the last few days.

'Wonderful. I'm sure there's much we could discuss. I've always found the criminal mind particularly fascinating.'

Boylan was delighted with himself, the inspector thought. And he'd barely looked at Tom. He only had eyes for the other professional. Not the lowly civil servant.

'It's a sorry business all this, isn't it?' the inspector said, inserting himself into the conversation. 'Finding Dr Howe's body like that. And his poor wife Miriam, not knowing all this time. Forty years. A lifetime of sorrow and regret.'

'Yes.'

Boylan uttered the one word and clamped his mouth shut.

Tom cast Linda a sideways glance. She looked equally askance. That one word was so bereft of feeling, Tom may as well have just asked did the doctor take milk in his tea.

'Have you contacted his widow at all?' the inspector tried again.

'Me? Contact her? No. Why would I?'

'Well,' Tom said, firmly on the back foot. 'You were her husband's boss when he went missing. You didn't believe anything had happened to him. I thought . . . I would want to apologise for not believing her all those years ago.'

'I am dying, Inspector.' Boylan patted his chest. 'I'm sorry if that makes my bedside manner seem poor but I have more pressing concerns. Conrad disappeared forty years ago. If Miriam Howe failed to move on in all that time, frankly, I'm astonished. I do not feel I have anything to atone for. I did not believe he had come to harm at the time. I had no reason to. I'm happy his body has been found but I'm not responsible for the feelings of his widow. Nor for the tragic accident that befell her husband.'

'It wasn't an accident,' Tom cut in. 'Most definitely not an accident. Conrad Howe was murdered. His body wrapped in plastic, dumped and hidden in a mass grave for nearly half a century. His wife and children left in ignorance.'

'You cannot shock me,' Boylan said, leaning forward, the discomfort of the movement written on his face. 'I have seen things that would give you nightmares, Inspector.'

'But she contacted you, didn't she? Miriam Howe. Years ago. She'd found her husband's diary and in it, he writes about his suspicions that a doctor was mistreating the patients. If that was true, it gave somebody a motive to murder him.'

'Stuff and nonsense. She told me her husband believed

somebody was subjecting patients in the asylum to treatments that were all completely legal. We each had our own allocation of patients and I, of course, oversaw all the treatment plans. Nobody was conducting any unnecessary procedures. If they were, I'd have come to know about it. I wondered, when she told me what her husband had written, if perhaps the man was having some sort of breakdown at the time and we weren't aware. That he might have been suicidal. It would have explained his disappearance.'

'But he didn't die by suicide,' Tom said.

Boylan shrugged, as though he was unconvinced, in spite of the facts to the contrary.

The inspector chewed the inside of his cheek and retreated in his own chair. He was sitting in front of a man who had one foot in the grave, and still he felt intimidated. The way Boylan's eyes lingered on the inspector made his skin crawl. What must this man have been like to work for when he was at the height of his powers? What must it have been like to be a patient under his care? Boylan had been able to switch off the warmth he'd summoned when speaking to Linda with such ease, it was unnerving. Schizophrenic, one might say.

The inspector had to gain control of this exchange or he'd leave with nothing.

Sitting forward again, he placed his cup back in its saucer and met the doctor's eye, unflinching.

'Did you get on well with Conrad Howe, Doctor?'

'Get on with him? I was his senior. We weren't friends.'

'You gave all your staff, from the top guys to the lowliest cleaners, a bottle of whiskey as their Christmas box. You weren't an unkind boss.'

Tom might have been imagining things, but he sensed a

softening in the other man's demeanour. Perhaps the trick was as simple as playing to his ego, as Linda had been doing.

'I was respected and I rewarded loyalty. Conrad was a good doctor in many ways. Extremely gifted. And he admired my experience.'

'What happened in the days leading up to Conrad's disappearance? Was everything as normal?'

'Normal? I spent my life working in an asylum, Inspector. We could sit here all night and try to define normal.'

'Were there any arguments? Not just in the immediate lead-up to Conrad's disappearance but in general. Had Conrad any enemies?'

Boylan paused and considered.

'Enemies? No, of course not. But it wasn't all peace and harmony. St Christina's was one of the country's leading centres for the treatment of the insane. Staff safety was always an issue and of course, there were disputes among the doctors themselves.'

'Over what? The running of the hospital?'

'I ran the hospital. The disputes were over the types of treatment, medical advances, diagnosis, that sort of thing. The lady doctor will know what I'm talking about. It could get quite heated. Not enough to murder a man. Not in a calculated way, anyway.'

'You believed at the time, you insisted, by all accounts, that Howe had left the island of his own volition. Why were you so sure of that when only one ferry left that day and nobody saw him on it?'

'He wasn't on it that day but he could have been on it the day before. Half the staff left on the 23rd and most of them were drunk after the hospital Christmas do. Howe was very good at keeping to himself. Making himself invisible. Like that child down the back of the class who manages to sink in their seat to avoid being noticed when they don't have their homework done.'

It was a strange analogy, but one Tom let go. There were more pressing matters.

'But a member of your staff saw him on the morning of the 24th. Out at one of the island's cottages.'

'Andrew Collins? He wasn't a reliable witness.'

'In what sense?'

Boylan shifted in his seat. Beads of sweat had broken out on his forehead.

'I'm sorry, I must . . . I need . . .'

'Where is it?' Linda said. She stood up and looked around.

'There.' Boylan nodded at a table in the corner and Linda approached it. She returned with a strip of pills. The doctor took the one she popped from its foil, washing it down with a sip of water from the glass beside him.

They waited a few minutes for the pain medication to have the desired effect.

'Andrew was a troubled soul,' Boylan said eventually, his voice a little less strong, more sluggish now. Anybody else, anywhere else, and Tom might have asked if the man wanted to stop and resume another time. But their case was forty years old and it looked like one of the star witnesses was about to exit stage left. They didn't have a second to spare.

'His approach to the patients was extremely strict, quite . . . regressive. He held no real hope for them. And I think that hopelessness started to seep into his wider view of the world. You have to have a strong character to work on an isolated island like this, in an asylum. Andrew grew depressed. I believe he was self-medicating. It can be common with doctors and he wasn't the first or last doctor to do it.'

'If he was that unhappy, why did he stay working at St Christina's?' Tom asked. 'Why keep a house on the island? He still comes here, doesn't he?'

'Perhaps there's something on the mainland he's avoiding,' Boylan said and shrugged, as if to imply, *I don't know anything more*, when the inspector sensed he was getting at something very specific indeed.

'He was correct back then, though, wasn't he?' Tom persisted. 'Andrew Collins. He must have seen Conrad. And Conrad hadn't left the island.'

'Perhaps he left and returned.'

'To travel on a ferry unnoticed once, perhaps,' Tom said. 'But twice? And in the end, that doesn't take away from the fact that the last time anybody saw the man was Christmas Eve and now his murdered body has turned up. Why were you so certain that he would have just upped sticks, anyhow? The man had a wife and two small children.'

'Ah. You assume he was content and settled because he had family. I never thought that. He chose to work here, on this island, away from home. And I never thought he was happy. Not Conrad.'

'Why wasn't he happy?'

Boylan sighed. 'The man was driven. It wasn't enough to treat the patients. He wanted to be their saviour. He was ambitious enough to want my job, eventually. People tried to create this myth of competition between us. It was just because he was so young and brilliant. Conrad saw what I was doing, trying to ameliorate the behaviour in the worst of our extreme cases, and he wanted to take that further. Yes, he had the makings of an excellent doctor. He would have looked up to me.'

'Sorry, you said "*take it further*". Further how?'

'He thought we could cure patients with deep-seated, chronic psychoses.'

'Wasn't that your job?' Tom asked.

'Inspector, don't be so naïve. Even if we could have cured patients, our real job in St Christina's wasn't to send patients back home. It was to keep them safe, here, to study the mind and its capacity for madness.'

'I see,' Tom said. 'It's just, it sounds like you believed your job was to make sure those poor people never left.'

Boylan shrugged.

Tom felt a shiver run down his spine.

CHAPTER 19

Ray had relented. Telling O'Hare to stay where he was, the detective found the least dirty glass on the draining board, rinsed it as well as he could and filled it from the tap with icy cold water that had a distinctive green hue. Ray hoped it was lime.

The sink was so full now that it threatened to overflow onto the floor. If the cottage's owner noticed, he didn't say anything. Instead, he refilled his whiskey glass and waited for Ray to rejoin him at the table. O'Hare was a doctor. Hadn't he heard of germs? He seemed to be incubating them in his cereal bowls.

'As I said, there were always little outbreaks of violence in the hospital. But the year I started, 1971, one of the patients started a fire in the basement.'

'In the basement?'

'Aye. Anyway, that was where we kept the no-hopers.'

'The what?'

'The patients who had no hope. They were kept in individual cells for their own safety. We even had treatment rooms down there so we wouldn't need to bring them upstairs and put the general population at risk. We had some sensitive souls upstairs. And by sensitive, I mean, well-paying.'

'I've seen the hospital,' Ray said. 'Including the basement.'

'Then you know. That was our equivalent of a high-security ward. On this occasion, the patient had managed to secrete a box of matches about his person. God knows how he got them. Some fool of an orderly or idiot of a nurse. Nobody 'fessed up, anyway. He'd been brought to one of the treatment rooms and a senior nurse left in charge. He was a lifer – had been at the hospital for decades. Apparently, he'd been a farmer before he was admitted. Displayed extreme delusion and often violent tendencies. But he was kept well-sedated, mostly. I don't know exactly what happened on that day, but somehow he managed to free himself from his restraints and push Dolores to the ground. She was knocked out. Then he pulled the mattress from the treatment bed and piled it with papers. He shut the door and set the mess in the middle of the floor on fire. Then waited, as it burned.'

'What happened then?'

'Conrad Howe happened. He had come downstairs for some reason and saw smoke coming out from under the door. Luckily, he had his keys. Apparently, when he looked through the door's glass grille the patient was sitting against the wall, hugging his knees while Dolores lay just at the edge of the fire. She was unconscious and seconds away from being burned to death.'

'What did he do?'

'He got the door open. The patient was weakened by smoke inhalation at this stage, but he still tried to wrestle with Conrad. Conrad was only trying to drag him to safety but the man was in a rage, he just wanted to kill him. So Conrad was forced to jab him with a sedative in order to rescue Dolores. By this stage the flames had spread and the side of her face had been burned.

'He dragged her from the room, then ran and got the fire extinguisher from the end of the corridor. By then we were all aware of what was happening. We got the fire out but it had spread to the archive office in the basement. Loads of files were lost. Still, Conrad had stopped the hospital from going up in flames and saved Dolores O'Sullivan's life.'

'What happened to the patient?' Ray asked.

'Oh, well, that was the sad part of the story. Most likely he would have died from smoke inhalation – that's what Lawrence tried to tell Conrad, afterwards – but he was devastated.'

'Because he didn't save him too?'

'No, because he killed him. In his panic, Conrad grabbed one of the syringes from the instrument table, believing it to be a sedative. It was sitting beside the bottle of Amobarbital, the drug we administered to extremely agitated patients. It used to put them into a long-term sleep, seven to fourteen days. But the syringe that Conrad picked up actually contained insulin. The patient was about to undergo insulin shock treatment. The insulin knocked him out and he would have required a glucose solution an hour later, but nobody realised what he had been given and with everything going on, well, time passed. The patient went into a coma, then had seizures. He died a few days later.'

'Jesus,' Ray whispered. 'That's awful. But Howe can't have been blamed for that, surely? Not in the midst of the chaos.'

'Nobody blamed him, but he blamed himself. In fact, he was overcome with guilt. You could see it in him. He became paranoid about safety, always asking us other doctors what we were doing, if the patients were being taken care of properly, all that lark. You'd think he was the only one who cared, the way he went on.'

'I suppose that's a natural reaction,' Ray responded. 'He probably thought if he'd gone to the treatment room earlier he could have prevented the fire from happening at all.'

'But it was just chance he was there at all.'

'He wasn't due there, anyway?' Ray was puzzled.

'To do what?'

'To treat the patient?'

O'Hare shook his head.

'Where are you getting that from? The man wasn't Conrad's patient. Conrad wasn't meant to be down there at all. In fact, there wasn't even a treatment scheduled.'

'But . . . I don't get it. Who was the man's doctor?'

O'Hare shrugged.

'His main doctor was Dr Boylan but he wasn't in the hospital that day and nobody knew who had decided to administer the therapy. It was a standard treatment; it just wasn't marked up on the patient's file. And when Dolores came to, she couldn't remember who'd instructed her to set up the treatment room or move the patient. But somebody must have been with her, because there was no way she moved that big fella by herself. For some reason the doctor, whoever he was, had left her on her own. She couldn't remember anything, not even her own name, for weeks. When it all came back, her memory stopped right after breakfast on the morning of the fire. Trauma blockage, I'd imagine.'

'Dolores,' Ray said. 'Wasn't she the nurse on the ferry on Christmas Eve, the one who left the day Conrad went missing?'

'Yes. But that was purely coincidental. Dolores had been looking to get off the island for a whole year before she left. Ever since the fire, in fact. She was desperate to leave. Couldn't cope with the patients. But she had difficulty finding a placement on the mainland and there was no way she was just walking out of paid employment. Not in those days. She and the head orderly finished up work that week. It was a shame about Dolores, though.'

'What was?'

'Well, she was gone on that ferry before we even knew Conrad was missing. If she'd known, she'd never have left. Dolores O'Sullivan would have searched high and low for Conrad. We never heard from her again. I guess she wanted to cut herself off, forget about this place and what happened. Though, it's probably a blessing. It means she never found out. God bless her, but she's probably dead now. You just knew, after the fire, that it had shaved about ten years off her life.'

'Why would she have searched high and low for Howe? Because he'd saved her life?' Ray guessed.

'No. Well, yes, but not just that. She would have wanted him found safe. I suppose she, more than any of us, knew what the patients were capable of.'

CHAPTER 20

Diary Entry

Hero. It's a funny word. Is anybody every truly heroic? When somebody does something everybody else considers brave, does anyone stop to consider the person's thought process? Think, perhaps, that the person wasn't being courageous but acting out of fear or panic or idiocy?

In fact, what else would you call running into a damned fire, but stupidity?

Still. I am happy to see Dolores safe. She is devastated by her injuries, that is true. But it would have been worse to burn to death than bear a few scars on her face. When she looks at them, she should remind herself of the alternative. She could be dead. She would never see the sky again or feel the sun on her skin or smell the salt of the ocean. She sees the wounds – we see her alive and well.

Of course, for some, I suppose, there is a fate worse than death.

I am not surprised that Padraic started the fire, that he would resort to such desperate measures. Anybody forced to endure the godforsaken conditions in the basement would be tempted to do such a thing. And if what the old woman told Minnie was true, Padraic's life ended when his landlord and that judge conspired to have him sent here.

He wanted to die. That's what I have to keep telling myself. He's at peace now.

Who knows what torture and pain he would have undergone in that treatment room? He wasn't scheduled for a procedure, that much we know. Whoever told Dolores to bring him there must have had something evil planned to keep it so secret.

The awful thing is, I suspect I know who it was.

But who can I tell?

I visited Dolores yesterday with flowers picked from the staff garden. Beautiful irises that I thought might cheer her. She was allowed to return from Kerry General but only on the promise that she rests up here for a few days. She's had the stuffing knocked out of her. The confident nurse is gone. She is scared now. A changed woman.

I tried to engage her in conversation. We've been told she remembers nothing but when I asked her about it, she looked pained and turned away from me. It left me wondering. Does she remember who gave her the order?

And is she afraid of him?

CHAPTER 21

Darkness had fallen proper and the approach as they returned to the asylum was particularly gloomy and eerie.

Once inside, Arnie switched on lights as they went, leading them towards Dr Boylan's office.

The hospital was daunting in the daytime. At night, it was a confusing maze.

Once they arrived at their destination, Arnie explained the lay-out of the doctor's former office and the adjoining room belonging to his secretary.

'The filing system is fairly straightforward, as I said earlier. If you want to spend a bit of time here, I can do a run back to the cottage and pick up a flask of coffee for you. Mum will be making dinner but we won't eat until later, whenever you're ready.'

'Perfect,' the inspector said. 'I hope we're not putting you out too much. Even letting us stay with you tonight is above and beyond. But we should be out of your hair tomorrow.'

'You hope. We'd best keep an eye on the weather. It's okay now, but if a storm comes in, Mannix won't run the ferry. You could end up moving in with me for a few days.'

'Jesus, I hope not,' Ray said.

'Eh, it won't be that bad,' Arnie said, looking a little offended. 'I've plenty of food in. It could be worse.'

'Don't mind him,' Tom said. 'He's just desperate to get home to the love of his life. Which reminds me, I wanted to ring my own wife this evening but my signal is patchy at best. Is it always like this?'

'It comes and goes. We're no worse than most of rural Ireland. Why don't you just use the landline? The hospital is still connected.'

'Really? Why, when it's not in use?'

'All of the buildings on the island have landlines and we all use the one provider. I just didn't see the point in going through the rigmarole of getting the hospital cut off, especially when nobody is up here making calls to China or anywhere else you'd worry about. It's handy for me, anyway. If I'm up here doing my rounds I can use the phone to get through to the others and they can get hold of me. There's even a fax, look.'

He pointed at the old-fashioned piece of equipment in the corner of the room.

'I don't suppose there's Wi-Fi?' Tom said.

Arnie smiled.

'Not even in the cottages. We're all on dial-up still. It's the one service we haven't been able to get. We have satellite for the television, but no broadband. Not that the hospital was ever set up for it. There's a primitive computer in one of the other offices, but you have to remember, St Christina's closed when the world was only getting used to technology. That's why those filing cabinets are about to become your best friend. They digitised nothing.'

'And is it just the filing cabinets in here and the secretary's office?' Ray asked. 'It's just, with the asylum being so old, I'd have thought there'd be more.'

'Ah, that's where you have a problem, if you're looking for

anything older. The archived records pre-1950 were kept in the basement of the hospital. There was a fire in the seventies and the whole lot went up.'

'Dr O'Hare mentioned that,' Ray said. 'I'll fill you in later, boss.'

'Fair enough. Arnie, you go do what you have to do. We'll get stuck in here.'

Tom sat behind the desk. Emmet had left out the records for the gravesite, so there was no need to go searching for them. The inspector began to read through the burial files while Linda and Ray went through the filing cabinets.

The office was silent as they worked.

Tom rested his chin on his hand, his eyes scanning names, a chilled feeling starting to settle in his stomach.

'Jesus,' he said, breaking the quiet.

'What is it?' Ray asked.

'Of the sixty deaths recorded here, only seven are listed as death due to old age,' Tom said, shaking his head.

Ray and Linda pulled up chairs on either side and began to read the records over his shoulder.

'These heart attack and organ failure cases, Linda – what's this reference beside them to purging?'

The psychologist sighed and planted her chin on her hand as she spoke.

'It was one of the many insane treatments for people with insanity. They used to make people vomit repeatedly, violently. They'd give them solutions to drink, saline, that kind of thing. Sometimes the heaving would take its toll on the other organs, like the heart. It would just give in, especially in weaker cases.'

'They vomited to death?' Ray asked, disgusted.

'Pretty much. These two cases here – the Metrazol related ones – they would have been patients injected with the drug to induce convulsions. It was a chemical form of shock therapy, the sort they used for Electroconvulsive Therapy later. The seizures caused by Metrazol were so vicious, the patients would often end up with compound fractures to the spine and skull. Of course, in those recorded deaths there, they may have overdosed the poor men.'

The inspector ran his fingers along the names.

'There seem to be a large number of patients who died from dysentery and pneumonia. I'm guessing that was common too?'

'There's a reason I entered the field of criminal psychology and not general mental health care, Tom. I wouldn't want to work in an institution like this, not even these days. They're still the poor relation of the health system.'

Tom was surprised. Linda's words were atypically bleak for a woman who practically breathed black humour and droll put-downs.

He closed the file in front of him.

'Right,' he said. 'A lot of these deaths occurred in the years before Conrad Howe's body was dumped in that pit. Which may be relevant. If you were a patient in here at the time and Howe was performing those *treatments* on you; if you'd seen other patients die at his hands, well . . . you'd be tempted, wouldn't you?'

'Unless he was a conscientious objector,' Ray said. 'Didn't you say that in his diary he seems a bit uncomfortable with what's going on? So, might one of his colleagues in that instance have had it in for him?'

'Perhaps,' Tom said. 'He found some of the procedures repulsive but we have to remember he was of his age, too. You wouldn't know what he deemed acceptable. I think we'll start with staff first, anyhow. Let's find out who worked here in 1972 and send the names back to HQ.'

'Fair enough, but you are right to consider the patients,' Linda said.

'You think so?'

'Of course. There would have been a lot of dangerous individuals here.'

Tom rubbed his beard.

'Yeah, I get that, but . . . I'm playing devil's advocate here, but think it through. I can see a patient lashing out at Howe and killing him, accidentally or deliberately, but why wouldn't that have been reported? And if it happened without a witness, could a patient have spirited his body into that pit unnoticed by the staff?'

Linda tapped her chin as she thought about it.

'I'd hazard a guess the patients were the ones who took care of the grave. One or two of the more reliable ones would have been set to work in it.'

'Set to work?'

'Of course. All of the patients, excluding the ones confined to bed or locked up, would have had jobs in the hospital. Gardening, laundry, cooking. They'd have aided the staff. That was how these places operated. So, say you had some fellow charged with working as an undertaker, he could have secreted Howe's body in there, or he could have done it for a pal.'

Tom considered this and then his brain began to leap to other, more fantastical options.

'Or, what if a patient killed Howe and the hospital wanted it covered up?'

'Yes, that's a good one,' Linda nodded. 'If they'd been on the receiving end of a recent government bollocking, which these places often were, they may have decided to keep Howe's death under the radar.'

'Then we'd have a rake of people conspiring to commit a crime,' Tom said. 'Hey, the more the merrier. Forty years past or no, one of them is bound to crack now Howe's body has been found.'

'It seems unnecessarily cruel to his widow,' Ray interrupted, 'that they'd deny her any knowledge of what happened to him to avoid getting into trouble with the State.'

The inspector pointed at the file he'd just closed.

'Ray, this place specialised in cruel and unusual. Look, we'll start with the staff. Sheer numbers dictate that route. Chances are, most of them are dead now anyhow. Let's try to narrow down the number of potential interviewees before we come up with any more theories.'

They set about finding the staff records. Tom approached the task with dread. They'd been in the same position a few years earlier, searching manually through boxes of records in an old convent. But in the end, Arnie had been right. Boylan's former secretary made it easy for them. One of the filing cabinets held all the files of formers employees in the latter part of the twentieth century. The second drawer from the top contained the personnel files of staff who'd started in the institution in the mid-1960s, continuing into the 1970s.

The trio worked diligently together, narrowing down those who were present in 1972 and, after an hour, had a list of eighty names.

After a while, Arnie called in with a large flask of coffee and a packet of biscuits stolen from the exhumation operation outside. They pounced on the coffee. They were all still in their coats.

It had been cold during the hours of daylight. Now, as evening fell, it was freezing.

They agreed that Arnie would go check on Emmet and his team to see if they needed more supplies, then return to collect them and lock up.

'Okay,' Tom said. 'We've fifteen senior doctors, five junior doctors, twenty-five nurses, fifteen orderlies, and twenty general employees. It doesn't seem like a lot of staff.'

'That was my point about the general patient population helping out,' Linda said.

'Okay. Got you. I'll ring Laura and let's see what she can turn up on these names. Unless you need to hear her dulcet tones, Ray?'

The younger man blushed.

'I spoke to her last night, I'm sure she can last without me for a day. Eh, just tell her I said hi.'

'What's that? Ask her if she'll marry you?'

Tom turned away from his mortified deputy, cradling the phone handset to his ear and waiting for Laura to pick up.

She answered the phone uncertainly, not recognising the strange number.

'It's me, Laura,' he said. 'I'm ringing from the year 1985, from a land where we rely on landlines and dial-up connections.'

'That explains things,' Laura said down the line. 'Moya Chambers just rang and said she was trying to get hold of you on your mobile.'

'Shit. She must have something important. I only spoke to her last night.'

'She has cause of death, but she didn't share it with me.'

'You're just an underling, Laura. Which reminds me. Have

you no home to go to? I hope your feet aren't getting too comfortable under my desk?'

'What? I'm not even at your desk! I'm just working late.'

'I'm joking. And I'm happy you're there, even if you are nuts. I'm going to send you some names and details and see if you can apply the magic of modern technology to track these people down. We've no internet access. There are eighty names, all people working in St Christina's in 1972. I suspect a good few of them are dead. I've put a tick beside the ones who still live on the island, don't worry about them. The cover sheet will have all of the names, followed by the first page of each of their files, where their personal information was filled in. That has addresses and the like, from the time. Might be of use.'

'Eh, okay. I can do that.'

'You sound unsure.'

'It's nothing. It's just . . . Kennedy wants to have a meeting in the morning. That's what I'm preparing for.'

'On 29th December? What about?' Tom bristled but didn't let the anger show in his voice.

'He said he has some ideas for a new approach to tackling the gang feud on the city's periphery. He wants us to bring our own suggestions, too.'

'Does he, now? Well, this is more important.' Tom would have laughed if it wasn't so tragic. He never thought he'd say the words 'this is more important' about a forty-year-old case versus an ongoing gang war.

'Boss,' Laura whispered, 'getting my hair done is more important than anything Kennedy wants to ramble on about.'

The inspector smiled. They'd be loyal until the end, his team. Every one of them. But you had to respect the chain of command. Sean McGuinness had instilled that in him and he, in turn, had trained all his staff the same way. Which is why Laura was sitting in the office late on 28th December.

'Anyhow, these names, Laura.'

'Yes, about that. How are you sending them to me if you've no internet? Carrier pigeon?'

'I said we'd no internet – I didn't say we'd no technology. Have you heard of a little thing called a fax machine?'

'I'm not straight off the boat. Don't we have another problem? Wouldn't I need a fax this end?'

'Oh, Laura. That big fat grey machine that Ray leaves the papers on top of in my office? Didn't you ever wonder what that was?'

'No?'

'Well, that's a fax. Now, the problem is, I haven't a clue what its number is. Will you mosey on up there and check? It should be stuck on the side of the machine. On a post-it.'

'A post-it?'

'Yes. Another one of those old-fashioned things we used before phone apps. It's pink. Sellotaped to the side.'

He listened as Laura ran up the stairs to his office, watching Ray and Linda fight over the last biscuit.

'Ray says hi, by the way.'

'He misses me, does he?' Laura said, breathlessly.

'Desperately.'

'Aw. Right, I'm here. Well, look at that, the number is where you said it was. Have you got a pen?'

The inspector took down the number and thanked her, before ringing off.

'Does anybody remember how to use a fax?' he said, holding up the page in front of him with the names written on it.

'Give it here, you great big lump,' Linda said, snatching the pages from his grasp. They listened nostalgically as the fax machine came to life, strange beeping and whirring noises filling the office as it dialled Tom's machine. The pages ran slowly through the feeder. It eventually churned out a sent receipt.

'That was incredible,' Tom said, in mock awe. 'They should have one of these in every home. Now, I'm going to place a quick call to Moya Chambers. I think she might have something good for us. Do you two want to locate Arnie and tell him we're ready to finish up? What time is it now?'

'Half seven,' Ray replied.

Tom dialled the pathologist's mobile number, while the others set off to find the caretaker.

Moya answered after two rings.

'Whatever it is you're selling, I don't want it and how did you get my number?'

'It's me,' Tom said. 'I'm on a landline.'

'A landline? From where? Space?'

'Oileán na Coillte. Or Caillte. Whatever you want to call it.'

'I call it off the grid. I've never seen that prefix on an Irish number before.'

'They've some group scheme. Anyhow, you were looking for me?'

'Indeed I was. I made an interesting discovery this morning. And as a result, I can tell you, it's official. Conrad Howe was murdered.'

Tom sighed.

'Well, I suppose we'd sort of figured that out. What was it? Poison?'

'Death by strangulation.'

'I thought you couldn't tell that with a skeleton.'

'Sometimes I can, if the victim was garrotted. Which, in this case, he was.'

'Tell me more.'

'Hold on. I need to stub out this cigarette. Somebody is in the corridor outside.'

'Are you smoking in your lab?' Tom asked, amused.

'Don't be so stupid. I'm in my office.'

'You're still at work as well? If only the public realised how diligent we public servants really are.'

'They still wouldn't care. It's our job, we're meant to do it with a smile on our face. All year round. Hence the cigarette.'

'You do know there's a workplace ban? I mean, I don't mind. I'm not inhaling your secondary smoke. But still. Anyway, can we hurry this along? I'm freezing my balls off here in a deserted insane asylum.'

'It's not much better here, Tom. The pipes froze this morning and they haven't got the heat going in our offices yet. That's why I'm smoking. Okay, the evidence. I know Howe was garrotted because I found minuscule traces of copper embedded in the fourth cervical vertebra. I missed them the first time, had to go look again.'

'Let's pretend for a moment I don't speak morgue.'

'In the neck, Tom, I found them in the neck. Please God, tell me you know what a neck is?'

'I know you have one like a jockey's bollocks. The copper?'

'From wire. It was looped and pulled. It must have cut through the skin and damaged the vertebra, though at that point, Howe would have been dead anyway. Suffocated from lack of oxygen.'

'Hmm,' Tom said.

'Hmm what?'

'If it cut through the neck, why weren't there blood splatters all over the remnants of his clothes? You said you only picked up traces.'

'Good point. He may have been suspended backwards or upside down when the deed was done.'

'Jesus.'

'You agree that's a possibility then?'

'I'm in an asylum and earlier we saw a spinning chair suspended from the ceiling that I suspect was used for some sort of torture, or as we are euphemistically referring to it, treatment. No, I wouldn't be surprised if Howe was hanging upside down when he was finished off.'

'Well, in light of that evidence, I'd conclude his neck broke when he was dumped in your pit, post-mortem. The other good news I have for you is that we've made a conclusive DNA match. Those blood traces on the clothing came in handy. We dragged one of our senior technicians into the lab this morning and he compared it to the kids' samples. This is Conrad Howe's body.'

'Good news at last, hey? Has somebody informed Miriam Howe we've got a match?'

'Not my area but I believe she is being told, yes. So, have you turned up any other bodies yet? Now we know there was a murderer who may have been operating undiscovered for decades?'

'Yes. Sixty of them.'

'What?'

'The ones in the grave. Their "natural" causes of death all look like homicide in one form or another to me. I'm starting to think the patients should have rebelled and murdered all the doctors.'

'I get you. Emmet said something similar. Kerry General is dealing with the bulk of them but I've sent down instructions. Tell me something before I go, Tom.'

'This sounds serious.'

'Have you still got that ridiculous beard?'

Tom swore and hung up.

He stroked the offending facial hair. He'd fought Louise long and hard for the right to grow the beard and because of that, he was stuck with the bloody thing. Just to make a point. That, and his wife now said she actually found it quite handsome. He wondered if she was playing mind games with him.

He tidied away the paperwork and checked the office one last time to make sure they hadn't left anything out where it shouldn't be. He was struck by how quiet the rest of the building was. There was no sound of his colleagues or their driver.

He was alone.

He felt a chill run down his spine. Alone in a place which some would say had too many ghosts to count.

And while Tom didn't believe in the supernatural, he still felt a pressing need to get the hell out of the asylum before his mind started playing tricks. Closing the door to Boylan's office behind him, he set off in search of the others, telling himself as he walked that the feeling he had – the notion that somebody was following him down the old, empty corridor, was all in his head.

But he didn't turn around to check.

CHAPTER 22

Arnie hadn't been exaggerating about the island's storms.

By the time they left the asylum for a second time, the thick mist had blown on and the silence it had brought was well and truly shattered. The wind that now lashed across the island howled and shrieked and battered against the Land Rover's windows, pulling at the vehicle as they drove.

They were grateful to get back to the cottage. Arnie's mother, Kitty, was there already and met them at the door with a lantern in one hand and bucket of turf in the other.

'Power's gone,' she greeted them. 'Come in quick. Arnie, I fetched this from your shed, get it on that fire before the heat goes out of the house.'

The lack of electricity didn't seem to have put a halt to her gallop on the cooking front. Arnie's home smelled of roasting lamb and rosemary, garlic and sweet spices.

'Gas cooker,' she said, as they followed her into the kitchen. 'We'd be lost without it.'

The fire burned brightly in the large kitchen. The candles she'd set out on the mantlepiece and table lent the room a warm glow, even giving the small effort at a Christmas tree in the corner the impression of being lit, the baubles and tinsel shimmering in the flickering candlelight.

'What's your tipple?' Arnie said, rubbing his hands together.

'I've a nice Malbec but I can open a white if you prefer. That's if you can have a drink? I figure you must clock off at some stage. I'll keep an eye on the suspect, make sure she doesn't poison you.' He nodded his head at his mother.

'What suspect?' Kitty said, stirring a large pot of gravy. Her dark hair, streaked with grey, was drawn into a tight bun but the heat from the cooker made the stray strands stand on end and her face was roaring red. Tom could picture her looking just like that at the helm of the large kitchen in the hospital.

'You, mum. You could have easily slipped something into that doctor's dinner. The inspector was only saying how you were top of his list.'

The old woman placed her hand to her breast, her heart beating so hard it was nearly visible.

'I never . . .' she said.

'I'm joking,' Arnie laughed.

'That's not funny, son. Jesus, you put the heart across me. You don't think I killed him, do you?'

'I'm sure you didn't poison him,' Tom said. That was true. He couldn't conceive of her garrotting him either, but you never knew. She was a large woman and even now the strength in her arms was apparent, built up from years of manual labour in an industrial kitchen.

'Well, good,' she said, lowering her hand, her face still blotchy from the heat but a little paler. 'I liked Dr Howe. The man never had a cross word with me. Some of the others, well now, they wouldn't spit on you if you were on fire.'

'Mum!'

'Oh, go away, you've heard me say worse.'

'Not in front of company.'

'I'll take a glass of the Malbec if it's going,' Tom said, and the others nodded in agreement.

Arnie poured the wine from a crystal decanter into four fine-cut glasses. It was obvious he was thrilled at having the opportunity to show off his best set.

'You're not joining us, Mrs Nolan?' the inspector asked. He took a sip of the deep burgundy liquid. It was an excellent vintage. Anomalous, that the caretaker on a near-deserted island should have it to hand, but, stranger things . . .

'Oh, no, I'm not a fan of the wine,' she said. 'Please, call me Kitty. I haven't been Mrs Nolan since I retired. No, the wine is Arnie's thing. I don't know where he gets his palate from. Neither me nor his dad drank it.'

'It's just a hobby,' Arnie said. 'I went on a wine-tasting course years ago, just a couple of days up in Dublin, and the bug caught me. I know, I'm strange. Most lads my age just drink beer but then, most lads my age aren't living on an island that's home to a former insane asylum.'

His glass, Tom noted, was already half-empty. While the rest of them sipped, Arnie took large gulps. The bug had caught him good.

His mother began carving slices from a large shoulder of lamb.

'What did you think had happened to Dr Howe at the time, Kitty?' the inspector asked. It was the perfect time for questions, while she was distracted with a task. Tom always found people answered more honestly when they were doing something else. It took real skill to lie when you were multitasking.

'I have to confess, I didn't really think anything had happened to him,' she answered, not missing a beat. 'It was a big deal, of course. That's why most of us would have strong recollections of it. Dr Howe was very important in the asylum and we knew he'd a wife and small kiddies. I went out and searched, along with the rest of the ones who stayed that Christmas. Even some of the patients helped – the ones from the top floors, anyway. Of course, this was where I lived, so I was always here over the holidays.'

'Did anybody speculate about what might have happened to him?'

'Sure we did. You see, all of us who worked there, the doctors and nurses, the orderlies and cooks and cleaners, we all got on okay. But there was still a class system, if you know what I mean. Like *Upstairs, Downstairs*. We all gossiped in our little groups about it. I would have known Dr Howe, but not very well. When we heard he was missing, I was certainly worried. We knew he hadn't gone on the ferry on the 24th, but then we looked and looked and couldn't find him. And then we heard that Dr Boylan thought Dr Howe had left earlier and that sort of fit. I felt so sorry for his family. We figured he'd done a runner. I mean, it never would have occurred to us to look in the grave. What sort of twisted individual thought that up, I don't know. It was filled in shortly afterwards, anyway. The poor man, though.'

'How do you feel, Kitty, about the hospital being knocked?'

'To be honest, I'm glad it's being demolished,' she said. 'I don't want the whole island redeveloped, mind. I signed the petition against that, for all the good it did. I want to stay living here. But that place . . .'

She shook her head and shuddered.

Her son rolled his eyes.

'She thinks it's haunted.'

'It *is* haunted,' his mother said, and momentarily ceased carving meat to bless herself. 'The number of ghosts in that place would put the catacombs to shame. They need to bring it down and erect something fitting – a monument of some sort. I hear they're planning to build a hotel on the site. Madness. The guests in that place won't get a wink of sleep.'

The inspector had to avoid making eye contact with Linda, who'd joined Arnie in theatrically throwing her eyes to heaven. Ray, on the other hand, took a large gulp of wine, eyes wide and scared.

The big wuss.

'But you stayed,' Tom said. 'If St Christina's is filled with ghosts, well, surely they're not contained to within the hospital's walls? Sorry, I don't mean that to sound as flippant as it came out. It's just, it's lonely here, isn't it? Your imagination could get quite carried away, I'd say.'

Kitty nodded. He noticed her knife work had become quicker, though her hands looked less steady. Not a good mix.

'That's right,' she said. 'The dead are everywhere.' She stopped and turned to look at him, her face sad. 'Including my husband. He was born on this island and he died here, Inspector. His father was the caretaker before him. He's buried in the graveyard on the far side. I was born on the mainland but I haven't lived there in over forty-five years. I came across when I was sixteen years of age, a slip of a thing. I'll die here too and be buried alongside my Enda. Arnie, now – well, he should move somewhere with a bit more life. France, where he can drink his wine to his heart's content and nobody will notice he has a sore head every morning and purple stains on his teeth.'

She turned back to the counter and studied the amount of meat she'd carved.

'That should do it,' she said, and moved the slices to a wooden board, arranging fresh sprigs of rosemary on top. Ever the chef.

'Arnie, lift those spuds out of the oven for me. Your poor mother doesn't have the back for it any more.'

Tom and Ray helped set the table as Arnie fetched more wine. When the roasted vegetables had been moved to a tureen and placed on the smooth walnut table alongside the lamb and gravy boat, Kitty settled down beside them and began to distribute the dinner.

'I can understand your reasons for staying here,' Tom said, accepting a generous helping of gravy. 'This looks delicious, by the way. What about the others on the island, though? What's your take on why they hung around so long after the hospital closed?'

'Ach, you know, Inspector, I suppose some of them had nowhere to go. And then the trustees needed some doctors to stay on and care for the patients who wanted to live out their days here. It's also true what they say, though – often the staff who work in these psychiatric institutions are madder than the patients. Maybe it's catching and they didn't think they could go back to mixing with normal people.'

'Is it, Linda?' Ray asked.

The psychologist arched a cool eyebrow.

'Again, for the slower members of the team, I'm a criminal psychologist. If any madness from our suspects is catching, you've been more exposed than me. But I know what you mean,' she said, turning to Kitty. 'It's actually quite common. First the institutionalisation. Then the mimicking of behaviour. Nurses, talking to themselves because that's what they become used to being around, that sort of thing.'

'That's right, she has it,' Kitty said, stabbing the air with her fork. 'Wait until you meet Carla in the morning. You'll see exactly what we mean.'

They ate companionably for a time.

'By the way, Linda,' Tom said. The wine had started to relax him and even with the wind howling and rattling the window panes, the hot food and good company was a tonic. 'About earlier. We got distracted so I forgot to ask – that chair we saw hanging from the ceiling in the basement. What the hell was that all about?'

Out of the corner of his eye, he saw Kitty pale and lower her cutlery. Her hand moved to the glass of water on the table, the slight tremor visible as she picked it up and took a sip.

Linda noted it too.

'You know of it?' she said to the old woman.

'I know of most of the things that went on there, God help me. God help *them*. The kitchen was always busy and I just kept my head down and did my job. The nurses could be uppity with me but the doctors were generally very courteous. I never saw another side to them. But with those patients. Dear Lord. The things they did to them. I wouldn't have seen the chair but I heard of it.'

'You sure you want to talk about this while you're digesting your dinner?' Linda said.

'I've a strong stomach,' the inspector said. 'It was a terrific meal, Kitty, thank you.'

'We'll wash up,' Ray offered, pushing his chair out from the table.

'You'll do no such thing,' Kitty admonished him. 'The dishes can sit on the side and Arnie can take care of them when you've all gone to bed. You're the guests. And . . .' She looked pointedly at the window, which was being pummelled by rain with such force it looked as though somebody was throwing buckets of water at it. 'I won't be driving home for a little while. It's a night for tales. I might even pour myself a small one if you promise you won't arrest me for driving under the influence, Inspector.'

Tom smiled. The woman was that big she could probably have a large one and it would still do nothing to her blood alcohol level.

They settled back in their chairs, glasses replenished.

'You know, treatment of the insane was never straightforward,' Linda began. 'Everybody knows the nightmare tales about places like Bedlam. Every country had places like it. Until the nineteenth century, anyway. Then a debate started in France and travelled to Britain and the rest of the world. This was before the era of psychiatry as we know it, but there were laymen working in the hospitals and they tried to introduce a system of what we refer to as *moral management* for the treatment of patients. They believed reason and emotion could be used with mentally ill people, that they could and should be treated humanely, despite their insanity.'

'Where was the compassion in a lobotomy?' Tom said.

'Well, they'd started to phase them out. By the 1980s, they'd more or less stopped worldwide. The doctors in St Christina's would have preferred to try some of the newer treatments. Like the chair.'

Arnie knocked back what was in his glass and reached for a fresh bottle. Tom observed him with pursed lips. Perhaps caretaking at the hospital had taken more of a toll on Arnie than he liked to admit. He was only a young man. He must have been curious and looked up the various things that had happened there. The inspector had only been alone in St Christina's for ten minutes and he'd been spooked. Arnie spent far more time there.

'The swing chair – that's what it was called – that was an Irish invention,' Linda said.

'An Irish person invented that?' Kitty said, her mouth forming an O of horror. 'I didn't know that.'

'Oh yes. A doctor called Halloran from Cork. He came up with the idea that spinning and swinging the chair at a great velocity could shake the madness out of people. They'd take somebody with, say, epilepsy, and strap them into this chair. The whole contraption was suspended from the ceiling, like we saw, and had pulleys attached on either side. Then they'd set it off. Invariably, the patients would vomit their guts up. Sometimes they'd be shaken into seizures. In some instances, the brain trauma killed them.'

'Was Howe performing all these treatments?' Ray asked.

Tom shook his head.

'He must have been. But again, in his diary he shows a distaste for what's going on. Not so much the medical side but the humiliation heaped on patients. The way they were treated like sub-humans.'

A sudden crash against the window made everyone jump.

The culprit was a broken branch from one of the trees outside.

They let out jittery laughs when they realised what had happened.

'I think it's the couch for you tonight, Arnie,' Kitty said. 'I might stay here and take your bed. Between that storm and these stories . . .'

'Good idea, Mum.'

'Maybe we should draw this conversation to a close anyway,' Tom said. 'I have goosebumps on my goosebumps. An early night is what's called for; we'll sleep out the weather.'

Kitty, under pressure, condescended to their helping with the dinner dishes.

As they dried and put away the crockery, Tom took the opportunity to raise the Emmet incident with Linda.

'Linda, about himself. It's been bothering me all day. I know it's not my job to apologise on his behalf, but I wanted to say it anyway. You were clearly making the effort to be civil and I, for one, appreciated it. I thought the way he responded to you was well out of order. I just wanted you to know that. I don't know what's got into him.'

Linda shrugged and took another plate from the draining board.

'I suspect he's just an unhappy man, Tom. I may not be living the life of my dreams with Geoff, but we make it work. Emmet, well . . . his wife was never a bundle of laughs. Not before and certainly not after she found out about me. And you know damn well he hasn't kept it in his pants since, either.'

'Unfortunately, I do. You wouldn't think to look at him . . . well, anyway. You're happy, though, aren't you?'

'With Geoff? Oh, Tom. You don't know how lucky you are with Louise. Most marriages survive because the people in them have accepted the degree of unhappiness they're willing to live with. I'm . . . settled. Don't look so sad, for heaven's sake. I'm fine.'

Linda pinched his cheek affectionately.

She took the stairs up to her room, leaving Tom to go into his.

But she had looked sad, he thought, as he sat down and watched Ray empty his bag on his side of the room. Arnie had left out a camp bed – the room only had one double bed and nobody expected the two men to share, nor was Tom offering. It was a luxury, a mattress all to himself, no Louise stealing the duvet or granddaughter drooling on the side of his head.

'I'm going to have a quick shower,' his deputy said, grabbing a towel and his wash bag. 'On the off chance anybody asks you to climb inside a big straw man while I'm gone, don't do it.'

'What?'

'*The Wicker Man*?'

'Oh. Ha! Yeah, I'd forgotten. A policeman on a strange island. I can't promise I won't, not if it's Britt Ekland doing the asking.'

'You might want to ring your wife and run that past her. See you in ten.'

'Get out,' Tom grinned. He picked up his phone, grateful to see he still had a signal. It may have been his imagination, but the wind and rain seemed to be quietening down a bit. Maybe the worst of the storm had passed.

He dialled Louise. She picked up after a few rings, a babble of noise accompanying her hello.

'Are you having a party?' he asked.

'Eh, yes, I'm having a party. You do remember your lot were due to call over tonight? I couldn't cancel their Christmas visit just because you're not here. I'd all the presents for the kids and a freezer full of vol-au-vents.'

'Oh . . . shit.' That was the only word for it. 'I had forgotten.' He'd had the date of the 28th in his head for weeks and one call on Christmas Day had wiped it clean. Now he was doubly annoyed. Missing all of his gang at theirs meant having to call around to them individually in the New Year. That was at least three weekends wiped out. He loved his siblings, but in small doses; hosting them all together diluted their impact.

'I'm telling you this, Tom Reynolds, I would only do this for you. And another thing, both our folks are here for dinner on

New Year's Eve and if you're still on that island – well, you can set up house there and get yourself a coconut for company.'

'Message received and understood.'

'What are you doing, anyway?'

'Right now? I'm going to bed.'

'At 9.30? Jesus wept. Your sisters here are looking for intravenous drips of wine.'

'Under no circumstances are you to open the Bollinger. That's for us when I return.'

'If you return. Love you.'

She'd hung up before he could reply. He sighed. Yes, they were a happy couple, even if he'd been a little depressed lately. Joe Kennedy had chipped away at him so much over the last six months it had affected him. How could it not?

But, despite himself, he was enjoying this case. They were no closer to knowing who had murdered Conrad Howe but at least they knew now how he'd died.

Forty-year-old secrets were starting to come to light. Everything they were learning about St Christina's was fascinating and repellent in equal measure. And in amongst all that history was a killer who'd been lucky enough to go undetected.

Well, maybe that streak of good fortune was about to come to an end.

CHAPTER 23

Tom was wrong. The worst of the storm had passed but that didn't mean it was over. The early night wasn't going to plan. The two men were still wide awake, unable to sleep with the clamour of the wind outside.

They'd been up since early that morning, though, and had had a long day. Eventually, Tom began to doze, slipping into a fitful, light sleep; half-dreams about the long empty corridors in the asylum and its eerie, deserted basement filled his head.

When the noise pierced his consciousness, he didn't know at first if he'd imagined it or if the wind had disturbed him.

'Did you hear that, too?' Ray said, and Tom woke up properly.

'It's the wind,' he replied, then sat bolt upright as a high-pitched scream sounded. 'What the hell was that?'

'It wasn't the shagging wind.' Ray made it to the window first, pulled it open and leaned out. The rain flew into the room, soaking the carpet.

'See anything?' Tom asked, arriving at his shoulder.

Another blood-curdling shriek filled the air, sending chills down both their spines.

'There's somebody out there,' Ray said, echoing his boss's thoughts. 'Being murdered by the sounds of things.'

Linda was already out on the landing, along with Kitty.

'What's going on?' The old woman was frightened. 'I knew something would happen when those graves were disturbed, God forgive us, it's the dead. They've come back.'

Kitty was wearing a neck-to-toe nightdress and a warm house-coat over it, but the older woman was still violently shaking.

'It's not the dead,' Linda said, calmly. 'That's very much the living.'

'Where's Arnie?' Tom asked.

'He had a few more glasses after you went up,' his mother said. 'He'll be unconscious.'

True enough, Arnie was in a deep sleep on the couch down-stairs; he didn't even stir when Tom and Ray pulled on their shoes and coats in the hall, making a racket in the process. Kitty found them torches and raincoats and then they were out the door.

'What direction?' Tom called over the storm.

'It was this way,' Ray yelled back. 'It sounded like it was com-ing from near the hospital. But that's a mile away at least; could it have travelled that far?'

'On the wind, yes. Come on.'

They started at a jog, hoping and fearing that whoever had made the din would decide to scream again – giving the two policemen a better chance of finding them.

They were drenched within minutes.

'Man or woman?' Ray shouted, not even out of breath. Tom struggled to keep pace with him on the uneven road surface and the incline. They were hemmed in on either side by trees and still the rain and wind found them. Out in the open, they'd be lucky to stay grounded.

'Woman,' he panted in reply.

And, there it was again. A hideous, nightmarish howl.

They both froze, trying to pin its location.

'It's definitely near the asylum,' Tom said, his hands on his knees as he caught his breath.

'Shit in a bucket!'

'What?'

'We should have taken Arnie's keys. He locked up earlier, remember?'

'Ray, if that person was in the hospital, we wouldn't be able to hear the screams. And it sounds to me like she's moving. It was closer to the cottage when we heard it first – it's somebody going towards the asylum.'

They started running again and turned the corner.

'Jesus!' Tom yelled, as his torch flew from his hands and hit the road with a bang and then a smash, the glass shattering. He'd barrelled into a large shape and almost floored himself. It was so solid, he thought for a moment he'd hit a tree somehow transported into the middle of the road, until he heard the replying 'What in Christ's name?' and realised he'd crashed into a man.

'Emmet?' he said, staggering back. Ray shone his torch at the grouping: his boss, the Tech chief and the assistant who'd come running with Emmet.

'You heard it, too?' Emmet said.

'Yes, but it came from closer to the hospital,' Tom answered.

'No. We just came from there and did a lap of the place before coming out this way. We thought it was nearer to you. This is the only road between the hospital and there unless you cut through the woods and I've sent men in there. They have our torches; that's why we're running blind.'

They stood in the middle of the road, rain-sodden, and looked about them. Sure enough, through the trees on the inland side,

Tom could see torchlight weaving a path, as Emmet's team searched for the person in distress.

'We're staying in a house near the asylum,' Emmet said. 'The main building was the first place we looked, but we thought the person was moving. It sounded like a woman.'

They strained their ears, thinking they might hear it again.

'We can't search this island all night,' Ray said. 'Not in this.' He pointed to the heavens.

Tom shook his head. Ray was right, but nor could they return to their safe, warm beds – not if somebody was in trouble.

'We'll continue on to the asylum and check all the doors are still locked,' the inspector said. 'Emmet, you keep going that way, but I really don't think the last scream came from over that side. We'll all take this road back and meet in the middle, see if we've come up with anything.'

'Let's go,' the Tech chief said to his companion. 'I can't see a thing through these glasses in the rain; you lead the way.'

'Take my light,' Tom said, lifting the torch from the ground. 'It's still working, just mind where the glass broke.'

The men parted, moving in opposite directions.

The trees thinned as they approached the hospital and, as Tom had predicted, the weather hit them with fuller force the more exposed they became. Without communicating, both of them dashed towards the asylum. As uninviting as it looked on the cloudy, moonless night, as the storm raged all around it still offered some protection from the elements.

'Could it have been a wounded animal or something?' Ray said, as they checked the front door of the building and found it locked. 'With the asylum giving us all the creeps, are we seeing the bogeyman everywhere? Or maybe it was on the other side of the island and the wind is really throwing us off?'

Tom shook his head. He knew the sound of human distress when he heard it. But maybe the geography of the island had caught them off guard.

They moved around the hospital quickly, checking each window and door until they arrived at the rear, where they followed the same process. Tom stood back and looked up the building, but there was nothing to indicate anybody was inside, no lights, no open windows.

In the distance, the material of the canvass tent that the Tech Bureau had erected flapped in the wind. Beside it he could see the vast hole where the exhumations had taken place, more canvass pulled across it.

'The bodies,' Tom said. 'The ones they took out today. There was no ferry tonight. Where the hell has Emmet put them?'

Ray looked blank, then shivered – both from the cold and the reminder that they were a few hundred metres away from a freshly dug mass grave.

'Let's head back,' Tom said. 'This place is empty and we've heard nothing in over half an hour.'

They met Emmet again on the road, almost in the same spot they'd bumped into each other on the way.

All of them were shivering in their wet, cold clothes by this stage.

'Nothing,' they said at the same time.

'Your team?' Tom asked.

'Nowt in the woods. We need to get indoors and dry off before we all end up with pneumonia. We can look again in the morning before the ferry arrives.'

'Where are the bodies?' Tom asked. 'The ones you took out today?'

'There's a storage shed at the port,' Emmet answered. 'I've two lads down there keeping guard on shifts. They heard nothing. You were right – it didn't come from that side.'

Tom nodded. They parted again, too cold and too tired to say any more.

It was a slower job getting back to the cottage and the inspector wondered how the hell Emmet was coping with the running around, let alone the conditions. The man was at least four or five stone overweight and the fellow with him had looked in his thirties and in Ray's league of fitness. The inspector was more than aware that Emmet was a heart attack waiting to happen.

Kitty made a fuss over them when they arrived back, sending them straight upstairs to change, even providing them with two over-sized tracksuits, gifted by her still snoring son.

Linda brought them up cups of scalding tea.

'Are you decent?' she said, knocking on the door and coming in before either had the chance to respond. She handed them the cups and plonked down on the end of Tom's bed. 'Himself downstairs never moved,' she said. 'So much for caretaking. Quite a taste for the drink, that one.'

Tom nodded.

'We didn't hear anything else,' she said. 'I thought I might have heard something but it was very faint, further away, more in the direction you ran in. Kitty rang this Carla character and woke her up. She's the only other woman on the island and we were sure it was a woman's voice.'

'Us too,' he said. 'She was definitely at home?'

'We rang on the landline.'

'Are we sure she's the only other woman on the island?' Ray asked.

Tom shrugged.

'We can be sure of nothing. The Nolans say she is, but that was definitely a woman screaming. We certainly weren't imagining things. It wasn't a collective psychosis.'

Linda smiled, grimly.

'And it wasn't a ghost, either, despite the woman of the house doing her best to convince me.'

Tom sighed.

'What the hell is going on on this island?' he said.

He glanced at Howe's diary where he'd left it, on the edge of the bedside table. He had to read more of it, see what other clues it might throw up.

CHAPTER 24

Diary Entry

Oh, Minnie! I warned her. I begged and tried to reason with her. For weeks now, she's been dragging herself around. Barely eating. Not talking to anybody, hardly able to string even a few words together for me, her best friend among all the staff. The weight has fallen off her, making her cheekbones more pronounced and her arms so thin they look like they'd break if you blew on them.

Just before it happened, I called on her in the patients' lounge. She had, at least, made the smallest effort to get out of bed and be amongst the others. I sat with her at the window as she stared out at the gardens of the asylum, her gaze vacant. She normally didn't like to look out that window. She told me once the grave gave her the willies and that as soon as she was home she was going to report the asylum for burying patients on site.

I explained to her that nobody wanted those poor souls back home and at least here they rested surrounded by nice gardens and trees and flowers.

'Are you feeling any better today?' I asked, the morning I joined her.

She shrugged, as much as her exhausted body allowed.

'What is it, Minnie? What is making you so sad? Is your prescription not enough these days? Do you need it increased a little?'

She sighed, a long, sorrowful sound.

'I don't want any more medicine,' she whispered. 'I just want to go home.'

'Home,' I said. 'Tell me about home.'

Something visited itself on her face. A memory, a smile. Better times.

'I have a little brother and sister,' she said. 'Maurice and Dinah. They're twins. Big blue eyes, curly black hair. When they were born, I was always holding one of them, because mother could only manage one at a time. And I was nine, a big girl. I was the only one who could tell them apart when they were very small. Maurice has a little freckle, just here.' She touched the side of her chin. 'But Dinah's skin is as smooth as Snow White's. They smelled of milk and clean and newness and I loved to just cuddle them. It was like holding happiness. And when they were growing up, they'd get into trouble for being so mischievous but I always found them funny. They'd just lie, you know – blatantly. *No, we didn't eat any jam*, and it would be smeared all over their hands and faces.'

'They sound like a right pair. You must miss them terribly.'

She nodded. It pained her too much to even say 'yes'.

'But you can go home, if you get better, Minnie. What age are your brother and sister now? If you were nine when they were born, they must be eleven or twelve, am I right? I'm sure your mother could do with the help, especially with them being characters. You have to be well, though. You weren't well before, that's why you came here.'

'Yes,' she said. 'I wasn't well. I couldn't explain it. I just felt so sad. Like nothing or nobody in the world could make me feel anything different. And I still loved my family – mother and father and the twins – but I couldn't make myself seem happy. I couldn't pretend, even for their sake. When I saw how upset I was making them, I thought it would be better if I went. If I died. Maurice and Dinah are young and so full of fun. They deserved better than me being around, old misery guts. And now they're probably starting to forget me. I'll just be the mad sister who was shipped off to the big house and never returned.'

'What about the flat in Dublin and the job in the hairdressers? How will you ever get revenge on the nurses if you just sit here forever?'

She smiled, weakly.

'I guess somebody else will have to pay them back.'

'But nobody could be as imaginative as you. Wee-ing in their shampoo!'

'Ha! Yeah. Yes, maybe one day.'

I was so worried about Minnie. It was the most words I'd had from her in weeks and, yet, the worst conversation we'd ever had. When she wasn't depressed, Minnie was like a little girl herself, full of fun and mischief and jokes. The woman who sat in front of me that morning was almost bent double under the weight on her shoulders.

'Please, Minnie,' I said. 'Let's just get you a higher dosage. We need you to feel well again, don't we? You need to try. For Maurice and Dinah.'

She nodded, half-heartedly.

'You know, you were right,' she said, just as I made to leave.

'About what?'

'The garden out there is peaceful. I don't feel so bad for the ones who've died, looking out now. All those flowers blooming around them. It's . . . restful.'

I wasn't there when it happened. I came back after a weekend at home and her bed was made, her locker empty.

'They moved her downstairs,' the nurse said. 'She was in one of the toilet cubicles. Tried to saw through her wrist with a broken link from the flush chain.'

'Downstairs to the third floor?' I asked, still hopeful that the worst hadn't happened.

'No,' the nurse said. 'She needs constant supervision. She's in a padded cell. She's going mental down there, though. I guess she's not happy she didn't get away with her plan. She tried to gouge the eye out of one of the other nurses. If she doesn't rein in it, she's going to end up in the basement. She'd want to watch herself.'

CHAPTER 25

Tom knew he was sick when, faced with the large breakfast Kitty had left out for them, he could only manage a bowl of porridge and even then, it tasted of nothing.

'You look like shit,' Ray greeted him. 'Only marginally less sick than Arnie, who tells me he thinks he has a stomach bug.'

Linda snorted, then stabbed Tom's cast-aside bacon with her fork, adding it to her own plate. The woman was rod-thin and had the appetite of a small nation, the inspector thought, miserably. She was like his driver in Dublin, Willie Callaghan. He could consume fifty thousand calories in a day and still maintain the physique of a greyhound.

Tom sighed. He'd end up just as thin, if he couldn't stomach a small bowl of cereal.

On cue, he sneezed. His throat hurt, his joints ached and his eyes were streaming. And the Lemsip and Nurofen Linda had rustled from the cupboards only served to mute his symptoms, not cure them.

'I'll drive,' Ray said. 'We'll leave Arnie to sleep it off. He's given me directions to Crowley and Lane's houses. Let's finish off our interviews and get you on that ferry. We can come out again in a couple of days, if needs be.'

Tom nodded weakly, happy to let somebody else take charge for a few hours. His desire to stay on the island as long as it took to find Howe's killer was wavering in the face of a head cold. He didn't have it in him to be a martyr to the cause. He just wanted to go home and be mollycoddled by Louise.

'You poor dear,' Linda said, feeling his forehead. 'I think the prognosis is death. It's the worst case of man-flu I've ever seen.'

Yes, home was definitely called for. Tom knew he'd get no real sympathy from this pair.

They decided that the inspector and Linda would call to see Carla Crowley and Ray would visit Edward Lane. Tom sat in the front seat, the heat from the Land Rover's engine blasting his legs, and let the island's sights distract him from his headache as Ray concentrated on getting them to their destinations.

The storm was gone. The only evidence it had hit at all was the stray branches on the road and the puddles that filled the potholes.

They turned way from the asylum when they left the cottage, taking a coastal route. The tall, leafless trees were sparser on this, the more exposed side of the island. Instead, the landscape was rockier, leading down to pebbled beaches on the broken shoreline, the sand so dark from the night's rain it looked volcanic.

In the distance, low, dark clouds rumbled, threatening the calm weather.

'I hope that doesn't turn and come back our way,' Linda said, nodding ahead. 'Your deputy here wasn't happy coming across on the ferry when the waters were still. It would be great craic in a storm.'

'If Mannix sails,' Tom said. 'If the weather changes, what we feared could come true. We could end up stuck here.' He sniffed, pitifully. 'At least it will give me time to read more of Howe's diary. I got a few pages in last night but it's like deciphering Sanskrit at this stage, the writing is so tiny. It makes my eyes hurt.'

Carla's cottage was tucked behind one of the hills a little more inland. It was sheltered from the wild Atlantic winds, but also missed out on the views. Tom reckoned he'd have sacrificed the shelter.

'Lane lives a mile up the road,' Ray said. 'I'll be back soon.'

Tom and Linda hopped out and made their way up the winding path to the nurse's front door. When Carla Crowley opened it, Tom immediately felt sorry for her. She looked worse than he felt, no mean feat.

'Thanks for coming over,' she croaked. 'I haven't been able to leave the house. It's dreadful being stuck in. I miss the company. Can I offer you some tea?'

Carla had to be at least sixty, but she looked far younger. Her hair was still dark, cut in a short bob and tucked behind her ears. Her skin, aside from the wrinkles around her eyes and mouth, was porcelain smooth. She would have been quite a beauty except for the fact one of her eyes roved to and fro, settling nowhere. She looked down frequently, a habit formed to try to disguise the impediment.

Linda looked from her to Tom and back again.

'How about I make the tea and you two sit down? The inspector here is a fellow sufferer, Ms Crowley. You can exchange remedies and . . . germs.'

The nurse smiled weakly and directed Linda to the kitchen.

The cottage was pristine. Only the small table beside the nurse's chair in the living room betrayed any sign of disorder – it was cluttered with a glass, tissues, foil strips of lozenges and a packet of paracetamol.

'It is true; we make the sorriest patients,' she said, slumping into her seat and pointing at the couch for Tom. 'There's you, Inspector, smothering, and you're traipsing around this island on your investigation while I can't even bring myself to get dressed.' She tugged at the belt on her housecoat as she spoke, shivering.

'If it makes you feel any better, I'd give anything to be in bed,' Tom said. He watched her closely, looking for signs that something had happened to her last night, something to make her scream in terror. There was nothing. Carla seemed fine, in the full of her health, albeit with the flu.

'You can take some of my supplies back with you,' she said. 'I doubt Arnie Nolan has anything in that house bar headache tablets. All of his illnesses are self-inflicted. Please, call me Carla, while you're here. Your colleague referred to me as Ms Crowley. Everybody on the island still calls me nurse, would you believe? Nurse or Carla.'

'You still are a nurse, from what I hear,' Tom said. 'Aren't you taking care of Dr Boylan?'

She nodded.

'Not very well this week, obviously.'

'Forgive me for asking, but you seem very young. When did you come to work in St Christina's? Were you actually here when Dr Howe went missing?'

'I was, yes. I started here in 1971, nineteen years of age. Myself and Dr O'Hare started at the same time. I'm sixty now and I'll take your lovely compliment. Anyhow, I knew Conrad but not very well. As a student nurse, I would have spent more time assisting the senior nurses and sometimes the junior doctors. It took a few years of practice before I started to move up the ranks. By the time the hospital closed, I was chief nurse. I stayed on with our remaining patients. I was the only nurse who did, but there were only a handful to treat and we had several doctors so it was fine.'

'It's unusual, is it not, to spend your whole working life in one hospital?' This came from Linda, who'd arrived in the sitting room carrying a tray of tea things. She settled them on the coffee table.

The nurse flushed at her question.

'I was content here. And Dr Boylan needed me.' She picked up her teacup. Tom watched, amused, as she stirred in the milk and tapped the spoon on the side of the cup and then the saucer, three times each. She set it down and her other hand moved to the arm of the chair. She began to pick at a half-knitted scarf she'd left there, the needles still attached.

'Feel free,' Tom said, waving at the scarf.

'If you don't mind,' Carla replied, pouncing on the wool. 'My hands get itchy if they're not busy. The devil find works for them.'

The inspector and Linda exchanged a glance but said nothing.

'You say Dr Boylan needed you,' Tom said. 'Do you mean at the hospital or personally? How long has he been ill?'

'Not so long,' she said. 'He got his diagnosis a couple of years ago. He was perfectly fine up until then.'

She clicked the needles together and it wasn't until she looked up that they saw the nurse had tears in her eyes.

'It was such a shock. I've worked so closely with Lawrence for so long. I'm just grateful to be able to give him the help he needs. It's so very sad.'

She looked down again, once more conscious of her unsteady eye, now filling with tears.

'Did you know Dolores O'Sullivan, then?' Tom asked. 'The nurse who left the day Conrad disappeared? I believe he saved her life.' Ray had filled them in that morning on the interview with Robert O'Hare.

'He did, yes. That happened the week I started working in the hospital. It was one of the reasons I came to know Dr Howe's name so well. I'm afraid, though, I wasn't here when he disappeared. I'd gone home that Christmas, on the ferry on the 23rd with many of my fellow staff. I was still young and a little homesick, even then, after a year. I didn't move onto the island properly until after my mother and father died. Then I got this cottage, purely because of length of service. They were normally reserved for the doctors.

'When I got back that New Year, they'd already searched the place for Conrad. Everyone agreed by then that he must have left the island earlier than planned. I mean, there was no reason to think anybody would harm him. He was a well-liked man and very respected.'

'So, in your opinion, Dolores O'Sullivan would have been a fan of Conrad's? She'd have had no reason to have been involved in his death?' Tom had been curious about the two people who had left the island that day. But after Ray had filled him in about the fire in 1971, it was hard to imagine that the nurse would have wanted to harm Howe.

Carla's eyes widened and even the roving one seemed to focus momentarily.

'Good gracious, Dolores involved in Conrad's death? Absolutely not. Dolores *did* leave the island because of Conrad, but not because she wanted him dead.'

'What do you mean, she left because of Conrad? Didn't she leave because she was still traumatised by what had happened the year previous?'

'Who told you that? Ah. One of the men no doubt. They

wouldn't have a clue. Dolores was very affected by the accident, true. That was apparent to all of us. But not because she was frightened it could happen again, or couldn't handle being around the patients. She was traumatised because of the damage it had done to her. Her face, her beautiful face; one whole side of it was completely destroyed. I only knew her for a few days before it happened, but she was a looker. Then, afterwards . . . Well, I have this,' she pointed at her eye, 'so I know how debilitating it can be to have an impediment. It's always worse for women.'

'I understand. So, what? Dolores was angry with Conrad because he'd saved her and left her to live with the scars? What, would she have preferred to die?'

Carla shook her head.

'No. Well, perhaps. She wasn't angry at Conrad. The problem was, she was *in love* with him. My fellow nurses told me she'd been smitten with him for a very long time, despite his being married. Conrad was an utterly brilliant doctor, by all accounts. He really had the patients' best interests at heart but he was also forward thinking. He had such a bright future ahead of him. And, of course, he saved Dolores' life and well, that was heroic enough to turn any woman. But she was left looking like that and he, of course, took a special interest in her because he . . . well, I suppose he felt a bond. She couldn't bear it, I guess. Him checking on her all the time, pitying her. When she looked like that and she really had no chance. She had to get away from St Christina's. She couldn't breathe here.'

'Ah,' Tom said. 'I see.'

Carla put down her needles and picked up her tea, tapping the cup and saucer again. If she realised the inspector and Linda found it disconcerting, she didn't let on.

'Anyhow,' she continued, 'if it's people who left the island on the 24th you're interested in, you should be paying closer attention to Owen Reid.'

'Right. He was the head orderly, wasn't he?'

'Yes. He finished up too, that week. Did you know that? And that was the last we heard of him, when he left. He was only at the hospital a couple of years but he was right up himself. He didn't even tell anybody he was going, just left his resignation letter in Lawrence's office. But he might have had a reason to flee, looking back now.'

'How come?'

'He hated Conrad. Absolutely hated him.'

Tom shook his head. This was new to him.

'Why? Everything we've heard so far indicated Dr Howe was popular. Professional.'

'Dr Howe was very professional, Inspector. He believed in what we were trying to do in St Christina's, and was even more ambitious for the patients, some would argue, than the hospital's ethos. All I can speculate is that he might have seen something happen, he might have known something was going on. That would explain the argument he had with Reid.'

'What argument? When?'

'A couple of weeks before he left. They had a huge blow up out by one of the cottages. One of the doctors saw it. Well, we all knew what it was over. We all suspected it was going on, but Dr Howe must have found evidence and confronted Reid. I was surprised, I admit. Reid always struck me as straight. He was outspoken, for sure. A little cocky for his position, reckoned he knew more than the doctors at times. Was always hanging around the patients. Perhaps it was more than cockiness, though. Maybe he was arrogant because he'd been getting away with it for so long.'

'Carla,' Tom interrupted. 'You've completely lost me. What did you all suspect was going on? What was Reid getting away with?'

'Oh.' She put down her tea and tucked a stray lock of hair behind her ear, tugging on the earlobe twice as she did. Kitty Nolan was right, Carla Crowley had picked up plenty of eccentricities working in the hospital. OCD among them.

'Some of the female patients said they'd been . . . touched, by one of the orderlies. We had quite vulnerable women in our care. And men, of course. It was our duty to protect them. But it was hard to know what was truth and what wasn't. The same patient might tell you one of the staff had interfered with her, then tell you she'd been talking to the little folk in the garden. The fairies, I mean. But what if Reid had abused somebody? Maybe Conrad confronted him and Reid killed him.'

She nodded decidedly and took up her knitting again, content that she'd just solved the case for them.

Tom looked at Linda, who shrugged with a *seems perfectly plausible to me* look.

'The doctor who saw this Reid chap and Conrad argue, Carla. You don't happen to know who it was?'

'Yes, I . . .' The nurse took a sudden deep breath and let out three loud sneezes, then fumbled for the tissue on the small table beside her. 'God bless. I really cannot shake this thing. It was Dr Collins. The funny thing is, he said he saw Conrad out at that same cottage the day he went missing, too. Isn't that strange? We thought he was imagining things at the time. Dr Collins could be – peculiar. A bit manic, at times. But . . . maybe he told the truth.'

'Maybe Conrad was out there that day meeting Owen Reid.'

CHAPTER 26

Diary Entry

I saw Minnie again today. She is barely recognisable. That's twice in the last fortnight, but from the look of her, you would imagine years had passed.

I've been kept so busy the last few weeks. A team of doctors and politicians from Dublin visited the asylum and we all had to ensure it looked its best.

It's almost funny. The team came to see how advanced St Christina's is, how we are at the vanguard of treatment when it comes to psychiatric care. Several patients near to securing day release were selected to showcase our talents as a potential teaching hospital. They were all patients from the top floor and most of them with hardly any need to be in here in the first place.

One member of the visiting team wanted to see the other wards and when I heard that, I prayed it would happen. Let them talk to some of the less fortunate in our care, I thought. Let them hear what I've heard about one of the doctors in here. And what he's been getting up to.

But then hospital management said that wasn't possible, for the safety of the guests and the stability of the patients, who would react with terror and mania if a troupe of strangers came marching down the corridors.

He's had Minnie in for treatment. She told me when I found her two weeks ago.

She'd been moved from the padded cell onto one of the wards. She lay in her new bed, her wrists bound to the side rails, even while heavily sedated. She'd torn clumps from her hair and her face was scratched and bruised. I sat with her quietly for a few minutes until she turned her head and looked at me through half-closed eyes.

'Want to go home,' she mumbled, her words drowsy and slurred.

'I know, Minnie,' I said. 'Soon. You have to get well. But soon.'

'No. Can't stay. Don't make me stay. Don't let him take me.'

'Who, Minnie?' I said.

She started to drift off again. I looked around. The nurses were busy with other, more alert patients. A few minutes passed, then Minnie came round again. This time she was more agitated.

'He does things,' she said. 'Choked me. I couldn't breathe.'

'What?' I said. 'Who choked you? Minnie, what are you talking about?'

She stirred in the bed.

'Says he'll make me better. No. No! Can't breathe.'

Minnie was coming out of sedation.

A nurse rushed over, her attention drawn by the sudden activity in the bed.

'Now Minnie,' she said. 'It's time for your next dosage.'

'Wait, Nurse,' I said. 'She's trying to tell me something.'

'Is this your patient?' the nurse said, eyeing me sternly.

'Well, no . . .' I started to say.

'Then please, let me administer her prescription. Her doctor will be furious with me if I don't.'

I moved out of the way, boiling with frustration. And I watched as Minnie strained against the nurse's firm grasp, protesting as the needle was injected. She turned to me, her eyes desperate and pleading.

And my gaze travelled down to her neck, where a necklace of bruises stood out like purple flowers on a white canvas.

Later that day, the visitors arrived and I was so busy, I couldn't get back to see her until today.

She's dying. She can't kill herself but still, her body is shutting down.

It's not for want of care from the nurses. They feed her through a drip. They wash her in the bed. Minnie might be deteriorating but her parents have still paid for good care.

But Minnie wants to go. There's something alongside her sadness now. She is terrified. Whatever her doctor is doing to her, it is not in her best interests. It is not helping.

I stood beside her bed and stroked her head as her teeth chattered and she stared at the ceiling – not even at the ceiling – just into the distance. Twenty years of age and the wrinkles and dark circles around her eyes speak of a woman three times that. Her dark hair is now flecked with grey, where she hasn't pulled at it. And her body is covered in lacerations. How, I wonder, is she harming herself when her wrists are permanently affixed to the bed? Has anybody asked?

'Minnie,' I said, giving it one last go. 'Remember Maurice and Dinah? I'm sure they would love to see you. Wouldn't you like them to come and see you? If you sleep and try to eat a little, you know, I'm sure something can be arranged.'

She blinked. I thought she might say something but she continued to stare upwards, eyes glazed.

I sighed. I was about to leave when, unexpectedly, I felt the lightest of touches on my hand, still holding the rail. I looked down and saw Minnie was trying to brush her fingers against mine.

I grabbed her hand and gave it a gentle squeeze. Then I realised she was trying to say something. It was nothing more than a whisper, blown through chapped, parched lips.

I leaned closer to her mouth and listened. I shook my head. 'I can't hear you,' I said. 'Just a little louder, Minnie.'

I suppose I guessed she might be saying, *tell them I love them*. A final message to her brother and sister, knowing that she was dying.

I was completely confused when she whispered again, a tiny bit louder this time, enough for me to hear her say: 'Rosita. M'friend. Rosita. Her. Please.'

'What?' I said, desperate. 'What do you want me to do for Rosita?'

'Keep her safe.'

The last three words were exhaled with such effort I thought it might be Minnie's last breath.

But when I looked down, her eyes were wide open and she was staring at me, imploring.

'Yes,' I said, nodding my head hard, trying to convince her. Whatever might bring her even a moment of peace.

I don't even know who Rosita is. We have over five hundred patients in St Christina's and, with the way we work, I know maybe only forty or fifty of them by name.

Is she one of them?

CHAPTER 27

The worst thing about Edward Lane was his inability to respect personal body space. The former chemist had chosen to live in the middle of nowhere, completely alone. Yet here he was, practically sitting on Ray's lap, as the detective sergeant attempted to interview him.

Ray had taken up position on the two-seater in the small sitting room, assuming the house's owner would take the couch across from it. But Lane had planted himself beside Ray, giving him the full effect of the rancid, stale breath that blew out from behind rotten teeth. There was no offer of tea or coffee, nothing that would have meant Lane getting up and Ray rearranging himself.

He was really getting the short stick in these interviews.

'Howe was an uppity little chancer,' Lane said, then broke into a hacking cough, wiping the accompanying phlegm with a filthy handkerchief. 'Like all those doctors. Fancied himself God. Thought he knew everybody else's job better than they did. Always sticking his nose in where it wasn't wanted. All those doctors, you see, were assigned a specific number of patients. Enough to keep them all busy. Didn't stop Howe from interfering in the treatment of others not in his care, I tell you.'

Ray was leaning back so far his spine hurt.

'And eh, did he claim to know your job better than you?' he asked.

'Mm-hm. You know, I was older than the little puck? Just by a year. I'm seventy-three. You wouldn't think it, would you? Ha! Anyway, it might have only been a year but it was probably by a few decades in cop-on, if you get my meaning. That Howe chancer would be under-prescribing for the patients and I was the senior chemist. I knew who needed what in that hospital. Took pride in it, I did. So I'd slip the right amount into the dosages. Well, he found out about it and kicked up a big fuss. We had a stand-up row, we did. Right in Boylan's office.'

'I see,' Ray said. 'When was this?'

The old man scratched his bristly chin, then coughed again.

'H-ha!' he spluttered. 'Not the week he was murdered, if that's what you're getting at, boyo. It was a year or so before that. I kept my distance from him after that.'

'Were you on the island when he disappeared?'

'Mm. Didn't bother to look for him, though. I didn't give a pig's fart where he was. I wasn't the only one, either. There's plenty who went out looking but weren't too bothered about finding him.'

'Oh? Like who? We've been given the impression Dr Howe was well liked.'

Lane leaned closer to Ray and the detective had to summon all his willpower not to heave when the chemist puffed out his cheeks inches from his face.

'His best buddy, Collins. Did he tell you Howe was liked? Pah! Not by him, that's for sure. And Collins was high as a kite that day. Bet he didn't tell you that, either. He had a thing for the Tofranil. Had done since we introduced it on trial in the late fifties.'

'Tofra-what?'

'An antidepressant. It's common, doctors self-medicating for depression. Collins was the opposite of Howe. He'd request too high a dosage for a patient and be lobbing the extra off for himself. That day, I could see in his eyes he'd been having a one-man party for the season. He tried to keep it together for the search party but then he was going on about having seen Howe that morning and nobody believed him.'

'Could he have been hallucinating? If he'd taken drugs?'

'One of the side effects of Tofranil is blurred vision. But seeing things that aren't there would be a first. No, he was either lying about seeing him or Howe was out there. S'pose we'll never know.'

Ray couldn't take it any more. He stood up.

'Sorry,' he said. 'Bad back. I need to keep moving.'

'I could give you something for that.'

'Eh. No thanks, you're okay. So – Collins. Why was he depressed? Was it being out here on his own? Working in St Christina's?'

'All of the above and none. I'm sure those things got to him but not as much as the primary reason. That's the problem with medicine these days. Treat the symptoms, not the cause. Collins' misery started with one problem.'

'Which was?'

Lane sat back and crossed his legs, his face a picture of smugness. He was thrilled, having information that the police did not.

'Well now, Detective. It could have been the fact he thought he was the best doctor in St Christina's but nobody else did. Then there was also the reality that he wasn't suited to work with the mentally ill. The man was unstable himself. It takes a deal of character to handle the insane and he wasn't up to it. He was weak. But his biggest problem was the final nail in his coffin, you might say.'

'Which was?' Ray prompted.

'He was in love with his best friend's wife, wasn't he? Collins fancied the arse off Miriam Howe. And she was married to his mate! You couldn't make it up. A recipe for disaster, that was.'

'God, he is a deeply unpleasant man,' Ray said, as Tom and Linda got into the car. 'How was yours?'

The inspector filled him in on the exchange with Carla.

'Did you pick up on anything at the start, when she was talking about Boylan?' Linda asked.

Tom turned his head.

'When she was saying how much he needed her?'

'Yes. She's madly in love with him.'

'Do you think so? You got that from that little exchange?'

'Oh, absolutely.'

'Well, funny that,' Ray said. 'Because we seem to have lots of hopeless lovers on this island. Lane insists that Andrew Collins was mad about Howe's wife.'

He filled them in on his interview.

'Lane says Miriam was over once or twice when Howe started in the hospital, as were a few of the doctors' wives. Said Collins couldn't keep his eyes off her. But apparently it goes back further. Collins and Howe were in college together and Miriam was the daughter of one of their lecturers. Apparently, they both fell for her.'

'Do you believe Lane?' Linda asked. 'Does he seem reliable? If he disliked Howe and Collins so much, how does he know their history?'

'I don't know if I'd describe him as reliable,' Ray said. 'He seems quite bitter and he absolutely despised Howe. Not just Howe, possibly all the doctors. Though he rates himself very highly. But he did say Collins was a fan of the drugs and Boylan told you the same thing. Since Lane was the chemist, maybe he talked to Collins a bit more and had something on him. And, when we went out to Miriam Howe's house the other day . . .'

'I know,' Tom said. 'I saw it, too. Collins is fond of her. To still be on the scene after all this time, it says something. Anyhow, he's the man we need to talk to next. He never told us he'd a cottage on Oileán na Coillte. And if he was fixated on his friend's wife, that's as good a motive as any for offing him. Though, it must be a fierce slap in the face to kill somebody in order to get your hands on his wife and then watch her mourn him for forty years.'

'And Reid?'

'Yep, he's high up the list now, too. Let's see if Laura found anything on him. If he's still alive, that is. There's a strong possibility the person who actually killed Howe is dead himself.'

'What are you going to do about those screams we heard last night?' Linda asked.

'What can I do?' Tom answered. 'I spoke to Emmet this morning – he'd sent his team out as soon as there was daylight to see if anything was amiss. They couldn't find anything. All of the island's inhabitants are safe. I don't see what more we can do. I'll ring over to Kerry, ask them to get some local uniforms to come over on the ferry and do another scout around before we leave.'

'So, we're definitely on the afternoon boat, then?' Ray asked, just as the first drops of rain landed on the Land Rover's windscreen.

Tom pulled his coat up to his chin and nodded. He'd need another dose of drugs to cope with the head cold, not to mention with Ray on choppy water.

CHAPTER 28

'Are we okay to sail?' Tom asked, looking up at the darkening sky. The bright morning had turned on its head, the fickle weather playing tricks again.

Mannix shrugged. The rain drummed on his mac, not bothering him in the slightest.

'S'alright,' he said. 'Rough, but not unmanageable. Have to get those bodies off the island, don't we? And the weather's turning. I won't be sailing for a couple of days after this. Can't leave them sitting in a cold storage shed all that time. Speaking of – your deputy don't look the Mae West.'

Ray had gone inside the ferry's cabin and Tom could see him through the windows, huddled into himself, his face turning all shades of green.

They'd only left port.

'He should be out on deck, getting some air,' Mannix said. 'I'm going in to make sure my apprentice keeps us steady. A ferry is a bigger ask than a fishing boat.'

Tom let him go. He'd met the new ferry hand, Mannix's sixteen-year-old son, when they were boarding; the young chap looked like he was about to loosen his bowels when his father said he could negotiate them out from the dock.

Linda was hanging on to one of the rails, looking back towards the island.

''m glad we're leaving,' she said, through a mouthful of scarf. 'Oileán na *Caillte* is right. Even Arnie, our gracious host. The alcohol will get him good and proper one of these years. He's far too young to already have yellow fingertips.'

'Hmm?'

'Cirrhosis.'

'Christ. Can you get it that young?'

'It only takes a few years of drinking too much. What the hell else would he be doing on that island all day long?'

'Poor Arnie. Poor Kitty. We're lucky to be leaving at all, by the sounds of it. Mannix told me the weather's deteriorating. This is the last ferry for a while. I don't think I'd have fancied staying on the island. Not least because Louise would have swum over to beat the shite out of me.'

Linda snorted.

'I believe you. Your wife is a paragon of patience but even she is allowed to put her foot down every now and again. It's easy for me to swan off over the Christmas holidays. I've no family, bar Geoff. It wasn't fair of Joe Kennedy to send you over.'

'It's caught my interest, though,' Tom said, watching the receding land mass. On the other side, in the distance, the Kerry coastline was visible, despite the rain. 'If we'd been able to figure it out very quickly – if Howe had enemies coming out of his arse – then I'd have been pissed off at having my holidays ruined. But this one is intriguing. I'm not sure anybody on that island is telling the truth. Well, except Kitty Nolan. She seems straight enough.'

'She must have killed him, then,' Linda said, and they both laughed.

'I read a few pages of that diary while we were waiting for the bodies to be transported on board,' Tom said, and shivered.

'I'm going to try to finish it when we get back to Dublin. Howe was not happy over there. He definitely had concerns about a fellow doctor. He doesn't name the bloody man, which is a bit of a nuisance. I wonder if he worried about the diary being found. Or maybe there's a name somewhere later. I scanned the pages but I couldn't spot one immediately. The handwriting is erratic, though, tiny and so bloody cramped in places.'

'How inconsiderate of the victim. You'd think he'd have found the time to carve his killer's name in blood on the final page. Why don't you get one of your minions to transcribe it? Save you squinting at every page.'

'I need to keep my team onside while Joe Kennedy's running his little campaign against me. I'm not sure giving them jobs like that would curry favour.'

'Tsk. Those detectives would walk into fire for you, Tom Reynolds. And don't you forget it.'

Tom nodded, knowing it.

'Here's Emmet.' He grabbed Linda's arm before she could make good her exit. 'No, don't you scurry off. We're having a conversation. Anyway, it's a small ferry. There's nowhere to hide.'

'Tom,' Emmet said, feeling his way along the rail. The deck was slippy from the rain and the sloshing waves. The Tech chief stood beside the inspector, ignoring Linda. 'I'm going to travel to Kerry General with the last of the exhumed bodies. Moya Chambers rang this morning. She reckons she's coming down with the flu but she wants some orders passed on to the pathologists there.'

'Flu? And what, she can't work?' Tom sniffed for effect. He was wrapped up warmly and Arnie had let him keep the raincoat he'd borrowed last night, but still, he felt wretched.

'You know what women are like.'

Tom groaned. He could feel Linda bristle beside him.

'No, I'm sure he doesn't. What are women like, Emmet?'

And the inspector had thought a runny nose and headache was as bad as it could get.

'*You* know,' Emmet said, pushing the wet fringe back from his forehead as he glared at her. 'Liars.'

Linda's response was temporarily delayed by the weather gods. A strong gust of wind hit the ferry sideways, rocking the boat and sending a large wave crashing onto the deck. Unfortunately, in the ensuing, slippery chaos, Linda slid bang into Emmet. There was nothing Tom could do to stop it. He'd swung sideways and landed on his backside, nearly dislocating his shoulder to hang onto the rail.

'Christ!' Emmet shouted, and pushed her away, roughly.

'Emmet!' Tom exclaimed in reply, using the rail to pull himself up. Even Linda looked shocked at the violent response. 'What has got into you? Apologise.'

'I will not.'

Tom's features hardened.

'For crying out loud, show an ounce of courtesy. She slipped, we all did. It wasn't intentional.'

'Tom. It's okay.' This was Linda. Her face had paled. Her and Emmet's eyes were locked in some sort of understanding. The inspector realised he was out of his depth. There was something going on between these two he wasn't privy to.

'Yes,' Emmet growled. 'Now you get it. *I know*.'

Linda's hand flew to her mouth.

'I know what you did in England.'

'Oh, God.'

Linda turned on her heel and moved away, hanging onto the side of the cabin to steady herself as she went. She almost collided with Ray at the door. Then she was inside and Ray had taken her place at the rail to throw his guts up into the sea.

'What . . . ?' Tom began.

Emmet held up a hand.

'Not now. I'm not the villain here. Just you remember that. Whatever way she tries to spin this, I'm not the villain.'

CHAPTER 29

It wasn't until late on New Year's Day that Tom had a chance to talk to his wife about the incident with Linda and Emmet on the ferry.

He'd received very little sympathy for his illness when he arrived home. More seasonal visitors had turned up, and once they'd left, Louise put her husband to work fetching things for their parents' stay over New Year's.

He abandoned all thoughts of dropping into what was probably an empty office, topped up on Lemsip and Berocca, and obeyed the most important boss he had.

'Fresh oysters, though,' he moaned, after their parents had gone home and the two of them had collapsed on the sofa. 'That was some ask on New Year's Eve.'

'You got them, didn't you? I always say there's no problem my husband can't solve. How did you lay your hands on them, incidentally?'

'A friend of a friend of a friend who has a boat out in Howth harbour. I'm almost positive he broke some licence condition for me.'

'They went down a treat with that tabasco sauce, though, didn't they? Right, are we opening this bottle of Bollinger or not? I am dying for a drink.'

They'd both stayed off alcohol while their parents were

there. Tom and Louise's fathers were, in their own domains, laid-back men. But when the two of them got together and whiskey was involved, they turned into argumentative, opinionated old so-and-so's.

'Go on,' Tom said. 'You can have the lion's share. I need to go into the office tomorrow.'

'I love the way you think you can gift me the champagne, like I wouldn't just drink most of it anyway.'

Louise got up just as Cáit toddled in, ready for bed in her Dora the Explorer pyjamas, dark hair tied in bunches on either side of her head.

'Come and give Granddad a cuddle,' Tom said, lifting the tot onto his lap.

'Mammy mean,' she said in return.

'Why is Mammy mean?'

'Me like bed.'

His granddaughter had taken to saying she liked things she didn't like and vice versa. It left outsiders very confused.

From upstairs, Tom could hear Maria stomping from room to room, looking for her daughter.

'You're going to be a big girl this year, pet. A whole two. You have to go to bed when Mammy says.'

'Nope. Oh! She coming!'

There was nothing wrong with Cáit's hearing. The lightest trip on the stairs and she'd dived into the tiny gap between Tom and the arm of the couch, attempting to hide under a cushion.

'Have you seen that bold baby?' Maria said at the door, hands on hips, eyebrows raised as she spied the giggling, moving cushion beside her dad.

'No, I haven't seen her,' Tom said. 'Oh, wait a minute. Do you mean *this* bold baby?' He flung the cushion to the floor and lifted the tot in the air as she screamed with delight.

'That's the one,' his daughter said, catching the struggling child around the waist. 'You're going to bed, munchkin.'

'No! Granddad do it!' Cáit yelled.

'Go on, then,' Tom sighed.

'Aw, thanks, Dad. You're the best. We're reading *Where's the Green Sheep?* About fifteen goes and she should nod off.'

By the time Tom arrived back downstairs, Louise and Maria had polished off most of the champagne between them. He enjoyed seeing his daughter happy and relaxed. She'd been so young when she'd had Cáit, just nineteen. It had come as a shock but she'd managed admirably, combining motherhood and college studies. Louise helped but had also learned to back off and let Maria raise Cáit her own way. They'd reached a happy equilibrium for their small family.

'Something happened on the ferry's return trip,' he said, as Louise flicked idly through the channels showing their pre-recorded schedules of bad films and worse soaps. She settled on *Eastenders* and sank back against his shoulder, watching the TV on mute. Two families appeared to be warring over an intended celebratory dinner. It looked like the gravy boat was about to be flung at a wall.

'Something happened? Did you have an epiphany about the case?'

'No. Not to me. Between Linda and Emmet.'

That was enough to grab her full attention.

'Linda and Emmet were there, together?'

'Of course. You knew Linda was coming across with me.'

'Yes, but I didn't know Emmet was over there, too. Are you

crazy? Why would you put the two of them on an island together? You ate the head off me when I had the two of them here for your party last year.'

Maria had arrived back with a fresh bottle and topped up the glasses. She sat on the armchair across from them, legs tucked under, ready for the story. She knew Emmet and Linda and was as curious as most about the history that had caused the discord between them.

'I was interviewing doctors about a murder that took place in an asylum. Linda is a clinical psychologist. It wasn't exactly left-field thinking. And I figured her and Emmet could play at being civil for a while.'

'You never learn.'

'No. But this was worse than normal. They weren't just sniping at each other.'

He told her about the exchange on the crossing – how Emmet had manhandled Linda and the words that followed.

'That *is* shocking,' Louise said, her brow furrowed. 'And he didn't say what he'd meant? Nor her?'

'Neither of them spoke for the rest of the trip. We parted company with Emmet in Kerry and Linda travelled back with us, but Ray was in the car so we just talked about the case. I was thinking, remember you told me how they'd split . . .'

'How did they split?' Maria piped up, seeing a chance to get all the gory details.

Louise had a few glasses of champers in her at this stage and was feeling more loose-lipped than normal. She gave her daughter the potted version.

'Holy shit!' Maria exclaimed.

'Yes,' Tom said. 'Holy shit. And don't mention that to anybody.

Remind me to never tell you anything in confidence, Louise Reynolds. Anyhow, you had a theory, do you remember, that there might have been more to the split?'

'Did I?'

'Yes. You said you couldn't get your head around why Linda would walk out on her marriage, knowing how it would hurt Geoff and the damage it would do to her relationship with her wider family. That she was of that generation who just had affairs and stayed in loveless marriages.'

Louise scrunched up her eyes. 'Yes. Yes, I did wonder about that.'

'Well, when Emmet said "I know what you did in England", I thought – what if Linda had been pregnant? What if that was why she wanted to go the whole hog? But when he rejected her, she went off and had an abortion. And she's never had kids since. That could be why she hates Emmet more than seems natural. And maybe he's gone and found out about it now.'

'Oh, God. You could be right. That would be horrendous.'

'Hang on,' Maria said. 'If she'd had an abortion, what, twenty years ago or something – how on earth would he have found out about it? That doesn't add up.'

Tom started to stay something, then stopped. He looked at Louise. He could see in her eyes she'd just had the same thought. Then they both looked at their daughter.

She was wasted in medicine. They'd make a detective out of her yet.

'I am so fed up of our families. I mean, I love them, but we just have too many relatives between us.'

Ray fidgeted until he was comfortable on the pillow, stroking Laura's hair, her head resting in the crook of his arm. It was the first few hours they'd had alone since he'd got back and they'd made the most of it by going straight to bed.

'Can you imagine what it will be like when we're married?' he continued. 'There'll be thousands of them looking to be fed – What? What did I say?'

Laura had stiffened. He'd felt it in her body, warm against his. She pushed herself up onto an elbow, her face flushed.

'You said, *when we're married.*'

Ray blushed.

'I didn't mean . . . I was just joking. I wasn't proposing.'

'I know you weren't, you big dope.'

'Not that I won't propose. I mean . . . I would propose. If you'd have me. But not now. Not that I don't want to.'

'Ray. Shut up.' She kissed him hard on the lips to see he did. 'We're together six months. I think we can leave that chat for another six months or so. A day when you can string a sentence together without sounding like you've just been released from the asylum.'

'Ha ha,' he said, but a pleasant feeling ran through him. He would ask Laura to marry him, he knew that. Waiting until they were together a little longer was just a formality.

'How did you cope here without us?' he said, changing the subject.

'Oh, please, no shop talk. I've to go into the office tomorrow to fill the boss in.'

'I don't want a report on what you've been doing. I just mean, in general, was everything okay?'

'Hmm.'

'That was a very uncertain hmm.'

Ray hooked his fingers under her chin and pulled it up gently so she was facing him.

'What is it?'

She sighed.

'Joe Kennedy. As soon as Tom knocked off for the island, he was down in the incident room. I don't think Tom knows, but one of the Sunday papers dragged up the whole Sleeping Beauties saga again a few days before Christmas. I know he was ignoring the papers at that stage, so hopefully he missed it. Kennedy gave us this big pep talk about preparing for big changes and how we have to be seen to be responsive to the court of popular opinion.'

'He used those words?'

'Those exact words. Then he told a couple of us that the chief would be off on a project for a while and that his return date was uncertain.'

The warm glow Ray had been feeling evaporated. It was replaced with something that felt pretty much like animalistic rage. He was going to find Joe Kennedy and smash the bastard's teeth in.

'Alright, big boy,' Laura said. 'I don't think we need to get the shovel and make room in the boot just yet. It's been unpleasant, yeah, but . . . I don't know. There's something afoot.'

'Like what?'

'Well, I was in the office the last couple of days to tie up some loose ends and get that job done for Tom. And it was pretty much a skeleton crew, as you know yourself.'

'Yeah.'

'And I saw some VIPs in conclave.'

'VIPs like who?'

'Bronwyn Maher, Sean McGuinness and the head of the Garda press office.'

Ray frowned. Sean was retired, so what was he doing

meeting with Maher, the assistant commissioner and second highest rank in the force.

'And did you listen to what they were discussing?'

'I'm no eavesdropper, Ray Lennon.'

'Well, why bring it up then? It's interesting that McGuinness was back in HQ and in that strange little grouping, but what's the relevance of it to Joe Kennedy? Or to Tom?'

'I said I didn't listen in on their conversation. I never said I didn't hear anything.'

'Ah. That's my girl. Tell me everything.'

'It was when Tom sent me up to get that fax from his office. I was on my way back and I heard somebody talking in one of the offices on that floor. I was surprised anybody was there so popped my head in. The head of press was sitting with his back to the door and didn't see me and I caught the tail end of what he was saying before the other two shushed him.'

'And?'

Laura smiled and rested her chin back on his chest.

'What will you give me if I tell you?'

'I'll give you a good spanking if you don't tell me.'

'Domestic battery now, is it? All right, I'll tell you, but only because I know I can't handle delayed gratification. If our sex life has taught me anything . . .' She screeched with laughter as he tickled her.

'Stop,' she begged, with tears in her eyes. 'Okay, okay, listen.'

Ray released her and they sat up in the bed, facing each other.

'He said, word for word, *It's a sackable offence but the important thing now is letting Tom know we've caught the leaker. He's been miserable. This will cheer him up no end.*'

'They've got the shithead who's been spinning to the press?'

Ray asked, smiling. 'That's the best news I've had in months. That will put a puncture in Kennedy's tyre. He can't continue to sideline the boss now. Not with those stories in the papers killed. But I still don't get one thing – what was Sean doing there?'

'That, I do not know. But Bronwyn Maher has huge time for him and for Tom, so it can only be good.'

'Come here,' Ray said and kissed Laura.

It was only a tiny gap in the clouds that had hung over the team for the last few months but it felt significant.

It even made him feel good about the shit case they'd been saddled with. A forty-year-old murder. He knew Tom wanted it solved, for Miriam Howe's sake, but Ray just didn't see the point. Everybody was dead or too old to matter anymore. There were far more important things to worry about. But, in the humour he was in now, Ray figured to hell with it. They'd look back on this investigation as the last of the crap ones they'd been assigned. His boss was going to be back on top. That made everything seem manageable.

CHAPTER 30

Diary Entry

We buried Minnie today. I helped carry her body to the grave in the hospital garden. A young woman, at times so full of promise and life, brought to her final resting place in a body bag, not a worldly possession to her name, not even a headstone to mark where she lies. Twenty years of age and she'll never experience the life she should have had. The children she could have borne. The husband she would have married. All that fun and wit and intelligence snuffed out. Will anybody remember her? Years from now, will anybody but me say, *Minnie Lehane – she was a lovely girl. She is missed.*

Two of us brought her down. Me and one of the patients. I could have carried her alone. She weighed almost nothing. That alone caused a lump to form in my throat and silent tears to slide down my cheeks.

I thought her family would want her brought back home. The way she talked about them, I assumed she was loved, even if they couldn't care for her. But no. They didn't even come over, not once.

Dolores said they probably found it too painful. And that they were most likely angry with her.

'Angry?' I said. 'Why would they be angry with her?'

'Well,' Dolores replied, 'she killed herself.'

I gave Dolores a funny look. She hasn't been the same since the fire. She's cross a lot these days, full of rage at the world. She's lost sympathy for the patients. I can understand all of this. But I felt so protective of Minnie, I had to correct Dolores on this.

'I don't think anybody can blame the girl for what she suffered,' I said. 'It was our job to keep her safe. Surely, if the family should be angry at anything, it should be at us?'

Dolores shook her head dismissively, annoyed at me.

'But the girl wanted to die,' she said. 'We did everything we could to cure her and still, she resisted it.'

Perhaps there was truth in what Dolores said.

But I didn't tell her about the last couple of conversations I'd had with Minnie. My fear that she was being ill-treated. That it might have pushed her over the edge.

I'm not ready to share that.

I need to make sure I'm right first.

If I accuse somebody of something so serious, I must have proof.

Especially if I'm to accuse *him*.

CHAPTER 31

'I'll tell you this much, there is nothing easy about tracking down people from forty years ago.' Laura pursed her lips and nodded to emphasise the point.

The office was still sparsely populated. It was the 2nd January, but people were stretching out the break. In headquarters, anyhow. Tom knew the ordinary police stations around the country would have been manned 24/7 throughout Christmas – with cold turkey dinners hosted in self-service canteens, crappy secret Santa gifts exchanged, drunken kisses at office parties with, downstairs, crowded receptions full of people reporting break-ins.

Thank Christ for seniority.

'We had more luck with the deceased,' Laura said. 'Michael Geoghegan came in and went through the online records for us. Unfortunately – or fortunately, depending on how you look at it – most of the staff from 1972 are dead. You gave me seventy-nine names excluding Howe's. Michael found death certs for forty of them, the majority being men. Chances are, most of the women are dead, too, but if they married post-1972 their names have likely changed. That's what we found when we tried tracking down women in a previous case, remember? Anyway, that will delay us.'

'Hmm.' Tom perused the sheet in front of him, looking at the names that hadn't been crossed out. 'Right, well, we know five of these are alive and living on the island. Boylan, O'Hare, Crowley, Nolan and Lane. Collins, too, though he's not a full-time resident. So that leaves thirty-three potential witnesses from the time, unless, as you predict, more of them are dead. Have you had any success tracking down these living ones?'

'A few. Those fifteen names with the ticks beside them? They were doctors and nurses who went on to work in Dublin hospitals when St Christina's closed. The medical council has them on record. They're retired now, in the main, but we have contact addresses. I can send a team around to talk to them over the next week or two. Bridget and Brian are due back in tomorrow. If they can fit it in with their other work, they'll do it. As for the rest – well, Michael is going to keep looking through the marriage records to track down some of the women. And maybe a few we've already found will know what happened to their coworkers. We might have luck with family members, too.'

'Needle in a haystack,' Tom said and sighed. He rubbed his jaw. 'Have we had no joy with Owen Reid or Dolores O'Sullivan?'

'Absolutely none. That's what I spent most of my time on. There are countless Owen Reids and Dolores O'Sullivans in the phone book. I had a couple of uniforms go through them with me. Most of them were too young. You could hear it as soon as they answered the phone, though we persisted with the whole rigmarole. I got one elderly Owen Reid who'd spent the seventies working as a brickie in London. His wife came on the phone to confirm it.'

'Right. Well, I guess keep doing what you're doing. Kennedy hasn't been on your back, has he?'

Laura hesitated just a beat too long.

'No. Not really. He hasn't been in much. I think he's upstairs today, though.'

'Well, I'm back now, so he shouldn't need to deal with you at all. He gave me this noose of a case. If he wants it solved, he can't take issue with me needing resources. Has everything else been quiet?'

'A man was shot in Galway yesterday. The local unit reckons they have the shooter. His brother.'

'Lovely. Christmas and families, huh? Nothing kicking off with the gangs?'

'Looks like they're all still hungover.'

'Thank heaven for small mercies.'

Tom sighed again.

'Something on your mind, boss?'

'Yes. You're not going to like me for it.'

'Uh-oh.'

'There was a patient in St Christina's. Sometime around the early seventies. All I have is her first name. Rosita. I'd like to track her down.'

'Seriously?'

'Yes.'

'Without a surname? That's hardly likely, even if Rosita is an unusual name. Wouldn't her full name be in the hospital records?'

'Probably.'

Laura blinked, realisation dawning.

'You want me to go over there. Can't we get the records sent here?'

'They're the property of the trustees and are staying in the hospital for now. Sorry, Laura. It should have occurred to me when we were there. But don't go yet. We may need another trip out ourselves.'

Laura sat back and tightened her ponytail. She rubbed her eyes, still tired after the late night with Ray.

'Ah, I don't mind so much. I am from that neck of the woods, after all. I've some family down there I could call in on. Take a few holiday days. I could go this weekend?'

'Okay. Let's aim for that, then. If I need to go back before then, that will save you the trip. Right, I'll go pick up Ray. We're going out to see Miriam Howe and then Andrew Collins.'

'He said. Are you going to ask Collins about Miriam Howe? Whether he's been nursing unrequited love all this time?'

'It might crop up. I'm going to speak to him about his cottage on the island. It seems like Dr Collins is weighed down with secrets. I'll have to prod them out of him one or two at a go. Otherwise he might clam up altogether.'

The inspector very nearly made it out of headquarters without being spotted.

Very nearly.

He was on the final flight of stairs when he heard his name being called from a couple of landings above. Chief Superintendent Joe Kennedy was leaning over one of the rails, holding his glasses at the nose so they didn't fall off.

Tom waved to acknowledge he'd heard him. Gritting his teeth, he turned and began the climb back up, taking it much slower than his jog down.

Kennedy stood at the door of his office waiting to usher Tom in.

'Sorry, Inspector, I can see you're rushing somewhere. This won't take a moment. Do you want a quick coffee? I had a new machine installed. I'm dying to show it off. It makes a lovely cup.'

As always, affable and friendly. Luring you in.

Tom was used to Kennedy's ways by now.

'No, thank you. I'm trying to cut down. New Year, new me and all that shite.'

'Ha! Yes, me too. €865 for gym membership and I promise I'll go this weekend. They've a lovely sauna, I'm told.'

Kennedy rubbed his hands nervously as he spoke.

Tom observed him with interest. There was something off about the chief. He was dressed in his usual smart fashion – full uniform and shoes polished to mirror perfection. His tight hair was neatly trimmed. He was the presentable face of the National Bureau of Criminal Investigation, the ideal representative in every way. Except, in the way that mattered. Kennedy reserved all his ambition and concern for himself, not for the force. And certainly not for ordinary members of the public.

The inspector had realised early in the chief's tenure that he saw Tom as a threat. And Tom had tried to manage it as best he could – by putting his head down and getting on with the work, content to concentrate on solving the Sleeping Beauties case. But it was during that case that Kennedy had gone out of his way to undermine the inspector.

The rift between them now was too deep.

So Tom was curious about what was worrying Kennedy – though as long as it didn't affect him, he wasn't too bothered.

'How did you get on out on Oileán na Coillte?' the chief asked.

'It went well,' Tom said. 'Considering the difficulties. We know now how Conrad Howe was killed. One or two possible motives have come to light. I've a couple more interviews to do and then a bit of legwork tracking down some people who were around at the time.'

'I see. Good, good.'

Tom waited. Was Kennedy going to land something else on him, now he was in the middle of a case he hadn't wanted in the first place?

'You're content to continue pursuing this, then?' the chief said, surprising the inspector. Was it a trick question? If he said yes, would Kennedy take it off him?

Tom sighed. He was too old for mind games. So was the chief, even if he was a few years younger than the inspector.

'Yes. I am. For now, while nothing bigger is on. It's an interesting case. I'm not sure if we'll get to the bottom of it but we should try. For Miriam Howe's sake, if nothing else.'

'Yes. Of course. And her brother will be happy too, if we bring some closure.'

'Ah, yes. The judge.'

Kennedy nodded earnestly, either not noticing or ignoring Tom's sarcasm.

He really was very distracted.

'Is everything okay?' the inspector asked, unable to stop nosiness from getting the better of him.

Kennedy tugged at his bottom lip and bit it.

'Yes. Just busy, as always. What about you? Are you alright? The last six months haven't been easy and then I give you this case over Christmas.'

Tom struggled to keep his face placid.

'Everything is tickety-boo. You know what they say, all publicity is good publicity. Even when the press are questioning every case you've ever investigated and rewriting your entire legacy. Not to mention your reputation. Apparently, I've avoided the media all these years in order to create the mysterious allure I now possess. How clever and strategic of me.'

Tom shrugged as if to say, despite the bitter words, the whole affair wasn't bothering him. It was. But perhaps more so because of the lack of support from his superiors. Kennedy didn't count, but others in the force – Bronwyn Maher, the Garda press chief, even his peers in other departments – they'd just ignored him. Stayed away, like they didn't want the stench of association. As if what the papers had said was true – Tom Reynolds was a man so caught up with himself he'd sell out his own colleagues in the force.

It stung because Tom had only ever thought of himself as a team player.

Kennedy's face was a picture of distress, distracting Tom from his own morose thoughts. He was never entirely sure when Kennedy was being sincere but in this instance, it really did look like the other man was upset about something.

'I'm very sorry you've had to go through this, Tom. I should have been more supportive. I realise that. Would it help if I assure you the person who leaked these stories will be weeded out? It will stop, I can guarantee you that. And you will return to doing your job the way things were. You'll be back in charge of the major incident room. Not that you weren't, but you know what I mean.'

The inspector waited for the *but*. It wasn't forthcoming.

'Eh . . . Yes,' he said. 'That would help. I'm not sure how you can guarantee it, but I'm happy to hear you'll try.'

Kennedy nodded.

'I will. I understand we didn't get off to the best start. And I know we had that clash last summer. But I'd like to think we're moving towards a mutual professional respect. Am I right, Tom? You do understand I only have the department's best interests at heart? Because I certainly hold your investigative abilities in high esteem.'

Tom was speechless. He wasn't capable of lying. He understood Kennedy's style too well and he didn't like it. And this apparent 180-degree turn was coming from a man who only days ago was trying to undermine Tom's leadership while he was off-piste.

Something had happened. Something that had made Kennedy nervous about his relationship with the inspector. Perhaps, Tom thought, the leaker had already been caught and it was who he'd suspected all along – the officer who Kennedy had defended in the face of Tom's accusations. That would explain why the chief was extending the olive branch. He felt guilty.

'Sure,' he said, going along with it anyway. 'I appreciate what you're trying to do here.'

Kennedy cocked his head to one side. The distressed look was gone, replaced with the shrewd, evaluating one Tom was more used to.

'I'll take that at face value, Inspector. I know you're man enough to tell me when you're unhappy or you think I've crossed the line.'

And again, Tom was left feeling like he was the immature one. What was it about this man that brought out the absolute worst in him?

'If there's nothing else,' he said, 'I'm popping out to speak to Miriam Howe again and one of the other doctors who knew her husband.'

'There's nothing else.' Kennedy straightened himself, the mask of professionalism in place once more. 'Work away. Check in with me, won't you? Let me know how you're getting on. I know it's an impossible ask, but if we solve this case, there'll be huge credit in it from high places.'

Tom nodded and left, thinking, *We?* There was no 'we' where Kennedy was concerned. He delegated blame and claimed credit. It was one of the things that made the man so bloody unlikeable.

CHAPTER 32

In the end, there was no need for two trips. When Tom phoned ahead to Miriam Howe, she informed him that Andrew Collins would be visiting with her that afternoon.

'We can kill two birds with one stone,' Ray said. 'He certainly does hang around there quite a bit. Do you think she's aware of Collins' feelings?'

Tom shrugged.

'It's hard to see how she wouldn't be. But . . . she's of that age, isn't she? Stifled emotions and what not.'

'What does that mean?'

'She might be good at ignoring the nose on her face. Or maybe there is nothing more than a familial affection on her side. They've known each other forever. Anyhow, there's no point in speculating. Those cars must belong to the son and daughter.'

They pulled into Miriam Howe's drive and parked up beside the extra vehicles now stationed there.

Sure enough, it was a man in his mid-forties who opened the door to the detectives this time, introducing himself as Jonathan Howe.

'It's good to meet you; Inspector Reynolds, isn't it?'

Jonathan extended his hand and shook Tom's firmly, then offered the same to Ray as introductions were made.

Jonathan had his mother's tall, upright bearing. Dark-haired, bespectacled, casual in a wool jumper and denims. He'd an intelligent, placid face. If there was any trace of the distress caused by losing his father so young, Tom couldn't see it.

'Mother is with my sister, Vanessa. Uncle Andrew has taken the children down to the Strawberry Beds for a walk. They've too much pent-up energy for this house. Every child does.'

'Sorry to be descending on you like this when your family is dealing with so much,' the inspector said. 'I am very sorry for your loss.'

Jonathan shrugged away the condolences.

'You've done us a huge favour, Inspector. Well, you and the team who excavated that grave and found our father. The loss took place forty years ago. I barely remember it and Vanessa has no memory of it. It did affect me, I won't lie. I spent most of my life feeling angry at our father and filling the void he left with fantasy. As a child I imagined all sorts. He'd been abducted by aliens – don't laugh, I was a big HG Wells' fan. He'd been kidnapped by pirates. He'd abandoned us. I couldn't conceive of him as dead, though in later years I suppose I knew that to be true. In finding him, you've taken a weight off my shoulders. I used to think, at my lowest, that he had gone off and had another family. You can imagine how devastating that was for a little boy, a young man. That's all been put to rest now.'

'I can understand that,' Tom said. 'Little boys hero-worship their dads. You were six, weren't you, when he disappeared?'

'Yeah. I actually have very few memories. Half of them I probably imagined. All of that, though, didn't affect me half as much as our mother's reaction to his disappearance. She just shut down. It was only as an adult I realised how badly she'd taken it. Shall we?'

They began to walk towards the rear of the house.

'Every Christmas, she turns that front room into a shrine,' Jonathan said, pointing at the sitting room door as they passed. 'Decorating it like she used to when Father was alive. What she won't admit is that the special occasions were the only times we really saw him. Our father sacrificed himself for his work – in every way, it turns out. Sure, he'd come home nearly every weekend, but most of the time he'd be locked in his study, reading up on medicine. He was obsessed. He loved us. But we very rarely saw him. Nor did she. Here we are.'

Jonathan led them into the cream-wood kitchen, its walls painted a duck-egg colour, where his mother sat at the table, stirring camomile tea and slowly turning the pages of a black and white photo album. Her daughter was unwrapping frozen pizzas and taking waffles out of a Birds Eye box.

'The police are here,' he said.

At the counter, Vanessa abandoned her task and wiped her hands on the sides of her jeans. She was tall, like her mother and brother, but fair-haired and big featured. She wore a rugby polo-shirt and her hair was tied back in a ponytail. From what he recalled of her uncle, the judge, Vanessa mirrored that side of the family more.

'I'll stick the kettle on for you gentlemen. Would you fancy a spot of lunch? There's plenty to go around.'

At the table, Miriam tutted.

'That's not lunch, Vanessa. You cannot offer anybody over the age of eighteen pizza and waffles and claim it's a substantial meal. I do have quiche and some home-made chicken soup if you are hungry, Inspector.'

Tom shook his head.

'Coffee is fine, Mrs Howe.'

'Jonathan, can you see to it? Not that nasty instant version you two drink. I have proper ground in the jar.'

Her daughter raised her hand to her head in mock salute, while her brother put down the jar of Maxwell House he'd just taken from the cupboard.

'Have you seen any photographs of Conrad yet, Inspector?' Miriam asked, beckoning the detectives to the chairs on either side of her. 'My brother suggested I get some out for the funeral. We'll be burying Conrad shortly, it seems.'

'Yes, our pathologists are just about finished,' Tom said. 'No, we haven't seen a picture yet, not a proper one. I saw an article from a long time ago but the photograph attached was poor quality.' Even as he said it, he realised how odd it was. One of the first acts in an active murder investigation was to secure images of the victim when they were alive. The differences in a cold case were marked. There was no real need to see a photograph of a victim who'd been dead half a century. You couldn't visually ID a skeleton. It hadn't occurred to him to ask Miriam for one the first day they'd called out. And he'd walked right past the framed photos in the hall on the way in.

'It would be great if we could see one now,' he said. 'These are all of your family, are they?'

'Yes. I kept everything. I've the wedding album upstairs but those photos were taken a good few years before Conrad went missing. We married when I was eighteen and he was twenty-four. These pictures here are our last Christmas together. That's my brother, Peter, and his wife with our Jonathan and Vanessa. Peter's wife couldn't have children, God love her. Polyps.'

'Excuse me?'

'In her womb. She had to have them removed when she was just sixteen. Tragic. Anyhow, she was very much involved with our two, when she was still alive. Cancer got her in the end.'

'That's terribly sad,' Tom said, though Miriam didn't seem distressed in the slightest. In fact, overall, she seemed quite upbeat compared to when they had last spoken. The news of Conrad's death seemed to have lifted the shadow that had been cast over the Howe household. It was the oddest feeling, as the investigating officer, to be told you'd brought relief to a family by telling them their loved one was dead.

Perhaps the inspector could get used to cold cases.

'This is Conrad,' Miriam said, turning the page, as Jonathan placed coffees in front of the detectives.

'Yes,' he said, looking over his mother's shoulder. 'That's how I remember him.'

'No, it isn't,' Vanessa scoffed, coming around to look. 'You think it is, because you've seen that picture so often. Nobody can recall the faces of dead people. Not properly.'

'Vanessa, don't be so uncouth. Your brother does remember his father, of course he does.'

'May I?' Tom asked, indicating the album.

'Of course.' Miriam pushed it towards him and the inspector peered closely at the picture. Conrad was tall and wore glasses like his son, and though the photo was black and white, he had a full head of dark hair. He stood in front of the house they were now in, hands clasped behind his back, one leg slightly to the front of the other. He was smiling, a pleasant-looking man. But Tom noticed that the smile didn't quite meet his eyes. They were intense, clever eyes, but they looked serious and sad.

'When was this taken?' Tom asked.

'The summer before,' Miriam said, not filling in before what. There was only one event worth referencing. 'Why do you ask?'

'Probably because Father looks worried,' Vanessa said, then shrugged and returned to the cooker.

'Is that it?' Miriam asked, squinting. 'Do you think he looks bothered by something?'

Tom tilted his head sideways, staring at the picture still.

'Your husband is smiling, but yes, it looks like he'd something on his mind. I've been reading his diary. I'm guessing he was writing some of the more traumatic entries around the time this photograph was taken.'

Miriam placed her finger on the image, the tiniest touch on her husband's cheek.

'Yes. You'll have seen, then, what I meant when we spoke last. Why I always suspected something had happened to him. That last year, he was very distant. He started to change when he began working on that island but it got steadily more noticeable. The final time he came home, that weekend a few weeks before Christmas, he wasn't himself at all. He was angry. Distressed. I could see that.'

She hesitated, swallowed. A sheen of tears covered her eyes.

'I could see it and I allowed him to go back. He insisted. He wouldn't speak to me, wouldn't tell me what the matter was. I was sympathetic but also angry. I was at home, to all intents a single mother, with two small children. If he wasn't happy in his job I would have preferred him here. He could have got a job in any of the Dublin hospitals. He could have gone back to St Bart's. But I didn't say that to him. Instead I snapped at him to pull himself together. I'll never forgive myself.'

At the counter, Miriam's daughter frowned and crossed her arms, uncomfortable with the display of emotion.

Jonathan was more responsive, crossing over to his mother and placing a hand on her shoulder. He squeezed it and said, 'You weren't to know.'

At once, Tom saw how far the tragedy had rippled out. Miriam Howe had blamed herself for allowing her husband to return to what would be the death of him, and punished herself by shutting down her emotions and refusing to move on from their life together. And in doing so, she'd forgotten to live for the present; for her children, who needed their one remaining parent.

It was tragic.

The back door opened and a gaggle of children poured in, all kitted out in raincoats and wellies, talking nineteen to the dozen.

Andrew Collins followed, cap in hand, looking somewhat shaken.

'They're getting faster and I'm getting slower,' he puffed, resting a hand on the counter to steady himself. 'Not a good combination.'

'Upstairs, washed and changed,' Vanessa bellowed over the noise. 'My lot, your father will be here shortly. Alice and Eve, your mummy is coming later. You need to get those bedrooms tidied and start packing up your gear. Lunch in ten.'

The children emptied out of the kitchen as quickly as they'd arrived. Tom would have, too. Vanessa was like a sergeant major when she kicked into action.

'Good to see you again, Inspector, Detective,' Andrew said, raising his hand in greeting. He was starting to get his breath back. 'Did you pick one out, Miriam?' He pointed at the album.

'I thought I had. This one of Conrad outside. But I think I'll find a nicer one. One of him with the children, perhaps.'

'Ah, yes. That would be better. Would you mind terribly, Inspector, if I just go up and source some dry clothes from my bag?' Andrew asked. 'The grass is so wet out there, I'm soaked up to my knees.'

'Go ahead,' Tom said.

'We'll retire to the sitting room,' Miriam proposed. 'The hordes will be back and it really does sound like feeding time at the zoo.'

They took her word for it and moved, back into the room they'd sat in when they'd first visited the house. The decorations were still in situ. Tom suspected Miriam Howe was the sort to honour the tradition of Little Christmas – leaving everything in place until the 6th January, when it wasn't bad luck to take the tree down.

'Jonathan referred to Dr Collins as Uncle Andrew when we arrived,' he said, taking a seat. 'Have the children always been close to him? A resident on the island mentioned that you, Andrew and Conrad had known each other since the two men were in college. Your father was a lecturer, I believe?'

'Yes, it's true. I met them both when I was sixteen. Daddy was a leading biologist. We all knew each other, but I wouldn't have said Andrew and I were very close. That didn't come until Conrad disappeared. I was fond of him but he was quite aloof in those days. My pal, Katie, had a thing for him but he had no interest.'

'Forgive me if this sounds impolite, but are you sure that wasn't because he was interested in you?'

Miriam laughed.

'Is that what you think? That we were caught in some sort of torturous love triangle with poor Andrew the unfortunate third point?'

Ray leaned forward.

'Were you?'

'No, my dear. Andrew wasn't interested in me. He was interested in my husband. No, that's not even correct. He was
interested in his work. All Andrew cared about in those days
was being a doctor. Please don't suggest such a silly thing to
him. He would be very distressed by it. Andrew has an awful
tendency to dwell on things.'

'All Andrew cared about *in those days*?' Tom repeated. 'When
did he stop caring about being a doctor so much?'

Miriam pursed her lips and scrunched up her forehead.

'I don't really know. I suppose, after Conrad went missing.'

Loud yelling, followed by a bang from upstairs, made them
all jump.

'Oh, my goodness, what now?' Miriam said, standing abruptly.

The door opened and Andrew stepped in.

'I'm afraid the children might have got into your room,' he
said, apologetically.

'Please excuse me, gentlemen,' Miriam said. 'The last time
they broke my grandfather clock. And listen.' The old woman
placed a hand to her ear. 'Do you hear the sound of parents
rushing to see what the crisis is? No, indeed. I don't know where
I went wrong.'

Tom and Ray stood as she left the room, while Andrew held
the door open for her.

'They're a handful,' he said. 'The lot of them. It is hard to
believe they share DNA strands with Miriam. Especially
Vanessa. She's the antithesis of everything her mother is. Fem-
inine, I mean.'

'Thank you for agreeing to meet with us again, Andrew,'
Tom said. 'We've been to Oileán na Coillte since we last spoke.'

'Of course. You said you were going. How did you find it? What did you think of the asylum?'

'The island is beautiful. Remote but pleasingly peaceful. St Christina's itself I found unsettling. Do you return to it much?'

'The asylum? No, never, actually. Too many memories.'

'So, your cottage. It must be a good bit away from the building? I can't imagine you'd like to wake up with a view of it, if it holds unpleasant memories.'

Andrew shifted, almost imperceptibly.

'I very rarely wake up on Oileán na Coillte. Who told you I'd a cottage there?'

'I think the question is, why didn't you?'

'It wasn't to the fore of my mind, Inspector. I live in Dublin. I only travel there very infrequently.'

'So, why do you keep it?'

'You've seen it. The island is a paradise for those in search of solitude. Sometimes, when I've a paper to write, that sort of thing, I go over. For the peace.'

'Do you live alone in Dublin?'

'Yes.'

'It seems a long way to go for peace when you've your own place here.'

'It's a different kind of quiet. Why do artists travel to retreats? Why do writers find themselves isolated cabins? Sometimes the silence must be physical as well as mental.'

'I see,' Tom said. 'And there is no other reason for you to return there?'

Andrew was now visibly uncomfortable. He sat forward on the edge of the chair and clasped his hands together.

'None that you would imagine, Inspector. I didn't keep a cottage on the island so I could visit a dead man's unmarked grave, if that's what you're getting at. But yes, there is another reason I keep the cottage on Oileán na Coillte.'

'And what is that?'

Andrew sighed.

'The need to atone.'

'Atone for what?' Ray asked.

'I dedicated my life to medicine, Detective. To treating people with the most incurable illnesses, the most stigmatised. The practices we used in decades of old – well, they were all we knew then, but they weren't right. They weren't . . . It's just – I swore to do no harm. That was my oath.'

'But you feel you did do harm?' Tom asked. 'We've seen the asylum. The operating theatres. The basement – the parts of it that are safe, anyhow. What you did to those patients, it does seem inhuman to me. Looking at it with a modern perspective.'

Andrew bowed his head.

'I know,' he whispered. 'I know that now. I lied, Inspector. I don't write papers when I'm out on the island. I couldn't if I wanted to. My brain is not steady when I'm in proximity to St Christina's. I hate the place. I go there and I pray. I ask for forgiveness. It's my punishment. I worked there until the hospital closed and I stayed on with the patients who didn't want to move, not because I felt an affinity to the place but because it was my penance. I did so many awful things, back in the day.'

Tom said nothing. He let the silence fill the room. The anguish.

When he did speak, it was quietly, directly.

'And spending all this time with Miriam and her children, was that also penance? Did you ever tell her how you felt? How much you loved her?'

Andrew's shoulders slumped. A broken-hearted man, folding in on himself. He shook his head.

'No. Of course not. She chose Conrad. Sometimes I wondered if he . . . oh, it doesn't matter now. Water under the bridge. I've been there for Miriam all these years not out of remorse, but because I wanted to be near her. Whether she acknowledged how I felt or not.'

'So you carried no guilt about her husband's death? You didn't see Conrad as a love rival?'

'How could I? To be a rival, you have to have a chance. They were married not long after they met. They had a child together soon after. I never got a look in. It was almost unbearable for me to stay in Conrad's sphere, but I did it out of a sense of duty to medicine. We ended up in St Christina's because it was our specialist field. I recruited him there because I respected his dedication and abilities. Yes, I suppose there was a part of me that wanted to stay in Miriam's life but there were times when I couldn't even speak to Conrad. I couldn't even look at him. I was green with envy.'

'I see. Miriam thinks you were a close friend of her husband's.'

'I was always more Miriam's friend, even if she didn't realise it. I did know Conrad first. He was a fellow student. But we didn't have a lot in common outside of medicine. What does it matter now, Inspector? I didn't kill him because I was in love with his wife. Has somebody said something?'

'They might have.'

'You won't tell me who?'

'It was just an opinion. One that you have now verified. Its owner is not important any more.'

Andrew frowned and moved his mouth as though chewing something unpleasant.

'I can't help but wonder who would be so mean-spirited. The person who told you about Miriam and me, they must have known it would make me look like I had a motive to kill Conrad. It's utterly ludicrous but no less vicious for it. I don't think it was Lawrence. He's never liked me but I doubt he noticed anything to do with any of our love lives. He was completely oblivious to that end of things.'

He peered from one to the other of the detectives. Tom was happy to let him stare but Ray started to blush at his roots. They could see the man mentally assessing potential enemies until he landed on the right one.

'Ah. Our chemist, I imagine. Mr Lane. A particularly nasty mouth on him. You don't have to say anything, Inspector. I don't need confirmation. It should have occurred to me immediately. You should know something about Edward Lane, though. He utterly despised Conrad. With a passion.'

'We're already aware Mr Lane had his issues with Conrad,' Tom said. 'Do you really think they were enough to want the man dead?'

'Somebody clearly did. Lane is a hateful man.'

'You have reason, though, don't you, to dislike the former chemist?'

Collins' face flushed again.

'More salacious gossip, is it? It seems none of us can escape the wretched past. What do you want me to say, Inspector? I had some difficult years in St Christina's. I've already told you – some of the work we doctors undertook, you couldn't help but be affected by it. I was only human. The things I've done . . .'

Collins broke off and put his fist to his mouth. He shook his head.

'But I wasn't the only one. It's just, I was the only one bothered enough to try to ease my conscience. I numbed myself, to make it more manageable. And whatever Edward Lane says, he wasn't exactly a paragon of virtue himself. Conrad caught him once.'

'Caught him doing what?' Ray asked.

'Administering drugs to a patient. It was completely illegal. I don't know what he thought he was doing. And we were positive it wasn't the first time, either.'

'What sort of drugs?' Tom asked. Ray had mentioned something along those lines after his interview with Lane.

'He claimed it was a routine prescription that a nurse should have provided. But he shouldn't have even been on the ward, you understand? He shouldn't have been near a patient. His job was at the dispensary.'

'Was this when Conrad went to Boylan?' Ray asked.

'Yes.'

'Was Lane reprimanded?'

'No. That was the odd thing. Lawrence said he'd punish him but all we saw was Lane continuing in his post. He should have been fired.'

Collins' voice was bitter, even after all this time. It was amazing how ancient injustices could still rankle so much.

'I'm sorry, you said something, Inspector. Earlier. I meant to ask you what you meant by it.'

'What did I say?' Tom asked, puzzled.

'Something about seeing the basement, the *parts of it that are safe*. What did you mean?'

Tom shrugged.

'We went down the first corridor in the basement but no further. Arnie said the rest of it is structurally unsound.'

Andrew shook his head.

'I don't understand. Nothing in that building is structurally unsound.'

Tom and Ray exchanged a confused glance. The inspector sat forward.

'How do you know that for certain? Arnie is the caretaker. It's his job to know these things, isn't it?'

'Yes, of course. But I am positive he's wrong on this. When the order came for the demolition of the asylum, Lawrence made a strong appeal to the trustees that the building be left untouched. The building and the grounds. He argued that the new owners could use the asylum itself because it was *structurally sound*. All of it. I saw the drawings.'

'Could he have been lying, just to keep it standing?' Ray asked.

Andrew opened his eyes wide.

'It seems like a daft strategy. If the developers moved in and discovered the hospital was about to collapse because of weak foundations, it wouldn't reflect well on Lawrence. He'd need to be extremely desperate to keep the hospital intact to fib so blatantly, wouldn't he?'

'He would,' Tom said. 'And the electrics in that part of the hospital – are they dodgy?'

'There's nothing wrong with any part of the asylum. That's what I'm telling you. The building is in sound condition. It was only ever the people who inhabited it, and I include myself, that were unstable.'

Tom rubbed his hand over his beard and shook his head. Somebody was lying.

'Andrew, I suggest you prepare yourself for a journey. I want to go back over to the island and this time you're coming with us. We've a lot more to talk about and I want you to show me some landmarks. Like that cottage you saw Conrad at, for one.'

And then, the inspector thought quietly, he and Ray could have a chat with Arnie Nolan.

Had somebody higher up told the caretaker that the basement was unsafe or had he made that call himself? And if he had, was it based on the truth or on something else?

Was there something hidden in the basement of the asylum?

CHAPTER 33

Diary Entry

I saw something today which has left me shaken.

For the last few weeks I've been all over the place. I've been trying to get my head around Minnie's untimely death. It's not unusual for patients to die but it's the shock of it with Minnie. She went from being this little vibrant thing to morose, to dead in just a few short weeks. I'm in shock and, I think, grieving.

Amidst all of that, I've been trying to keep an eye on the doctor who has roused my suspicions, who I believe was mistreating her. He's been more secretive than ever. I think he, in turn, suspects somebody is watching him. Perhaps he knows it's me. I might have asked too many questions about the patients and their treatment plans.

I had started to wonder if perhaps he has somebody helping him. Patients disappear from the wards and when they come back, I know they've received some sort of treatment. But could one man be moving grown men and women around the hospital on his own?

Now I think I might know what's happening.

Today, on my rounds, I thought I heard whimpering in one of the supply closets on the fourth floor. I opened it and a man barrelled past me. He was of such bulk that I was spun into the wall and hit my head. By the time I righted myself, I could only see his back disappearing down the stairwell at the end of the corridor. It was his uniform that made me realise he was an orderly.

For a moment, I thought it was him who'd been crying and I wondered, did he feel as I did? Was he distressed by what he'd seen in St Christina's? We all have to keep up this front of being professional and being in control but, beneath it all, aren't we all a little sickened by what goes on here? Most of us, anyway?

I was about to lock the door to the supply cupboard when I realised there was somebody still in there. I turned on the light and found one of the female patients lying on the floor. Her nightdress was pulled up to her waist and her under-wear discarded. She was visibly trembling. I understood what had happened immediately. A willing participant in any sexual act would have attempted to cover herself when her partner ran off.

She had been raped.

Trying to put my own shock aside, I attempted to help her from the floor and it was this act that spurred her to life. She screamed and jumped up, her nightdress falling to cover her modesty. Pushing past me, she ran off into one of the wards.

I followed and found her in her bed, the blankets pulled up to her chin.

I approached like somebody trying to quieten a fright-ened horse.

'What was he doing to you?' I asked.

She was a pretty girl, no more than eighteen. Her eyes were big, cornflower blue, and filled with great, fat tears. She shook her head and lifted a hand out from under the bedclothes to place a finger over her mouth.

'Ssshhh,' she said.

'It's okay,' I persisted. 'I can help you. Just tell me who it was and what he was doing. He's not allowed to hurt you like that, do you understand? That is not allowed. What did he do to you?'

She turned in the bed to look over her shoulder, checking to see if anybody was listening. The ward was virtually empty, bar one old lady down the far end. All the patients were in the day room.

'It's okay,' she whispered, hoarsely. 'He's promised. He said if I let him put his thing inside me, he'd help me get out. I just want to get out of here. I didn't realise it would hurt so much, that's why I was crying. But he said it won't hurt like that next time.'

I felt a rage rise in me, an anger that made me feel murderous.

'No,' I said, shaking my head vigorously. 'He's lying. He's not allowed to do that to you.'

We were disturbed, then, by the arrival of one of the nurses, a crotchety woman who only ever has harsh words for both patients and staff. She should have been retired years ago.

'What are you doing in here?' she said, both to me and the girl. 'Rosita, you're supposed to be in the sewing room. Are you ill?' She looked at me, as if that was the only reason I would be in the ward talking to a female patient alone.

My head was spinning.

Rosita. Minnie's friend.

She'd asked me to take care of her. Had she known something was happening?

'Sorry, Nurse,' Rosita said, eyes downcast. 'I had a stomach ache but it's gone now.'

'Let's go, then.'

The girl was out of the bed and the ward before I'd even stood up properly, the nurse throwing me an evil look on the way out.

I remained there, shocked, furious, still wondering about the identity of the man who'd abused the girl.

I'd failed Minnie. Rosita was barely three wards down on the same floor, but I hadn't noticed her before. Look at what was happening to her!

And my head was filled with another thought.

Was Rosita the only patient being abused in the hospital? Or were there others?

CHAPTER 34

Tom mused on his plans to get back to the island as they drove away from Miriam's house.

'Do you want to ring your sweetheart and tell her you've been called back into action?' he said.

Ray sighed.

'Jesus, we're together six months now. When are you going to stop slagging us off?'

'Ray, it's the gift that keeps giving. And as long as you are happy together, I'm going to enjoy it. Just promise me that if you split, it won't be a Linda and Emmet scenario. There's no room in the force for that to happen twice.'

'I can't imagine anything that would drive us to that. Anyhow, I think it's you who should be nervous about breaking the news to your missus.'

Tom had to nod at that. Louise was going to kill him. The 2nd January and he was planning to disappear again. She'd resumed her PhD studies last October with him promising to be around more. At the time, Joe Kennedy had been happy to help him keep his promise. Now, everything had turned on its head.

'We'll fly down to Kerry airport in the morning,' he said. 'That will shave time off the journey. Give us the evening with our respective spouses.'

Ray opened his mouth but before he could utter a word, the inspector jumped in.

'I don't want to hear it. There's a ferry crossing to the island tomorrow afternoon. I rang the B&B. Turns out there hasn't been one since we left the other day. The weather has been too rough.'

Ray sighed.

'This isn't your way home. Where are you going now?'

'I'm calling in on Emmet McDonagh first. He's back up in Dublin. He was on that island for a few days. I want to see if he noticed anything odd when he was there. That, and find out what's going on with him these days that's made him more cantankerous than usual.'

'What do you want, Tom? I've two officers in court tomorrow and we've just got new evidence that the man they're testifying against may have been involved in another death. Some of us have work to do in the present as well as the past.'

Emmet was his usual chirpy self.

'Nice to see you, too,' Tom said, standing aside to let the young man who'd just been in with the Tech chief out the door. The bloke looked upset. He'd probably been on the receiving end of an Emmet special, too.

Emmet sat up straight and looked over his glasses.

'I don't have anything more from that grave, if that's what you're after. No smoking gun.'

Tom plonked on the chair in front of his desk, uninvited.

'I have cause of death. It was wire around the throat. Anyhow, it's the drunk driver in court tomorrow, isn't it? Killed that pensioner on the quays? Don't tell me he was involved in another hit and run.'

'Have you been reading the court listings again?'

'Only when there's a special sitting. It's unusual to see a judge this early in January.'

'Yes, well, the pensioner was a former GAA All-Stars player and the judge was on his county team.'

'There we go again. People in high places.'

'Indeed. And no, boy racer wasn't involved in another hit and run, not that I know of. He did, however, have a lump hammer in his boot that just happened to have been used to batter a gang member to death last month.'

'Are you actually telling me we can kill two birds with one lump hammer?'

'Yes. It will be nice to take him off the streets. You look like you're getting comfortable there. I'm not lying. I have nothing for you.'

'From the grave, I know. I was wondering if you picked up on anything else when you were down there, though? Any strange comings and goings to that hospital? Any of the island's residents down at the site asking questions, that sort of thing?'

'I was a tad busy overseeing the exhumation of dozens of bodies, Tom. The caretaker fellow, we saw a good bit of him. He sorted us out with accommodation, supplies, that sort of thing. He was in and out of the asylum a couple of times.'

'Right. To be expected.'

'Actually, I saw one of the other chaps there – one of the former doctors.'

'Robert O'Hare?'

'No. The other one.'

'Not Lawrence Boylan? He can barely walk.'

'Yes. I noticed. Some woman drove him. Youngish-looking,

bobbed hair. Funny eye. He was in and out. She helped him over to the site and we spoke for a couple of minutes.'

'Did he say what he went in for?'

'Nope. I didn't bother to ask, either. Didn't see anything unusual in it.'

'I see. Thanks. That's interesting. Another thing – one of the bodies in the pit might have had Minnie as a first name. I can't remember reading it on the list. Did you make a copy of all the names? I know we can't take records out of the asylum.'

'Of course I did.'

Emmet pulled something up on his screen.

'Minnie Lehane. Twenty. Heart failure.'

'That's it. Where was she positioned, do you know?'

Emmet frowned.

'Why are you asking about her?'

'Can you tell me where she was or not?'

The Tech chief sighed.

'Obviously. She was one of the last in. Hers were one of the sets of legs Howe was hidden under.'

Tom shook his head. He told Emmet the tragic story he'd read in Howe's diary.

'Jesus!' Emmet said, when the inspector had finished. 'That's too sad.'

Tom pursed his lips.

'Even for me,' he said.

Emmet sat back.

'I sense there's more.'

Tom shrugged.

'So, Linda,' he said.

'There was a time – I remember it fondly – when you

wouldn't dare utter that woman's name to me. What changed?
When did you become so . . . kamikaze?'

'I don't know if it's ever occurred to you how damn awkward
it is for me and every other member of the force to have to work
with two warring colleagues who are frequently flung together
on cases. There have been times when my bosses have ordered
me to bring a psychologist in and I've run rings around myself
to solve a case quicker just to avoid listening to you two sniping
at each other.'

'What's your point?'

'My point is, I've known you a long time, Emmet. And my
wife knew Linda before we even met. What's changed, you ask?
Well, discovering the circumstances of your split, for one. Look,
there's blame on both sides. You can equally despise the other,
or you can be adults and accept that the past is the past. Linda
was trying to be an adult over on that island and you threw it
back at her. Now, tell me if I'm wrong, but that seems out of
character for you, even as unpleasant as you can be at times.'

Emmet planted both his hands on the table, red-faced.

'Are you in marriage counselling now, Tom?'

'You're not married. Never were, which makes it all the cra-
zier that you still hate each other. Haven't you an ounce of
sympathy for her, Emmet?'

The other man removed his glasses. Tom felt himself wince
in anticipation of what was to come. Removing his glasses –
was Emmet planning for this exchange to end in a fistfight?

But the other man surprised him.

He didn't roar, or shout, or lean over the table and grab Tom
by his lapels to give him a good shake. Instead, Emmet rubbed
his eyes and when he took away his large, pudgy fingers, it
looked like he was about to cry.

'I *did* have sympathy for her. At times. Once. From a distance. When I didn't have to hear her snide remarks and bitter vitriol, I could feel very sorry for the woman. When we were together, I loved her, Tom. Adored her. That fire, her passion. Her mind. So utterly brilliant. I would have crossed hot coals to spend an hour with her. But it wasn't to be. And she showed nothing but selfishness when she discovered how ill my wife was. How could I walk out on a woman who, at the time, we thought was dying? Would Linda have done that to Geoff? I couldn't understand how she could feel no compassion for another member of her sex in those circumstances. She wanted me to run off while my wife was receiving chemo. I wouldn't have thought she was capable.'

'She didn't know your wife was sick until she turned up at your house and confronted you for not leaving, Emmet. I'm sure she felt differently when she realised.'

'No. No, that's where you're wrong. I could have forgiven that. But she still wanted me to leave. Even then. She insisted on it. She was a different woman, like somebody possessed. I tried to reason with her but she was illogical. She turned on me, then. That was when the rot started. But what she did afterwards – what I know now – I can never forgive her for that.'

'What did she do?' Tom barely dared breathe, let alone ask the question. He had a feeling he knew already. Maria had helped him and Louise arrive at the revelation the other night.

Emmet placed his head in his hands.

'She was pregnant. She never told me. It makes sense, now, I suppose. Her determination, her insistence I walk away from my marriage, from a gravely ill woman. It wasn't just about Linda. Why didn't she tell me?'

Tom exhaled loudly. It was as he'd suspected, with worse to come.

'Perhaps she needed to know you were leaving for her and not a pregnancy,' he said.

Emmet raised an eyebrow.

'That sounds straight from the Louise Reynolds handbook on relationships.'

'She's always been better than me on affairs of the heart. And all things female, obviously. My world was black and white before she started colouring it in with shades of grey.'

'Ha! Well, maybe she's right. Perhaps that was Linda's thinking. But then – afterwards, when I didn't leave – she could have told me what she'd done. Twenty-one years, lost. You must understand why I'm so angry, Tom. We never had children, the wife and me. I always wanted a child.'

The inspector was struck by a sudden revelation.

'Emmet, the young man who left here looking upset just as I arrived. Who is he?'

Emmet sighed. He reached for his glasses and put them back on his nose, then coughed to clear his throat.

'That, Tom, was my son.'

CHAPTER 35

'Is it my imagination, or does Arnie seem more hostile this time around?'

Ray handed Tom the last of the boxes Mannix had just lifted from the ferry's hold. Tom was passing them along the line to Andrew Collins, who in turn was lugging them up to a sullen Arnie. The caretaker had made a pile beside the island's storage sheds.

'He's definitely off form,' Tom answered. 'I'm glad Andrew brought his car. I wouldn't like to ask Arnie for a lend of his, not with him in that mood.'

'Hangover, do you think?'

'Maybe. Or perhaps it's something more.'

When they'd finished unloading, they made their way up the pier to join their fellow labourers.

'We're going to be staying over with Andrew tonight,' Tom told Arnie. The caretaker dropped the box he was carrying and Tom winced, imagining all sorts of fragile items within being damaged.

'Sorry. I'm clumsy today. What's that? You're staying with Dr Collins?'

'Yes. It was very good of you to put us up last time but we want to have a look at the other side of the island on this trip. Maybe get a gander at that graveyard.'

'What's that got to do with anything?'

Tom shrugged.

'Probably nothing. By the way, there's something I wanted to check with you.'

'What's that?'

'When you gave us a tour of the asylum the other day, you said there were structural issues in the basement. What exactly is wrong down there?'

The caretaker began to break out in bright red blotches, his hair turning even redder at the roots.

'It's just, there was damage done, because it was never updated to cope with the building work going on above. I told you that.'

'Yes, but how do you know that for certain? Did engineers come in? Is there a surveyor's report we can see?'

Arnie stood up straight and puffed out his chest.

'Are you calling me a liar?'

'No. It would be extremely stupid to lie to us about something that could so easily be checked. I believe you actually think there's something wrong with the foundations. And the electrics. What I'm wondering is why? Who told you that was the case?'

Arnie's shoulders slumped.

'It's always been that way. Since I started working there, I mean. It's just something I was warned about when I started the job, after Dad died and the asylum closed.'

'By whom, Arnie?'

'By my mother.'

The west side of the island was wilder, more rugged. The woods here were at their densest and large stone cliffs rose up from the sea, their rock faces jagged and uneven from centuries of pounding Atlantic waves.

'Kitty Nolan lives up the road from me,' Andrew said as he drove. 'So you can drop in on the way, ask her what Arnie meant. I can't understand it myself. What the hell would Kitty know about the foundations of St Christina's?'

'Maybe it's like Arnie said,' Ray suggested. 'His dad, as the last caretaker, was the authority and he told his wife.'

'But it's still not true,' Andrew protested. 'It never was. The trustees of St Christina's were never short a few bob. The building was always kept up to standard, even when they knew it was closing. Like I said before, I've seen the drawings.'

'Let's check with Kitty,' Tom said. 'There's no point in speculating. She struck me as an honest woman. She must have had her reasons for telling her son what she did.'

'See over there,' Andrew said, slowing the car to a halt.

'Is that her house?' Tom looked across to the unkempt cottage atop one of the headlands, surprised.

'No. There's a coastal walk along the bottom of the cliffs and from it, you can see up to that cottage. That's where I saw Conrad the day he went missing.'

'And he was alone?' Tom asked.

'Yes.'

'It's just, you had seen him there previously, hadn't you? With somebody.'

Andrew frowned.

'No.'

'Somebody told us you did. They said you saw him fighting with Owen Reid.'

The man looked blank for a moment then his face fell and he clamped his hand over his mouth.

'Yes. Yes I did, actually. God, how could I have forgotten? Everything about the day he disappeared and the months afterwards is so clear. But I'd forgotten I'd seen him here weeks before.'

'Perhaps, Andrew, the pills you were taking at the time affected your memory. If you were self-prescribing quite heavily . . .'

Tom watched as the doctor blushed bright red.

'I . . . yes. It was a mad time. It didn't even occur to me back then when Conrad disappeared. They weren't physically fighting, it was nothing like that. I couldn't hear what they were saying either, not from that distance. But there was something about the body language . . . yes, I remember it now. Reid was leaning into Conrad, threateningly. I wasn't surprised, as I recall. That is – I was surprised to see them there, but not to see them arguing. There was an animosity between them. I'd picked up on it before. Conrad didn't like Reid. I don't know why. We wouldn't have had much interaction with orderlies socially, so it must have had something to do with a patient or maybe Conrad had caught Reid sleeping on the job, something like that.'

'And when Conrad went missing, when you and Miriam were wondering if something had happened to him, why didn't you think of Reid? If there was history there, surely he would have been the first person you suspected. Especially as he left the hospital that day, never to return.'

Collins shook his head.

'The way you say it – it seems so obvious. But at the time, Inspector, yes, while we did think something might have happened to Conrad, it was more along the lines of an accident. Certainly not that he might have been murdered. I never thought of Conrad as unable to stand up for himself. He could be quite formidable when he wanted to be, for all his hail fellow, well met charm. When he got an idea into his head, he pursued it.'

'Do you know where Reid was headed when he left St Christina's? Did you try to find out?'

Andrew shrugged.

'Why would I?'

Tom stared at the man. Was he really that oblivious?

'Did you read Conrad's diary, Andrew? The one Miriam found? You know he mentioned suspicions about an orderly in it?'

Andrew shook his head.

'I know this sounds incredible, but I never actually read it. Miriam read me sections from it, over the years, to prove her point that something must have happened to Conrad. But I never thought it right, that I should be reading the man's most private thoughts. It was enough that I . . .'

'What?' Tom said. 'Coveted his wife?'

Andrew nodded.

'Yes. As you so eloquently put it. I don't remember her reading anything about an orderly. What did Conrad suspect him of?'

'Something Miriam Howe might have found indelicate to read aloud.'

'Oh. I see.'

A few minutes later, he dropped them outside Kitty's house, telling them he'd go on ahead and get his cottage opened up.

'She should be in, her car is there. If by any chance she's not, I'm only a five-minute walk up the road.'

'We'll find you,' Tom said. They waved as the doctor drove off.

'I wonder what else he's forgotten over the years,' he said, as the car vanished around the bend.

'What, like murdering his pal and secretly dumping his body?'

'Ha! I wish we could lay our hands on this Reid chap. It's nagging at me.'

'Yeah, me too. Here, this interview. I can't believe for a second Kitty Nolan is involved in something funny.'

'No. But I do get the distinct impression her son is up to something. He was happy to accommodate us coming down during Christmas week, when he'd been given a few days' notice. But he only knew we were coming across on today's ferry when Mannix rang ahead. If I didn't know better, I'd say he has the look of a guilty man about him.'

'Guilty of what?' Ray said, as they crossed the road to the cottage's gate. 'He's too young to have murdered Howe.'

'Obviously. But what is he hiding? He's up to something. Like that wine he served us the other night – it struck me as high quality so I looked it up. It's €50 a bottle. Now, he's not buying that on a caretaker's wage. And it's ridiculous money to be spending on wine when you're really only drinking it to get drunk. That's not a man with a hobby. It's a man with cash to spend.'

'You think somebody is paying him to keep a secret? Like something at the asylum? Is that why he told us we couldn't go into the basement? But why involve his mother?'

Tom stopped, his hand on the iron gate.

'I don't know. But I'll tell you this much, we are going to look in that basement on our own tonight. If Arnie knows there's something awry down there, he'll try to steer us off course, like he's done so far. I want us to check out that place undisturbed.'

'I had a bad feeling you were going to say that. Do we need a warrant?'

'To go into an asylum we've already been in, that now belongs to the State? I don't think so. The only reason I want to go at night is to possibly catch him in the act of something.'

'Gentlemen. Are you going to stand down at the gate all day chinwagging? If you're waiting for some dancing at the cross-roads, I can assure you there are no pretty *cailíní* coming this way any time soon.'

Kitty had thrown open the door and was standing in the entrance with her arms across her chest.

'Well, you just arrived,' Tom said, smiling.

'I see you've recovered from your flu. Flirting and all, now, is it? Go away out of that. Come in. I've the kettle on.'

The room Kitty brought them into was a large sitting room with bay windows curling around one entire side. The view stretched from the woods inland all the way to the cliffs and the sea in front of the cottage.

'Ah,' Tom said. 'I can see why you had your heart set on this place.'

'Aye. It's magnificent. I reckoned I was due it, after all those years cooking down below, slaving over hot stoves and break-ing my back heaving sacks of spuds about the place. That, and I wanted some peace and quiet. I know there are mothers who never want their brood to leave but by Jesus, I never saw myself house-sharing with an adult son nearly thirty. Great big lump of a fellow. God, if his father hadn't died ten years ago – I think he'd have gone to college. But he was eighteen, old enough to take on the job and . . . well, he just got stuck here. Hold on there now, I'll get the tea.'

'This would be my chair,' Ray said, relaxing back into an armchair, perfectly situated to avail of the panoramic view.

'You and Laura could probably pick up one of these places

cheap enough. Use your inside knowledge and buy one quick before they go on the open market. She's from Kerry originally – it would be like moving home.'

'Not a chance,' Ray said, aghast. 'Sure her folks have lived in Dublin for years. There's no way she'd want to move back to Kerry. Is there? I couldn't hack living outside Dublin. Imagine having to drive somewhere every time you wanted a pint of milk.'

'The inhumanity!'

'Leave off.'

Kitty wasn't one for dainty tea services. She handed them each a large mug of builder's tea and plonked herself on the couch.

'Rob my grave as quick, would you?' she said to Ray, nodding at the armchair.

'Oh, sorry. I'll move.'

'Don't be daft. I get to sit there all the time. Best seat in the house, it is. What are you doing back over, anyway? Are you in love with the island or are you hoping to find Dr Howe's killer this time? It's the definition of madness, you know. Repeating the same task over and over and expecting a different result.'

'Then we're mad,' Tom said. 'Kitty, there's something we wanted to ask you.'

'Fire ahead. I've *Loose Women* recording on the Sky Box. Aside from that, I've nowhere to go and nobody to see.'

'Eh – okay.' The inspector couldn't decide what he found odder. Her choice of programme or the notion that anywhere on this island was hooked up to technology. He'd noted a large flatscreen in Arnie's house, yet another curious object, but the unreliability of mobile signal on the island and the fact everybody was still on dial-up, not Wi-Fi, had left him thinking the island was stuck in the 1990s.

'I've a satellite dish, Inspector,' Kitty said, leaning forward and whispering conspiratorially. 'A present from Arnie. We're not a total backwater.'

'I see. Makes sense now. Anyhow, look, speaking of your son. He seems to think that parts of the basement in the asylum are structurally unsound. He says you told him about it? Is that true?'

'Oh yes. My husband shut the door on everything beyond the east corridor back when St Christina's got its orders to close. The basement hadn't been used in years, anyway. It wasn't so bad that the building risked collapsing in on itself but Enda said you couldn't risk anybody going down there, for health and safety reasons. They could get hit on the head with loose debris if somebody was moving something heavy about upstairs. He told me there were leaks and rats and what not. You'd run the risk of electrocuting yourself if you turned on a light. I was glad it was made off-limits. Everybody knew the basement was the worst in that place. I was happy to know it was being locked up for good. Anyway, why are you asking about that?'

'And, was it just your husband who decided it needed to be closed?' Tom asked, avoiding her question.

Kitty scoffed and took a gulp of tea.

'Not at all, Inspector. We knew our place in St Christina's. Enda didn't do anything unless the big boss told him to.'

She took another sip of tea.

'The big boss being . . .' Tom prompted.

'Dr Boylan. Keep up. He wanted the whole basement shut down, Enda said. Told my husband he'd had engineers in to check it out. The problem was, the water mains are in the basement so part of it had to be kept open for access. Boylan was fine with that, as long as it was just Enda going down there, and later, Arnie. He'd no problem leaving my men at risk of getting a bang on the head. Not that Arnie would notice.'

'I see,' Tom said. 'That was all, really.' He had to cut Kitty off at the pass before she asked any more questions. 'We'd best be off, so.' He took a quick slurp of the scalding hot tea for politeness' sake.

'If your plan is to go from here to visit Dr Boylan, you'll have to change it,' Kitty said. She sat back and rested the tea on her chest, stuck out her legs and crossed her thick ankles.

'Why's that?' Tom asked.

'He took a turn yesterday. Carla left her own sick bed – though to be fair, she's on the mend – and went up to mind him. She rang this morning and told me. Just before ye arrived on the ferry. Said Boylan was in a bad way.'

'Indeed,' Tom said.

'Interesting that, isn't it?' Kitty continued. 'Him suddenly becoming very ill after we all heard you lot were coming back.'

'How would he have known we were coming?' Ray asked.

The old woman clicked her tongue.

'Lad, this is a small island, with a tiny population. We always know what and who is coming across on the ferry. Up to now, the most excitement we had was Dr Boylan's visitors. He's our resident celebrity, you know. But you've taken it to new levels.'

Tom smiled.

'Well, if Carla calls again, please feel free to tell her we're safely ensconced with Dr Collins for the evening and if Dr Boylan is well enough, we would like to see him in the morning. And if he's not well enough, we'd still like to see him.'

'I will delight in passing on that message, Inspector,' Kitty said, her face aglow. 'And watch yourself with Dr Collins.

I rarely see him when he's over these days, even living down the road from him. But that suits me just fine. He always had a bit of a temper on him, did the doctor. You wouldn't guess it to look at him. All intense and studious and stuck into his work. But he could flare up all right. Just mind that, won't you?'

Tom nodded. It was nothing he hadn't considered himself.

He'd felt something shift in the air when they'd crossed on that afternoon's ferry. People were starting to let down their guard.

It was only a matter of time.

Once outside, he and Ray set off in the direction of Andrew's house. They'd gone a few hundred metres up the road when Tom stopped short.

'Forget something?' his deputy asked.

'Carla Crowley told me she'd been in bed all over Christmas with a cold. Said she was dying from it.'

'Yeah. And? She's better now, that's what Kitty said.'

'Yes, but Emmet came over a few days before us and I asked if he'd seen anybody going in and out of the hospital besides Arnie. Boylan was in, he said. And Carla brought him.'

'She lied?'

'She lied. Another one.'

'Hmm,' Ray said. 'Boylan and Carla. An ageing Bonnie and Clyde, you think?'

Tom shrugged.

'That man didn't look like he was capable of walking more than a few feet when we met him. He's eighty-two and riddled with cancer. So he says. But then, when we arrived at his house, Linda and I saw a curtain twitch upstairs – and the door opened a minute or two later. Interesting, right?'

'Maybe,' Ray said, starting to walk again, 'he was experimenting on the patients for all those years to figure out the secret of eternal life. In fact, he's not eighty-two. He's two hundred and two. It's all a big act. This place is so creepy, nothing would surprise me.'

Tom raised an eyebrow and fell into step with his deputy.

Him neither. But Boylan wasn't faking cancer or his age. If he was at the back of something going on at the hospital, somebody younger, and fitter, was helping him.

CHAPTER 36

Diary Entry

I know now what's been going on.

And I know who's behind everything.

I am appalled. Shocked. There are no other words for it.

There's a level of persecution and torment in this place that even I have become accustomed to. But what has been happening – the sadistic, evil acts that have been carried out on these patients – it is as though we are sharing this island with the devil.

I have no choice. I must confront the perpetrator.

And all those who help him.

He does have help. I'm sure of that.

In his own twisted, unnatural way, I think he believes his torture is actually treatment.

These are just some of the accounts of unscheduled 'treatments' I have finally managed to extract from the patients:

- He strapped Joseph into the spin chair every day for two weeks. Joseph vomited so much he lost a stone in weight over the fourteen days. His death is believed to have been caused by a bleed on the brain. The doctor had recorded just two episodes in the swing chair, but Joseph's fellow patients told me the actual number.
- He poured water into Vincent's mouth and lungs through a cloth and almost drowned him. Vincent said this was

done to him three times over the course of two days and that he passed out each time. He has developed a nervous stutter since the treatment and his split personality disorder is still not cured. In fact, he seems to have had more episodes in the weeks since. I can find no medical reference to justify this sort of procedure.

- Bernadette was made to sit in an ice bath for several hours – so long, in fact, she sustained frostbite in four of her toes. Bernadette was admitted here for matricide – she suffocated her ill, elderly mother to death. The doctor claimed the bath would cool her murderous inclinations. All it did was lose the woman her toes.

What he is doing is abhorrent. And I have to confront him about it. I have to draw the line in this place. For Minnie. For Rosita. For all of them.

They say the darkest place in hell is reserved for those who do nothing, who remain neutral when evil abounds.

I know it's me who people will think mad when I tell them. It's my reputation that will be at risk. But I don't care anymore.

I won't remain neutral.

CHAPTER 37

Despite Kitty Nolan's warning ringing in his head, Tom still found it hard not to enjoy being in Andrew Collins' company. As they stood in the small galley kitchen preparing an evening meal, the doctor regaled them with his fonder memories of St Christina's.

'It's never easy working with the mentally ill,' Andrew said, handing peeled carrots to Tom to chop. 'And, obviously, I went through a pretty bad period there. But there was light as well as dark. The patients could be hilarious at times. Intentionally and unintentionally. We had this one lady, Grace – in her forties and sex mad, she was. Every night she'd try to hide herself in the line of men heading to their separate wards. The nurses would pull her out and she'd hiss at them while the men booed. Jesus, you couldn't let her go with them, no matter how much she thought she wanted to. Anyway, the odd night, she'd break in. Mainly when narco Nancy was on.'

'Who?' Tom asked, amused.

'Narcoleptic Nancy, we used to call her. One of the nurses. She didn't actually have narcolepsy, just a tendency to fall asleep on her watch. And when she did, Grace would have the nightgown off and be down in the men's ward in minutes. Nothing would ever happen. You'd be alerted by the screams and hollers of the lads. It was just a bit of titillation for them.

She'd usually be dancing in the middle of the ward, that sort of thing. One night, though, she quietly climbed into bed with this chap. She couldn't have known how he'd react. The poor man leapt out of it, screaming, his blanket wrapped around himself like a shield. He fancied himself good for Holy Orders. By the time we got up there, he was yelling about Eve tempting him in the Garden of Eden. The fellow in the bed beside him was near crying with hysterics, saying he'd happily bite into them apples. I shouldn't laugh – our holy man was utterly disgusted to see a woman in the full of her flesh. Not a bad figure on her, mind. Is that all the potatoes? Hang on. I should have more out in the shed.'

Tom stood aside for the other man to pass.

'You're awful quiet,' he said to Ray, who was standing at the window, his back to him.

'Come over here a minute,' Ray responded.

Tom joined him at the window.

'What am I looking for?'

'Over there, between the trees at the end of the garden, see it?'

The inspector stared out the window but he was at a loss.

'What am I looking at?' he asked.

The moon shifted in the sky. It was then he saw it. The changing reflection of light on glass.

'It's a windscreen,' Tom said. 'A car.'

'Yeah. It's not Collins' and it wasn't there earlier. We're being watched. Will I go out and see who it is?'

'If the driver is watching and sees you leave the window, he'll be gone in a heartbeat. His view of me is obscured by those trees. Just stay standing there. I'll go upstairs, see if I can get a better look.'

Tom made his way to the bedroom at the front of the house, the one Collins had allocated them for the night. He flicked off the landing light before entering the room in darkness, and felt his way to the window.

He'd a better view from up here. On the other side of the trees he could make out a Land Rover.

Arnie's car.

What was he playing at?

And more importantly, was he intending to stay there all night?

Back in the kitchen, the doctor had returned with the extra provisions.

'Chops, mash and carrots coming up. I'm afraid that's the extent of my culinary abilities. When I'm feeling adventurous I alternate from pork chops to lamb.'

'Sounds perfect,' Tom said.

Arnie, he mouthed to Ray.

His deputy raised a puzzled eyebrow.

They talked some more about the hospital over dinner but declined the offer of a nightcap from Andrew.

Up in the room they were sharing, Tom and Ray studiously ignored the window, pretending to be oblivious to the spy outside.

'Do you think he's keeping watch for the night?' Ray said, plumping the pillow on his single bed and propping himself against it.

'No,' Tom said. 'I think he's just making sure we settle in. We'll look out in a few minutes.'

He knocked off the light.

'You think he's keeping tabs on us so he can head down to the asylum?' Ray asked.

'Maybe. Or maybe somebody has him on the payroll.'

'Yes, but for what? To keep a forty-year-old secret that only came to light in the last couple of weeks? That can't be it – he didn't just buy his mother that satellite dish over Christmas. It sounds like she has had it a while.'

'I know,' Tom said. 'Shush, listen.'

They both fell silent. The sound of an engine quietly purring to life filled the room.

Ray moved to the end of the bed and looked out the window, just in time to see tail-lights rounding the bend.

'Yep, he's gone. Right, when's our expedition?'

'Let's give it a couple of hours. I want to go in the dead of night, when everybody on this island is asleep. Whatever is going on at the hospital can't be moved or sorted in a short time or they'd have done it already. Set your alarm for 2 a.m. and put it under your pillow. You got Collins' car keys, didn't you?'

'Yep. I think he's the least of our worries, anyhow.'

Tom listened to the loud snoring already drifting out of the room across the landing.

Could you fake snoring like that, he wondered?

The inspector must have been tired. When he closed his eyes, they stayed closed and it took a good poke from Ray to wake him up.

'I'm awake,' Tom said, yawning loudly and rubbing his eyes.

'Ssh. We're in Andrew Collins' house, remember?'

Tom opened his eyes properly and sat up.

'Sorry. I was out for the count. Is the doc still asleep?'

'He's not snoring but I looked in – he's fast asleep.'

Neither man had undressed, so it was just a matter of putting on their shoes before creeping downstairs.

'Drive with the lights off,' Tom whispered when they were outside. 'We don't know for certain whether or not we're still being watched. There's a good moon, we should be able to see where we're going.'

'An Audi,' Ray said, tapping the car's bonnet. 'One of the least noisy engines around. Good of Andrew to sort that for us. Are we actually stealing a car right now?'

Tom smiled.

'He said we could have the use of it. Just take care not to scratch the bloody thing. This car cost more than my annual salary.'

They pulled out onto the road and started to drive, slowly, in the direction of the hospital. It was a cloudless night and the moon shone bright, but on unfamiliar roads and without headlights, Ray was taking no risks.

'I don't want to be a killjoy, but how are we getting into this place? Arnie keeps it locked up. We know that much.'

Tom turned to his deputy.

'We're halfway there, in the middle of the night, and it's only now you're wondering how we get in?'

Ray looked flabbergasted.

'Was I supposed to figure it out?' he asked.

The inspector shook his head.

'You're joking, right? As if I'd leave that to chance. I'm just getting my head around you not having considered a plan until now.'

He took a set of keys from his pocket.

'What are they?'

'Spare keys.'

'Yeah, I'm not a complete dunce. Where did you get them?'

Tom smiled.

'Arnie's house. When we stayed there, I figured we might need to get back into that hospital at some stage, un-chaperoned.'

'But . . .' Ray frowned. 'He was happy to leave us there on our own the day we were over. If there was anything to hide, why do that?'

'He showed us what we needed to see and steered us clear of what we weren't allowed to see. We weren't so curious then. We are now.'

'And you still had the foresight to take the keys.' Ray whistled. 'I bow to your genius.'

'Yes, well, don't get ahead of yourself. I know the front door key is on here, but I've no idea if there's a key for that door in the basement. We could be snookered yet.'

'I have every faith. Do you think we should have let somebody know we were doing this? It could be dangerous.'

Tom shook his head.

'Ray, Ray, Ray. Firstly – I told Laura what we'd planned and I can't believe you didn't. Secondly, half the residents on this island could star in the cast of Dad's Army. I feel like a spring chicken over here. I'm pretty sure we can handle ourselves.'

Ray slowed the car to a crawl as they approached the gates of the hospital.

'I didn't tell Laura for the same reason I bet you didn't tell Louise. You told a fellow officer, not your wife. Laura is my . . . you know what I mean. She did make a fuss of me when I was leaving, now I think of it.'

'You can thank me later. Pull up here outside the walls. I don't want the car to be noticeable from the windows. Let's not get caught out like Arnie was earlier.'

They left the car, taking with them the torch they found in the Audi's boot.

'Doesn't look like there's anything much happening inside,' Ray said, as they approached the dark building.

'That we know of,' Tom replied.

He took out what he suspected was the front door key and inserted it in the large, old-fashioned lock.

Just before it turned, the inspector hesitated.

'There definitely wasn't an alarm system, am I right?'

Ray smiled.

'So you're not that prepared. No, there isn't an alarm. We came out this way when we left you in Boylan's office the other day. I didn't see anything even resembling modern technology.'

'That's good.' Tom turned the key and breathed out as the door opened easily.

'Looks like it's easier to break into this place than it would have been to break out,' Ray said.

'I think things would have been a little different back in the day. Stick that torch on so we can get our bearings.'

Instantly, light filled the large entrance hall. Ray shone the beam around the walls and across the Edwardian-patterned tiles.

'It's grand, isn't it,' he said. 'Linda mentioned the receptions in these places were always nice. Lured families into thinking their loved ones were being dropped off somewhere pleasant.'

Tom nodded. At the mention of Linda, the memory of what Emmet had told him yesterday sprung to mind. He'd gone home last night, completely distracted by it. And for the first time in his married life he found himself deliberately not telling his wife the significant thing he'd learned that day. Emmet had asked him not to. It wasn't fair, he'd pointed out, for other people to know before Linda did. He would tell her, Emmet had promised. When he thought he could be in the same room with her without wanting to kill her.

Louise would understand his silence when Tom eventually told her. He hoped.

'Which way to the basement?' he whispered.

Ray pointed at a door in the corner with his torch.

'There might be a faster way but that's where we came from.'

'That's it, then.'

They met their first obstacle at the door, which was also locked.

'Seriously,' Tom said, trying one key, then the next. 'Why the hell would you lock all the internal doors as well? What exactly does Arnie think is going to happen?'

'Maybe he's worried somebody will break in,' Ray said wryly, as his boss landed on the right key.

'Got it! That was lucky. There are about thirty keys on this chain. If this keeps happening we could be going through them all night. It will be like the Crystal Maze.'

'There aren't as many doors on the other side,' Ray said. 'One to the corridor that leads to the basement, from what I remember, and then the rest are up to the wards and offices. It was worth bringing me, wasn't it?'

'Always,' Tom said, opening the door. 'I'm completely lost. After you.'

They halted temporarily at the next door. Once through that, they found themselves back on familiar turf.

They walked the corridor slowly, their shoes clipping softly on the hard floor.

'The last time I was here, I had the feeling I was being watched,' the inspector whispered. He gave an involuntary shudder. Even now, in company, the walls of the asylum screamed at him.

Andrew Collins had talked about some of the more pleasant times at the hospital over dinner but Tom had known he was giving them the superficial gloss. The man himself had admitted he returned to Oileán na Coillte to atone.

God knew what he had witnessed.

God knew what he had done.

'Yep,' Ray said. 'Even Linda was spooked here and most of the time I reckon that woman could put the shits up the Devil. Tom, what exactly are we looking for? How could there be anything still in this hospital connected to the murder of a man forty years ago?'

'That's what we're here to find out. I feel it in my gut, Ray. They, whoever they are, have blocked off that basement for a reason.'

'You don't think . . .'

'What?'

'There could be another body?'

The inspector hesitated.

'It's crossed my mind. Two people left the island that Christmas Eve – Dolores O'Sullivan and Owen Reid. They were never heard from again and Laura can't track them down either. Are we even sure they were on the ferry? That both of them were on it? Mannix's father is dead; we've no way to check he wasn't paid to say that. Or even to say that Carla left on the 23rd. Who can we confirm that with? And we know from what we've heard that Dolores was a fan of Conrad's. If somebody was willing to murder him to hide what they were doing at this hospital – they might have been happy to kill again to keep their secret. So, yes. Maybe there is something down here. But a dead body, I'm not sure. Those screams we heard the first night – that was very much a live woman. Uniforms came over on the ferry and searched but found nothing. They wouldn't have tried down here, though.'

'We're about to find out if we all missed something. Any clue about the key for this one?'

'I do, actually. I noticed Arnie locking it behind us that time. Direct that beam over here.'

Ray shone the torch at Tom's hand. He sifted through the bundle until he found the right one. He was just about to insert it in the lock when, from beyond the doors, they heard a crash.

The two men looked at each other.

'Kill the torch,' the inspector said, quietly.

Silently, he opened the door. Nothing met them on the other side. No light, and no more noise.

Instinctively, Tom took the steps ahead of his deputy. He moved stealthily, barely making a sound, feeling along the wall with his hands. At the bottom step he paused and sniffed the air.

Yes. He was sure of it. That smell . . .

Horrified, he turned to Ray.

Before he could utter a word, a shape emerged from the darkness and sent him crashing sideways into the wall.

The figure tried to shove past but Ray was waiting. He hit his moving target with a well-aimed smack of the torch. The thump was met with a low guttural groan.

Winded, Tom tussled with his attacker, already knowing when he grabbed at the thin frame who it was.

Ray flicked on the torch as Lawrence Boylan fell to the ground, moaning.

They both stared at the man on the floor.

Boylan was huddled into himself, his hand shielding his face from the light.

'Tell me I'm seeing things,' Tom spat. '*You* are meant to be dying.'

'Please,' Boylan whimpered. 'I'm very ill. Help me up.'

'Stay where you are. Ray, is there a light switch up top?'

His deputy handed Tom the torch and bounded back up the stairs, feeling along the wall until he found the switch and flicked it on. He then sprinted back down.

Boylan looked deathly in the light that now filled the corridor, cowering at the inspector's feet. Tom wasn't fooled. Seconds ago, the man had shown plenty of life.

'Where are the extinguishers?' he demanded.

The old man said nothing.

'Now!' Tom shouted.

Ray looked at his boss, confused.

'I don't know what you're talking about,' Boylan answered.

'I can smell it,' the inspector hissed. He pulled out his sidearm and pointed it at the doctor.

At first Boylan winced. Then he sneered.

'Go on, then. Shoot me. I'm eighty-two and sick, Inspector. Do you think I care if I die at your hand and not God's?'

Tom cocked the gun.

'Don't tempt me,' he said. 'And don't be an idiot. Do you really think I'd shoot dead an un-armed man? My plan is to wound you and leave you screaming in agony, if you don't tell me where the *DAMNED FIRE EXTINGUISHER IS.*' His voice rose on the last few words, furious.

Ray sniffed the air, finally picking up on the smell.

'Boss, there's definitely one upstairs.'

'Run,' Tom said, nodding. He bent over Boylan and grabbed one of his bony wrists, slapping a handcuff on it and fixing its partner to an old length of pipe running along the wall. Then he checked the other man for weapons. The inspector was still smarting after being floored by a dying old man. He wasn't taking any chances. Boylan, though, was empty-handed, bar a single lighter and a set of keys.

'You can't leave me here,' the doctor said, finally showing some fear.

'Why not?' Tom said. 'You said yourself, you're dying anyway. What's down here that you need to destroy, Boylan? You've only just started that fire. What will I find when I open the door?'

The old man clamped his mouth shut. But his eyes said everything. Tom was now desperate to see what lay further into the basement.

'Why?' Tom persisted. 'What are you doing out here? What would drag you from your sick bed to put yourself at risk like this?'

He asked the questions more to himself than the man on the ground.

Then Ray was back, taking the stairs two at a time and loosening the nozzle on the extinguisher as he approached.

Tom didn't need to search for the right key this time. The door at which Arnie had called a halt to their tour was closed but unlocked.

The inspector tapped his hand gingerly against the handle.

'Cold,' he told Ray. 'I'm going to open it. If the fire has caught hold, we'll need to get out of here and take that sorry sack with us.'

'Understood,' Ray said.

Tom opened the door.

Immediately the acrid smell of smoke filled their noses.

But it wasn't overpowering, not yet.

'There,' Tom covered his mouth with his hand and pointed. 'One of those rooms at the end.'

They raced along the corridor until they arrived at the open door.

In the middle of what seemed to be an old office, Boylan had stacked a table with piles of paper and what looked like old ward curtains. The fire was busy consuming the centre of the room but had yet to spread beyond.

Ray pointed the discharge hose at the flames and sprayed the foam, not stopping until he'd beaten the blaze.

'I think that's it,' he said, waving the smoke away from his eyes and mouth. He crossed the room and used the bottom of the extinguisher to smash the window near the ceiling, providing the smoke with an escape route.

'Go check on Boylan,' Tom said, 'and open the other doors wide so we can clear the corridor. That window alone won't do it.' He approached the smouldering pile. It was still too hot to touch. He looked around him, seeking something to prod the embers with. He spotted an old pair of scissors on a cabinet on the far side of the room and fetched them.

'He looks out of it,' Ray said, coming back in. 'He shouldn't even be walking around, let alone committing arson.' He took his phone out. 'Who will I ring? Is the station in the village manned at this time of night or will I just ring HQ?'

'HQ,' Tom said, combing through the debris. 'Let them sort out the locals.' He was distracted. 'It looks like this is just blank paper. No files or anything like that. There's no writing that I can see.'

A cold chill settled in his stomach.

Slowly, he turned to Ray.

'Boylan is too ill. He came here either because he's desperate to get rid of something or . . .'

'Or what?'

'Or somebody made him come. This could be a trap. We need to . . .'

The rest of Tom's sentence never made it out. A spine-tingling scream reverberated around the walls of the basement. Ray, already on edge, dropped his phone, then flinched, listening for its crack. He was lucky; it survived. He swooped it from the floor as Tom passed him, sidearm back out of its holster.

'That's the same scream,' the inspector said. 'Where did it come from?'

'Off this corridor,' Ray said, close on his heel.

They ran through the basement, throwing open doors as they went. They could see nothing in any of the rooms.

'There,' Tom said, pointing at a door further along, the shadow in its frame revealing it was open.

The room they entered was larger than the others. It was dark. Another small window, high on the wall and criss-crossed with bars, was the only source of natural light, like the office they'd just come from.

But even unlit, the inspector could see the shapes within. And then the woman wailed again.

Behind him, Ray felt along the wall until he found the light switch, and flicked it on.

Three ghostly, skeletal faces met theirs; wrinkled, shrivelled hands tried to block out the sudden brightness. All of them had their other hand shackled to the safety rail on the sides of their hospital beds.

Two men and a woman.

Patients.

Prisoners.

Ray held the door frame, lightheaded with shock, while Tom tried to make sense of what he was seeing.

And then the woman opened her mouth – broken, yellow teeth within – and screamed.

And screamed.

CHAPTER 38

'You've been travelling over and back on a ferry when there's an emergency helicopter,' Linda shouted, her corkscrew curls still gyrating wildly in the wind generated by the rotor blades. She'd greeted them with a jibe, but her face was deadly serious.

'This is Dr Lucy McQuaid,' she said, introducing the stern-faced woman to her left. 'She's a senior psychologist at the Central Mental Hospital. And this is Dr Adi Basu from the College of Surgeons. There's a paramedic team with the helicopter but we need to assess the condition of the patients first.'

'They need to be in hospital,' Ray said, as they shook the doctors' hands. 'A proper hospital.'

He was still shaken, his face white; the early morning drizzle had deposited a sheen on his skin that made him look sickly. Every time he closed his eyes he could see Boylan's victims. The key to not falling apart was to stay angry. But he kept remembering . . .

As soon as they'd recovered themselves, Tom and Ray had moved to unshackle the prisoners. It was instinctive, but all three reacted with distress. Back along the corridor, Boylan started roaring, too. Ray had gone down and uncuffed him, half-walking, half-dragging him to the room. When Boylan tried to look away, the inspector had taken his chin and turned his face towards his captives.

'Don't untie them,' the doctor had croaked. 'I know you think it's the right thing to do but you don't understand. They are very ill. They won't understand either of you touching them and they need the chains for themselves as much as for us.'

Ray looked like he was going to punch the old man, and made to move towards the beds anyway, but Tom put an arm out to stop him.

'What? Like he cares about their well-being,' Ray said. He turned to Boylan. 'You were trying to burn them to death. You're an animal.' He hissed these last words in Boylan's face.

But, despite himself, the inspector knew that what the doctor said made sense.

'Ray. We're strangers. We're frightening them. She stopped screaming as soon as she saw him. You,' he grabbed Boylan again. 'Get them water. Make them comfortable.'

Tom watched as Boylan approached the woman first. If she showed any sign of discomfort, he would remove the doctor from the scene. But he needed to assess the situation first.

As he expected – and feared – the woman's body relaxed as Boylan approached.

A caged bird, happy to see her jailor.

Boylan stroked the woman's head.

'There, there. I'm here now. It's time for sleep. Everything is okay.'

The woman settled down on the bed, murmuring garbled words.

'Turn out the lights,' Boylan said.

They did, and then they all left the room.

*

They'd walked away. In his head, Ray knew they'd done the right thing. The rest of him felt like vomiting.

'I just checked on them,' Tom said. 'They're awake. Boylan says he'd normally feed them about now. But I'm happy to hand over to the experts on this, Linda. I'm still in shock.'

She placed her hand on his arm.

'Let us deal with the medical requirements. What's your plan now?'

'I want to arrest everybody on this damned island. How the hell could those poor souls have been kept down there without the knowledge of those who lived here?'

Linda shrugged.

'How many of them would have had access to the hospital and been in there frequently?'

Tom shook his head.

'I don't know. But I'm going to find out. We've more officers en route. Myself and Ray are going up to Boylan's house now to go through it. There are no food supplies in the hospital so Boylan must have been bringing their meals down. When he did feed them. And given the state of him, there's no way he was driving down here or cooking for three people by himself all the time.'

'Carla Crowley?'

'We were already starting to suspect she'd more involvement than she let on. I'd no idea how much until now.'

'Okay. Good luck. I'll report to you as soon as I have something.'

'Collins will be awake by now and wondering where his car is,' Ray said as they left the hospital.

'Let him.'

'Boss – you don't think . . . Is it Dolores O'Sullivan?'

The inspector pursed his lips.

'I really don't know. Only a very sick mind could conceive of keeping people prisoner like that – keeping them alive that long in captivity. Doing that to Dolores O'Sullivan, a former nurse to boot, would have been worse than killing her. I'm struggling to get my head around it.'

'Having killed Howe, why wouldn't Boylan just kill Dolores? If she knew what Howe did, I mean?'

Tom shook his head.

'Can we apply logical thought processes to the man? Anyway, I suspect we'll find out for definite, up in Boylan's house, who those poor souls are.'

'How?'

'There were no files in that room. No patients' files. Boylan will have kept notes. He must have them at home. I imagine that, all this time, Boylan has been telling himself it was just medicine. And in that case, he'll have ticked the box and kept records.'

'But would they not be in his office?'

'They might. But I suspect they're not. He's too ill to be in that hospital for long periods of time. I'm sure feeding the three in the basement and doing whatever else he was doing to them – Jesus, it makes me sick to say it – would've been enough. He'd have brought the paperwork home. When we visited him, it looked like he was living in two tiny rooms in the back of that huge house. Boylan didn't commandeer that place as head of St Christina's so he could live like a church mouse. So what does he use the rest of it for? He must have an office there, too.'

They pulled into the gravel drive of Boylan's home. The inspector had left the ailing man in the care of the doctors who'd arrived on the island. He was being kept in a locked room, but Tom figured the danger he posed was done with now.

In fact, he was still trying to get his head around the reactions of the prisoners to Boylan's presence. He hadn't detected fear. Just familiarity.

But the three had not been looked after that well. They were deathly thin and bore the scars on their faces and bodies of people who had been ill-used. Tortured, in fact.

Could any human being become so used to that treatment that they wouldn't cower in the company of their tormentor?

'You have Boylan's keys?' Tom asked, as they climbed out of the car.

'Yep.'

Ray opened the front door.

They stood inside the house, listening for a moment.

It was silent.

'Where do we start?' Ray asked.

'You take downstairs. Look for evidence in the kitchen of extra supplies. Hospital-type food.'

'What the hell does that look like?'

'I don't know. Puréed. Tinned. And keep your eyes out for any paperwork. Wear your gloves if you find anything so we're not messing about with fingerprints later. I'll search upstairs.'

Tom made his way through each of the rooms on the second floor, starting with Boylan's.

His bedroom looked like a hospital ward. Starched sheets, a blue cellular blanket, IV drip set up beside a small chest that contained a water jug and small vase of flowers. On the cabinet under the window, bottles of prescription pills and syringes. Nowhere to hide files.

In the room of the sick man, Tom wondered again how or

why Boylan had kept going with his crime all this time. How had he even managed to move about in the hospital last night, unaided? He was at death's door.

Was that the reason? Boylan was about to croak so he decided he had to kill his 'patients'?

As Tom moved on to the next room, he pondered the lunacy of a man's brain that would think burning people alive an act of kindness, rather than setting them free or even medicating them into a sleep from which they wouldn't wake.

Most of the bedrooms were unused, a light sheen of dust covering their furnishings.

Excepting two. In one room, Tom found signs of a very recent inhabitant. The bed was neatly made, the corners tucked in tight. A woman's housecoat hung on the back of the door. Beside the bed, on a chest of drawers, were a packet of tissues and tray of lozenges.

Carla Crowley's room. She must have stayed over some nights to nurse Boylan, including recently.

The next room was a double and again, appeared to have been used frequently. There were no personal items, so the inspector assumed this was where Boylan put his visitors.

The very last room upstairs was what he'd come looking for.

An office, not dissimilar to the ones he'd seen at the hospital, except this one had a much nicer view, looking out at the woods that dotted the island.

Tom sat at the teak desk and tried to open the drawers underneath. They were locked. He looked around for a key, cursing when he couldn't see one.

'No time for this,' he muttered, and stood up. Clearing the top of the desk, he toppled it on its side.

The drawers were a thinner wood than the table's surface. He was able to break through the underneath of the first one with the butt of a heavy ornament he found on the windowsill.

He was removing the folders inside when he thought he heard a sound. Standing upright again, he crossed the room and opened the door.

Ray was on the landing.

'What was that crashing sound?' Tom's deputy asked.

'I'm disassembling furniture. Did you hear a noise just then?'

'Yeah, I just said.'

'No. After that.'

Ray shook his head.

'Maybe it was just you on the stairs,' Tom said. He looked about him suspiciously, but saw nothing awry. 'Right, I think I might have found the files. Come with me.'

Back in the office, Ray helped Tom turn the desk back on its feet.

'I hope Laura hasn't had trouble sorting out that search warrant,' the inspector said, placing the files on the table top.

'I shouldn't think so,' Ray answered. 'Retrospective warrants are her speciality. She's definitely flirting with somebody downstairs in HQ that I don't know about.'

The words were jokey but Ray's expression was serious. Neither he nor Tom could take their eyes off the files on the table.

There were three. Tom separated them out so they could read the names on each. The inspector swore and placed his hand over his mouth when he saw the name on the third.

'What is it?' Ray said.

'Remember I told you Howe had written in his diary about catching one of the orderlies raping a young woman?'

'Yes.'

'Her name was unusual. Rosita.'

Tom pointed at the name on the file.

Rosita Moore.

'Fuck!' Ray slammed his hand on the table. 'What sort of sick bastard . . . She's been here nearly her whole life?'

'I can't imagine it's another Rosita.'

'The others – George Bonner and Henry Arnold – he didn't mention them in his diary, did he?'

'Not yet. Here. Take one. Let's start skim-reading.'

Even though he didn't want to, Tom picked up Rosita's file.

Ten minutes later, he regretted it.

'It's so clinical,' Ray said, quietly. 'Every procedure is noted with such precision and . . . so unfeelingly. What is this? What was Boylan hoping to achieve? Is he a sadist or insane?'

Tom closed Rosita's history and placed his hand on the cover.

She'd endured years of the same medical interventions long after they went out of fashion or were declared in contravention of human rights. Insulin treatment. Purging. Starvation. Force-feeding. Ice-baths. Scalding hot baths. ECT.

Over and over.

Each page in her file noted the date of the treatment. The length of time it was applied. The results, which ranged from 'calm' to 'violent response' to 'no improvement'.

How had they survived, Rosita, George and Henry?

The assaults on their minds and bodies had stripped them of their dignity. Invaded every inch of their persons.

Rosita had been sterilised. Before her hysterectomy, Rosita's child had been aborted.

'I don't think she was even ill, when this all began,' Tom said to Ray, his voice sounding a little dazed. 'Not properly, if Howe's diary is anything to go by. She might have been a little simple, but she didn't belong in there.'

'We should have rescued those people and left Boylan to burn,' his deputy answered. 'It was as you said, downstairs. There are cartons of stuff in the fridge and freezer. Smells like baby food. Potatoes and veg, that kind of thing.'

This time they both heard the noise.

'There's somebody downstairs,' Ray said.

Tom nodded. He moved towards the door, hand on his holster. He imagined it was Carla Crowley, come to check on Boylan, but they had to be careful. They'd just learned what one of the island's occupants was capable of.

'Hello?' a voice called out.

'It's Laura,' Ray said, surprised, as Tom exhaled the breath he'd been holding. 'We're here,' he shouted down.

They met in the hall.

'You got here fast,' Tom said. Less than six hours had passed since they'd rung headquarters. Linda had only arrived speedily because she'd used the emergency air vehicle.

'I was already in Kerry,' Laura said. 'I was due some time off so I drove down last night. Figured you could do with some help going through those hospital files and I brought the warrant over you needed. Michael Geoghegan phoned me after you rang through to HQ. The local uniforms had already organised a ferry crossing so I hopped on it with them. They're down at the hospital, by the way. They've taken Boylan into custody but they're not going to move him until they get your say-so. I told them you'd want to speak to him first.'

'I will,' Tom said. 'And fortunately we don't need help finding those files – they're right here. But we will need you to help us question the other islanders. We have to get to the bottom of what they know. So I'm very glad to see you.'

'That's great. Because the Chief Superintendent won't be happy that I'm here. He was putting me on another job when I told him I was overdue about three months of overtime. I said he could let me take the week or I'd have to make a complaint to my union. Oh! I have an update on Dolores O'Sullivan and Owen Reid.'

'I'm very interested in that. What do you have?'

'Well, I tracked down their families. Dolores had a sister. She says the nurse came home from St Christina's that Christmas alright. But she went to work in England then, which explains why I couldn't get hold of her. Her sister said she'd been in love with some bloke on the island but it hadn't worked out and she just wanted to flee. She hasn't heard from Dolores in decades and reckons she's dead. They weren't very close. It shouldn't take me long to source a death certificate in Britain if she is.'

Tom looked at Ray.

'Well,' he said. 'That's one avenue closed down.'

'Yeah, well, Owen Reid is a different story,' Laura continued. 'He had quite a large family. Unfortunately, all of his siblings are dead but he has tonnes of nephews and nieces. One of them, the eldest, remembers him very well. Says he was a very intense man, and huge. Hands like shovels. He says Owen spent years working as an orderly but that he had notions. His nephew was a bit unkind in the telling of this – a little scathing – but basically I got the impression Owen fancied studying for a medical degree. Apparently he used to come home and tell them all about medical procedures like he was some sort of expert. He said he was learning a lot at the asylum.'

'Okay,' Tom said. 'What else?' He knew Laura was building up to something.

'Well, here's the thing. Owen travelled home regularly from St Christina's. He wasn't married, so home was still his parents' farm in Galway. Then, in 1972, he stopped returning. He sent letters for a while, but then those stopped. The last of his siblings went to the grave assuming Owen was still working in St Christina's.'

'And we know he wasn't,' Tom said.

'So, where is he?' Ray puzzled.

'There are two options,' the inspector said, rubbing his jaw. 'One, he went into hiding because he'd murdered a man. Or two, he's dead. Either naturally, or because he knew or saw something and had to be disposed of.'

Ray rubbed his eyes, tired and frustrated.

'I don't understand. It's obvious Boylan killed Howe, surely? Howe must have figured out Boylan was subjecting the patients to unnecessary treatments and had to be silenced. What has Reid got to do with it? He and Howe were seen fighting – so they were hardly on the same side.'

Tom sat on one of the bottom steps and pondered the possibilities.

'Reid was a big man, that's a known. Boylan could have been using him as muscle. Especially if he was the orderly that Howe caught assaulting Rosita. Maybe Howe reported him to Boylan. The doctor could have blackmailed him to murder Howe.

'Or,' Tom continued, 'Howe and Reid were on the same side and were fighting over how to tackle Boylan. Or somebody else . . .'

'What do you mean, somebody else?' Ray threw his hands in the air. 'How much more convoluted could this get? Who else could be involved?'

'There's something not right,' Tom replied. 'If Howe's diary is anything to go by . . . it doesn't read like he was keeping an eye on Boylan. He describes the doctor he was watching as senior, but not in charge.'

'Well, what doctor was Howe watching, then? Somebody we don't know of? Robert O'Hare was a junior doctor, so it can't be him, surely.'

'Andrew Collins started before Howe. He was senior, technically. He got Howe the job out here. Miriam told us.'

'And there might be a reason he's kept his cottage over here,' Laura suggested. 'I mean, outside of what he claims.'

'So two of them?' Ray asked. 'Collins and Boylan torturing the patients?'

'Or him and Reid,' Tom said. 'And Boylan just following orders. I don't know. I just didn't see anything in the victims' reactions to Boylan to think he's the one who's been undertaking all these experiments. Rosita didn't recoil when he touched her, as you would have imagined.'

'Rosita?' Laura asked, puzzled. 'Isn't she . . . ?'

'Yes,' Tom nodded. 'We found her. Look, we're going around in circles just speculating. I'm going to talk to this . . . specimen. Why don't you two go over to Carla Crowley's house? And if you get done with her, move on to the chemist – Lane. He sounds nasty enough to give up anything he has on Boylan and Crowley, if it's his neck or theirs. I'll have O'Hare and Collins brought down to the asylum. Laura, I take it you brought your car across?'

'Yep, it's outside.'

'Right. Let's go.'

They locked the door of Boylan's house before getting into the two cars.

None of them noticed the person watching from the upstairs window as they drove away.

CHAPTER 39

Diary Entry

I have confided in someone. I was reluctant at first but I started to feel that I too would go mad if I didn't tell another person what has being going on.

Perhaps it was unfair of me to choose Dolores. She has already suffered so much. And while she cannot remember who put her at risk on the day of the fire, I believe it is the same man who is responsible for the campaign of terror in this asylum.

And I chose her for another reason. Dolores was the first person I met on this wretched island. I have seen nothing but professionalism in her, which I haven't in many others here. She may be the only one I ever speak to again when I leave.

When I leave. When I return to normality. Home, to family. God, I miss that.

All the great plans I had. I've put them aside now. I don't think I ever want to work in medicine again. Part of me thinks I should have left when Minnie died. I took her death too hard. I don't have the courage to surround myself with such sadness, with such hopelessness. Everything I've learned about medical advances and treatments, all that confidence I had, and it turns out I'm just not cut out for it.

I believe Dolores is fond of me and I couldn't leave

without saying goodbye, anyway. She has been thinking of leaving for quite some time. I will press the issue with her. When it all comes out, when I reveal what this doctor has done, the consequences will be dire. I cannot see how what's been going on at St Christina's can be covered up.

What has been happening to the vulnerable human beings in our care goes against God and nature. He is experimenting on them, like they are his animals and he a demented ringmaster.

Rosita is the final straw.

I have been watching her closely for the last couple of months. I was terrified her abuse was continuing. More than that, I was frightened she would come onto *his* radar. He chooses them carefully. They are always the weakest of our patients, the ones least likely to fight back.

I promised Minnie I would keep Rosita safe. That promise has become the only way I can redeem myself. But I cannot be here every minute of the day.

I knew Rosita was pregnant. I could see it. The nurses could too, I'm sure.

Nobody said a word. Nobody asked how she had fallen that way.

Then I had to go home for a weekend. When I returned, she'd been moved from her ward. I sought her out. I looked in all the treatment rooms, searched all of the floors.

Finally, my heart sinking, I looked in the basement.

When I found Rosita, she was in shock. Through half-sentences and whispers, I managed to establish what she had endured. He had strapped her to a gurney and inserted a tube into her mouth and down into the stomach. There he had poured concoctions designed, as he told her, to flush out her system.

She vomited, of course. Repeatedly. And then she said she felt horrendous pains in her stomach.

Obviously not satisfied with the results at that point, he'd strapped her ankles into stirrups. She felt a terrible agony between her legs. When she awoke, the floor and the sheet she lay on were covered in her own blood.

Rosita has no concept of what was done to her, only that it was bad. I don't know if she thinks she's still pregnant or if she realises the baby is gone and has lost her mind with it.

Minutes after I found her, he arrived and spoke to me as if it were the most normal interaction in the world.

'Excellent, you're here. Could you bring her back to her ward and see the nurses clean her up? Good man. Rosita, I will check on you again next week. We must make sure that little incident doesn't happen again.'

They were his only words. There was no apology for what he had done. No explanation to her, or to me, as to why she was there.

I've told Dolores I will confront him. I have been carefully noting what he's doing. All the unplanned treatments. The lack of peer knowledge or consent, the lack of patient knowledge and consent.

There is little enough accountability in St Christina's, in the entire field of treatment of the insane.

But abortion, for one, is illegal.

I've let one young woman die on my watch. While I'm here, I won't have another on my conscience.

I will give him an option. Leave, or stay and deal with the consequences of my revelations.

He is so well respected in his field. He may think he can challenge my assertions and face me down. But I will plant the seed of doubt that his legacy may be affected, even if he protests my claims, and that may be enough.

What matters more than him being punished is that he is stopped.

He must be stopped.

CHAPTER 40

Carla Crowley was waiting for them.

She had been due to pick up Lawrence Boylan. But when he hadn't rung up from the asylum to be collected, she'd realised something was wrong.

She made no attempt to deny what she'd done.

When Ray put it to her that she had helped Boylan get down there on multiple occasions, and cooked the additional food he requested, she just nodded.

'So, you know what he has been doing?' Ray said, appalled at the conspiracy.

'No.' Carla's steady eye looked straight at him. Her other eye flitted from side to side.

'What do you mean, no? You just said . . .'

'I just did what he asked me to. I always have. Is he in trouble?'

Ray and Laura looked at each other and back to the nurse.

'Who did you think all that extra food was for?' Laura asked, her voice thick with disbelief.

The nurse shrugged and pursed her lips.

'I didn't ask. My entire life I've worked for Lawrence, taken his orders. When he requests something, I just do it. In the last few months, as his illness progressed, he asked me to make up batches of puréed foods. I did think it was rather a lot but I didn't inquire as to the reason for it. And I saw nothing wrong with him wanting to visit the asylum. I suppose I presumed he preferred to work at night.'

Laura shook her head.

'No,' she said. 'You're lying to us.'

Ray clasped his hands and leaned forward.

'Three of the inmates from St Christina's are still in the basement,' he said. 'They never left. I doubt they knew it was an option. They've been down there since the asylum closed. He's been experimenting on them.'

The nurse paled. Her hands began to shake.

'No,' she said, weakly.

'Yes,' Laura answered. 'And you are an accessory by facilitating Dr Boylan. Nobody is going to believe that you had no knowledge of what was going on. Saying *I didn't ask any questions* won't get you far with a jury, Ms Crowley. So the best thing you can do now is start talking to us. Honestly. And perhaps your cooperation will be taken into consideration.'

'I . . . I didn't know.'

Carla's eyes began to water, her whole body trembling now.

'Not good enough,' Laura said.

'I didn't! I swear it. Oh, God, I knew there was something wrong. I knew something was going on. But I didn't want anything to change. You don't understand.'

'Try us,' Ray said. 'You need to tell us everything, Carla. For your sake and maybe even for Dr Boylan's.'

The nurse looked down.

'I'd do anything for him. For Lawrence. I love him. I always have. But nursing him and assisting him is as close as he's ever allowed me. I asked Lawrence to confide in me. But he wouldn't. Or couldn't, I don't know. He changed, when the visitors started to arrive.'

'What visitors?' Ray said.

'The ones who came to talk about his work. Lawrence would spend hours discussing things with them. The history of St Christina's. The medical advances he made. It was like we were back there again, like he was back in his prime. He could pretend, if even for a little while, that he was the great doctor and not a frail, old man. I was happy to see him like that. So I didn't ask any questions. You must believe me? I didn't want to know.'

'The problem is,' Laura said, 'wilful ignorance is a poor defence. I suggest you call yourself a solicitor, Ms Crowley. It's likely you'll need one.'

'Will it come to that?' Carla looked frightened now.

'Of course it will come to that. What did you think?'

'I . . . I haven't done anything wrong.'

'You know,' Laura said, 'you haven't asked us once who is in that basement.'

Carla looked at the floor.

'Who is it?'

'Rosita Moore, George Bonner and Henry Arnold.'

The nurse looked up, entirely confused.

'But that can't be right! They're dead. We buried them. You must be wrong.'

'Stupid, stupid, stupid,' Laura said, as they drove away from the nurse's cottage. 'She's obviously lying.'

Ray cocked his head and scrunched up his face.

'I don't know. People do funny things for love.'

Laura furrowed her eyebrows.

'That's not love. That's obsession. How much would she have been willing to turn a blind eye to if he'd actually loved her back? I shudder to think. She knew there was something going on in that building. She was driving him down there every other night with containers of food, for heaven's sake. And she helped medicate him to ensure he could carry on with what he was doing. That's complicity right there. She kept her mouth shut hoping to curry favour, not giving a shit at whose expense. She deserves everything she gets.'

Ray just nodded and kept quiet.

He'd noticed a change in Laura since the summer. Mostly for the better – after all, she'd admitted she was in love with him and he with her, and they were now together –but since her brush with the Sleeping Beauties killer, she'd become tougher. She'd always been more cynical than he, but she'd had more sympathy, too. That balance seemed to have faded.

It was natural, in the job they were in. He understood – a couple of years ago, he had trusted somebody; discovering how wrong he'd been had sent him into a tailspin.

But he wished Laura hadn't suffered through what she did. He would have given anything to have protected her from that.

She still had nightmares. He knew, because he often lay awake at night looking at her, thanking God she was alive.

'Am I going to like this Lane chap any better?' she asked, as Ray pulled up outside the next house.

'Absolutely not,' he said. 'Do you have any mints in this car? Anything strong smelling?'

Laura smiled, bemused.

'I've Polos in the glove compartment and a tub of Vicks. Are we calling in on a live one or a dead one?'

'Something inside him is dead and you can smell it every time he opens his mouth,' Ray explained. 'Dab some of that under your nose. You'll thank me for it.'

When Lane opened his door and bared a mouth full of yellow, decay-ridden teeth in greeting, Laura appreciated the advice.

'Sorry to call on you unannounced like this,' Ray said. 'We've had a bit of a development.'

'No problem at all,' Lane said, and stood aside for them to enter the house. In the sitting room, Ray guided Laura onto the two-seater so they'd be sitting together and not be at the mercy of Lane's personal boundary issues.

The former chemist followed and sat across from them.

'A development, eh?' he said, scratching at the bristles on his chin. 'Have you found who whacked Howe, then?'

'Have you noticed anything strange going on up at the hospital?' Ray said, getting straight to it.

'Strange? Like what?'

'Any peculiar comings and goings? Dr Boylan spending time at the asylum, stuff like that?'

Lane sat back and sucked in hollow cheeks.

'Dr Boylan? Now, why would you ask that?'

Ray sighed.

'Mr Lane. Can you answer my questions and not keep coming back with questions for me?'

The other man cackled.

'Right. Fair enough. To answer your question, I don't know. I'm not down at the asylum at all. I don't tend to see much of my neighbours either, if I'm honest. There may only be a handful of us here but that don't mean we live in each other's pockets. I had my fill of that shower when we worked together.'

'So why stay here, then?' Laura asked.

Lane looked around him.

'I live here practically rent-free in peace and solitude. And I'm a misanthrope. So shoot me.'

'You weren't aware of what Lawrence Boylan was up to in the hospital?' Ray persisted.

Lane desperately looked like he wanted to say yes, because he knew everybody's secrets. But in this instance, he couldn't.

'No. I know about some other funny goings-on on this island but not what Boylan was doing, if he were doing anything. I could tell you what he used to get up to.'

'What does that mean?'

'Boylan is no saint. He likes the finer things, don't he? You need money for the sort of life he wanted. He was good at finding it – wherever and whenever. He used to give us all a Christmas present. A bottle of Jamesons. Showing off his largesse. Well, I knew how he was buying it, where he got his money from and it weren't his wages.'

'Where was it from, then?'

'He was shaving money off the hospital budget for himself. Every month. His budget would say one thing and the actual spend would be another.'

Ray shook his head. Where the hell was Lane going with this?

'Can you explain what you mean, Mr Lane? And why didn't you mention this the last time I was here?'

'Ye never asked, did ye? You wanted to talk about Howe and Collins and all that ancient history. But now you want the dirt on Boylan and I can give it to you. I'll tell you what I mean. Cheap drugs. That's what Boylan was up to. He had this nice set up as the head doctor of this progressive institution. Well, when the rest of the world had moved on to

Chlorpromazine and Valium and Prozac in the sixties, the good doctor instructed me to keep ordering in Chloryl hydrate and bromides and barbiturates. That was what he insisted his staff continue to use to sedate their patients – even though he knew, *he knew*, that there were better drugs on the market for the treatment of psychosis. He saved a fortune, so he did. The manufacturers were thrilled to get rid of their ageing stock; they were happy to sell it on cheap.'

'And what about you?' Laura said. 'What did you get out of this? Were you pocketing money, too?'

Lane straightened up.

'How dare you? I never took a penny that wasn't mine in my life.'

'So why?' she said. 'Why facilitate Boylan, if you knew he was doing something wrong? Was he that powerful, that intimidating, that the entire bloody staff just cowered to him?'

'I didn't cower!' Lane almost shouted.

'Mr Lane,' Ray said, holding up a warning hand. 'Do you not understand what you've just told us? You've admitted to helping Dr Boylan skim from private funds. You must have had a reason to follow his orders, if it wasn't for your own financial benefit?'

Lane looked sideways, out the window.

'I had to keep my job, didn't I? That bastard Howe went complaining about me administering drugs to the patients and Boylan said if I didn't fill out the order forms as he instructed, he'd sack me. '

The chemist looked down at his fingers, winding them in and out of each other.

'I didn't intend any harm. I knew those poor creatures were

going down to that operating theatre barely out of it and that, afterwards, when they were in pain, the rubbish they were getting was barely sufficient. I was only trying to top them up. I knew what I were doing. I wasn't some amateur experimenting on them.'

Ray rubbed his jaw and stared at the chemist.

Could he have got this man wrong? Was the seemingly most unpleasant resident on the island perhaps the one who had tried to be the kindest to those who'd suffered in St Christina's? Or was he spinning his role in events?

'You said something else,' Laura said. 'You said you knew about funny things going on here on the island, but not to do with Dr Boylan?'

'Aye. Well. I'd be afraid to open my mouth now. You might arrest me for withholding knowledge or whatever the correct term is. Seems I can't do right for doing wrong. Any time I try to tell the truth, I'm the one that gets in trouble.'

'You're not going to get in trouble with us for telling the truth,' Ray said. 'Not unless you've willingly been involved in the commission of a crime. Please, Mr Lane.'

'Hmm. Well, it's Arnie Nolan, isn't it? He's been stripping the hospital of copper and valuables and anything else he can take. He's selling it on the mainland. Little shit doesn't think anybody knows but I've seen him and Mannix loading that ferry the first Tuesday of every month. It's when I go to visit my sister. Big bloody boxes and Mannix gives him a brown envelope every time. He dropped one a few months ago and the thing opened. Loads of those old medical tomes that collectors buy. I realised then what was going on. You wrecked it for him this month, coming over on that ferry yesterday.'

So, Tom had been right. Arnie had been up to something.

And with him down at the asylum all the time, surely he couldn't have been ignorant to Boylan's frequent visits, nor to what was happening in the basement.

Exactly how many people on Oileán na Coillte, Ray wondered, had known what was going in St Christina's, and turned a blind eye for their own benefit?

CHAPTER 41

'I have been kind to them. That's what you don't realise. If they had been moved to one of the large hospitals on the mainland they would have become anonymous, don't you see? I gave them my personal care and expertise – me, a leading expert in the field of mental health. I'm still a qualified doctor. I renew my medical cert when necessary. I haven't done anything wrong. They are my patients.'

Tom felt his jaw clench. He turned to Linda and gave his head a little shake. He was struggling to stay calm in the face of such obstinate denial. She had to take the reins and give him a moment to compose himself.

Linda placed her hands on the table, palms up. Accepting, understanding.

'Dr Boylan. I hear what you're saying. But what you did is still completely illegal. You registered their deaths. My colleagues found the death certificates in your office. You created a whole fiction about their burial on the island. And more. You tortured them. You submitted them to repeated medical trauma, unnecessarily. They are all underweight, severely lacking in several vitamins, dehydrated. Their nervous systems are barely functioning. They have bedsores. They live every day of their lives in pain and fear, and for what? You have not been their doctor. You are their persecutor.'

'No!' Boylan tried to slap his hand on the table but the movement was weak. 'It wasn't to harm them. It was to try to cure them. They would have been living miracles. If their psychosis had been beaten, it would have been written about in journals and papers all over the world. And even if it couldn't be done, they were better here, with me. How would their lives have been improved had they moved? They've always been here. This is their home. I am their protector, not their abuser.'

'If you felt that way, why did you fake their deaths?' Linda said. 'You hid them away. The asylum trustees were happy to let patients stay on who didn't want to leave – there was no need for the subterfuge unless you wanted to perform illegal procedures on them.'

Boylan opened and closed his mouth. He had no answer.

'You're quite mad,' Tom said. 'Madder, possibly, than anybody you've ever treated. You tried to burn those poor people to death last night. Your wards. You left them shackled to their beds and set a fire to kill them.'

Boylan's shoulders slumped.

'It was to bring an end to it. To give them relief. They'd have died from the smoke inhalation first. I made sure of it, by lighting the fire so far away. I didn't want to do it. I had to.'

'Jesus. Only somebody with a sick and twisted mind could even conceive of that as charitable. Wouldn't it have been cleaner to do what you did with Howe? Choke them to death with wire?'

Tom sensed a change in the doctor. He'd been caught red-handed trying to murder three people. There was no denying his involvement. But his posture altered when the inspector mentioned Howe.

He was going to deny it, Tom realised.

Why? What would be the point, now, after all this time and with so much guilt on his hands anyway? Did he think his sentence would be lighter if the charges against him were merely for imprisonment and attempted murder rather than actual murder?

'Howe,' Boylan spat. 'I didn't kill him.'

Tom felt like his whole body was about to cave from tiredness. To come this far and be denied at the last hurdle.

'Of course you killed him,' he sighed. 'You, or somebody you asked to do it. Maybe you didn't want to get your hands dirty. Perhaps your method of killing is the more cowardly hit and run, like that fire you started.'

'I did not kill him. You think Howe was an innocent. A slaughtered lamb. My God, you have no idea.'

'We already know you hated him. And he hated you, by the sound of things. He confronted you, didn't he? About what you'd been doing to the patients. He confronted you, so you killed him.'

'Confront me? What are you talking about, man? I was Howe's mentor. I guided him as a student. He respected me. Yes, we differed on the outcomes for patients but that was the extent of it. Howe had many enemies on this island but I wasn't one of them.'

Boylan shook his head, slowly, with great effort.

'I didn't kill Conrad Howe. If you think that, Inspector, then you have a long, long way to go in your investigation. A long way.'

'He has no remorse,' Tom said, amazed. 'Absolutely none. The way he speaks about his victims – it's incomprehensible. I don't know. Maybe he'll start to see how serious this all is when he's banged up in a cell over in Kerry jail. Imagine, eighty-two years of age, dying from cancer, and living out your last days in jail.'

'And still denying his role in Conrad Howe's death,' Linda added. 'Even now, he won't give the man's widow some peace. You are right, by the way. I suspect he is absolutely insane. Clinically so. And also, looking at him, that he'll be dead before there's ever a trial.'

'And what of his victims?' Tom asked. 'What's the latest there?'

Linda clicked her tongue.

'Well, unfortunately, there was an element of truth in what Boylan said. To move them now would be a cruelty. The paramedics are in the process of stabilising them and they've been made as comfortable as possible. A full care unit is en route from Kerry General. But it will be a while before they will be in a position to be moved, weeks even. And when it happens, we will have to sedate them and hope the shock of waking up in different environs doesn't result in heart attacks. Their bodies are so weak, Tom. It's a miracle they're alive. In some awful way, he actually was caring for them. Quite well, in fact. It's not unusual for people to be cared for into their old age in psychiatric institutions but considering what they've been through, they should be dead.'

The inspector said nothing. It was mid afternoon and already the light was starting to fade from the day. He hadn't eaten since last night and, just to remind him, the hunger pangs made themselves heard.

'Let's get some food into you before we move onto Collins and O'Hare,' Linda said. 'What do you plan on asking them? Do you think they might have known what he was doing?'

'I don't know, is the honest answer. It was Collins who alerted us to the fact there was nothing structurally wrong with the basement. That was all Boylan's creation. He obviously wanted to prevent the hospital being knocked for as long as possible. At the same time, for decades he'd been telling the people with access to the building that the basement was off-limits. We were down there the other day, Linda. Just think of it. A few corridors away from the three of them.'

'I know it, Tom. I wondered why we hadn't heard them but my colleagues tell me there are a lot of sedatives down there. He was obviously keeping them out of it when we were on the island. He wasn't expecting you back yesterday. It must have shocked him, when you arrived unexpectedly. By the way, do you really think Arnie Nolan didn't know? Or his father before him?'

Again, Tom found himself shrugging.

'No. I can't believe they didn't. And if they did know, there must be a reason they chose to ignore it or let it continue. Money, probably. It will come out now, anyway. Everything the people on this island have been hiding will come out. Including who murdered Howe. I just don't know if it's as straightforward as it being Boylan. I want it to be but something doesn't fit. Something about that diary. Boylan as Howe's killer jars with me.'

'Hang on,' Linda said. She walked to the door. 'Officer Fleming, is it? Would you be so kind as to secure some food for me and the inspector?'

The lad nodded, then looked blank, wondering where the hell he'd rustle up lunch on the island.

'There's a local woman, Kitty Nolan,' Linda said, seeing his face. 'She's probably down in her son's house at the pier, wondering what all the commotion is. Ring your colleagues there and get one of them to pass on the message. Say Linda McCarn asked if she could make up a couple of sandwiches and that we'd be very grateful.'

The young officer nodded more confidently this time. That, he could do.

'So, do you think Collins or O'Hare might be involved?' Linda said, returning to the conversation.

Tom placed his fingers to his temples and rubbed. The hunger was giving him a headache.

'Yes. Perhaps. It would sit better with me, I think. And I won't feel comfortable until we know for certain what happened to Dolores O'Sullivan and Owen Reid. Something in my gut tells me they're involved. Ray thought Rosita might have been Dolores but of course, now I think of it, we should have realised immediately that it couldn't have been her.'

'Why's that?'

'Her face. We only saw it fleetingly, but according to the diary, Dolores sustained bad burns in a fire.'

'Another fire?'

'Yes, but started by a patient that time.'

'Are you sure?'

Tom raised his eyebrows.

'No. No, I'm not sure. We only have hearsay to go on.'

'You know what's very sad about Boylan's victims, Tom? I mean, aside from what they've gone through all these years?'

'What?'

Linda folded her arms across her thin frame.

'According to those files you brought back, Rosita was admitted to St Christina's because her parents believed she *had a want in her.* The family probably wanted rid of this independent young thing with a tongue she couldn't keep in her head. George seems to be bipolar. And Henry. Christ. He's an epileptic. That was his "insanity". Rather than his seizures being treated, he has been subjected to a lifetime of forced seizures. Did you see the lacerations around his mouth? That was him biting through his gums during ECT.'

'He recorded it in his file. Boylan. Administration of ECT. Frequently.'

Linda sighed.

'These days, all those men would have been given is the minimum of care and medication, and less than that in Rosita's case.'

Tom felt the acid in his empty stomach rise. He put his head in his hands. 'No more, Linda. I can't. I can't bear it.'

'Nor me,' she said and placed a hand on his shoulder. 'But we must. They did.'

The young officer arrived back to tell them he'd sorted a late lunch.

Tom had lost his appetite.

CHAPTER 42

Nobody could fake that shock. That's what the inspector hoped. Robert O'Hare was either telling the truth or he was a complete psychopath.

The doctor had spent more or less the whole short interview with his mouth hanging open.

'I had no idea,' he kept repeating.

'At one point, Rosita, George and Henry were in your charge,' Tom sighed, exasperated. Was everybody on this island going to plead ignorance? 'All you doctors stayed on Oileán na Coillte because you volunteered to care for the patients who didn't want to leave. Surely three couldn't go missing without your knowledge?'

'They didn't go missing,' O'Hare insisted, shaking his head. He'd arrived at the hospital with his old doctor's case, thinking, because of the urgency of the call, that somebody had been hurt. He sat with it still, resting on his lap, hands clasped around its front. His lifeline. He was sweating profusely, though it was cold, and his large pudding face was red and glistening. 'They died. Dr Boylan certified their deaths. I helped carry the coffins out to the hearse, each time. We had a funeral vehicle in those days. We drove them to the cemetery. We buried them.'

'You buried them?'

'Yes. In the cemetery.'

'Right,' Tom said. 'And just how, exactly, did these supposed bodies get from their beds in the hospital wards to the coffins? Who performed the death rituals, embalmed the bodies, that sort of thing?'

'Dr Boylan.'

'On his own? Was he moonlighting as an undertaker?'

'It's not a joke, Inspector.'

'I'm not laughing,' Tom said. He hadn't smiled once in the last sixteen hours. Not since he'd seen Boylan's victims.

'We were all capable of readying a body for burial. We had to be, in the hospital. Back then, there were whole weeks when people couldn't travel to and from the island, when the ferry couldn't cross if it got too bad. And the village undertaker would never come across. He wouldn't set foot on the island. We had an onsite undertaker for a good many years but he was gone by the time we'd the last of the patients. Lawrence would have been more than capable of doing what was necessary.'

'So he did that, three times, on his own and nobody suspected a thing?'

'They were . . . the three of them had been in the hospital their whole lives. When we agreed to stay on and care for the ones who remained, we knew we were just caring for them until their deaths. There were no more treatments to perform in those days, just prescriptions for various drugs. And he wasn't on his own. He had help.'

'Who?'

'Carla.'

Tom sat back and nodded, slowly. Carla's name was recorded as a witness on the death certificates they'd found.

'My colleagues rang a short time ago, following an interview with Carla Crowley. She claimed, like you, that Boylan's victims were already dead. She didn't let on she knew anything different.'

'Well, either she's not being truthful or she agreed to back Lawrence without seeing the bodies. He needed a second person to record their deaths. Either way, you should be talking to her.'

'Hmm. How many patients stayed on in total?' Tom asked.

'There were twenty in all. They all died here. They were all buried here. Their families were long gone or had long forgotten them. But now you're telling me three of them are still alive? I can't believe it. I just can't . . . can I see them? I can help.'

O'Hare sat forward, nodding at his bag.

'I'm a doctor. I can assess them.'

'They've been assessed,' Tom said, coolly. He still didn't know if he could believe O'Hare. An idea was forming – one that could let him check the veracity of what the doctor was saying. But should he? Would it be ethical?

Linda touched his elbow.

'Perhaps, Inspector, if Dr O'Hare was to just look in on the patients. He knew them when they were here. He could confirm their identities. I could go down with him?'

Tom raised an eyebrow. She'd read his mind. If O'Hare had been near the three in the basement over the last few years, they would react to him in some manner, good or bad. And in the inspector's head, he still felt they were looking for a second player in this case. He wasn't sure it was Carla Crowley.

'Yes,' Tom said. 'That might be a good idea. We need their IDs verified.'

Linda gave him a brief nod as she stood up, a look of understanding passing between them.

She and O'Hare left just as Ray and Laura arrived back.

'Well?' Tom asked. They'd spoken briefly earlier; now it was time for the full rundown.

'Carla knew,' Ray said. 'She knew but claims she didn't know. She was running him down here for his nightly visits, making up the food and so on. But she never came in. She has deniability. I'm not sure if she's actually committed a crime.'

'She has,' Tom said. 'She helped him forge their death certs. Her signature is on the ones we found in the hospital files and O'Hare is under the impression she helped Boylan embalm Rosita, George and Henry's bodies. She shouldn't have signed them. O'Hare, on the other hand, says he only saw closed caskets. He helped transport them to the cemetery.'

'Have we put in a request for an excavation order?' Laura asked.

'I have. The warrant is being sent across. It will be interesting to see what or who is actually in those coffins.'

'That's what I was thinking,' she said.

'And, with his illness, there had to have been times when he couldn't come down here, or see to his victims' needs. She might have stepped in then.'

'That makes sense,' Ray said. 'By the way, you were right about Arnie Nolan.'

They told the inspector what Lane had revealed.

Tom tutted.

'Idiot. His mother will kill him. You know, I think she might be the only one on this island who's not been trying to pull the wool over our eyes?'

'I'm not sure about that,' Ray said.

'You think Kitty has secrets?' Tom asked, surprised.

'No. I don't think she's the only honest one on the island. I think I got Edward Lane wrong. I think he might be okay, if a little flawed. So, are you going to speak to Andrew Collins now?'

'Yes. Why don't you go and have a chat with Arnie? I've a bad feeling he knew what was going on here, too. Or something of it. Boylan may have found out what he was up to in the hospital and blackmailed him into keeping his mouth shut. You look one way and I'll look the other, that sort of thing. Have you eaten, by the way?'

'No.'

'Kitty sent up enough sandwiches to feed an army. Get stuck in, then go quiz her son.'

'Sorry about your car. We needed a vehicle . . . in a hurry.'

The inspector slipped into the chair in front of Andrew Collins. He ran his finger around the rim of his suit jacket collar and rubbed his eyes. One of the uniforms had sourced a couple of old Superser heaters and hauled them up to the asylum. The patients downstairs and Tom's interview room were the first to benefit. The inspector had gone from freezing to boiling and his eyes were itching from the fumes, but he wasn't complaining.

'I was surprised when I woke this morning to find it and yourselves missing,' Andrew said. 'It isn't what you expect to happen when you invite policemen to stay in your home. A quick check, though, and I could see no other valuables had been taken.'

Andrew attempted a half-smile. He kept tugging at the ends of his beard, nervously, unable to sit still.

'I can't believe it, Inspector. I wasn't here when any of them . . . when Boylan said they died. I didn't think anything of it. They were among the last. At that point it was really only Boylan and Carla working up here. There was no need for the rest of us. And I was over in Dublin, mostly.'

Quick to lay out his defence, Tom thought. Collins felt guilty. But for what? His absence? Or his involvement?

'Did you suspect something was going on here?' the inspector asked. 'Is that why you kept returning? Is it why you maintained the cottage here?'

Andrew shook his head.

'I'd like to claim I was that observant, but sadly, no. I didn't maintain a presence on the island to conduct a private investigation or to monitor Boylan. Believe me, Inspector. After what I saw happen over the years in this building, if I'd thought for one second there was something amiss, I would have been down here like a shot. I would not have allowed Boylan to get away with this. I already have too many sins on my conscience. No. I avoided this place. To my shame, I avoided it.'

Andrew looked at the walls around him. They were sat in Howe's former office, closest to the basement.

'I want to believe you,' Tom said. 'I want to believe you didn't know what was going on downstairs. You would hardly have made me aware of the lie about the foundations if you'd been involved. But there *is* something you haven't been entirely truthful about.'

Andrew straightened in his chair.

'What's that?'

'What are you not telling me about Conrad Howe, Andrew?'

The other man blushed.

'I don't know what you mean.'

'I think you do. When I spoke to you in Miriam Howe's home

the other day, we discussed your feelings for her. You began to say something about Conrad – that sometimes you suspected he . . . then you trailed off. Finish the sentence.'

Andrew closed his eyes. He sighed.

When he opened them, he looked defeated.

'We were in college together. We weren't close. Miriam always thought Conrad and I were friends because that's how we presented ourselves to her. Amiable, jokey, nice fellows. We were rivals. I saw her first. This tall, graceful beauty. She was unlike anybody I'd ever met, even then, at sixteen. I fell for her. Harder than I'd ever fallen for anyone or anything in my life, including medicine. Conrad – he was handsome and charming and popular. He could have had any girl he met. He was even courting another young woman at the time. I think he saw how I looked at Miriam and he took her. Just because he could. To hurt me.'

'Did you hate Conrad Howe?'

'Yes.' The short word came out as a long breath, a release.

'Because he stole the love of your life, even though she wasn't aware?'

'There was more.' Andrew blushed. 'When you say it like that, it makes me sound like a halfwit. I loved her but I know what true love is. It's allowing somebody to be happy. If she had been truly happy, I would have learned to live with it. If they had enjoyed their life together. But I offered him the job here and he took it so quickly. He leapt at it. He couldn't wait to be on a campus with me again, competing. Conrad ran from Miriam and then from the children. And I suspected . . .'

'What? Andrew, look at me. What did you suspect?'

The doctor made a steeple with his hands and rested his chin on his fingertips.

'I suspected he was unfaithful to her. Every nurse in this place hero-worshipped Howe. I think he might have . . . taken advantage of it.'

Tom blew out his cheeks. Every time he scratched at the open wound of this island's history, it gave up more pus.

'Are you positive about that or is it your dislike of the man speaking? Did you have any proof?'

'No, but he was especially close to one or two of the nurses. The senior nurse – Dolores. I saw them whispering together. A lot. Blushing, like they had secrets. I don't know, maybe she made him feel special, but I got the sense with Dolores that that was her way. She was the flirty type. Strict with the patients but manipulative with the doctors. She even tried it on with me. This was before her accident, of course. That put an end to the charm offensives.'

'You mean when half her face was burned off?'

Andrew looked up. While he'd been speaking, it looked like he'd drifted, back to the time when all of it had happened. Tom thought his opinion on Dolores was unnecessarily harsh. Had he wanted this Dolores woman and been jealous of a friendship she had with Howe? Yet another woman Howe had taken from him?

'Did you kill Conrad?' the inspector asked.

'No. I swear I didn't.'

'But you wanted to.'

Andrew blinked.

'Maybe. Sometimes. Yes. But I didn't kill him.'

'Who did then?'

'I don't know. I genuinely do not know. If you'd known Conrad like I did, Inspector, you would never have imagined somebody murdering him. He was too confident. Too alive. Too arrogant. Always thought he was right. He got away with what he did to Miriam because of that personality.

'He got away with everything until he got his come-uppance.'

CHAPTER 43

Linda, Ray and Laura arrived back in Howe's former office at the same time.

'That ferry is coming back in an hour,' Ray said. 'Are we leaving on it or are we staying again?'

Tom rubbed at his beard.

'I don't know,' he said. 'I just don't know. I feel like I'm not finished on this island. There's something . . .' he shook his head. He couldn't articulate whatever was plaguing him. And he wasn't entirely sure he was being logical. He'd left the other day feeling unsettled about the screams they'd heard the previous night. And it turned out he'd been right to suspect there was more at play on the island. If they hadn't returned, Boylan's victims would have died an ugly death. Was that why he was unsure about leaving now? In case they missed something else?

'What happened when you brought O'Hare down to the basement, Linda?' he asked.

'Nothing. I couldn't see anything in the three that would lead me to think they remembered O'Hare, even from years ago. They reacted like he was another stranger. He seemed very distressed when he saw them. They look a bit better. It looks more like a proper hospital room down there now. But it's still disturbing.'

Tom nodded.

'And Arnie?'

Ray and Laura looked at each other. She went first.

'He folded as soon as we put it to him. He was drinking when we arrived and ready to make a confession. He knew it was coming to an end. He's not a criminal mastermind, by any stretch. But he has been robbing from the building for years. Says he knew the caretaking wouldn't last and he was trying to get a fund together, just taking what was owed. He claims he didn't know exactly what Boylan was up to but knew there was something going on. Boylan knew about the stealing and told Arnie that if he wanted to keep his job and his home, not to mention prevent his mother from finding out, he'd keep his nose out of the doctor's business.'

'That all sounds about right,' Tom said. 'I'd mark him down as stupid rather than bad. But he'll still have to answer for the robberies and for turning a blind eye. Boylan hasn't said anything more?'

'Not that our colleagues in Kerry are reporting.'

The inspector sighed.

'What else?' he said. 'What are we missing? There's something. I can smell it. There's no reason for Boylan to keep denying his role in Howe's death.'

'There's no *reason* for what he did in that basement,' Ray pointed out.

'No,' Linda said. 'In his head, there's a twisted logic to that. Tom is right. Boylan is not stupid. If he murdered Howe, he's only refusing to tell us in order to keep something else hidden. Maybe he murdered another person and we don't know about it yet.'

'We stay,' Tom decided. 'We stay until those graves are exhumed. There's a team coming over in the morning. Let's see what's in those coffins. And let's sleep on what we found out today, see if anything comes to us. Shit!' He slapped his hand on the table.

'What?' Laura said.

'I meant to ask Boylan about the screaming the other night. It came from outside the hospital. So what was he doing?'

Ray nodded.

'You're right. Was he trying to move them? But how . . .'

'How could an eighty-two-year-old man move three bed-ridden patients? Exactly. We need to ring over to the mainland and get them to ask him.'

Linda shook her head.

'There's no point until the morning. Boylan has been hospitalised – in a proper hospital, I mean. He's drugged up to the eyeballs. That's what I meant when I said he hadn't said anything to our Kerry colleagues.'

Tom swore.

'Right, well, in the morning then. But that just proves it. We still don't have the full story of what is going on here and we're not leaving until we do.'

'So, which suspect are we staying with tonight?' Linda asked.

'We don't have to stay with any of them,' Ray answered. 'Let's stay where Emmet's team were put up.'

'You're a killjoy, Ray,' Tom said. 'Right, let's stay there. And before the exhumation in the morning I want to get back up to that cottage on the headland where Collins saw Howe fighting with Reid. I just want to look inside and see if there's anything there.'

'Like what?' Ray asked.

'I'm not sure,' Tom answered. 'Like, maybe Owen Reid in hiding. You never know. Maybe his family was right, that all this time he's being working as an orderly in St Christina's. Perhaps that's what Boylan is keeping quiet about.'

CHAPTER 44

Diary Entry

I confronted him.

It went as well as can be expected. He threatened me. Tried to intimidate me. I finally saw what his patients see. Not a man. A monster.

I am still shaking and I do not scare easy. But I stood my ground. He tried to attack me but I fought back, even though I was injured. I gave as good as I got.

I told him he might have the rest of the world fooled, but not me.

I've given him his options.

I had planned to go home for Christmas anyway but it is my intention, if he takes what I have said seriously, to also leave permanently. I have drafted a letter of resignation and told Dolores what I have planned.

I have one final meeting with him to see what his answer is.

He is convinced he has done nothing wrong. He even asked me for proof of my assertions.

I have it. I have noted everything in this diary, but more importantly, I know where he keeps the private records for the procedures he performs. When I return home next week, I will bring the diary with me and hide it. The only person I will tell of its whereabouts is Dolores. If anything happens to me, she can read it and bring my full suspicions to the attention of the police.

I think, when I return to my old life, I will move on from Dolores. I will try to forget the feelings I have for her, the ones that crept up on me so unexpectedly. It's for the best if we all move on from this without looking back.

And so it is. The dice have been cast.

We will see where they fall.

CHAPTER 45

The view of the Atlantic from the cottage on the clifftop was magnificent.

But that was all there was to see.

Tom and Ray had driven out first thing to the old house to scout around. They'd found an empty shell, with holes in the roof and birds' nests in the walls. There was certainly no sign of anybody having lived there, secretly or not, for a good many years.

'No Owen Reid, anyway,' Ray said, coming carefully down the rickety stairs.

'No,' Tom agreed. 'Let's go out to this graveyard and see if he found somewhere more permanent to rest.'

'Why are you so convinced he has something to do with this? There were plenty more people working here that we still haven't found – that doesn't mean they were involved in some way.'

Tom hesitated at the door and rubbed the back of his neck. It was sore from the tension. He felt like he was carrying every unanswered question slap bang between his shoulder blades. He reached into his coat pocket and fished out the cigar he had tucked in there. When he had it lit, he stood at the cottage window, looking out at the sea, and puffed – the tension easing in his joints with each mouthful of smoke.

'It's Reid and Dolores leaving on the 24th,' he said. 'I finished Howe's diary last night. The last entry is very disturbing. He was desperate to get off this island, to get away from every-thing. It was definitely a doctor he suspected and we can be certain now that it was Boylan. But did Boylan have it in him to kill Howe? Howe was a young, fit man. Fair enough, Boylan would have only been forty-two himself, but he's not a big man. And Howe would have been on his guard around the man he was confronting. In a straight fight, could Boylan take him? In the second-to-last entry, Howe says he'd already confronted the doctor and been attacked. I presume that's when his arm was broken. But he gave as good as he got. The only way I can see him being compromised and strangled like that is if Boylan took him by surprise, or had him taken by surprise. For the lat-ter, he would have needed help.

'He said he planned to hide the diary and tell only Dolores of its location. If Boylan suspected Dolores knew what Howe was up to, maybe he sent Reid off to sort her out too, as well as giv-ing him a route off the island for good. Her family says she came home but then they didn't see her again. Reid might have followed her.'

'We should read his file,' Ray said. 'His staff file, I mean. See if there's anything in his past that would indicate violence – a criminal record of some sort. I'm not entirely sure that would have stood against him getting a job out here. Also, the file might shed new light on where he might have gone, if it wasn't to his family. All Laura did was try to find his whereabouts now, but there might be something more in his records to help.'

'You're right. We'll go back to the hospital after the exhuma-tion and see if there's anything there.'

Activity was already afoot when they arrived at the old

cemetery on the west of the island. It wasn't a huge distance from Andrew Collins' cottage and he emerged as he heard the car approach.

'I see you're out joyriding again, Inspector,' he said, when Tom rolled down the window.

'Not likely with this lad,' Tom said. 'His idea of speeding is sixty-one in a sixty zone. We've commandeered one of our detective's cars this time.'

'There were a couple of vehicles along the road before you. One of them looked like it had serious equipment in the back. What are you doing?'

'Just digging up more ghosts. We're exhuming graves.'

Andrew's face blanched.

'God almighty. Why would you do that?'

'Boylan buried something in those three coffins. We want to find out what.'

'I . . . I see. Sorry, I'm just shocked. It seems like such an unholy thing to do. Wouldn't he have just stuck rocks in the coffins or something?'

'We have to find out for sure,' Tom said.

'I'll let you go, so.'

He stood away from the car, his face still worried.

'A bit nervous, isn't he?' Ray said.

'He is a bit,' Tom said, watching Collins slope off back into his house.

Laura was overseeing the operation at the graveyard.

The place already looked like a bomb had hit. The inspector could see beyond the debris – the cemetery, before they'd ridden in, had been old and pretty, with small headstones partially covered in moss and lichen, the greenest of grass, and wildflowers sprawling over the stone wall that surrounded the yard. A peaceful place.

Now, a small digger was positioned on one side of the yard. A mound of muck had been heaped by another. A satellite forensics unit was assisting three men who were hoisting the first of the coffins from the disturbed earth.

The headstones had directed them immediately to the patients' alleged graves.

'He went all out with the charade,' Ray said. 'And meanwhile, he was colouring in a different picture in the records.'

'He's a bizarre character,' Tom nodded.

They waited until the coffin was on solid ground before approaching.

'Do you want us to open her up now, Inspector Reynolds?' one of the forensics officers asked.

'Go for it,' Tom said.

His stomach clenched as the officer broke the seal on the coffin and forced open the lid.

'Christ!' the officer said, standing back.

'What is it?' Tom asked, coming closer.

'Rocks. Is that what you were expecting?'

'We weren't sure what we were expecting.'

Tom looked in at the bed of rocks in the base of the coffin, packed tightly so they wouldn't rattle. Just like Andrew Collins had suggested. Boylan had thought of everything.

'Are we still bringing up the other two?' the grave-digging team asked.

Tom nodded.

'Please.'

It took just under two hours to exhume the other graves.

The second coffin bore the same cargo as the first.

When it came to opening the third, everybody was tense. There was a feeling that this one could be the one to contain something more unexpected. A body, for instance.

'Open it,' Tom said, giving the forensics officer the nod.

The man had raised the lid a couple of inches when a vehicle came screeching down the road towards the cemetery.

'Shit-fuck-shit!'

The howled curses came from the poor sod as he dropped the heavy lid with a bang and trapped his fingers.

The inspector took a quick look at the oncoming vehicle before falling to his knees and getting a grip under the lid so the man could slide his fingers out.

'Broken?' Tom asked.

'Just bruised, I'd say,' the other man winced, clasping his hands to his chest. 'The coffins are cheap and it was just the tips.'

One of his colleagues fell into position beside the inspector as the injured party stepped back.

The car came to a halt outside the graveyard.

Some instinct told Tom they had to get the coffin open quickly, before the car's owner descended on them.

'Now,' he said to the woman beside him.

Together, they lifted the lid.

Inside, there were more rocks.

'How dare you!'

Kitty Nolan marched towards Tom, her face roaring red with rage.

Where she wasn't red, she was white – covered in flour, in fact. Whatever she'd come to say, she'd broken away from a massive baking session to do it.

'Mrs Nolan . . .' Tom began.

'Don't you *Mrs Nolan* me. You've had my son arrested. And

now you're committing this sacrilege! Digging up bodies and tearing the cemetery apart.' She looked around her, then howled, pointing at the mound of muck spilling over from the wall.

'That's my Enda's grave! Have you dug up my Enda? How could you?'

'Kitty,' Tom said, louder, trying to be gentle and forceful at once. 'We haven't gone near Enda's grave. The only coffins we're looking at are the supposed coffins of the three people we found imprisoned in the hospital basement. Are you listening to me?'

Kitty had been wringing her hands at her bosom, her distress obvious. She stopped when the impact of Tom's words hit.

'We had to see what Boylan had buried, do you understand? We needed to find out if he'd murdered somebody else and buried them. We still don't know what happened to Dolores O'Sullivan.'

The old woman dropped her hands, her mouth forming an astounded O.

'You think Dr Boylan murdered Dolores O'Sullivan? Are you completely mad? Dolores idolised Dr Boylan. The only person on the staff who couldn't stand Dolores was Dr Collins. And that's because he thought – well we all did – that Dr Howe was getting his leg over with her. I don't know, maybe he was jealous or something. Why on earth would you think Dr Boylan would kill her? Why do you even think she's dead?'

CHAPTER 46

'Let's get both their files out, then.'

Tom walked straight to the filing cabinet where the staff records were kept.

'Owen Reid's and Dolores O'Sullivan's. They were here, weren't they, Ray?'

'Yep. Second drawer down. Take this coffee, Tom, before it goes cold.'

Ray held out a mug from the flask they'd brought down to the hospital.

The inspector took the cup and sipped distractedly.

'Collins is still in his cottage, isn't he?' he asked, as he flicked through the files.

'Still there and we've a uniform keeping watch. But you've something else on your mind, haven't you?'

Ray and Laura's eyes met. They both knew when their boss was close to arriving at a conclusion in a case. He disappeared into his own mind. Talked less and mumbled more. Which was what he was doing right now.

'They're not here,' he said, putting down the coffee and practically climbing into the back of the drawer.

'What?' Laura asked.

Tom didn't answer. Instead he opened the drawer underneath

the one he'd been looking in and started sifting through that. Frustration growing, he opened the one above.

'They're gone,' he said, throwing his hands in the air. He started to pull out the drawers from the cabinet before placing them on the floor.

'Their files?' Ray said, kneeling on the ground.

'Of course their bloody files.' Tom got on all fours and looked into the hollow of the now empty cabinet. 'They haven't fallen out, anyway. Let's go through them separately in case I overlooked them. But I can't see how I'd have missed both.'

'What's in these other cabinets?' Laura asked.

'More records,' Ray said. 'These drawers covered all the staff from the 1960s to the 1970s.'

'Should we start looking through those as well in case the ones we're looking for were misplaced?'

Tom and Ray looked at each other. They knew that wasn't what had happened.

'They've been removed,' Ray said.

Tom nodded.

'Somebody has taken them,' he said. 'Shit.'

'What exactly are you looking for, though,' Laura said, opening one of the other cabinets. 'The whole file or just the names, addresses and personal info?'

'The whole files, but anything would help. Why do you ask that? Have you found something?'

'I haven't even started to look. But you faxed me the top sheets of their files the other day, remember? That's how I tracked down most of the family members – through the old addresses.'

'Of course!' Tom slapped his forehead with the palm of his

hand. 'Well, let's get those pages back, at least. Who's in the office today?'

'Michael's in,' Laura said. 'I'll ring him.'

Laura got Michael Geoghegan on the phone and told him where the pages were on her desk, explaining about the antique fax machine in Tom's office.

They waited, drinking their coffee, for the machine to come to life at their end. In the distance, they could hear doors opening and shutting, muted conversations. The asylum was alive again. Linda had returned to Dublin that morning, but the psychiatrist from the central mental hospital, and the medical team, would be staying until the patients could be moved.

A whirring sound started up over by the fax machine and Ray walked over to it.

'It's asking if I want to accept a document?'

'Hit OK,' Tom said.

The pages came through at a snail's pace.

'Here's Reid's, anyway,' Ray said. 'He's filled in his name, age, address, DOB and religion. There's nothing else. The rest of the pages must have contained the references and work history. We're going to have to find those original files.'

Tom took the page. He started to read the details, then stopped just as he got to Reid's DOB.

'No,' he said. His heart thumped in his chest. 'It can't be.'

'What is it?' Laura said, taking the second page from the fax.

The words swam in front of the inspector's eyes as he swallowed. He was seeing things, surely? Tiredness maybe, though he'd slept fine last night and the coffee had given him a further boost. He blinked. He wasn't mistaken.

He put the page down on the desk and rested his hands on either side of it, looking calmer than he felt.

'When you were talking to Carla yesterday, what did she say about Boylan's visitors?'

Laura scrunched up her forehead as she tried to remember the exact words.

'She said that they'd brought Boylan back to life. That it was like he was back in his prime, the head doctor again, when they started to come over.'

'Did she say who they were?'

'No.'

'Sex, age, anything?'

'No, but we can ring her . . .'

'Why?' Ray asked. 'Do you know who they were?'

'I think I do,' Tom said. 'And I've a feeling they're in Boylan's house right now. We need to get down there.'

Ray frowned.

'It's not . . . It's not Reid and Dolores, is it? Is that what you think?'

'Let's just go,' Tom said. 'I won't believe this until I see it with my own eyes.'

Two squad cars accompanied the detectives to Boylan's house.

'You two go round the back,' Tom issued orders to the officers in the first car. 'And you pair come with us. We'll search the building systematically. If I'm correct, we're dealing with a man and a woman in their late sixties, early seventies. But they're still dangerous, so be careful.'

'Do you really think you're right?' Ray said, when the uniforms were out of earshot and it was just himself and Laura with the inspector. 'That the three of them were in on it together?'

'I'm as amazed as you,' Tom said. 'But, yes. It makes sense.

And it also means Carla Crowley knows more than she's letting on. Dolores O'Sullivan is distinctive-looking, because of those facial injuries. Carla couldn't have seen her and not known who it was.'

Ray nodded. It still seemed ludicrous to him but if Tom was certain, he believed him.

'Yesterday, I thought I heard a noise upstairs,' the inspector said, when they were standing in the hall. 'And now I suspect it wasn't just you, Ray. I'd been through all the rooms so it could only have come from overhead. The attic in this place must be huge. But how do you get into it? I didn't see any access point.'

'A house this size,' Laura suggested, 'would have a walk-in staircase. One of the rooms upstairs must lead to it. Let's look.'

They headed up to the first floor and split up, making their way around the bedrooms until Ray called for them.

'This door is locked,' he said. 'Was it locked yesterday?'

'Yes,' Tom said, remembering. 'But I thought it was just an airing cupboard or something. It seems too narrow to lead to a room.'

'A room, maybe,' Laura said. 'But a staircase, perhaps. Let's see Boylan's keys again.'

Ray took out the ring and they went through the keys until they found the one that fit the lock. He shoved it in, only to hear a clink and then a thud on the other side as an object hit the floor.

'It was locked from the inside,' he said, eyebrow raised.

They unlocked the door, sidearms cocked and ready.

The door opened out into the room they were standing in.

Ray spun around from the side of the doorframe, aiming his weapon inside.

'It's clear,' he whispered.

Tom and Laura followed at his shoulder.

A narrow set of stairs led up to the attic, closed off at the top by another door.

'Move aside,' Tom told Ray, and led them up the stairs.

At the top, he rapped on the door.

'Dolores,' he called out. 'We know you're in there. We're armed and ready to fire. I want you to unlock this door. Then you and your companion need to move a few feet away and have your hands by your sides so I know you have no weapons; is that clear?'

There was silence from within.

Then a click.

Tom waited a second and then opened the door, his pulse racing.

On the other side of the attic space stood a woman and a man, both elderly, arms hanging loosely by their sides.

The attic floor was lived in, with a sitting area, a double bed, even a small TV. And that was just the space they could see. Tom imagined it was plumbed for a toilet – they probably even had a kettle and fridge up here.

Dolores O'Sullivan, former nurse at St Christina's, wore her grey hair neatly plaited around her head in a Grecian style. One side of her face was still quite beautiful. Strong cheekbones and an attractive eye. The other side was covered in burn scars; the eye drooped at the edge and the corner of her lips was missing.

The man beside her was tall and strong-looking, even now, at seventy-two. He stared at Tom with pure hatred in his intense, angry eyes.

'You did the right thing by cooperating,' Tom said. 'I'm Detective Inspector Tom Reynolds and these are Detective

Sergeants Ray Lennon and Laura Brennan. Dolores O'Sullivan and Conrad Howe, I'm arresting you for the murder of Owen Reid in December 1972 and for the unlawful detention and torture of Rosita Moore, George Bonner and Henry Arnold.'

CHAPTER 47

The atmosphere the next day in Tom's incident room at Dublin headquarters was jubilant.

For six months, the man the murder team in the NBCI looked up to had been sidelined, as his reputation was smeared. Their routine had been thrown into disarray and line management was unclear.

Now, DI Reynolds was back. The insinuations had dried up in the tabloids. And he'd only gone and solved a forty-year-old case.

Downstairs, in the interview room, Tom didn't quite share his team's buoyant mood.

He'd yet to break the news to Miriam Howe and her children that they'd found her husband and their father alive and well, having lived with another woman for almost half a century after committing the most heinous of crimes.

Tom had asked Linda to sit in with him for the initial interview with Howe. Ray and Laura were in with Dolores O'Sullivan. As soon as they were finished, both suspects would be transported to the criminal courts for an emergency session. The inspector didn't think they'd struggle to find a judge to conduct the bail hearing. Not once Howe's brother-in-law was informed who was waiting to be processed.

Conrad Howe sat across from the inspector, his expression

inscrutable, an overwhelmed duty solicitor beside him. The doctor had gone for the cooperation route. The police knew almost everything; there was no point in denying the charges and being further penalised for it. Howe was nothing if not calculating.

'The diary,' he said, shaking his head. 'I should have burned it. I didn't realise when I hid it on that first trip home that I wouldn't be returning. I suppose I could have watched the house, waited until Miriam was out, and retrieved it. But it was safer to stay away from Dublin altogether. Did you realise, when you were reading it, that it was Reid's? His handwriting was quite like mine, I thought.'

'I assumed it was yours,' Tom said. 'Miriam – your wife – had kept some of your earlier love letters. Remember them? It's similar handwriting, that's what confused her, but there were subtle differences. It wasn't until I paid proper attention to a sample of Reid's actual handwriting that I realised how wrong I'd got it. And out of context, the diary read exactly like the thoughts of a doctor. Reid wanted to train as one and he'd been studying all the medical books he could get his hands on. But more than that – he showed a real compassion for the patients in St Christina's. Something you lacked.'

'You're correct about the orderly in one respect, Inspector.' Howe adjusted the glasses on his nose and straightened his jacket. It was one of the things Tom had noticed about him when they found the couple in the attic. Howe wore a full suit, jacket and tie included. He was still clinging to an air of respectability, despite the life he'd chosen for himself. 'Reid fancied himself as some sort of medic in training, just because he'd read a few books. He didn't know his place. The man was a manual worker. His job was to wheel trolleys and clean up shit. Not to challenge the work of the doctors. Not to challenge me.'

'Yes, that was a mistake on his part, wasn't it?' Tom said. 'Going up against you. Did you know he was watching you?'

Howe made an exasperated sound.

'Yes,' he said. 'I became aware a short time beforehand. Dolores had told me one of the orderlies was fixated on her, but also on me. She said he had all sorts of crazy theories about what I was doing. She was using his obsession with her to grow closer to him, find out what he knew. I didn't see any danger in him. It was none of his business, after all, how I chose to treat the patients and nobody would believe his insane accusations. When he approached me directly, I was taken by surprise.

'He asked to meet at the cottage out on the headland. Once he mentioned that place, I knew he must have seen me going up there with Dolores. We could never meet at mine because I lived on the hospital grounds. I thought, foolishly, that it was some sort of ham-fisted attempt at bribery. Or perhaps he wanted to challenge me about Dolores. She had that effect on men. The poor idiot had fallen for her, hook, line and sinker. But when I met him, he accused me of torturing the patients. Torturing! How dare he?' Howe shook his head. 'He told me he had been making notes. I went to strike him and he assaulted me. That's when I knew he was deranged.'

'He assaulted you?'

'Yes. He broke my arm.'

'Ah. I see. You must have realised at that point there was no reasoning with him?'

'None. But I saw a way out: Dolores. She played up even more to his affection for her. And he told her everything. How he'd force me to resign and how he planned to leave as well. He'd already written his resignation letter. We got hold of that and made sure it was in Boylan's hands before Reid could change his mind. Then it was just a matter of planning.'

Tom sat forward.

'You stole his diary and hid it in your own home before he could leave the island with it. His "evidence" against you. Then you destroyed your own patient files. You arranged to meet him again. What for? Were you going to tell him he no longer had anything on you? Shock him by revealing the fact Dolores was complicit so he'd be too heartbroken to fight you? What actually happened?'

'I organised to meet him back up at the cottage. Dolores was waiting up there, but he didn't know it. She told me that he'd become very despondent, that he didn't think I was taking him seriously. She said he was planning to leave the asylum and report me when he got home. He had the diary packed in his bag, that's where she found it. He was a true coward – accuse and run. He would have done untold damage to my reputation. When he came to the cottage, I told him I had his *proof* and his resignation letter had been submitted. He had no actual evidence I'd done anything wrong other than some childish stories in a diary. Whereas I had actual, physical proof that he'd assaulted me – a broken arm. I *hadn't* done anything wrong. It should have ended there. He should have taken the opportunity and left.'

'But he wouldn't stop.'

'No. He was furious when he realised I had his precious diary. He kept ranting about a patient who'd died, Minnie somebody or other. Then he claimed he mightn't be able to prove I'd harmed the patients but that he would report the abortion I'd performed on Rosita Moore. It was ridiculous. As if a sluttish idiot could be allowed to continue with a pregnancy.'

'That girl was raped. If you read his diary, you must know that?'

'Raped?' Howe scoffed. 'She spread her legs for an orderly, Inspector, in the hope he'd help her escape from the care her family had found for her. She was probably giving it up for Reid, as well. Rosita is and always was a simpleton.'

Tom felt obliged to grip the side of the table to stop himself from punching Howe.

'You are going to spend the rest of your life rotting in prison for what you did to that woman,' he said, slowly, gravely. 'So I'd be careful how you speak about her.'

Howe looked at him dismissively.

'You aren't a doctor. You wouldn't understand.'

'No,' Linda said. 'He's not a doctor. But I am. You broke your oath, Mr Howe. You swore to do no harm. What you did to your victims was not medicine in any sense of the word. No more than what the Nazi Mengele did. And you did break the law when you aborted that woman's child, however it was conceived, as well you know and whatever your views on the pregnancy. That's when you decided you had to murder Reid. You knew you'd crossed a line that you couldn't explain away. The hospital trustees – most of them likely from religious orders – would have come down on you like a ton of bricks. Reid was a threat to you and to your sick plans. You are a disgrace to your profession.'

Howe coloured.

'That's your opinion. I was trying to cure lunacy. All great medical advances require sacrifice and experiment.'

'My opinion will be the opinion of your peers for all time. Your legacy will be as a madman, not a doctor. You didn't cure anybody. You cannot cure insanity. You can cause it, as you did, but you cannot remove it. You, perhaps, are living proof of that.'

For a moment, Tom thought Howe was going to lose himself. But the doctor regained his composure. The snarl slid off his face and he appeared calm again. In control. Arrogant. He'd confessed to Reid's murder as if nobody had the right to judge him for it. The man thought he was God.

'So, you realised Reid would have to die, but you had a broken arm,' the inspector said. 'That's why Dolores was there. To help you take him by surprise.'

'Yes. She hit him and when he fell, we choked him with the wire.'

'But you'd already decided to disappear at that stage, to leave your own life, your wife and children. You decided he would take the place of your body, were he ever found.'

Howe nodded.

'An unpleasant necessity. When he was dead, we dressed him in my clothes and put my wallet in his jacket. Then we put him into the pit at the hospital. It was to be filled in that week anyway. I thought, on the off chance he was found, he'd be mistaken for me.'

'Not if he'd been found immediately,' Tom said.

'No. But I did what I could to disfigure his face before we dressed and buried him.'

The inspector shook his head. They'd only found a skeleton; there'd been no face to identify.

'You even went to the trouble of breaking his arm in the same spot,' he said.

The doctor nodded. He was serene. Nothing he had said repulsed him. The inspector could feel the bile churning in his stomach but this man, who'd desecrated his victim's dead body, could have been talking about the weather.

'We picked up your blood on the coat you buried him in. That's why we thought it was you. But you couldn't have known about DNA back then.'

'I didn't. I worried about DNA later. But I'd cut myself when we attacked Reid. I must have been still bleeding when we dressed him.'

'And then you kept writing letters to his family, so they would think he was still alive.'

'Yes.'

'And the trip out to the cottage on the 24th? Why did you come out of hiding?'

'How do you know about that?'

'You were seen.'

'Ah. I had to make sure it was clean, you see. We made a bit of a mess when we killed Reid. There was a lot of blood.'

Tom shook his head.

'The lengths you went to,' he said. 'The things you've done. Don't you feel any remorse?'

Howe blinked.

'I did what I had to do. I didn't think of myself. I thought of my patients. That's all I've ever thought of.'

Dolores O'Sullivan was unnerving. In the interview room next door she was giving Ray and Laura more or less the same account as Conrad Howe. And it had become apparent to both detectives, despite her cool tone and articulacy, that the woman was as mad as a bag of cats.

'Why did you return to the island?' Laura said. 'The address you've given us is in rural Mayo. You were obviously content to live there anonymously for a good many years. Dolly O'Sullivan and her husband, Con O'Sullivan. Why did you get in touch with Boylan and risk him finding out about Conrad?'

'I had no choice,' she said and sniffed. All her answers were succinct, efficient, to the point. She spoke to them like they were halfwits. 'We lived in England for a long time and when we returned I needed to find work. Con had worked over there, but he couldn't risk it here. He might be identified. I wanted Lawrence to provide me with a reference so I could get a job.'

'Why didn't you just stay in England?'

The nurse looked down at her nails. Cut short and spotlessly clean, she still studied them for specks of dirt.

'Con's expertise wasn't as valued over there as it had been here. They were changing how they treated patients. As doctors always do, even when the new methods are no better than the old. He was unhappy.'

'I see,' Laura said. 'So you came back and you contacted Boylan.'

'He invited me out to the island. I'd been his favourite nurse. He told me he had a private job that I could take on, that some of the patients had chosen to stay at St Christina's, though it was closing. I saw an opportunity.'

'An opportunity to imprison and torture three people?'

Dolores raised an eyebrow.

'A chance for Con, and Lawrence, as it happens, to continue their work. At that time, Lawrence didn't know what had happened to Reid, just that Con had left. He was surprised to discover we'd left together, but the old codger had suspected something of the sort all along. He just hadn't been able to figure it out. I lied and told him the ferry operator had been drunk on the 23rd and must have missed Con getting on board, because I'd waved him off myself.'

'When in actual fact he was with you on the Christmas Eve ferry, pretending to be Reid, wasn't he?'

'Yes. Con just threw on an old suit of Reid's and wrapped a scarf around his face. I made a point of talking to the captain several times and mentioning my travelling companion, Mr Reid. He was none the wiser. The only problem we had was Con had to act as though there was nothing wrong with his arm and take it out of its sling. He was still recovering and in a lot of pain.'

'God love him,' Laura said, an eyebrow raised. 'So you presented your little plan to Boylan – to pretend three of the inmates had died and allow your boyfriend to carry out experiments on them?'

'He's my husband. We married in England.'

'Well, he's still married here,' Ray pointed out. 'So we can add bigamy to the litany of charges against the pair of you. Did you even think of his wife, or of his children?'

'They're dead to us,' Dolores said and sniffed again. 'Con was only with that woman for a few years. We've had a whole lifetime together. He only married her to prove a point to that sop Andrew Collins. That, and she came from money. Her family's wealth helped him pay for his medical training. And in answer to your question,' she turned her gaze to Laura, 'yes, I suggested to Lawrence that rather than letting a once great hospital limp to a sorry end, there was still the potential to do something magnificent. To show the world that the advances he and Con had made could cure madness if they were given sufficient time. He swore he'd keep Con's identity a secret. We went over for a short time, then we started returning more frequently until, eventually, we were staying in the house with him.

'When Reid's body was discovered, he pieced it together but at that stage, our work had come too far for it to matter. I told him, when you lot were up sniffing around the asylum, that we would have to end things – we would have to put the patients to sleep.'

'So, you told him to kill Rosita, George and Henry, the night he started that fire?' Ray said.

Dolores gave one short nod.

'We tried Lawrence's way first – moving them to the house. That was a disaster. Ultimately, we really couldn't do any more for them. It was over. We'd achieved as much as we could.'

She sat back, lips pursed.

'You achieved nothing,' Laura said. 'Absolutely nothing. All you did was torture innocent people. But I think you're too mad to even realise that.'

It happened in a split second. Dolores leaned across the table and slapped Laura hard across the face.

The officer at the door jumped forward as Ray also leapt into action, both of them restraining the former nurse. Her duty solicitor looked like she was about to vomit, as the full realisation of who she was meant to be defending sank in; and now with an assault charge against an officer to boot.

'Nice,' Laura said, clutching her stinging cheek. 'Try that with your cellmate in prison and see how far you get. The thing is, Dolores,' she leaned over the table and got as close as she could to the other woman's face, 'I'm not afraid of you. Not even a little bit. Nobody is ever going to be afraid of you again.

You're going to see what it's like on the other side now. And trust me. It's not pretty.'

And there it was. A hint of fear in the nurse's eyes.

She understood it had come to an end, all right. For her, rather than her patients.

CHAPTER 48

'So, they were trying to move Rosita, George and Henry up to Boylan's house,' Tom said, when they gathered in the incident room later that day. 'That night we heard Rosita screaming. After we'd been in the hospital that day, they arrived at the conclusion it was unsafe to leave them there. The patients, and the records that would reveal Reid's handwriting. Dolores and Howe wanted to murder them but Boylan insisted they be moved to his house.

'I think, over the years, he was the only one who actually cared for the three. Howe and Dolores were the real sadists. Anyway, that night they started with Rosita. She'd been sedated but they obviously misjudged the dosage or gave her an amount that would have worked if she was safely ensconced in the basement. When the cold and the rain hit her outside, it must have brought her around. She tried to escape the car and when that didn't work, she got the window down and screamed. She's so terrified of Howe, being in a car with him must have given her the strength required to fight. Boylan couldn't calm her so they panicked and got her back inside the hospital. Then we left the island but we returned before they could carry out Dolores' plan – burning the hospital down with the three inside and hoping they'd be lost in the rubble.'

'How did none of us see them that first night?' Ray asked. 'We came from one direction and Emmet from the other.'

Tom shook his head.

'We thought we heard the screams between the hospital and the pier. The sounds were travelling on the wind, like you guessed at the time. Boylan's house is inland. They got her back in through the rear of the hospital when Emmet and his team had moved on towards us.'

'It's utter madness,' Laura said. 'The whole thing. Who's telling Miriam?'

'Bronwyn Maher has gone out,' Tom said.

'The assistant commissioner?' Ray said. 'Bit high up, isn't it? Is Kennedy not jumping all over this?'

'You'd think he would be, wouldn't you?' Tom said, scratching his beard. 'He seems to have gone off the radar. He wasn't in his office when I called and I can't get him on the phone. Anyhow, Maher knows Miriam's brother so I think it's a courtesy. She's breaking the big news to her and I'm to call out tonight with the details.'

'Makes sense,' Ray said. 'She'll be devastated.'

'That's one word for it.'

'Where are you off to now?'

'I want to pop in to see Emmet. We started a conversation the other day but we need to continue it.'

'What about?'

Tom sighed.

'Don't ask.'

Tom was practically at Emmet's door when Linda caught up with him.

'Shit,' he mumbled under his breath, hearing her call his name.

'Tom, darling,' she called again.

He spun on his heel. He could walk her back down the corridor to safety, then come back up later.

But Emmet had heard her, too.

He emerged from his office, with a head like a bull's.

'Linda,' he barked. 'Inside.'

Tom turned around again and headed towards the office.

Emmet held out a hand to stop him.

'Is your name Linda?'

The inspector gritted his teeth.

'Look, I'm no happier than you are, but this one needs a referee.'

Linda had arrived beside the two of them.

'What is it?' she said, nervously, all of the confidence Tom had witnessed earlier in the interview room gone. She had been such an asset on the investigation. He'd grown fond of her, this last year. Which made what she was about to hear all the worse.

'Let's go into the office,' Tom said.

'Should you be here?' Linda asked, eyeing Tom.

'Definitely not. But I am.'

It *was* private. It should have only been between the pair of them. But there was too much bitterness on both sides. Tom didn't trust Emmet to break the news gently to Linda and that was what was needed in this situation.

The inspector had to take one for the team.

Emmet rested his large backside against the front of his desk while Tom and Linda hovered anxiously by the door.

'So . . . so you know,' Linda said. Her hand moved to her curls, where she wound a finger into one of the corkscrews and tugged nervously.

Emmet gave a curt nod.

'Yes. I know. Tell me. Who does that? Who gives up their child?'

Even though his words were derogatory, Tom could see the big man was doing everything in his power to remain calm. Long may it last.

'I had no option,' Linda said, her voice no more than a whisper. 'If I'd told you I was pregnant and you'd left your wife, I would have spent the rest of my life fearing you resented the child. I couldn't inflict that on any of us. And you were so cruel, Emmet. You broke my heart.'

The veins on the side of Emmet's neck pulsated; a sheen of sweat covered his brow. Tom wanted to caution Linda. Tread carefully. But she didn't know what was coming.

'You could have kept the baby. I could have supported you.'

'So I would have been alone, a single mother, dependent on your charity while you were still shacked up with your wife? You, having the best of both worlds? I lost my whole family when I told them I was leaving Geoff for you, Emmet. When he said he'd have me back, I cried with relief. At least I wasn't on my own. But he wouldn't have me with another man's child. That was too much to ask.'

'So you chose yourself over your child.'

'I had no choice!' Linda's voice had risen. 'You gave me no choice, you . . . you selfish wanker! I wouldn't have taken your money and I couldn't have worked. I wasn't earning enough back then to pay for full time childcare, even if the college kept me on, which they wouldn't have. You know the male lecturers in there were dying to get rid of me. A baby would have been the perfect opportunity to stab me in the back. I wouldn't have been able to give the infant anything. My family had already turned their backs on me. I had nothing and nobody. I had to give him up. I had to put him first.

'I never had another child, Emmet. Do you know why? Because I couldn't bear it. I couldn't bear the agony of giving birth again and rearing that child while always wondering about the one I'd given away. When I gave him up, I gave up my future, my life. There isn't a single day I haven't thought about him. Not a single day. I thought I did what was right. I tried to do what was right.'

Linda threw her hands out in despair.

Tom wasn't sure, but he sensed he saw something shift a little in Emmet. Linda's distress was real and it was painful to witness. It was as Tom had suspected, and even Emmet, in all his righteous anger, was smart enough to see it.

'How do you know?' Linda said, suddenly. 'How did you find out?'

Red blotches broke out on Emmet's neck and cheeks. He removed his glasses and rubbed them, his eyes on the floor.

'He found me.'

Silence.

'He . . . he found you?' Linda said, eventually, her hand on her beating breast. 'He came looking? You've met him?'

'Yes.'

'I—' Linda's whole body sagged.

Tom crossed to the desk and pulled a chair out. He raised an eyebrow at Emmet, who still didn't move.

Linda sank onto the seat when it was offered.

'What is he like? What does he look like?'

Emmet opened his mouth to try to form some words, but Linda stopped him.

She looked up, her eyes boring into his.

'Why didn't he look for me?'

Emmet turned away, unable to meet her gaze.

'He doesn't want to know you,' he said. 'You're the woman who gave him up. He read your note. He knew I didn't know about him; that's why he came to find me. He can't forgive you, Linda. And nor can I.'

As soon as the words were out of his mouth, Emmet looked around him, trying to figure out what to do, where to go.

It was his office, but still he strode from it.

Tom was left there with Linda, as her mouth hung open. When the door shut behind Emmet, she put her hands over her eyes and let out one intense, heartbroken sob.

The inspector recognised the sound and it cut through him.

It was the sound of a mother who'd lost her child.

CHAPTER 49

'I'm glad you told me,' Louise said.

Tom sat at the kitchen table, his head in his hands, elbows propping him up. Louise was behind him, rubbing his shoulders distractedly.

'Are you sure that tea is strong enough?' she asked. 'I feel like I need something stronger after that and I didn't even witness it.'

'Tea will have to do,' Tom said. 'I'm calling out to Miriam Howe's in an hour.'

'God, it's horrendous.' Louise came around to sit beside him. 'It's not Linda's fault. Maybe she should have told him about the baby but he should have told her about his wife too, before she marched around there to scream at him. She couldn't have known about the baby then – maybe if she had, she would have approached the whole thing differently.'

'How do you know she didn't know about the baby when she did that?' Tom asked.

'Because she'd had half a bottle of vodka, remember?'

'That's what she told you. She might have wanted to make her irrational response seem rational – without explaining that she was furious because she'd been dumped while pregnant.'

Louise exhaled the air from her cheeks.

'You could be right. What's going to happen now?'

'I don't know. I don't have a whole lot of faith in Emmet playing peacemaker between Linda and her son. And he's the only one who has the lad's ear.'

'Well, he's going to have to, Tom. That boy needs things explained to him properly. Not some idealised version where Emmet comes out smelling of roses and Linda is the only baddie in the tale. You'll have to tell Emmet what's what.'

'I think I might have interfered enough,' he replied. His phone buzzed on the table. 'That's Ray outside. I'd better go.'

'Fine. But remember what I said. Don't stop nosing around their business now. You're far too good at it. I've known Linda for years and sure, I might have suspected there was more to the story than I knew, but that was it. You figured it all out.'

'I was just in the right place at the right time,' Tom said.

'You always are,' Louise replied. She leaned over and hugged him tightly.

'What's that for?' he said, brushing her hair from her face.

'I love you.' She smiled.

'I love you, too.' He stared at her, puzzled. 'You look oddly happy, considering the conversation we just had. Anything you'd like to share?'

'Everything is going to be okay,' she said.

'Eh . . . is there something I don't know about?'

'Of course not. Go, do your job. See you later. Buzz me if, you know, anything comes up.'

'I swear to Christ if you've organised another surprise party for me, I won't forgive you.'

'You're having a laugh, aren't you? Your birthday has come

and gone, Tom Reynolds. Get over yourself. As if I have nothing better to be doing. Feck off to work; go on.'

He smiled and kissed her head as he stood.

'That's better. I love it when we bicker. Secret to a happy marriage. Now, I'm off to talk to a wife who has real cause to be upset with her husband. I am not looking forward to this.'

CHAPTER 50

Miriam Howe was angry. Fuming, in fact. And drunk. Very drunk.

Andrew Collins let them in. He had dark bags under his eyes and anguish writ all over his face.

'She's been drinking since I got here,' he said. 'She rang as soon as your boss left. I was waiting for her call. I knew I couldn't be the first to tell her. I thought she'd blame me and think I knew something when I hadn't. I really hadn't. I thought she'd still hate me, just for being here, for being Conrad's peer. But she asked me to come right over. She'd already started on the brandy when I arrived.'

'Well, it's understandable,' Tom said. 'Where is she?'

'Out in the garden. She had me build a bonfire.'

'What is she burning?'

'Christmas ornaments.'

Outside, Miriam was wrapped in a shawl, her hair loose, the flames dancing in her eyes. She was muttering to herself when Tom approached, intermittently slugging from the bottle she gripped tightly. The inspector guessed it was the first time in her life that Miriam Howe had ever drank straight from a bottle.

'Mrs Howe,' he said. Andrew hung back at a safe distance, Ray beside him. Tom's deputy was trying to talk the other man into joining him in the kitchen to make coffee, but Collins didn't want to take his eyes off Miriam. It was like he was afraid of what she might do.

'It's Ms Mythen,' she said. 'I refuse to bear that bastard's name for a minute longer.'

Tom stood beside her and looked into the fire. A Christmas tree was burning fast alongside various baubles and wooden decorations. Everything would be gone in minutes.

'You're right to be angry,' he said. 'Have you told your son and daughter?'

'Yes. They're on their way. It's just a pitstop for Jonathan. He's going to find his father and murder him, when he's done consoling me. I don't need to be consoled.' She glared across at the inspector. 'I need to be compensated. I want every penny that man has, if he has anything. And then I want his head on a plate.'

Tom nodded.

'You will,' he said. 'He's going to spend the rest of his life in prison.'

'The rest of his life!' Miriam snorted. She took another slug. 'I'm sorry, where are my manners? Do you want some, Inspector?' She offered Tom the bottle. He politely declined.

'He's already lived his life,' she continued. 'He's had the best forty years of them living with some . . . some whore, while I waited for him here, raising his children and doing everything to keep his good name alive. Well, this is what I think of him, now.'

Miriam turned her head and attempted to hock up a globule of sputum. She wasn't practised in the art. A dribble ran down her chin and she wiped at it roughly with the shawl.

'Did he . . . did he ask after his children? Even once?' Her voice was a little meeker now. Less angry, more sad. Tom preferred the rage. It would keep her strong. She'd spent too long crying for the man. He didn't deserve a single tear more.

'Not once,' he answered, truthfully.

She gave her head a violent shake.

'That . . . *bastard*,' she repeated, and never had Tom heard such contempt in the word. Conrad Howe was lucky he was in custody. It wasn't his son he had to fear. If his wife got her hands on him in this state, he would be a dead man for real this time.

'What about Andrew?' he said, nodding over his shoulder.

'What about him?'

'He must be angry, too. He's here, though.'

Miriam snorted.

'Do you think we're going to embark on a love affair, Inspector? At our age? God, you don't have to tell me how tragic my life has been. If I'd known what Conrad had done, chances are I might have found something with Andrew. But now? After all this time?'

'Is it ever too late to start afresh?' Tom said. 'Can you even conceive of wasting another day?'

'So, that's to be my lesson after a life given over to mourning a husband who abandoned me? I'm sorry, Inspector. Maybe for another time. Not today. I'm too bitter.'

Tom sucked in his bottom lip. She was right, of course. It might occur to her at a later point that it would piss Conrad off to be in jail while she was happy with Collins. Then things might change.

'Do you want to know how we figured it out?' he asked.

Miriam flinched as something on the bonfire cracked and exploded.

'No,' she said, staring straight ahead. 'I don't care how he did it. It's enough to know that he did. I believe she's disfigured. The nurse?'

'Yes. She has burn marks on one side of her face.'

'And still he chose her,' Miriam said. She reached for her neck, stopped as she felt the pearls.

In one swift move, she yanked them free and threw them into the bonfire.

'It was better when I thought he was dead,' she cried. 'I was happy, when you told me that. After forty years, I was happy that he was gone and it was over. I always thought I wanted to know. That nothing could be worse than not knowing. I was wrong. This is worse.'

Tom placed a hand on her shoulder.

'Don't let it be,' he said. 'Time served, Miriam. You've done your sentence. Free yourself.'

She nodded once, an obligatory response.

She wouldn't, Tom knew. She'd never get over what he'd done to her. She was his final victim.

CHAPTER 51

There was an odd atmosphere about headquarters when Tom arrived the next morning.

He'd gone home the night before to a slap-up meal prepared by Louise. Caít was with her great-grandparents and Maria was out for the night so they'd retired early to bed with a bottle of wine. Most of it had been left un-drunk, as they caught up with each other.

He'd awoken refreshed and happy and gone to work, ready to share in the good mood of yesterday. But the incident room was strangely muted. He walked over to Ray's desk. His deputy had his head down and was typing furiously.

'What are you doing?' Tom asked.

'Typing up notes for the chief.'

The inspector had momentarily forgotten he had a stone resting in his stomach. They were only just back, they'd successfully wrapped up a case, and Kennedy was already sticking his big bloody nose in with Tom's staff. It wasn't Ray's job to type up the case notes for the Chief Superintendent. Well, it probably was, but it was down to Tom to delegate the task to him. Nobody else.

'He wants to see you, by the way,' Ray said, still typing.

Tom swore.

'Marvellous,' he said. 'Bloody marvellous.'

He dragged his feet up the flights of stairs to Kennedy's office on the fourth floor. What could the man throw at him now? What had he done wrong this time? Surely even Kennedy had to be happy with this case being solved?

Unless . . . unless, Tom realised, it had been another attempt to embarrass the inspector. Give him an unsolvable case related to a senior judge and watch as Tom messed it up. And then it had backfired spectacularly on the chief superintendent when Tom did figure it out.

The inspector sighed as he reached his boss's door. This couldn't go on.

He knocked and entered.

Kennedy's chair was turned to the window, its back facing the door.

The inspector cleared his throat.

'You wanted to see me?'

'Christ, I only wish I had a white cat for this occasion,' a familiar voice said. The chair swung around and Tom gawped at its occupant.

It was Sean McGuinness.

'I could be stroking it, on the arm of this ridiculous hydrolic chair,' his old boss said. 'Who, for the love of God, signed off on this expensive monstrosity?'

'What . . . ?' Tom couldn't even finish the sentence.

'Take a seat, Inspector,' Sean said. 'Now, the Howe case –'

'Woah! Sean, what the hell is going on?'

'It's Chief McGuinness to you when we're on the job, Tom. As I was about to say, I think you did an excellent job on that island. Judge Mythen thinks so too. I suspect a commendation is in the offing. Everybody knows cold cases are virtually unsolvable.'

Tom shook his head.

'Are we?' he said. 'On the job? What's going on? Where's Kennedy?'

'Ah. Yes. Kennedy. Now, that's where you've been falling down, Inspector. You seem to find it fierce hard to bring your detection skills to bear on your own life, as you've proven time and time again.'

'Sean!'

'It's all fallen apart around here since I left, hasn't it? This lack of discipline and respect for authority is shocking. Right. Time to fix things.' The smile slid off Sean's face as he pulled the chair closer to the desk and leaned forward.

'Joe Kennedy has been suspended pending a disciplinary hearing. Leaking information to the press from your own department is a serious offence.'

Tom scrunched up his features, confused. Then the penny dropped.

'It was him?'

'It was him. We suspected it for a while. He tried to cover his tracks, but the press office were already on to him. It was unlike him to be so stupid. I thought he'd wait in the long grass for you, Tom. You must have done something to force his hand.'

The inspector stood up and started to pace. He had too much pent-up energy and anger to stay sitting still.

'After the Sleeping Beauties case, I threatened him. I told him if he kept pushing me, I'd tell Bronwyn Maher I wanted a promotion. I didn't even mean it seriously. I just wanted him to back off.'

'Well, that didn't go as planned,' Sean said. 'We all know what happens when you corner a rat. Anyway, it's out now. You should know, he won't be fired, Tom. He'll worm his way out of this somehow and it would be too embarrassing for the force if it came out. He'll be shifted sideways but he'll still be around, so you'll need to keep an eye out for him. You've arrived, Tom. You're not doing your job properly if you haven't made an enemy somewhere in the ranks. Now sit down, will you? You're upsetting my digestion, stalking around like that.'

'But why are you here?' Tom stopped. 'You retired. And it's so soon after June.'

A cloud passed over Sean's face. It was gone as quick as it had arrived.

'It's been six months. And June would have wanted this with all her heart. I've come out of retirement, my friend. But only for a short time. I'm sorry, Tom, but this is the sting in the tail – you won't be able to keep running on your comfy treadmill. I told Bronwyn Maher I'd come back only if there's an express commitment that you will take over in eighteen months' time. It's time to move up the ladder. We can't have another Kennedy incident.'

And now Tom did sit down.

Shit. Chief superintendent. He'd been dodging that bullet for so long.

'I suppose I've no choice in the matter,' he said.

'None,' Sean said. 'I checked with your wife and she's agreed for you. And your buddy in high places, Jarlath Kearney, has asked about you one too many times for you to keep kicking around under the radar.'

Tom nearly smiled. They'd sewn it all up – even the *Taoiseach* of the country, who'd been trying to promote him since they'd met on a case a couple of years ago. And yet, instead of being annoyed, Tom felt relieved. They'd caught him at a good time. Even taking on a job he wasn't ready for or sure he wanted was preferable to having another mind-numbingly frustrating meeting with Joe Kennedy.

'This time,' Sean said, clapping his hands together and rubbing them, 'we're not taking "no" for an answer. Eighteen months. Then you're Chief Superintendent Reynolds. Congratulations. Now, go on back downstairs. I believe your team have a bottle of champagne in. Only have a half glass, mind. We've intelligence the Reilly gang are planning a retaliation killing for the last hit against them. We could have a body on our hands any minute.'

'They all know, downstairs?'

'Like I said,' Sean smiled. 'An excellent detective. Except when it comes to your good self. That's all, Inspector. Oh, actually, do me a favour. Give Moya Chambers a call. She's been giving herself a really hard time over that blood DNA match to Howe. The bone analysis came back and, obviously, proved it wasn't him. I've told her she can't dwell on it. The damned results only came back yesterday, when the lab technicians returned from their Christmas break. She was pushed to make that identification and our man Howe made it easy for her with the broken arm. But, still . . .'

'I'll speak to her,' Tom said. 'I knew she'd be hauling herself over hot coals. It was our collective fault; we all rushed to the same conclusion. If we hadn't solved it so quickly, she'd have been able to correct it. She can blame me for being so good.'

Sean smiled.

'Tell her that, why don't you. Patch me in on that call, I have to hear her response.'

Tom smiled and stood up.

'Oh, yes, and Tom?'

'Yeah?'

'Shave that thing off your face. You're a high-ranking officer and public servant. Not a bloody rock star.'

The inspector grinned. Well, if Sean was giving him a direct order . . .

For the first time in a long time, he felt relieved.

Things were almost back to normal.

The dynamics in the team were changing. And his career was about to take a sudden leap into the unknown.

But he could live with all that if the people closest to him were happy.

And he could especially live with it if it meant an end to having to deal with Joe Kennedy.

If that really was the case.

ACKNOWLEDGEMENTS

Ireland is very good at coming up with institutions for those society doesn't want. The Magdalene Laundries, the Mother and Baby homes, the industrial schools, psychiatric hospitals. Latterly, Direct Provision centres.

There's a lot of talk about the stigma surrounding mental health. Well meaning. Not always genuine. Faced with the very real and frightening symptoms of mental illness, most people back off. We, as a people, not unlike others, backed off big time. And we put our ill, our most vulnerable, into homes. In prisons. In hell. We let them be tortured. And we looked away. Shame on us.

Much has changed. Much stays the stay. Mental illness is the forgotten branch of the medicinal tree when it comes to resources.

Much research went into the facts of psychiatric care for this book. Mary Rafferty's *Behind the Walls*; Hanna Greally's *Bird's Nest Soup*; *Asylums, Mental Health Care and the Irish: 1800–2010*, ed. Pauline M. Prior. The investigative reporting of the *Irish Examiner* and *Irish Times*. Type 'mental health care in Ireland' into Google yourself and read the shocking, disturbing stories and statistics.

This is just a crime novel. The story is fiction. The texture is based on fact.

And now to the thanks.

My beautiful, loving family stand beside me while I beaver away on these tales. Martin and the kids, the Smiths, Spains and extended layers!

My friends, Michelle, Aine, Nina, Catherine, Kathryn, Natasha, Louise, Mary, Pam, Kathleen, Sinead, Declan, Brian, Kyran, Martin, Tommy, Doreen, Larry, Marie, Andrea, Margaret, Aengus, Aisling . . . good God, too many of you – you hang on in there when I disappear, lend an ear when I'm stuck, turn up when I break out the wine and cry party. I know there's more, I'm typing fast. DM me for next book, I'll get you in there. Or maybe you're already a character. I'll just leave that there.

My publishers, Quercus, are on this journey with me, every step of the way. You can only dream of publishers like this. The whole amazing team, but Rachel, Hannah, David, Bethan, Jon and most importantly, Stef Bierwerth – you make me want to work harder and reach a higher standard with every book. Stef, you're one of my best friends.

My agent, Nicola Barr – nowadays when your name pops up in my email, I drop the cup, toast, baby, break out the champers, and this is before I've checked the subject title. Because you are the bringer of brilliance. No pressure for 2019, so.

And the readers. Nikki and the whole gang; the Warrenpoint, Limerick and Youghal libraries. I've missed out several thousand of you. Seriously, there'll be more books, don't worry. And the bloggers. Okay, way too many here. But they love the books and they shout about them and . . . wow.

Thank you, from the bottom of my little, sinister, plotting heart.